THE QUEST FOR THE TEMPLE KEY

BOOK ONE:
THE GARGOYLE CHRONICLES

BRANDON KING

PREPARE FOR RAIN PRESS

THE QUEST FOR THE TEMPLE KEY
Book One: The Gargoyle Chronicles

For inquiries, please contact:
Prepare For Rain Press, Boise ID
prepareforrainpress.com

Edited by Stacy Ennis: stacyennis.com
Cover by the graphic design team at Prepare For Rain Press; background image by Meranda Devan
Interior Design by Fusion Creative Works, www.fusioncw.com
Key illustration by Jessica Lund

ISBN: 978-0-9889537-4-1

First Printing, 2014
Revised Cover, 2023

Published in the United States of America

To our beloved Watson,

who was Tiny in our house.

ACKNOWLEDGEMENTS

This story began as the shred of a dream, nothing more than a scene unfolding in my slumbering mind. Waking, with the sound of the antagonist's name lingering in my head, I puzzled for a minute or two about its spelling. Then, many years passed by, but the idea for this book never quite left.

The greatest influence upon this story is Jessica, my daughter. Not only did I write it for her, in many respects the main character, Danielle, is based upon her. Jessica got wildly involved in this tale, making many excellent sketches of several characters and important scenes, including one that this cover design is based upon. To top it off, she contributed many plot ideas, twists and turns, as she'd eagerly read a chapter immediately after I'd completed it. I'm very grateful! And proud, too. You see, she's written her first fantasy novel, *NeverSeen*.

Few authors write in abject isolation, even though most write in abject something, whether it is misery in general, battling writer's block, working in a cold writing closet or what have you. I experienced none of those. My wife has been a constant support in all of my writing endeavors, often stealthily bringing in something to snack on when she hasn't seen me emerge from my writing cave for a while.

I have been blessed by many, many supporters. A select few need to be recognized: Shane, Linda, Pat, JT, Morten, Bastian, Alice, Lori, Kim and Marti. Your warm smiles and encouragement mattered.

Naturally, you would have nothing better to look at than a poor, typed document were it not for the awesome professionals that assisted me in bringing something better, much better, to you.

Stacy Ennis is a novelist's dream copy-editor, providing in-sightful comments, brilliant suggestions and demanding cri-tiques. She was a firm backstop for me, and was invaluable.

Our original cover designer, Martin Maceovič, created an epic illustrated cover. No longer creating covers, we thank Stuart Bache for his amazing cover design training, which provided the tools for our publishing team at Prepare For Rain Press to create the cover you have in your hands now.

Robin Bethel is a superb proofreader. Anything she may have missed must be attributed to me.

Shiloh Schroeder masterfully took a plain manuscript and designed it into a beautiful interior.

My heartfelt thanks to all of those named above, but most of all I thank you, my readers, for making this journey as a novelist so maddeningly fun and fulfilling.

Brandon King
Boise, ID
2014
Revised 2023

CONTENTS

CHAPTER ONE

THE HOUSE
WITH THE PORTICO

There was really nothing special about the house at the end of the cul-de-sac. It looked very much like all the other split-level, mostly stucco homes on Larch Drive, with two stories, a two-car garage, one lamppost in the front yard and a chimney rising above the black shingle roof. It had a three-color paint scheme like all the other houses on the street, with beige as the main color and the remaining colors lighter or darker. The trees and bushes around the front yard all looked slightly unhealthy. What made the house different was that it was the very last house on the street, and it was the only one with a portico.

But Danielle Wheelen didn't notice any of this. Since this was the first day to collect payment from the people on her paper route, she was too nervous to notice much of anything. So far, she'd mostly enjoyed having a paper route, but she'd been getting increasingly nervous about collection day.

She'd also noticed her parents had started acting differently towards her. Her father had talked about having "grown-up responsibilities" at dinner the night before, and he seemed to be quite proud of her. Naturally, this made her feel good. But that was yesterday.

Her mother had suggested she dress "nicely," so Danielle wore her new jeans, a pretty blue and green plaid top and her white patent-leather shoes and tied her long, blond hair in a ponytail. The people on her route had been pleasant, which pleased Danielle, but her feet hurt from wearing the stiff shoes. *Next time I'll wear my Keds!* she said to herself. Now that she'd been collecting for her route for almost two hours, Danielle's nervousness was beginning to come under control, although she really just wanted to get home.

So when she hastily walked up to the last house on the cul-de-sac, she didn't notice that it was the only house with a portico. Because she delivered newspapers before school and early in the mornings even on weekends, all she knew was that everything looked very different now, just before dinnertime, with lengthening shadows from the soon-setting sun. No one wanted to have their newspaper delivery girl collecting early in the morning when they were still in their pajamas. Of course, she didn't want to see them in their pajamas, either.

The portico's walls were slightly taller than Danielle's blond head, so she couldn't see over them. The walkway to the house went in between two walls, directly to a dark red front door. Had Danielle not still been a little nervous about collecting, she may have looked longer at the walls. She might have no-ticed that each wall had a vague shape or design in it. Neither wall had a uniform, stucco surface; the lines in the walls may have been cracks, but looked more like they'd been lightly carved in. It almost appeared like a very large wing had been pressed into it before it dried.

As Danielle marched between the fence-high stone walls, towards the door, she glanced at the walls and thought it very curious that each wall had a single, amber-colored circle of glass, about the size of a quarter, embedded in the surface. So intent was she on making her final collection, she failed to notice the house number above the door was not on her list. As she reached up to use the door knocker, she was startled by a rustling noise behind her.

Spinning around to look for the cause of the sound, she saw feathers littered all around the sheltered area, between the portico walls and the front door of the house. She'd never seen feathers so big, and she thought they might be as long as her arm. However, now that her attention was on the walls, she thought they looked odd. *Why would someone go to the trouble of carving wings into them, on both sides?* she wondered.

The sun was glinting off of both amber-colored glass circles. With a shudder, she realized they looked almost like eyes. As she looked down again at the feathers, one gently fell from the top of the right wall, landing with the same rustling sound she'd heard.

Relieved to find the source of the feathers, Danielle turned back to the door, happy she was nearly through with the collections and eager to hurry home to count the money. She was already visualizing her father helping her sort out the bills, dividing what she could keep and what had to be paid back to the newspaper. So when she lifted the knocker away from the door, her attention was only on the door, not the peculiar portico behind her. The portico walls quickly collapsed without a sound, dissolving, melting into weird, grotesque shapes.

At the sound of the crack of the knocker on the door's metal plate, Danielle heard two more cracks, like rocks splitting. At the same moment, there was a bright flash of amber, and a storm of feathers blew up around her. Something brushed by her right ear. Just as she turned to look—and felt an enormous talon squeezing into her shoulder—there was another crack, followed by a scream. Her scream. The red door vanished. The house vanished. She shut her eyes, unbelieving. Her heart pounding, her shoulder aching, she opened her eyes, surrounded by darkness…and four amber orbs. The orbs slowly changed shape, becoming more like the shape of a football. Then blinked. And Danielle fainted.

CHAPTER TWO

BAD DREAMS

"Oh, I hate this dream," Danielle muttered. Even though she was dreaming, she could tell she was dreaming. And it was a dream she'd had before, but more like a nightmare. It always started with being chased. It always ended with a dark, cold, cavernous room. In between, there were flashes, scenes, faces. Things just beyond the reach of memory. It was the in-between of her dream that she couldn't remember. She'd had it several times this summer, in the weeks following the end of seventh grade. Danielle wasn't sure if it was normal to have strange dreams at her age. When she'd mentioned it to her mother, she'd been told not to worry about it and something about hormones. Still, she hated this dream, especially when in it, and she'd wake up breathless and sweaty. She never could remember why she was breathless. The dream always ended in the cool cavern. Yet, the chasing ended somewhere earlier in the dream. Or did it? It was confusing.

With a start, Danielle woke up. It was dark. Too dark. She must have awakened earlier than normal.

Why aren't the birds singing? she wondered. It was cold. "That's weird. I'm not sweaty," she said quietly. Thinking she'd thrown off her covers during the dream chase, she reached down to the foot of her bed to grab her blankets. There were no blankets. And she wasn't in her bed.

The amber orbs in her dream blinked again.

Danielle screamed. She hadn't been dreaming, after all. This was real. She *was* in the dark, cold cavern.

"What is 'sweaty'?"

Danielle jerked at the sound of the low, rough voice. She didn't move, and hoped the pounding of her heart wasn't loud enough to be heard beyond her own head.

"What is 'sweaty'?" said the hoarse voice again.

"Yes, what is 'sweaty'?" The second voice was much like the first, gravelly, but it was a higher pitch than the other.

She was certain the hammering of her heart could be heard by anyone—or anything—within ten feet of her. But was there really something out there? Was she still dreaming? Was she dreaming she was aware of her dreaming?

"Is there someone there?" she whispered.

There was only the sound of her heart slapping around in her chest.

"Please…am I dreaming? Is there someone there?" she said a little louder, listening for a sound, a voice, anything that would explain what she was experiencing.

"What is 'sweaty'?" said the first gravelly voice a third time.

This time, Danielle was looking directly at the amber orbs on her left, which blinked. That was where the low voice was coming from.

So, stammering from fear and the encroaching cold of the cavern, Danielle said, "Uh…you know… it's when you get all wet from working real hard, like from running."

"Hm," said the higher voice. "Like when it rains?"

"I suppose. Sure," said Danielle, with very jangled nerves.

"Are you always sweaty?" said the lower voice.

"What? Well, no. Of course not," Danielle replied.

"Then you dry off when the sun comes out?" said the deep voice.

"Uh…what?" Danielle said, puzzled.

"No, Kimar, you twit," rumbled the higher voice. "It— she—dries off like we do, I bet. From heat. From the sun. Or from fire. Isn't that right?" The other orbs blinked at Danielle.

"Who are you?" asked Danielle, ignoring the question. Her heart was still pounding hard. She'd wanted to ask "*What* are you?" but was too afraid.

The deep voice replied, "I am Kimar, of course. You heard Ercen say so."

"And who are you?" the higher-pitched voice asked. Danielle assumed it must be Ercen's.

"I'm Danielle. Where am I?"

"You are in our home, the ancient cavern of Osberg the Great," said the deeper voice of Kimar.

Danielle grew more alarmed with each passing moment. Now, learning she was in a place she'd never heard of before, it was very hard to keep her voice calm. "Why can't I see? How did I get here? Why am I here? Did you bring me here?" Suddenly, Danielle's fear was overcome by anger. "I want to go home! Now!" Immediately, she regretted making a demand.

"Ah. Of course, Kimar," murmured Ercen. "She can't see us. Her eyes are not like our eyes."

"You are here because we need you. You are here as our…
guest. When we…once we have…it is not possible for you to
leave just yet." Kimar's voice echoed slightly in the dark.

"But we can help you to see," said Ercen.

Danielle's hazel eyes were very tired from trying to pen-
etrate the darkness around her. In fact, she wasn't even sure
what direction she was looking. A golden light grew around
her feet. It spread slowly away from her, chasing shadows further into the cavern, until she could just make out the cavern's roof hundreds of feet above her. At first, Danielle was
apprehensive. But as her surroundings became visible, fear
was quickly replaced by wonder, for the cavern was now glittering in golden light, with stalagmites and stalactites every-
where. Except directly in front of her were two large boulders.
Danielle thought they looked out of place. Where everything
else in the cavern was sparkling gold, the boulders didn't re-
flect any light at all, but seemed to absorb it into their mottled
gray and silver stone surface.

Danielle's eyes followed the gentle curves running up the
side of the boulders. The colors reminded her of the mottled
shapes and sweeping lines in her parents' Italian marble kitch-
en countertops at home. She was sitting very close to the stone
masses, so it took several moments for her mind to notice
familiar forms within the stone slabs. Tipping her head to one
side, she squinted hard.

Well, that's odd! she thought. *It nearly looks like an arm,
here…but it's too big.*

Her eyes drifted further up the boulders. Doubt crept
through her mind, like a cold fog on a winter's day.

That…resembles an oversized shoulder. But if that's so, then…

Her eyes stopped abruptly, wide with panic, on two amber orbs near the top of each boulder. She gasped, "Oh…oh…oh, my! Oh, no!"

"Welcome, I am Kimar."

"Welcome, I am Ercen."

Her mind had, indeed, made sense of the stone shapes, even though her heart desperately fought accepting the conclusion. Danielle was staring at two enormous gargoyles! She didn't have any idea what to say, so she said nothing. Getting stiff from the cold, she shifted around on the floor, backing away a few feet, feeling frightened but very curious at the same time.

Then, Ercen, who Danielle took to be a girl, said, "Look, Kimar, the human child is cold." She turned towards Danielle, then said, "Please, do not be afraid. We mean you no harm."

Without saying anything, Kimar stood up. Danielle had not realized until that moment that both gargoyles had been on their knees. Kimar reached his hands over his head to the ancient stalactite nearest to him and held it very close to its tip. Danielle could see that he didn't touch it. About a minute later, he stooped down to the floor and held his hands against the smooth area where Danielle was sitting. Without understanding what had just happened, Danielle was pleased to feel the floor warming under her. She looked up and noticed Kimar's hands were glowing with a soft golden light. It quickly faded.

Not knowing what else to do, and feeling that it wouldn't help to repeat the same questions again, Danielle struggled with what to do next. She didn't know if these creatures were to be trusted. She didn't know if she could trust herself! Was her mind playing tricks on her? Her head hurt. Her nerves were jangled.

Finally she just blurted out, "How did I get here? The last thing I remember was...well, I was just about finished collecting for my paper route. And there was one more house—it was strange, though. Like no one had been there for a few days, maybe even weeks because the grass and bushes looked dry..."

She talked quicker when she was nervous. Even so, she observed that Ercen and Kimar watched her intently, like they were waiting for...what?

"...and the house had these strange walls in front of it, and just behind the walls were these huge feathers littered around just in front of the—"

She stopped abruptly, unable to utter a sound. A huge feather, very much like the ones she had seen at the house she'd just been describing, fell from Kimar's shoulder and fluttered onto her lap.

CHAPTER THREE

PARTING

"You…" Danielle whispered. She wasn't sure if she meant it as a statement or a question.

"Yes, Danielle," replied Kimar, "we brought you here." Ercen nodded, knowingly.

"But how? It was—it *must* have been!—your feathers in front of the house. But I didn't see you before…well, before I ended up here."

"Didn't you?" asked Ercen quietly.

"Uh, like I said, there were these two walls blocking my view of most of the entryway to the house. But the walls, they didn't look quite right for the house. No one else in that neighborhood has them, at least on my route, anyway." Danielle noticed Kimar's eyes glint a little when she said this.

"No other house had such an entry," he said, "because we *were* the walls."

"But how? How can you be made out of stone—like when you were walls—but then be *alive* like you are now?" Danielle murmured while tugging at her dark, strawberry-blond hair.

"Child," said Ercen, "when we are stone, we are still alive. But changing from one state to the other often will dislodge a feather or two."

"I saw lots of feathers littering the courtyard, though," replied Danielle. She wasn't sure she wanted to know the answer to the question buzzing in her head, but she had to know. "So, when you change from stone to, uh, not-stone, feathers can get knocked out?"

"Yes," answered both Kimar and Ercen.

"OK, but there were quite a few feathers, maybe twenty or more, so wouldn't that mean you changed back and forth a bunch of times? How long have you been...walls?"

Kimar, who had been looking at the glittering roof of stalactites overhead, slowly dropped his eyes until he was looking intently into Danielle's face. "We'd been waiting two of your lunar cycles for you to come."

Danielle felt a weird tightness forming in her stomach, and almost a shortness of breath.

"'Two lunar cycles'—do you mean you've been waiting for *me* for two months?" Danielle asked, trembling. Her hazel eyes shimmered and welled up with tears, frightened by this thought but determined to learn more about these creatures.

Kimar nodded.

Nervously, Danielle asked, "How did you bring me here? I was knocking at the door of the house and...then I remember the darkness...and then just being here."

Kimar nodded again and replied, "The realm between your space and our space was parted. It is not unlike stepping through one of your doorways."

"I'm sorry. What? You 'parted' *space?*" Danielle had seen plenty of science fiction programs on television but couldn't believe what she was hearing. The shows that were popular with her friends she thought were silly enough, but this was too much.

"Yes," said Kimar. "It does not matter."

"Of course it matters," replied Danielle, testily. "It matters a lot to me how I got here." She pulled her denim jacket tight around her shoulders and hugged her knees tightly to her chest.

"You misunderstand, Danielle," said Kimar. "The realm between our lands matters, naturally. We simply asked it to not matter so that the space could be parted quickly."

Confused, Danielle thought of her science teacher, Mr. Johnston, and what he would say to this crazy statement. She replied, dismay lining her forehead, "You…parted space? By asking it to?"

Kimar tilted his head just a little before answering, "Of course."

"And you have been waiting for two months to do this—this 'parting'?" she asked.

"Yes," said Ercen.

The tightness inside was growing stronger. Danielle just wanted this dream to end. It was becoming more frightening than any dream she'd ever had. She heard herself ask, "This is the first time I've gone collecting for my paper route. In fact, I've only had the route since a week ago Saturday. So"—she took a deep breath—"how did you even know where to look for me? Why did you wait for me? Why...*me?*" she cried.

"You were foretold to us," Ercen answered quietly. Her wings lifted and then spread wide, as if she was stretching. Danielle was astonished at how far they reached. She thought they must span the width of her two-car garage at home.

"It is time for us to leave here. It won't be long until we're followed," Kimar said, his amber eyes narrowing.

And before Danielle could say anything, Kimar reached out to take her right hand, while Ercen took hold of Kimar's and Danielle's left hand at precisely the same instant. They vanished, just as the glittering light in the cavern fled into darkness.

CHAPTER FOUR

EXCAVATION

Peter Wheelen cried out, "Drat, Amy! Watch where you swing that thing!" A small avalanche of stone and scree had just fallen onto Peter's hard hat, startling and annoying him.

Amy Wheelen, the recipient of Peter's umbrage, just smiled and continued humming. She was so happy that even Peter's yelling couldn't diminish her joy. "Sorry, Pete!" she purred.

Amy balanced on a rock face about eight feet above where Peter was digging. She'd just been gently hammering the surface of the stone. They were pursuing further evidence of a strange prehistoric fossil, which appeared to be an unknown creature. Other archeologists had found exciting traces of this creature in the three years prior to their arrival at the dig.

Peter and Amy had been in graduate school for a year before they met. Peter had at once fallen in love with red-haired Amy James, the beautiful, freckled transfer student from California. How couldn't he? She was very smart, equally pretty and could go toe-to-toe with any professor in their science department, and often did. In fact, she had the first day Peter met her.

Peter smiled as he swept off the dust and rock from his sweat-lined helmet. Even though it was nearly four years ago, it was like it had only happened yesterday; he still couldn't decide whether it had been funnier to see "Ol' Smitty" at a loss for words, or to witness Amy angrily flush the color of a ripe cherry tomato in a room full of mostly male physical science majors. Peter recalled that Dr. Smithers—the brilliant, contentious and sometimes condescending head of their prestigious university's archeology department—had been droning on about fossil timelines, competing theories and his antiestablishment argument for the potential appearance of "hominids" during the Cretaceous period. Amy wouldn't have it—either his condescending style or his unsupported position—and she challenged him. Dr. Smithers was unaccustomed to being challenged by students, especially female students; he hadn't responded well to Amy, at first thinking she was red from embarrassment. Only the class bell brought their monumental intellectual—and loud—battle to an end. *More like an enforced truce!* Peter thought.

His smile faded quickly as his mind drifted back from his memory to the very real, stifling heat of the midday sun. Grumpy again, Peter called up to Amy, "Ah, never mind. Let's knock off for now and grab some chow, huh? I'm dying here." He pointed to his drenched sleeveless shirt, as if she needed help understanding how hot it was.

"No. I'm not ready yet. I want to get to the base of this section of wall. Go on, and I'll catch up in an hour or so. Maybe less," she replied, cheerily.

"Should have guessed that, Honey. You're never 'ready' until you want to be," Peter muttered under his breath. He tromped away towards their meager camp, pulled his helmet off and poured the remainder of his canteen onto his head. He shook the water out of his shoulder-length blond hair, then refilled his canteen from the water jug sitting on their dilapidated camp table, draining half the contents in one huge swig.

Peter sighed as he fell heavily into the rattier of their two canvas-back chairs. Disappointment and weariness washed over him like the sweat dripping through the grime on his face. *Could it really be three years that we've been here?* he wondered, bitterly. They had so little to show for it. Their excavations impacted rock faces all around the small valley south of Ghorlikharka, a tiny village in the southeast corner of Nepal, near the border with India. Sure, they'd found enough evidence to confirm that the scientists that came before them had, in fact, found something strange, a creature apparently unlike any found before. What was so tantalizing was that the creature didn't seem to be a bird, nor did it seem to be a mammal. Just a few months earlier, Amy had discovered a fossil revealing a wing. A big wing! If they postulated the scale of an individual wing based upon the partial fossil piece she found, the creature's full wingspan could be ten feet or more.

The most curious thing about the fossil, though, was that its wing was not like a bird's wing, at all. Its structure appeared much more like a bat's wing, but there were, obviously, no known bats that stood well over six feet high with a wing span taller than the inside of a house.

Peter admired his wife's boldness, though even he considered her a bit rash at times. Especially when Amy proposed, around one of their evening campfires a few weeks earlier, that the wing represented an entirely new species. Their excavation supervisor, Dr. Hector Ramirez, had vigorously argued with her. He vehemently contended that her findings did *not* represent a single animal, but comprised at least two layers of fossils—one bird, the other mammal—and that she'd jumped to a false conclusion. Although he didn't say anything, Peter was inclined to agree that there simply was not enough evidence to support the assertion that they had discovered a new—and exceedingly remarkable—species.

It had taken Amy more than a week to calm down after Hector had gone back to the United States. Peter grinned to himself as he realized that Dr. Ramirez probably needed at least a week to calm down, too. Amy had a way of getting herself in trouble with people in authority. But then she had since the first time he'd met her.

Hearing shuffling dirt and stone behind him, he turned to see Amy tromping into camp, wiping her face with a filthy kerchief, sporting an enormous smile across her lovely, nut-brown face. A welcoming smile was just beginning to form on his own face when he noticed what she was holding. Then his jaw dropped.

CHAPTER FIVE

DISCOVERIES

Amy, who had not been watching her step, nearly fell into their camp's fire ring. In her right hand was a stone, about the size of a football. The shape of it was nothing like an animal's body part, like Peter would have expected from the area that Amy had been excavating. In fact, he never would have expected her to be carrying anything away from the dig site until they'd—together—determined whether it was safe to remove. Their work was called "laborious and painstaking" for good reason.

"What on earth do you have there?" he asked, a little harshly.

"Boy, the heat sure has gotten you sideways, hasn't it?" she replied, flopping down in the other canvas chair.

"Yeah, I guess it has. Sorry." Peter poured the remainder of his recently filled canteen onto his head and again shook the water out of his hair. "That's better."

Peering over Amy's knees, which she had folded up in front of her to cradle the object in her lap, Peter again asked, "So, what do you have there?"

For a long moment, Amy did nothing. She said nothing. She continued to stare into her lap, at what it held. "Well, Honey," she said quietly, "I don't rightly know what it is. As I was brushing away the dirt around the end of the wing—you know, around the tip of the feathers," she paused to watch Peter nod, "I could see a small crack in the rock face about an inch beyond the wing's tip. So I brushed the area just a bit, wanting to see how serious the crack was and whether it might jeopardize my dig site…"

Her voice trailed off, and as she looked up at him, Peter could see Amy's eyes sparkling in a peculiar way. He felt his breath quicken, and he gripped the arms of his dilapidated chair.

Not seeming to notice, Amy continued. "Like always—you know how careful I am, Peter— I brushed at the crack with only the slightest force. So, obviously, I was alarmed when it suddenly widened. And it was odd how the crack widened *away* from my dig. Without thinking, I kept brushing bit by bit along the direction of the fissure. Each time I did so, the crack lengthened, twisting down and around until it circled all the way back to where it had started. It was almost as if I had been chiseling the rock face, instead of gently brushing it. Before I knew it, there was this roughly oval crack in the wall, just to the right of my excavation, in the shape you see here." She lifted the jagged object out of her lap with both hands. "Now there's an oval hole where this used to be."

Peter, trying to be careful not to sound critical of his wife, asked, "Uh, why did you cut it out of the wall?"

"I didn't," she replied, distractedly.

Confused and a little annoyed, Peter said, "Well, it didn't exactly fall out by itself, did it?" After he said it, he realized, too late, it didn't come across as he intended.

Surprisingly, Amy tipped her head to one side, stared hard at the chunk of rock in her lap, and quietly replied, "Yes. Yes, it did."

"Huh?" Peter's forehead wrinkled.

"That's the thing. I didn't pry at it or pull at it. At first, I just reached up to probe the crack with my finger—you know, to test the strength and integrity of this section of wall—and then I, well, I laid my hand across the oval, and it just came out of the wall, just like that. Like a cake out of a pan."

Peter stared at the void in the rock face where she must have had placed her hand. He could still see the area from where he sat.

"Was there any evidence of a fossil behind this chunk? Anything damaged by its removal?" he asked.

Although Peter had asked the question without a hint of criticism in his voice, this question seemed to irritate Amy.

Snapping her head up at him, she retorted, "No, there was nothing behind this chunk of rock besides more rock! But"— her eyes sparkled with an odd glint—"there is something on the *back* of this rock."

Turning the stone in her hands so Peter could see the side she had been staring at, he saw the unmistakable shape of a key. A large *metal* key, embedded in an ancient rock wall in southeast Nepal, just inches from a fossilized creature never seen before. A key found in the wrong place, in the wrong era, and that defied explanation.

CHAPTER SIX

FARM FRIENDS

Paign Macy had never liked school much. It seemed like a huge waste of time to him; he'd rather be doing than sitting. He was often in trouble with his defensive skills teacher, Alistair Murdoch. "You are not—once again—PAYING ATTENTION!" Professor Murdoch would bellow. Although when his teacher called out like this, he pronounced it in such a way that it sounded more like "pain" instead of "paying." So there was never a question of which student, in the class of eight, the good professor was annoyed with. Nevertheless, Paign excelled at the art of defense, even if he didn't often remember the details surrounding the history of it. What did it matter? He was very, very good in archery and excclled in sword fighting.

His best friend, Anders Knutson, knew everything about the history of defense. In fact, Anders knew everything about everything. It had always been so. They had been friends for so long that Paign could not remember a time when he and

Anders weren't best friends. Some people said that it couldn't have been otherwise, their always being best friends, because Paign's mother was the older sister of Anders's mother. But both Paign and Anders knew that their friendship went beyond, far beyond, simply being cousins.

For one thing, they were only three months apart in age. Anders had been born in May, while Paign was born in August. In addition, neither boy got along well with his own older sister, or with the other's sister. Both boys, now almost thirteen years of age—their upcoming "Age of Becoming" celebration only a few weeks away—had thick hair the color of charcoal and pale blue eyes, like their mothers'. Each boy, regrettably, had lost their fathers to the War of Dominance. Anders's father, Knute, had died when he was not quite five years old, while Paign's father, Roald, was killed just two years ago. Even now, it was difficult for Paign and Anders to talk about Roald's death because Anders took it almost as hard as Paign, since Paign's father had really become like a surrogate to Anders. Both boys had taken on more and more of the responsibilities of their dead fathers, until at this point in their short lives they were the men of their households. Each was nearly full-grown, strong and skilled in the ways of farming and herding.

Where they differed most was in their temperaments. Paign preferred testing his physical skills against any and all comers. He was often in fights, not always of someone else's making. Anders was exceptionally smart and loved to read, learning most everything with ease. He didn't really have much competition intellectually, since he was usually top in their class, with one exception: Freida Skulstad. Although she was a year older than the boys, the three spent most of their time together after school and on the weekends, after they all finished their chores. Anders and Paign, each in his own way, were quite smitten with Freida, with her bright grey eyes, easygoing personality and wavy, rust-colored hair. Anders worked very hard all the time at impressing her with all the things he knew. Paign, of course, attempted to impress her with his strength and agility. Freida, being very smart herself, knew this about both boys and pretended not to notice. It wouldn't do to let either boy think he was winning her over.

The farm Paign's family owned was set against the western rim of the Honellaken Valley, only a mile from the Knutsons' dairy farm, where Anders lived. Freida's home was farther up the east rim than Anders's family farm. Her father raised sheep and goats, grazing his flocks high up in the mountains above the valley, and she helped him herd the flocks down from the mountain each Saturday. They would rise early in the morning and trudge high above the valley, listening for the jingle of bells on the collar of the lead animals. By then it would be light out, although most often it would remain gloomy from the cloud cover, which only dissipated in the warmest weeks of summer. Once they had gathered up the flocks, Freida and her father, Johann, would turn back towards home, munching on their stale hard breads, an apple and enjoy a long drink from their water flasks.

After their last class was over, on the last day of term, with the excitement that only a two-week winter break can bring, Freida rushed up to where Anders and Paign were waiting for her, at the canopy of oak branches that marked the beginning of the wagon path leading up to their farms. They didn't care whether their desks were messy when they came back from break, like Freida did.

"I *found* it!" she gasped, breathless from running the quarter mile from school. "I am sure I have found it!"

Anders gaped, unbelieving. He knew that the odds of Freida finding the Cave of Parting were, well, nonexistent. Explorers had been searching for the most famous cave in the Highlands for centuries. Of course, they had been searching, too, for as long as Anders could remember.

"Huh. Right, Freida." Paign tilted his head as he said this. "Look, I have to get home to get our cows milked."

"Paign, I'm telling you I have found it! I *have* found the cave," she retorted, throwing an annoyed glance at Anders.

"OK, fine, Freida," replied Anders. "I have to go, too. Why don't you tell us about it while we walk?" He smiled, but she could tell he still didn't believe her.

"Fine!" she snapped, falling in between the boys, as they began the hike up the valley towards their farms. A light snow began to fall.

"Last night, my father needed to check on a nanny he'd tended last weekend. He wanted me to go with him, even though we'd be out until well into the evening…"

"So, that's why you look so tired," quipped Paign.

Ignoring him, Freida continued. "The flocks were sheltered on the lower slopes of the central ridge, but spread over the southernmost rise. It was nearly dark, so we needed our lanterns to follow their tracks to the individual animals, looking for the injured nanny goat. My father went up the steepest slope, while I slowly tracked the gullies. The final set of goat tracks I followed took me around a steep, ice-blown shelf. The snow was deep powder there and the passage was difficult, even in snowshoes. In a gaping cavity on the rock face, I could see the glint of our little goat's eyes from my lantern light.

She was trembling at the mouth of a small opening into the mountain. I scooped her up and hiked back to where my father's lantern was on the higher slope."

"But," interrupted Paign again, "wouldn't that have put you somewhere below Ruar's Peak?" All of the villagers, farmers and herders living in the Highlands territory were very familiar with Ruar's Ridge, the tallest saddle of rock amongst the Honellaken range, which rose up between them and the territory to the north. Ruar's Peak was the tallest peak along the saddle's spine.

"If you were paying more attention, Paign, you'd have heard me say that it was by then very dark, even by lantern light, and dangerous going, so I wasn't exactly keeping track of my position on the ridge," she snapped. "But, yes, I suppose I was somewhere below Ruar's Peak."

"Well," Anders chimed in, "there are no cave entrances anywhere along that ridge. We've climbed all over that rock face, Freida, especially last summer."

"Don't you think I know that?" sighed a dispirited Freida. She'd expected an enthusiastic response from her friends, not the third degree. "What I'm telling you is this: there is a cave opening now. I'm convinced it wasn't there before when we searched for it."

"Oh, come on, Freida!" Paign sounded more irritated than he meant to, but this was getting out of hand. "People in our village have been looking for the Cave of Parting for nearly three hundred years. Our fathers searched for it when they were our age. Their fathers searched for it, and so did their fathers. It hasn't been seen since old hermit Sandersohn wandered into the village, delirious and wild-eyed, declaring he'd seen Widow Vellhelmina vanish into the mountain—that the mountain had, in his words, 'devoured her, robes, staff, witch and all!'"

Of course, all the children for miles around their village—perhaps all around the country—had heard the Tale of Vellhelmina and the crazy Hermit since they were wee tots. For Anders, it had become nothing more than a fable elders would tell children to scare them from wandering off into the mountains until they were of age. So, it was difficult to take Freida seriously, except for the fact that she appeared to be as set in her belief as the cold, hard ice crunching on the path under his feet. He could see her face was red, and he didn't think it was just from the cold wind blowing down the valley.

"OK, Freida, let's say you have found it." He shot a glance at Paign, who appeared to choke on something. "We're almost home. Paign and I have chores to do tonight. You'll be up in the mountains most of tomorrow with your flocks. Why don't we all meet Sunday, at noon, behind your barn, and you can take us up and show us what you think you saw?"

"Wha—what I *think* I saw?" Freida's eyes were blazing. Her face flushed even redder than before.

"Uh, well, sorry, that's not what I meant to say," replied Anders, who thought he heard Paign quietly mutter under his breath, "Yes it is."

"Please show us the place. Show us on Sunday afternoon. OK?" Anders continued.

"Hm," Paign said, looking unconvinced that Anders's plan was worth much. "Come on, Freida. I'm not trying to question you. It's just that this cave has been the most sought after thing in our country for a very long time. What makes you think you found a cave, especially this cave? Couldn't it just be that a chunk of rock broke away from the face?"

The cousins could see Freida was quaking, even though her fur-lined hood pulled up tight over her head. Her eyes welling with tears, she stared at both of them in turn and, quietly but fiercely, replied, "Fine. I'll show you. I'll show both of you. Sunday, noon, behind my barn. Then you can explain to me how it is that a fallen chunk of weathered granite reveals a glowing light deep within the passage where no cavern should be!"

With that, she abruptly turned and ran up the path towards home.

CHAPTER SEVEN

FREIDA'S FIND

Paign was in a foul mood as he walked across the valley to Anders's farm. He hitched his daypack a little higher on his left shoulder to better distribute the weight of his gear, which included extra layers of warm clothes, enough food and water for the afternoon—and night, if it came to it—and his bow and quiver. His sword was strapped to his belt and swung off his right hip. Tromping through the fresh snow, he replayed in his mind the intense conversation from two days earlier, when Freida told them about discovering the legendary Cave of Parting. Still convinced it was a wild goose chase that Anders had committed him to, he grumbled while he trudged along, looking at the ground and dragging his boots through the snow. At the last moment, he looked up, just in time to slow himself enough to not crash through the Knutsons' gate.

Cursing under his breath, he carefully opened the gate and paused to admire Anders's farmhouse. It included the four-color pattern common to the farmhouses around the Highlands.

But these colors were more vibrant than most, with a deeper green, richer burgundy and lighter yellows. The paint still looked fresh and bright, giving the house a sense of spring-time warmth even in the winter gloom. Admiring the farm was bittersweet for Paign, since it was his father, Roald, who had painted it a little over two years ago, before he was called into the battle from which he didn't return. Paign's mother had asked her husband to help Mrs. Knutson with her farm, and he had done so willingly. He was that kind of man, and he'd enjoyed spending time with his nephew, Anders. He also knew that Knute Knutson would have done the same for his family, had the tables been turned.

Paign had lost track of how long he'd been standing there, but it must have been a few minutes, since he'd accumulated about a quarter inch of snow on his coat. Shaking it free, he walked up to the house, stepped onto the porch and knocked. Just a moment later, Anders pulled it open.

"Where have you been?" Anders asked. Without waiting for an answer, he hollered back into the house, "Mom, we're leaving and won't be back until after dark. See you later!" He pushed Paign back out the door, at the same time hoisting his backpack onto his shoulders.

"Come on!" he yelled at Paign, as he jumped off the porch at a run. "You know how Freida gets when we're late!"

It was a marvel how fast Anders could be. Since he was also already a brighter student, it annoyed Paign that he couldn't quite catch up to Anders. *Well, I have a sword swinging into my knee!* Paign thought. But he didn't say anything and just kept running after Anders.

Nearing the gate of the Skulstad's farmhouse, he could see Freida stomping in the snow behind the barn. Their huge mastiff, Tiny, chained to the porch's corner post, yawned lazily as he watched Paign run by. Paign smiled to himself at the notion of such an enormous dog being named Tiny, but he knew it was because Freida had fallen in love with the runt of the Olson's mastiff litter. While Tiny gave no heed to Anders or Paign, since they were around Freida so often, he was truly fearsome to strangers.

"You're late!" Freida said to Anders, who had already jogged around the corner of the barn. Without even looking at Paign, she turned on her boot heels and strode up the snow-covered pasture towards the edge of the tree line that marked the base of the ridge. High above, dominating the horizon of their little valley, the ridgeline erupted more than three thousand feet into a jagged sky.

They hiked along the existing snow trail made by the trampling of Freida's goats and sheep, for more than an hour without speaking. Freida led them with a ferocious pace. Anders, just ahead of Paign, was puffing like the steam train that went through their valley twice a month. Paign's throat felt like it was on fire from his hard breathing in this bitter-cold landscape. He was sure that Freida felt every bit as much discomfort as he did. Her pace was her way of showing she was still angry with him for not believing her, Paign was certain. Had he asked, he would have learned how right he was.

Climbing up a steep pitch of snow, kicking the toes of her boots deep into the crusty snow, one above the other until she reached the crest, Freida looked back down to where Paign stood. He thought she looked equally determined and weary. When Paign reached the crest himself, he could see she was nearly finished making a small campfire for them.

"I hope you brought something to eat." She spoke while rummaging in her pack, without looking up at him.

Paign was quiet. Instead, he pulled out his snow parka, put it on without zipping it, tugged it as low as it would reach and sat down in the snow. He knew he'd cool off pretty quickly now that they weren't hiking, and he needed to control his core temperature by keeping the heavy coat unzipped and open for only a minute or two. Once they started hiking again, he'd overheat if the parka was zipped, but chill too quickly without it. He'd noticed Anders had already done the same. In fact, so had Freida.

"Yeah. I brought food. Um, thanks for building the fire," Paign replied, trying to catch her eye.

"Right, then," said Anders. "Thanks, Freida, for making the fire."

"It's not a big deal, you know," she said, glaring at them.

"Hey," said Anders quietly, looking at the crackling little fire, "we're here with you, OK?" He stole a sideways glance at Paign. "It was just a surprise when you told us you'd found what is arguably the most famous and elusive thing in the land, right? It wasn't like I—we—were calling you a liar or anything. We wouldn't be here if we didn't trust you."

Paign would have sworn that Freida's grey eyes welled with tears, but with the cold and wind his eyes were starting to water, too. He simply nodded his support to what Anders had said.

A few moments passed before she grinned slightly and said, "Come on and eat whatever you are going to. We need to get to the rock overhang in the next hour if we want to have any time to explore it—the cave—before turning back."

For the next few minutes, they ate with only the sound of the wind in their cold ears. Quickly, they bundled up their packs and slung them over their shoulders. Freida kicked snow into the fire and it sizzled out abruptly.

Nearly an hour later and many hundreds of feet higher, threads of cloud swirled around them before blowing down the steep ridge they had just climbed. They had all tied on their snowshoes about fifteen minutes earlier, and Freida continued to lead them with confident steps. She'd begun to traverse the slope laterally, in the direction of the escarpment the boys knew to be to the south, even though they could not see anything but the shifting whites of cloud and snow.

Suddenly, Freida stopped, dropped her backpack on the snow and fished out a rope. Tying it around her waist, she played out about twenty feet and then handed the rest of the rope to Anders. He tied a loop of rope to his waist and then handed the remainder to Paign, so there would be about the same rope distance between them. When he'd also tied into the rope, Freida hoisted her pack and began to climb again. Looking off to his right, Paign could see far below, between the shifting clouds, shreds of sunlight on the valley floor. He walked directly into the back of Anders before realizing the group had stopped walking.

"Hey!" cried a startled Anders, who was knocked over onto his back.

At the same moment, Paign yelled out, "Sorry!"

As Paign reached down to help his friend up, he noticed an odd look on Anders face. Turning his attention in the direction of Anders's gaze, he saw for a moment a ghostly Freida, shrouded in vaporous snow and cloud. Then, suddenly, she darkened and came into sharp focus as the cloud shredded, leaving only a few swirling flakes around her face, which was engulfed in an enormous, triumphant smile. He heard Anders breathe out a low, long "Whoa!" Paign then saw immediately behind Freida the unmistakable mouth of a cave he'd never seen before. It could be the ancient Cave of Parting. Maybe Freida *had* found it, after all.

CHAPTER EIGHT

THE WIDOW'S CAVE

Huddled close together in the cave's opening, Freida couldn't help but blurt out, "See! I told you so." Her face glowed with triumph.

Anders shrugged and nodded, kicking a clump of ice into the blowing wind outside.

Paign slipped off his pack, pulled out a lantern and said, "OK, Freida. You *did* find an unknown cave opening. But how do we know it's the Widow's Cave?"

"Uh, well, what else could it be?" Anders interrupted.

Paign was surprised to hear this from Anders, who prided himself on his knowledge. "Couldn't this cave opening simply have come from the forces of a freezing and thawing cycle over hundreds of years?"

Freida, who had by now removed her lantern from her pack and trimmed it to a brilliant yellow flame, said, "Truth is, Paign, I just know it is the Widow's Cave. It's the only explanation that makes sense to me. If this is just a hole in the side of Ruar's Ridge, this won't take more than a moment to explore. Otherwise…" Her voice became muffled as she turned away from the opening and began scrambling inwards, through the piled-up snow.

Since Anders was in between the lanterns carried by his friends, he pulled out a little parchment journal from his pocket in case he needed to take notes of their journey. Paign considered this almost ridiculous, expecting this trip to be short. He'd concluded that there was a small void behind the chunk of stone that must have fallen out of the rock face during a recent storm, and was now covered in snow. So he was very surprised when Freida—and her lamp—disappeared up ahead.

Dropping almost to his knees, Paign crouched to get below a nodule of rock that jutted down from the ceiling, snickering because it reminded him of the uvula at the back of his throat. Not far ahead, he could see Freida had stopped. Her light revealed they were in a much larger opening than they had just come through. The roof rose nearly twenty feet over them, with the walls retreating into the far reaches of the lantern's beams. Towards the back, a few stalactites dangled down. Paign could dimly see there were three corridors, or tunnels, branching off of the open hall they had just stepped into. Even though it was warm inside the chamber, he shivered.

"So, what do you think now?" Freida asked Anders.

"It's obvious this is a cave, and it's been here a long time. It could be the Widow's Cave, I suppose. But I don't know how we can be sure…if there's a way to know it is, you know, *that* cave," he replied, looking around the chamber as he spoke.

"Hm." Paign looked at Freida. "Don't you suppose there'd be clues, like something left by the Widow Vellhelmina? There must be signs that she was here…hey, I wonder whether she could *still* be here?"

"Come on, Paign! Really? Three hundred-odd years after the legend began, you expect an astonishingly old woman to come shuffling down one of these tunnels?" Anders asked. The way Paign was peering around the chamber, Anders thought his cousin expected a shriveled carcass or skeleton to fall out of an alcove in the cavern.

Paign's fist clenched tight.

"She was supposedly a witch—according to the legend, anyway," Freida piped up.

Anders shook his head slightly. "Yeah, I know the story. A weird little old widow woman, so old that no one living then remembered when she'd been born, or where she'd come from. Lived high in the mountains above Paign's farm. Didn't seem to have any way to support herself, yet she never seemed wanting. Wandered all around the valley, always muttering under her breath like she was casting spells and incantations, tottering along with a long, gnarled walking staff."

Pausing for a moment, Anders sighed. When he began speaking again, he sounded agitated. "She didn't seem to have any friends but no one thought ill of her, just thought her plenty peculiar and eccentric. Then, according to the ever-reliable crazy Hermit , Helmut Sandersohn, the little Widow Vellhelmina climbs the ridge we just did, in similarly nasty conditions, and then shuffles into the cave below Ruar's Peak, only to have the cave's opening snap shut behind her with such force it could be heard all the way into the village. So complete was the cave's closure that no one could be sure where the opening had been. And the Widow Vellhelmina was never seen again…perhaps until today, when her skeleton falls onto

Paign!" Anders laughed at his brilliant new ending to a story they'd all grown up with. Paign slugged him.

"Not funny, Anders," Paign said, his fist still clenched.

"OK, sorry. I'm just kidding around. This place is kind of giving me the creeps. It feels sort of like we're being watched. So, what's next?" he said, looking to Freida.

Freida, slowly surveying the chamber, finally said, "It's getting late. We should start heading back." She unslung her pack onto the floor, rummaged in it a moment, and pulled out a canteen and an apple. "We should eat and drink something, though, before leaving the cave. Once we leave here, we'll need one hand free for the lanterns and the other for balancing."

The boys nodded. Without saying anything, they fished out food and drink from their packs, quietly eating and drinking as they hiked back to the mouth of the cavern. Anders stopped to get out his lantern and trim it for maximum light. They could all hear that the wind had picked up while they were inside, so they dug out their extra clothing, donned it, pulled their fur-lined hoods tight around their faces and marched out into the deepening gloom.

Had they looked back into the depths of the cavern, in the dimness left in the center tunnel, they'd have seen the vague and perplexing movement of what would have certainly appeared to be rock stepping out of rock, until a pair of blood red orbs opened nearly seven feet above the floor…and blinked.

CHAPTER nINE

THE KEY OF KAHRNAHRGX

Danielle lay still for a moment. She realized she was in that fuzzy state of mind between dreaming and waking. Slowly, she opened her eyes, expecting to see her mobile of clouds gently bobbing above her head. Even though she'd had the mobile since she was little, because it came from her grandmother, she hadn't been able to put it away. So she gasped a little when—instead of a mobile dangling from her bedroom ceiling—she saw real, crimson-tinted clouds drifting high above. They floated above a ring of treetops. Was she still dreaming? Even as she thought it, she realized that, no, this wasn't a dream.

"Where are we now?" she asked, not even bothering to look for Ercen or Kimar.

"In a different place," replied the deep, grumbling voice of Kimar.

"Well, that isn't especially helpful, now is it?" quipped Danielle.

"Child, we needed to part from the cavern of Osberg the Great. We were being followed." Ercen spoke quietly, looking intently at Danielle with her large amber eyes.

"OK, fine. We had to leave in a hurry, I get it. You took me from the cul-de-sac I was collecting on for my newspaper route, because I had been 'foretold' to you. And you waited two months to snatch me, right? What's that all about, then?" Danielle's voice sounded jittery. She realized her hands were shaking noticeably, so she sat on them.

Kimar, who had been standing, sat down on the ground. The tops of the huge firs were glowing red from the setting sun. Aimlessly, Kimar pulled a fallen tree branch to his lap and began peeling the bark off of it, like Danielle had seen her father do many times on their family camping trips. The difference was that her father's branches were twigs, and he used a pocketknife. Kimar's was the size of the branches her father cut for firewood to bring home, and instead of a knife, Kimar used the talon above his first finger. First, he drew his talon the length of the branch, angling it into the bark so that, as it cut away from the branch, it curled tightly. When he reached the end, his talon twisted in such a way that the angle was perfectly reversed. A moment later, another curled ribbon of bark dropped from the opposite end of the branch.

Ercen paced nearby. Her movement reminded Danielle of the motion of herons she'd watched near her school. Slow. Elegant. A bit awkward.

"You were foretold to us in the early days of our people," Kimar began. "For millennia, we had been creatures of peace and beauty. But many generations ago, there was a rift amongst us. We had been a unified tribe. But, as with many races of creatures, there arose one gargoyle who worshiped strength over peace. Instead of harmony, he desired domination. So great was his lust for power, he swayed others to follow him. He led a revolt against his own kind, but was eventually defeated and banished—he and his followers—from the realm of Osberg. So strong was his thirst for domination that he continued to delve deeper into the dark magics. In time, he became a very powerful wizard, conjuring the blackest of incantations…"

Kimar paused for a moment and peeled more bark from his tree limb. There was a large pile now in front of his feet. At first, Danielle smiled at the strange sight of a massive gargoyle idly stripping a huge branch of its bark. She found it to be oddly comforting. Then, her eyes widened as her brain slowly computed that Kimar's feet—very much like her own, but enormous by comparison—also had talons. His slab-like feet had four long talons that protruded through the skin just behind the toes and arched forward ten inches or so. Only now, she also noticed that a single talon thrust out behind his feet, beginning just above his heel. Danielle guessed that his "human" foot must be around twenty-four inches long, with the talons adding another twelve inches in both directions, front and back. No talons protruded over his big toes.

"The member of our tribe who was banished from among us—his name is Kahrnahrgx," Ercen said, with her back turned to Danielle and Kimar. Her head was lowered and facing the ground, but her voice was strong. Then she turned and faced them.

Kimar glanced up from his tree limb, now completely skinned of bark, and stared at Ercen. Danielle could not place the expression on his face.

Her amber eyes glistening in the falling dimness engulfing the forest, Ercen continued. "The gargoyle Kahrnahrgx rebuilt his forces and remounted his attack on our realm. Before he was defeated a second time and cast out of our lands, our leader, Osberg, was killed by Kahrnahrgx, as were many of our kind. Those of us who survived were scattered." A tear dribbled down her leathery face.

"What does this have to do with me?" Danielle was confused, tired, hungry and wanted desperately to go home. Yet something stirred deep within her at the pain and sadness in Ercen's face. "These things you're telling me are terrible, to be sure. But I'm just a kid and have no special powers. What can *I* do?" she asked, softly.

Kimar spoke. "When Osberg was fighting Kahrnahrgx, talon against talon, Osberg seized a key hanging from his enemy's belt. In fury, Kahrnahrgx thrust a talon deep within the chest of Osberg. Moments before he died from the mortal wound inflicted on him, Osberg parted, still holding the key."

Ercen continued, "As far as we know, the Key was to a special chamber in the evil Temple that Kahrnahrgx had built for himself. We believe the room this key opens holds the secret of Kahrnahrgx's power. We believe this because he has sought nothing else since the key was taken from him. He and his minions have been searching for hundreds of years."

"How is it possible they wouldn't have found it by now?" cried Danielle. "You are so...strong!"

Kimar replied, "It is always difficult to trace a parting. Not only is space parted by our asking, but strong gargoyles can also ask time to not matter, and thus part it, along with space. So it is difficult, but generally not impossible, to trace a parting. Only the strongest can leave no trace of their parting.

Osberg was one of those strong ones, perhaps the strongest. Because he was dying the moment he parted, there has been no sign of him since."

"But you have been looking all this time?" Danielle quivered, feeling a sudden chill down her back. "You and, um, Kahrnahrgx?"

"We have," said Ercen.

"You must believe, then, that I have something to do with the answer to what happened to Osberg?"

"We do."

Danielle, torn between a desperate desire to help and a gnawing fear of what that could mean, snapped. "But have you not been listening to me? I'm a kid with a paper route. That's it! I'm in the eighth grade and don't have a single interesting thing about my life. I haven't been anywhere special. I've never been any farther than Minnesota to visit my Gram and Gran. I don't have lots of friends, either, and the ones I have don't have mysterious lives any more than I do!"

Ercen quietly replied, "Child, we didn't say that you know where Osberg died or that you found the key he plucked from the belt of Kahrnahrgx."

Kimar added, "But you know who did."

"Wha...I *do*?" Danielle blurted. "Who?"

"Child, your mother. She found the Key many years ago. Have you not seen a large key, engraved with strange runes, somewhere in your house?" replied Ercen.

Suddenly, Danielle recalled a Plexiglas case, sitting on the lowest shelf of one of several enormous bookcases in the corner of her parents' home office. She hadn't looked for it in years, but assumed it was still on that same shelf. As best she could remember, it had been surrounded by piles—mountains—of books, journals, diaries, binders and the various detritus of their many adventures. On the shelves above and below the plastic case surrounding the odd key were other artifacts from the early years of their marriage, when they had traveled all over the world excavating various archeological sites. She knew the key must have been important enough to encase it the way her mother did, but she knew little else about it. However, she vividly recalled that when she was younger, around seven years old, she had picked up the case to study the huge key inside, puzzled by the curious markings upon it. Her mother had come into the office, seen what Danielle was holding, looked very alarmed and yelled, "Not again! Put it back at once!" Her mother had rushed over to her, hoisted her into her arms, squeezed her tight and told her to never pick it up again. And Danielle hadn't.

With the vision of that case still in her mind's eye, she focused again on Ercen. "Yes. Yes, I have seen such a key. I mean, yes, we have a key like that in our house. At least, we did. It was in my parents' office."

Although she was very distracted by her situation—at first feeling she was in great danger from these gargoyles, then believing that Kimar and Ercen meant her no harm, then understanding that she was in great danger, after all, but from a different gargoyle—Danielle was suddenly struck by a question, like a clap of thunder. Plucking up her courage again, she asked, "So, if you are able to locate this Key of Kahrnahrgx, won't he also be able to?" Once she's said it out loud, she shivered at the idea.

"Yes," Ercen replied.

"No," countered Kimar.

"Huh?" Danielle blurted, confused. "Which is it?"

Ercen looked at Kimar, but said nothing.

"Both," Kimar said, flatly. "Although he created the Key, it was wrought with such terrible power his ability to sense it across time was severely blunted. So, the answer to your question about his ability to locate the Key is, as I said, 'No.' However, we did not trace the Key here, either. While our ability is not blunted as is his, Osberg—with the Key—parted into such a far, distant past none of our kind could trace him nor the Key. But we were able to eventually discover *you*. Our impressions of where we could find you were only strong enough to get us into the area in which you live, not directly to you. Thus, we had to wait until our impressions strengthened. Of course, we had no idea you would come to the very house where we hid. Yet, you did. We do not believe this was a chance meeting. So, the answer Ercen gave you is also true. We believe it is only a matter of time before Kahrnahrgx locates you."

Danielle shivered more than before.

"Now that we have located you, we must have the Key," Kimar said. "Soon."

CHAPTER TEN

CURSED

"Honey, what have you got there?" Peter peered up from the pile of papers stacked precariously on their small desk.

Peter rubbed his eyes for a minute and ran his fingers through his long, wavy blond hair. He disliked this week of the fall semester more than any other. The freshmen archeology students seemed to pay less attention to his instruction each year. When it came time to complete their term papers, roughly half the students would do a fair job of simply regurgitating pages and pages of things he'd taught them about the history of archeology. The students seemed to believe their grades werc measured by the ounce, and the more ounces of paper, the higher their scores would be. What he wanted to see was clear thinking and strong correlation—connecting the themes between eras, drawing bold conclusions, even if they ran against the prevailing beliefs of science. In fact, more than anything, he hoped to instill this value in his daughter, Danielle. But he rarely got this from his own college students.

Most of his students gave evidence that they had been asleep all semester and didn't care enough about what their grade would be to include solid content in their massive papers. So, Peter graded their papers accordingly.

Amy's eyes were darting around the small office. Her voice sounded tight to Peter. "Well, I finally had this thing boxed up today. You know, like I've been saying I would."

"Ah! OK, I see what you have inside there," Peter said, squinting in the dim banker's light shining on their dark mahogany office desk. He could see, through the plastic, the key lying unceremoniously on a piece of burlap.

"Didn't want it lying about any more?" he said with a wry smile on his face.

"Now, stop it," Amy said with some heat. "You know that thing has bugged me since the day I found it."

"Yeah, I know, Ame. But you haven't mentioned it for the longest time, so I thought it must have, you know, stopped bugging you," Peter replied.

Peter cast back in his memory to the day Amy had returned to their Nepalese camp, holding onto the enormous key that had been mysteriously lodged in a stone nearby the fossil dig. It had made them somewhat of a celebrity couple for a few months, almost three years earlier. What a day that had been! They'd argued about the key and whether or not it dated back to the era of the fossil. Neither believed it possible that the key could actually be as old as the fossil it was buried beside, but they also had no explanation for how it got there. Both had argued various points of view, all the way through their meager dinner, which was mostly rice. To this day, Peter still didn't like rice.

While still facing Amy, his mind lost focus on her while his recollection of that day sharpened. He remembered that as the evening cooled, along with his temper—*I never did that well in heat*—Amy had snuggled up to him, and in the flickering light of their dying campfire, announced to him he was going to be a father. Even now, he regretted that he laughed and blurted out, "Good one, Ame! How would you know that?" He'd thought Amy was starting up another round of arguments about the key and using this announcement to put him off his guard. *What an idiot I was! What woman would joke about having a child? Certainly not Amy.* She'd sneered back at him, "Trust me, I know!" After half an hour of apologizing, including on bended knee, he'd finally convinced Amy he was, in fact, delighted by this news. Because he was. Even though it meant leaving their excavation about six months earlier than planned, they had agreed early in their marriage that as important as their scientific research was, they wanted to have a family.

He was horrified just a few hours later when, in the darkest hour of the night, Amy had sat suddenly bolt upright and screamed out from the depths of a nightmare, "Nooooo! You *can't* have her!" She shivered in his embrace the rest of the night, even though the air was still warm.

Snapping out of his strong memory, Peter observed his wife. Holding the plastic-walled box as if it was more than a little toxic, apprehension lining her gentle features, she appeared much older than her twenty-six years. But he understood how it could be so, because every year since that first bad dream, Amy had the same nightmare. It was not always as intense or frightening, but it always came, like a horrible anniversary present no one wants.

He'd thought it strange that Danielle had come into the office, yesterday of all days—the third anniversary of Amy's unwelcome dream—and went to the shelf where the strange key laid…the key that defied scientific explanation, the key Amy had found just hours before that initial, terrifying nightmare. Granted, Amy had even odds of guessing they would have a girl. But as she'd told him in the hours following each return of the nightmare—every single year of its horrible visitation upon her—Amy always cried out for the return of their *daughter*. In her dream of terror, Amy *knew* they were parents of a girl, about seven months before their only child was born. And now, of course, they were parents of a growing toddler girl. Peter hadn't been prepared for the overwhelming sense of joy that washed over him at her birth. He'd wept when he first held her in his arms. Even now he was misting up, deep in his remembrances. Amy shifted her feet, pulling him back to the present.

Quietly, she murmured, "I thought so, too. It's just that yesterday, when I found Danielle in here…you know how fast she moves since she's been walking by herself. She was right next to me in the kitchen while you were out jogging. I was busy cleaning up. When I looked down, she wasn't there. I checked the gate to the basement to make sure it was closed. Then I checked here in our office. That's when I found her holding…this." She was staring at the now-boxed-up key. "I don't want her touching this ever again." Peter saw the look in her eyes grow more intense, even manic. "Ever!" she yelled. "That's why I had it boxed up."

"Should we dispose of it, Hon? Give it to a gallery, maybe?" Peter replied.

"I've thought about that. A lot..." Amy responded, with a wan smile. "No. We don't get rid of it. Not yet. Not until we've learned what it is. You know, Hector is still deciphering the runes. Maybe he'll finally have a breakthrough."

"Fair enough," Peter said quietly, as he reached over to retrieve the clear box his wife was clutching, pushed aside a huge pile of magazines and placed it on the most open shelf in their office. He didn't tell Amy that he was thinking Hector was already plenty busy with running his scientific research lab in La Paz and since he'd not broken the runic code yet, he probably never would.

CHAPTER ELEVEN

FINAL PREPARATIONS

Danielle had grown up hearing about the mysterious key and how her mother experienced an annual torment in the form of a bad dream. She knew that her parents, in ways even they could not express, believed there was a connection between the two events. Her Mom had discovered the garish, rune-covered key embedded in the same wall of Nepalese rock that they'd been excavating an unknown fossil from. She also knew that the fossil—when they had finally unearthed it from the stone wall several weeks later—had proven to be quite a sensation. At least, at first. By the time her parents had returned to the United Srates with it, the fossil—and consequently, her parents—was famous. Many reporters came to interview "The Doctoral Students Who Found a New Species!" There were several copies of a magazine in a corner of their home office featuring her parents right on the front cover. Her Gram and Gran had the same magazine cover framed in the front room of their home in Minnesota. In fact, their notoriety eventually found them their current teaching positions. Her father had ruefully declared it was a good thing that the hire happened when it did, because eventually a collaborative group of scientists from various fields of study concluded that their "new species" was just a mishmash of fossils that coincidentally looked like something new. But, by then, her parents had completed their doctoral dissertations, been granted PhDs and become university professors.

But as she considered what Ercen and Kimar were telling her about the origins and history of the key that was found with the fossil, she remembered what had happened when she was seven and her mother had screamed at her for picking up the plastic box. Since that day, Danielle could not recall seeing the key box. Was it still in her parents' office? It was always such a mess in there, more like a storage room for dusty old stuff.

Her stomach growled loudly, and she could see that Ercen had heard it.

"Kimar will return soon with human food and drink for you," Ercen said.

"Thanks. I'm famished," replied Danielle, scooching closer to the fire that Kimar had started before he'd parted in search of food. All that bark he'd peeled from the tree limb had come in useful. *Did he mean to do that all along?* she wondered.

A moment later, Kimar appeared on the other side of the small fire ring, startling Danielle. No sound of footsteps—just "poof," and there he was! She did notice that, just a moment before he appeared, there was a little rustling of the leaves and pine needles beneath the spot he parted to. He walked around the crackling fire and handed her a small tin bucket filled with water, as well as a loaf of bread as long as her arm and a round of whitish-colored cheese, the kind her mother bought from time to time for holidays. Danielle wasted no time in digging in to her long-overdue meal. With no knife, she had to take bites out of the cheese round, as if it was an apple. She followed up with a chunk of the bread loaf and washed it all down with a swig from the bucket. She repeated the process, eager for the growling to stop. A bit of fruit would have been nice, but she wasn't complaining.

"We regret not providing you sustenance until now," said Ercen, smiling. "You see, we find nourishment from the earth and sky, from stone and cloud."

"Hmphf," mumbled Danielle, mouth stuffed full of cheese and bread. So many bits of bread had fallen around her lap, it looked like she'd had a small snowstorm go over her.

Ercen and Kimar said nothing else while she ate. Kimar's attention was directed towards the sky above, his amber eyes casting a slight glow, scanning the stars, back and forth. Danielle noticed the moon beginning to peak over the treetops. Ercen, she noticed, seemed amused at watching her consume her very late dinner with such vigor.

Finally full, Danielle put the leftovers on a flat rock. "Thanks. That's the best cheese I've ever tasted!"

"Are you strong now?" asked Kimar.

"Huh?" replied a puzzled Danielle.

"Are you strong enough to go?" he clarified.

"Um, I guess so," she replied, a great weariness washing over her. "If you mean, am I full…yeah. I am. But it's really late. I've been gone for hours now. My folks are sure to be frantic, my mom, especially. I just want to go home and then go to bed. Do I really have to go with you in search of—of whatever…" Her voice trailed off.

"Child, we are going to your home. We must retrieve the Key of Kahrnahrgx at once." Ercen answered with an urgency in her voice that snapped Danielle back from the drowsiness stealing over her.

"Your parents are in grave danger, Danielle," grumbled the deep voice of Kimar. "If you are strong now, we must go at once."

Reaching out his left hand to Ercen, Kimar took Danielle's left hand in his right. As soon as Ercen completed the circle by taking Danielle's other hand, they parted without a sound. A few leaves and pine needles floated down onto the small fire and the leftover food that was lying on a flat rock. A family of local mice enjoyed a delightful feast of leftover bread and fine-tasting cheese.

CHAPTER TWELVE

EXPLORATION

The next morning, Freida woke to a very foggy day. There was a ghostly pink tinge to the fog, so she knew the sun would eventually burn off the gloom. The sun could not have cleared the eastern ridge, though, because it was just a little after six. She could hear her father puttering down in the kitchen. Still a bit groggy from the full day of hiking she had the day before with Anders and Paign, Freida realized it must be Sunday, because she could smell pancakes. Her father always made pancakes on Sunday morning. It had been a tradition for as long as she could remember.

She cracked open her bedroom window to let the fresh and very cold air help wake her up. The flannel curtains her mother sewed fluttered gently in the breeze coming from outside. She watched the clouds of fog roiling slowly around, with light dancing at the edges and the sun momentarily beaming through, unfiltered. Her rooster, Grumpy, was angrily crowing at the dawn of the new day. He was probably hungry, she realized. She'd been staring at the ebb and flow of the fog for almost half an hour!

Hastily, she threw on her work clothes and woolen socks and hurried down the steep stairs that led to the first floor from her room and the "guest room" that never had a guest in it. That's why the other room might just as well have been her room, too, because it was where she played and kept her games and playthings.

Giving her father a quick peck on the cheek, she took three fast steps and then slid in her stocking feet across the hardwood kitchen floor into the mudroom and, with the perfected timing that comes from months of practice, stopped directly in front of her farm boots. Plopping down on the narrow bench, she thrust her feet into her muck-crusted boots without paying heed to what fell off, jumped up, grabbed her heavy woolen coat and ran outside onto the porch. Just as she closed the mudroom door, she heard her father call out, "I'll keep the pancakes warm for you, dear."

"Thanks, Papa," she yelled through the small kitchen window, just a few feet from the mudroom door, and waved at him.

By the time she got to the barn, she'd buttoned up her coat high around her collar to keep out the biting cold. She didn't mind her chores so much as some kids at her school did. They seemed to think it was a real hardship, if not an evil injustice meted out by wicked parents. Freida figured it was just her way of helping out. Although she wouldn't mind if her father got rid of the pigs. They smelled!

About forty minutes later, Freida walked back to her home, carrying a basket, with a little less bounce in her steps. But then she had fed the chickens, cuddled with Grumpy and slopped the pigs. While they were eating, nosing noisily about their breakfasts, she cleaned out the stall they were penned in at night. During the day, the pigs gratefully ran around a much larger outside pen. She'd never understand what a pig's attraction was to mud, especially the nasty, fouled mud of their outside pen.

The fog was beginning to burn off, but it looked to Freida that they'd be replaced by threatening clouds. *Bother!* she thought. *I wanted to visit the boys...*

After brushing off her filthy boots with an even filthier boot brush left outside for that one purpose, Freida stepped into the mudroom and kicked them off. After hanging up her coat, she slid back into the kitchen, deftly placing the basket gently onto the table mid-slide.

"Perhaps you should become a ballerina, Freida," her father said, smiling behind the coffee cup stalled between his lips and the table.

She frowned. "Oh, Papa! Don't make fun. You know we don't have any teachers in the village…even if I did want to learn." Freida also knew her parents did not have money for such luxuries as private lessons for anything, and certainly not for something like ballet. But even as she said it, she felt an ache inside.

"Little One," her father said, smiling —still calling her this *at her age*—as he put down his cup. He got up, walked over to his daughter, and placed his large, gnarled hands on her shoulders. Looking her square in the face, he continued, "I wasn't kidding or making fun. Your mother and I have eyes in our heads. And we use them, too! We see the joy and wonder that fills your pretty face whenever you dance. And you know that our little farm doesn't provide for much more than just what we need, with a wee extra, once in a while. However," he said, gently squeezing her shoulders with his knobby fingers, "I always want you to dream your dreams. Do not let them go! You may not see all of them fulfilled, it is true. Those times can be difficult. But, my darling, you are certain to not ever reach a dream you abandon."

Just over her father's left shoulder, Freida saw her mother dabbing a kerchief to her eyes. She must have heard the whole thing.

"OK, Papa," replied Freida, fiercely hugging her father.

He smiled and patted her head. "Ready for those pancakes now?"

Freida had tried catching Paign's eye during the hymn singing. She'd wanted to silently mouth that he should meet her after the service concluded. But he seemed distracted. Maybe he'd already gotten into trouble, even this early; he seemed to be constantly at odds with someone, especially at home. At least she'd succeeded in alerting Anders, so she'd have to trust Anders to bring Paign outside to their meeting tree. Everyone in their village considered the enormous black oak to be the oldest living thing in their valley, possibly even in all of the northern realm. *The stave church must be almost as old*, she thought. It had been a part of village life for generations. Though not large, it was magnificent, with rooflines vaulting up like the tallest peaks of the nearby mountains, whimsically competing for dominance.

She especially loved the inside of the church, with the ceiling so high over her head that she had to lie on the floor and look straight up to take it all in. The music and singing sounded so sweet, it often brought tears to her eyes. *Dazzling,* she thought, *are the intricate designs created by the interlocking beams that support the massive roof system.* Even the best craftsmen marveled at how complicated it would have been for them to build. And this church was over nine hundred years old!

Of course, everyone had loved ones buried in the cemetery that ringed the church. Many of the headstones were so old and weathered, it was hard to tell who lay beneath. Most of the grave markers were modest stone; some were quite meager, carved from hardwoods, but they were still no match for the harsh winters. A few graves were marked with enormous stones, revealing the wealth that had been reserved for the small ruling class of eras long past. There had been no new stones like that for hundreds of years.

As the final hymn ended, Freida stole out through the tall, intricately carved doors and ran back to the black oak. She watched as the families inside wandered out, chatting with friends only seen on Sundays, and eventually climbed into their waiting buggies. The single farmers congregated together for some time, laughing and slapping each other on the back. Freida knew some of those farmers to be quite funny, but that her mother often didn't approve of the jokes. The men eventually either rode home on their waiting horses, or simply hiked off in the direction of their farms.

Finally, Anders and Paign came out of the church and straight over to where Freida stood; by now, she was stomping around in a vain attempt to warm her frozen feet.

"What took you so long?" she asked, heatedly.

"I stopped the parson to ask him about the Widow Vellhelmina," Paign said, with a sheepish grin. "Anders heard most of it."

"Why on earth did you ask him about her? What would he know?" Freida asked, as she pulled her coat collar up high. She continued stomping.

"You'll be surprised!" replied Anders.

Paign added, "He's a bit of a historian around here, you know."

"Well, OK. Fine. I'd heard something of that nature about Old Parson Pearsson." Freida's cheeks were flushing. "I thought we were going to meet now and finalize plans for our next trip to the cave tomorrow afternoon. Have you learned something that changes that plan?"

"Uh. Yeah, I think so. Don't you, Anders?" Paign asked his cousin. "He seems to know something, anyway."

"Look, Freida. Don't get mad at us. At least not at Paign," Anders replied. "After we got back from our journey last night, I couldn't sleep. It was pretty exciting, you know, you finding the long lost Widow's Cave. At least, I'm almost certain now that you have found it. I kept tossing and turning for the longest time. Finally, after midnight, I got up and started reading some of the history books my dad had collected. You know that's where I got my love for history… Anyway, he had this really old tome, up on the top shelf of his bookcase. I guess I'd never opened it before because it was covered in dust. When I got it down, it got me choking and coughing so hard, I was sure it would wake my mum.

"I carried the old book up to my room and quietly shut my door. Even threw some dirty clothes at the base of the door to block any light getting through, in case Mum got up."

Anders paused, as if collecting his thoughts. He kicked a few rocks into the side of the oak. Freida realized she was holding her breath.

"So…?" she murmured.

"Here's the thing. We knew that Widow Vellhelmina was old, and that she'd been a widow a long time, right?" Anders continued.

"Yeah, sure," Paign responded, trying to look knowledgeable.

"Of course," replied Freida, with more conviction than Paign.

"And we know that she had been peculiar in her old age, to the extent that many in the village called her a witch, based largely on a few 'eye witnesses' who saw her talking to herself while wandering around the outskirts of the Highland Valley." Anders paused, took a deep breath, and added, "At least, that's what we were told."

"What do you mean by that—'what we were told'?" Paign asked.

"According to what I read last night, she was harassed by one particularly nasty old woman, the wife of the wealthiest landowner at that time. So none of the villagers dared challenge her assertions about the Widow Vellhelmina. A few brave farmers tried to provide shelter for the old woman. But they could see that the vile things being said about her were having a terrible effect on her mind. So, her muttering and wandering around at all times of day and seasons of the year simply reinforced the notion that she was evil, or in league with evil." Anders voice trailed off.

"Why, that's horrible, Anders! Really, really horrible," cried Freida. "Was there anything else you learned?"

"Oh, yeah. Loads!" Anders kicked another rock against the oak tree. Paign thought he looked angry.

"See, the reason we were taught that the widow was a witch was because there were so many people in town guilty of treating her like one! No one wanted to be found out later. Their descendants are people we go to school with…shop owners our parents buy from, even people we worship with!"

"And you learned all this from that dusty old book you read last night?" an unbelieving Paign blurted out.

"Yeah! Yeah, I did, Paign! You know who wrote that old book I studied last night? It was your great, great, great, grandfather, Olaf. He wrote the true story about Widow Vellhelmina. He was one of the farmers who tried caring for her as best he could. So did my ancestors. And Freida's, too. In fact, our three families were the only ones that Olaf records as extending kindness to her. But it wasn't enough to save her! It's painfully clear from his journal that he regretted that to the end of his days." Anders had worked up a head of steam, enough so that Freida could see his breath as he spoke.

"When crazy Helmut, the hermit, told all the townspeople about the widow's being snapped up into the cavern, they all laughed. No one went to look for her. No one cared enough to even search for her on the ridge. At first, they mockingly called it the Cave of Departing, saying that she departed them through it. Almost immediately, they shortened it to Cave of Parting. Olaf doesn't say why, but he clearly considered the shortened name a great evil. And he was incensed that the townspeople just went back to what they were doing…and she was never seen again." Anders's voice cracked. He savagely kicked another rock. It flew well past the oak and thudded into the snow.

"Wow," Freida said. "That's incredible. How could people be so hurtful, especially to an old woman? And a harmless old woman, at that! It's horrible! But, you know, I am so proud of our ancestors for standing up for her…for trying to take care of her." Freida's eyes glistened.

"I know, Freida. I feel the same way. Can you imagine how we'd feel right now if they'd been like the rest of the villagers? That would be awful. I'd be…so ashamed," Anders replied.

"But there's one more thing. Something really important. Something that's been hidden from us…hidden for generations," he continued.

"What?" Paign rubbed his hands together, impatiently.

"The Widow Vellhelmina had to have been married, right, to be a widow?" replied Anders.

"Stands to reason!" Paign stated, sarcastically.

"Well, of course," said Freida. "So, who was she married to? One of the farmers? Or one of the merchants?"

"Neither!" Anders replied. "She had been the wife of the town's parson!"

"What?" cried Freida and Paign, simultaneously.

"Exactly!" Anders could tell this news had really surprised them. It pleased him. "She was the wife of the village's minister for a great many years. And his death seemed odd to our ancestors. Olaf says so in his book. The Parson Vellhelmina *also* died in a mysterious fashion."

CHAPTER THIRTEEN

PANIC

"Honey!" Amy bellowed from the kitchen. "Will you call Dani down? I'm ready to dish up." This announcement was followed by an explosive clattering of pans.

Peter's head was nearly walled in on both sides of his small desk, surrounded with his senior students' midterm papers, two enormous stacks teetering on the ends of his desk. He'd been at it for several hours, and it showed. Though he was weary and, like in all his years of teaching, frustrated by his students' general lack of enthusiasm, he was so proud of Danielle. Her pretty face smiled at him, from the mahogany frame next to his desk lamp. Now in junior high, he could see her ability to creatively think through complex issues growing daily. What really pleased him, though, was her willingness—even boldness—to ask challenging questions of her teachers.

Smiling at the thought of his daughter intellectually—but graciously, he was certain—poking holes in her teachers' assertions, he slowly sat back in his old, creaking office chair and laid his bifocals in the small remaining open area of the desk. Arching into the chair, he leaned back, stretched his arms over his head and rocked back and forth a few times. Finally, he pushed his fingers through his thinning, salt and pepper hair—more salt now than he wished—and hollered back to his wife, "Okay!"

Trudging up the stairs to Danielle's room, he realized he'd been so focused on grading papers that he hadn't heard her come in from her first route collection. He was proud of his daughter for her spunk. Most of the parents in their neighborhood considered it strange that not only was a girl delivering their news, but that her parents encouraged her! But Amy had made a strong case to him about Dani being up to the challenge, and frankly, Peter couldn't think of a good reason why his little girl couldn't do what boys her age were doing. "Really! Why not? It's the sixties , right, with equality of the sexes and races."

He reached her bedroom door and paused to knock. There was no response. He knocked again. Still no response. The door was ajar.

"Dani, can I come in?"

Still no answer. She must be listening to her Beatles album with headphones again.

He pushed the door open and could see the evidence that she'd not come back yet, since her books and homework were tossed on the bed the way they always were when she came home from school. Dani wasted no time getting to the next thing she wanted to do.

He leaned over the upstairs banister and yelled towards the kitchen. "Ame…she's not upstairs in her room! Come to think of it, I don't remember her coming back from her route yet, leastways not through the front door. Is she in back?"

Another small explosion of pans erupted from the kitchen. Amy came out, wiping her hands on a kitchen towel, and looked up the stairs. "Hm. She's not in back. I didn't think it would take this long for her to complete her collection. Maybe someone's being difficult—probably the Smithers. They live on the corner—the house with that big maple, the next street over. Will you go check on her, Pete? I'm about ready to dish up."

Peter could see the anxiety on his wife's face. He realized there was probably a similar look on his face.

"Sure, Hon. She's fine. Took one of her legendary shortcuts, I imagine, and lost track of time poking around the gorge behind Larch Drive. That was her last street to collect on. You know the saying, 'The apple doesn't fall far from the tree.' We can't expect the offspring of two archeologists to not lose track of time when she's exploring. Throw everything back into the oven. I'll be back in a little bit!" Peter hoped he sounded convincingly calm as he trotted down the steps to Amy.

"Check the Smithers' place first! He's a grumpy old man… and kind of creepy," his wife said, clearly worried.

He smiled and gave her a little peck on the cheek, quickly grabbed his baseball cap and a flashlight from his office, and headed out their front door.

A moment later, he stood staring into the front window of the Smithers' home. Two elderly people were watching the Ed Sullivan show. He ran up and down their street. And the next street. And the next. It took him less than ten minutes to run down to Larch Drive. Quickly walking up the north side of the street, he scanned each door on both sides of the road, still expectantly looking for an open one, with light streaming through, framing a quarrelsome homeowner being difficult for his enterprising girl. Like the streets before this one, no one was outside.

An evening like this would normally have been very pleasant to Peter, making for a great jog. Now, though, with his daughter unaccounted for, he saw each street as increasingly foreboding. Every house seemed darker than before, their front room blinds looking like rows of narrow teeth. Trotting, he moved more quickly up the narrow drive, his head turning back and forth until there were no more homes to check.

The last house must have had a broken porch lamp. He could see no light emanating from behind the closed curtains of the twin windows in front. Even though dusk had nearly surrendered to night, Peter could see this house's yard was very poorly cared for, which did nothing to reassure him. As he walked closer to it, he flicked on his flashlight, glad he had recently replaced the batteries.

Shining the light across the expanse of the front of the house, he could see the bushes and trees were, indeed, probably dying. There was an astonishing amount of debris around the entry area to this dark house. Certain no one was home and determined to find his daughter quickly—and so close to panic he was fighting the urge to start wildly screaming out her name—Peter ran up to the left side of the front door. Flicking his light back and forth in the corner of the porch, he noticed feathers and was struck by how out of place they were. Enormous feathers!

"What's this about?" he said, startled at the sound of his own words.

Spinning around, he shone the light at the other end of the entry area. More feathers! He squatted down to inspect one, laying the flashlight on the concrete patio. Peter slowly twirled an immense feather into the beam coming from his powerful light, surprised by how beautiful it was, stunned by the subtle nuances and layers of silver and grey hues. Tipping his head to one side, he tried to remember where he'd seen something like this before. The shape. The size. Why did this feather seem familiar? He tapped his forehead, distracted. Suddenly, he remembered why he was here in the first place and jerked his head up. That's when he saw it, in the one place he hadn't noticed yet. The feather he'd been holding had blocked the beam of light as it hit the front door of the gloomy house at the end of the cul-de-sac. Directly below the door was Danielle's purse!

"Oh, God, no!" Peter cried out, seizing the purse after leaping to the front door. A wave of terror washed over him, chilling his sweaty skin and caused him to shudder. He felt suddenly nauseous. He banged on the door with the side of his fist so hard the door knocker bounced up and down. "Dani! Danielle!"

Jumping over to the front window, Peter pressed his face to the dusty glass and peered into the structure. He could only make out the shapes of furniture enough to determine they were all covered with blankets of something, like the house hadn't been lived in for a long time and the owners wanted to protect everything from dust.

Frantic, he ran beyond the right side of the porch and kept calling his daughter's name. He tried the fence gate. It opened, so he ran around to the backyard. He ran to the back windows, peering in like he had in front. Pounding on the back door, he continued to call out, "Dani! Dani! Are you in there? Answer me!"

Finally, crushingly, Peter realized his daughter wasn't there. Only her purse was, squeezed under his left arm. Choking back the fear attempting to burst out of him, he broke into a sprint and ran for home, swearing to find his daughter. Visions of horror flooded his mind. Peter ran faster than he'd ever run in his life.

CHAPTER FOURTEEN

A TRAP IS LAID

Gahrspat swore under his breath. Loath he was to let the human children leave the cavern his master had set him to watch. Long he had waited. Time had little meaning to him, but even so, he knew that, measured in human "years," he had lingered in the Cave of Parting for hundreds of them. Eons.

The temptation to follow the children into the howling snow—to maim, to kill, to feed—was very strong. He nourished the feeling, strengthening the temptation so that it acted like a fever, warming up the frigid stone that his body had been in for so long, embedded in the walls of the grotto. It pleased him to have this elemental, throbbing hatred pulse through his body.

Arching his back so that his slab-like head faced upwards, Gahrspat thrust his fists towards the ceiling and murmured an incantation fitting his dark mood. Abruptly, his massive wings stretched out from his sides and swung up over his head, forming a canopy. Savage light burst from the ceiling as several stalactites ruptured from the rock overhead and crashed to the floor all around him. Withdrawing his wings from over his head, Gahrspat surveyed the destruction he'd wrought, a smile widening across his face. His crimson eyes glowed so fiercely that they cast a bloodred glow on the shattered stone at his feet.

He reveled in his strength and the surging return of raw power in his veins. Oh, his need to destroy was great! But orders were orders. His commander's instructions had been abundantly clear, even though uttered generations ago. "Wait until someone comes. Do not be discovered. Then report immediately. Do not fail me! Now, go!"

Gahrspat wondered for a moment if all the other scouts his master had sent out so long ago, to guard all the caves of access, had returned. If so, what had they reported? Or was he the first to come back?

"Argh! What does it matter, you fool?" he swore at himself. "Tarry any longer and Master will teach me the way of pain!"

Immediately, the obsidian-shaded gargoyle sped down the middle passage that Anders, Freida and Paign had considered taking just minutes earlier.

CHAPTER FIFTEEN

THE HUNTED

"Look!" Paign declared, swinging his arms wide. "It's freezing out here, if you haven't noticed. This is all very interesting, talking about the Widow—and now the Parson—Vellhelmina. But isn't the best thing to stop talking about this and just go back to the cave? Let's search around up there, see what we can find out. Maybe we can solve whatever is mysterious about how the parson died. Besides, I'm tired of standing here in the cold and feeling my stomach twist with hunger. So, what are we going to do?"

Anders looked from Paign to Freida, both now dappled in the partial sunlight breaking through the clouds and broken up by the massive oak's branches. He shrugged.

So the decision was left to Freida. "Um. Yeah, I suppose that's right. OK, then. Let's meet tomorrow—after we're all done with our morning chores—behind my family's barn, like we did last time. Bring everything you did last time, and make sure you have your lanterns filled up. And bring some rope, too. Might be important if we go deeper into the cave. OK?"

Paign nodded curtly and turned for home.

Anders watched him for a few seconds, then turned and nodded at Freida. "Sounds like a plan."

Freida stood by herself for a moment, thinking. "Hey!" she yelled before they were both out of range. "Bring extra food!"

Both boys waved back, indicating they'd heard her advice.

Freida shook her head and started back for the warmth of her home and a hearty lunch.

The next morning, Freida had finished her chores with plenty of time to spare, but was feeling sleepy, even in the chill of another gloomy winter morning. She'd kept turning it over in her mind, all the news they'd learned the day before from Anders. Why had people been so cruel to the widow? How had the parson died? Was there any connection between his death and her disappearance? Was the hermit's story true or the mutterings of a madman?

She was grateful it wasn't a long wait for the cousins. It was cold! Freida rubbed the sleep from her eyes and looked up to see Anders and Paign rounding the corner of her barn.

"Good morning!" she said, as cheerily as she could manage. "Ready?"

"Hmphf," was all she got from Paign, as he shifted his large pack into a different position on his shoulders.

"Sure. Let's go!" replied Anders. He, too, was carrying a bigger pack than a few days ago. "Are you bringing Tiny along?" he asked, looking at the huge mastiff, which had been making a misshapen snow angel next to his master, with his fluffy tail swishing a partial wing into the fresh powder that had fallen in the night. Tiny barked at the sound of his name, his back half wagging the front half. *This must be an adventure. I love adventures!* the canine chattered to himself. Anders was certain the dog was smiling at him.

"Uh huh. He's got a good nose, and that might be useful as we search around the cave." She also thought about the good set of teeth he had, and that might also come in useful if they ran into any trouble. But she didn't say so out loud, certain the boys would make fun of her for being afraid—of what, exactly?

"OK, sounds good," Anders agreed.

Freida hiked up her overstuffed pack onto her shoulders, wondering whether bringing Tiny along, with the necessary extra water and food the dog needed, was such a good idea after all. *Bother! A change of plans means I'll have to explain it to Paign.* She began trudging up the frozen slope of her ancestors' pasture. Tiny trotted up ahead. Anders and Paign followed behind.

Her father, Farmer Skulstad, watching for them from Freida's bedroom window, finally saw them appear in the distance, just over the top of the barn roof. A few moments later, they were lost in the clouds roiling down the ridge.

The fresh powdered snow made their journey slower than their first trip. Where the snow collected to a few inches, it gave them more traction, but where the mountain breezes whipped it about, it actually fooled them into expecting better footing over the icy crust. So it took almost three hours to retrace their way back to the entrance to the Cave of Parting. Again, the lighting there was ghostly, the result of a dimmed sun unable to break through the swirling cloud rolling off Ruar's Peak hundreds of feet high above them.

Freida lurched over the uneven heaps of snow and ice into the cave's entrance, kicking crusted snow off her boots, while also brushing it off her coat. Pulling back her hood, she waited only moments before Paign and Anders stomped into the opening together. With the added benefit of midday light pouring into the narrow fissure, all three pulled out their lanterns, lit and trimmed the wicks, and walked into the chamber they'd discovered just a few days earlier.

Now that they were out of the cold wind, they stuffed their coats into their packs and re-hoisted them.

"OK, Freida. What's the plan now?" asked Paign.

"Well, I've been thinking we should go inside to the chamber we found, so we can get away from the howl of the wind here at the entrance. Then Anders can finish telling us what he discovered about the parson's death," she replied.

"Right, then," Paign agreed.

Anders shrugged and led the way down the tunnel, which spanned the thirty meters from the cave opening to the chamber within. When he reached the entry to the chamber, he stopped and put his lantern on the ground, waiting for the others to catch up.

After Paign and Freida caught up to Anders, Freida carefully picked her steps over the loose rock and shale that partially blocked the opening to the chamber. She immediately sat down on the largest rock, set her gently hissing lantern on the stone floor and looked curiously at Anders.

"Hey, you know, I realized you never told me what you and Paign had talked about with *our* parson yesterday, except that Paign wanted to ask him about the widow. That's why it took you so long to come out after church, right?" she asked, the warm yellow light from her lamp gleaming in her eyes.

"Uh, yeah. That's right. I waited for Reverend Pearsson to finish chatting with folks. You know how he is—and how most folks in the congregation are—about wanting to chat before they head home. Anyway, Paign found me there and waited with me, until we could talk to him alone." Anders finally sat down on another bucket-sized rock.

"Pretty boring, too, I might add!" Paign fired off before sitting down.

Anders' eyes narrowed a moment, looking at his cousin. His attention on Freida, he continued. "Like I was saying, Reverend Pearsson knew we were up to something, waiting for him. So once he had the elderly Lindquists finally shuffling off to their farm, he hurried back into the church to find out what we wanted. Boy, was he shocked when Paign asked him what he knew about the Widow Vellhelmina! It was as if we'd punched him in the stomach, he sat down so abruptly into the little side pew in the vestibule."

Tiny, who had been lying quietly next to Freida, with all four of his paws tucked underneath him, simply flopped his tail on the floor twice to indicate his excitement at this news. *When can we go home?* he wondered. *It is time for lunch.*

Paign piped up, "You should have seen how pale he got, Freida! With his head framed by those dark mahogany panels behind the pew, and his black robes cloaking the rest of him, it was like seeing the ghostly head of Death just floating in the church lobby! It was creepy." He looked at Anders for support, who nodded vigorously.

Freida shuddered a little, but kept quiet and waited.

"Right," Anders continued. "So, the Reverend takes a deep, slow breath and says, 'Why do you boys ask a question like that? You already know the story of what happened to her.' I thought he seemed kind of dodgy."

"'Well,' Paign said, recounting his conversation with the parson, "I said, 'We think—that is, Anders, Freida and me—we think we have found the Cave of Parting. You know, the one that widow is supposed to have disappeared into. If we trust the word of old Helmut, the hermit, that is!'"

"Freida," Anders interrupted, "you just can't imagine how pale the Reverend became when he heard that bit of news!"

"Yeah, he just sat there and spluttered for a moment, but no real words came out of his mouth," Paign added excitedly.

Tiny thumped his tail once, his dark brown eyes following which child was speaking.

Anders continued, "He looked a bit off, you know, like something had gone wrong inside of him…sort of a mad look in his eyes. 'What makes you believe you have found her—found the Cave of Parting? It was closed—I mean, it was supposed to have been shut, according to the legend.'"

"I was getting pretty hungry by this point in the morning, right?" Paign interjected. "I mean, you know how I got with you a few minutes later, out at the old oak. So I said to the Reverend, 'Look, it doesn't really matter, OK? We're pretty sure we have found it! We know that you are about the most educated man in all these parts and that if anyone knows anything else about the Widow Vellhelmina, it would be you. Can you help us, Parson?'"

Anders spoke up. "Freida, this peculiar change happened to the parson when he learned from Paign that we'd—you'd—found the Cave of Parting. The color flushed back into his face and he seemed to relax a little. 'Maybe I can help you,' he said quietly to Paign. 'What is it that you need?'

"'We need information,'" I said to him. "'As much as you have. You see, Reverend Pearsson, I've learned that the Widow Vellhelmina had been the wife of the Reverend Vellhelmina…'"

"Which knocked me for a loop, of course," Paign said enthusiastically, "since Anders hadn't had a chance to tell me this tiny bit of critical news."

Tiny raised his head at the sound of his name. *Hm?*

Paign smiled at the dog. "I probably looked like Death warmed over, at that point, like the Reverend had just a few minutes before!"

"'How have you come into this knowledge?' the Reverend gasped," Paign continued. "At least, I thought he gasped, didn't you, Anders?"

"Yeah, I guess so," Anders replied. "So I told him that I'd found Olaf's journal the night before and read a lot of it, especially about the Vellhelminas' history in our village and their very strange deaths. He asked me, 'How do you know about this journal, Anders? I thought it was lost. I'd *hoped* it was lost.' I told him about how I'd discovered it on the top shelf of our bookcase, and then I recounted to him all the things I'd learned from Paign's ancestor, Olaf."

Paign continued, "'Hm,' he said. 'At last, that which was lost has been found. All the parsons since the time of Victor Vellhelmina have sought the journal of Olaf Macy. Now it is recovered!' But he didn't seem real thrilled about it."

"When I asked him why it had been sought and what it was all about," Anders added, "he told us that even the Reverend Vellhelmina knew Olaf had been keeping notes about the goings on in the village and recording the cruelty of some of the merchants towards his family, especially his wife. But he'd pleaded with Olaf to stop writing in it, to stop telling people about it, in fact…to get rid of it, because it could be dangerous…"

"How's that?" Freida interrupted. "How could the journal be dangerous?"

"I asked him that same question," Anders replied. "He explained that Olaf had named names. He'd listed in his journal who had done what. Some of the names were of the most influential and powerful farmers and merchants in all of the Highlands. The Reverend Pearsson also said that Olaf had a way of shooting off his mouth—often—but wasn't always clear, so a few folks came to believe that the Reverend Vellhelmina was actually putting him up to it. That's why so many of our village ancestors were so unkind to the parson and his wife."

Anders stopped for moment and pushed some dirt and gravel around with his boots. Tiny started pawing at Anders's boots, thinking he was starting a game.

Looking up at Freida, he quietly added, "Reverend Pearsson asked if I'd gotten to the section in the journal that discussed the poisoning…the poisoning of the good Reverend Vellhelmina."

"What? The parson was…poisoned?" Freida cried out. "Did Olaf know who did it? Or how?"

"No and yes," replied Anders. "I mean, yes, no and yes. That is to say that, yes, according to the information that Reverend Pearsson has, the Reverend Vellhelmina was poisoned. He is not certain who did it, but he made it clear that he has strong suspicions about who was behind the murder. He believes several were involved but one man was behind the conspiracy, as well as the cover-up that followed. And, finally, yes, he knows how it was done, because the ladies that helped with Communion hid the chalice afterwards."

"Oh, no. Please, no. You are not saying that the Reverend Vellhelmina was murdered in his own church, during Holy Communion, are you?" she gasped.

Freida's face looked like the Reverend Pearsson's had yesterday, Paign noticed: ashen. Tiny squirmed, concerned about his mistress.

"That's precisely what Reverend Pearsson is saying happened. Apparently, right after the congregation had been served Communion, the Communion elder gave the cup to the Reverend so he could commune...just like we do now. Parson Vellhelmina drank from the cup, then set it on the altar. He was just beginning his blessing when he began choking and coughing violently. The congregation was already alarmed, but then he fell to the floor, convulsing. At that point, several ran up to the altar area. Olaf was the first to reach him, just as he vomited. By now, the parson was twitching uncontrollably, coughing and retching over and over again. Within a few minutes, he was dead, lying in Olaf's arms. According to what we were told yesterday, Olaf then started yelling, 'Where is he? Where did the jackal run to?' even while clutching the lifeless body of his pastor."

"I don't understand, Anders," said Freida. "Who was Olaf talking about?"

"He was looking around for the assisting elder. That's who Olaf thought poisoned the Communion wine just before the Reverend drank from the cup. Made sense, I suppose, since that was the last person to touch the cup before the parson was killed," Anders replied.

"But…it wasn't him? Is that what you're saying?" Freida asked.

"Not according to Parson Pearsson, no," Paign chimed in. "He believes the elder was set up…and"—his head dropped so that his eyes were too low for Freida to see—"he thinks it worked because of Olaf jumping to conclusions the way he did."

Now it was Paign shoving the dirt and gravel around the cavern floor. Tiny started pawing at Paign's boots, his tail thumping hopefully.

"What happened to the elder, then?" she asked him quietly.

"He was…he was run out of town, Freida." Looking up at her, his eyes welled up with tears, he repeated softly, "He and his family were run out of town."

"Oh. I'm so sorry, Paign," Freida's eyes were downcast now.

Anders was quiet a moment, observing his friends. He felt bad for Paign and the terrible discovery of what his ancestor had caused, but realized it had nothing to do with Paign. Besides, Olaf was his relative, too.

"Here's the rest of the story. Anna Vellhelmina was, of course, in the sanctuary during all this and watched her husband die before her very eyes. Some of the women of the church had run to her side when Olaf and two other men ran to the altar area to help the pastor. But when the Reverend Vellhelmina died, Anna shrieked out hysterically and ran out of the church. It was almost a week later when she was first seen again. By then, her mind was gone, and she had taken to muttering and aimless wandering around the valley.

"One of the women who had comforted the widow, though, had the presence of mind to remove the cup from the altar, hide it in her heavy winter coat, and take it with her so the wine could be tested for poison. Freida, that woman was your great, great, great grandmother, Edith Skulstad." Anders stopped to let that sink in.

"Oh, my! How did she test the wine?" asked Freida.

"She was clever, that one," replied Anders. "She poured some of the remaining wine into a dry trough and let one of her pigs drink the wine. You know, they'll eat and drink just about anything. The pig died in just the same fashion as Reverend Vellhelmina, only quicker because, of course, it was smaller and weighed less than he did."

"How sad!" Freida said, conflicted by the news that her ancestral grandmother was a woman she was sure she would have liked very much, and distressed that her quick and brilliant investigation resulted in the death of a poor pig. But she was also proud of her for discovering the cause of death was poison, and therefore proving the Reverend had been murdered. But that raised an unanswered question.

"So, who was behind the murder, then?" Freida said out loud what had been bothering her for many minutes.

"Great question! Wondered when you'd come around to it!" Anders replied.

Freida saw Paign roll his eyes and scowl at his cousin. She had to admit that Anders, for all of his intelligence, could be a royal twit. She ignored the insult and waited.

"From what we learned yesterday from Reverend Pearsson, the few people in town that dared to discuss the matter—and cared about the poor Vellhelminas—eventually determined that it was the wealthiest merchant in town that wanted the parson murdered. And that would be the great, great, great grandfather of Mr. Pers Olson, currently the Highland's wealthiest merchant and also the only breeder of mastiffs in our small valley. Including your Tiny," Anders finished, with what Freida took to be a sense of triumph.

Having been expecting some playtime from all the boot movement over the past several minutes and hearing his name again, Tiny finally got to his feet, his tail sweeping back and forth like a leafy tree limb in a brisk wind.

Absorbing another bit of pompousness from Anders, Freida ignored the dig about Tiny's heritage and replied, "But why would he want to see the Reverend murdered?"

"Sure. I was puzzled by that, too," he replied. "I suppose that parsons back then were like parsons now—pretty much everyone goes to them with problems they're having. You know, it could be stuff about their faith, but sometimes it's about just day-to-day things like not getting along with your family or your neighbors, or that your crops aren't growing properly and does the parson have any idea how to fix it. No, really! In loads of places, the most educated person in town is the pastor of the church. So people just figure they'll know the answers to just about any questions they come up with. I guess that's really common. At least, according to Reverend Pearsson, that's most of what his week is about—dealing with stuff like this.

"By now, we'd been talking to him for a while and knew you'd be getting annoyed, so we made ready to leave. That's when he said, 'Anders, there is another journal, similar to the one Olaf wrote, but this one has entries from every reverend that has served this church since the Vellhelminas. We must get together, privately, and compare them. It is imperative that we confirm what my journal says is the reason the ancestor of Pers Olson had the Parson murdered.' His eyes got very big, and then he told Paign and I, 'According to the secret investigation of the first parson to come after Reverend Vellhelmina's death, it was determined that the parson had learned about a secret order—an evil sect of village leaders, most of them merchants—led by Pers Olson. He learned this from the wealthy merchant's tormented wife, Maria Olson. She'd blurted out to him, during a fierce argument with her husband, that she'd told the pastor about his wickedness and she was about to leave him. We need to confirm that Olaf's journal has a similar story.' Frankly, I don't see why it is that important."

"Because," Freida replied with some heat, "it could mean the downfall of an important family in our community. Can you imagine what that news would mean to the Highlands, now, after all these generations?"

"Hmphf," Anders snorted. "I suppose so."

"So, are we ever leaving this place? We're burning through lantern oil like we have all day. How about a quick lunch, and then we explore, eh?" asked an eager Paign.

Tiny barked, approvingly.

CHAPTER SIXTEEN

HURRY UP AND WEIGHT

Peter's chest was heaving as he burst through the front door of his home. He tried shouting for Amy. Except he had run so hard that his very short breaths were making it extremely difficult to speak, let alone shout. He settled for slamming the front door behind him, nearly doubling over as he gasped for air. For a few moments, he stared down at the tile floor of their entry, waiting for his breathing to slow enough to attempt speaking.

Glancing up, finally, into the front room of their home, Peter was puzzled to see Amy sitting on the couch. She faced the stone fireplace, so her head was turned away from him.

"Honey! We've got to call the police!" he squawked, not sure if his words were yet understandable. He still had a terrible stitch in his side from running so hard.

Amy sat, unmoved. She didn't even look his way. *What the...?* he wondered. It was then Peter noticed his wife was the color of ash, and even from his side view, he could see that she had a vacant expression on her face. She was still staring towards the fireplace.

"Hi, Daddy!" he heard Danielle say.

No one could blame Peter that it took a moment for him to process that he'd just heard the voice of his daughter—the girl he'd just been frantically searching for—because, except for this evening of terror, it was completely normal to hear his daughter's voice in their home. Still panting heavily from his run, and at a complete loss from Amy's behavior, it only took a moment.

Peter's head snapped over in the direction of where he'd heard Danielle's voice. And then he reared backwards into the corner of the entry, knocking over the umbrella stand and slipping on the handwoven carpet that welcomed their house-guests. Slamming heavily into the corner walls, Peter slid to the floor. He was vaguely aware of the sound of glass shattering beside him, as the large framed picture of their Nepalese excavation site crashed down onto the tile.

"Daddy," he heard Danielle say again. "It's OK. They're friends," she continued, rushing over to help him up.

Peter, whose face was now ashen like his wife's, watched his daughter smile at him. Then, he turned his face towards two goliath statues of gargoyles towering in their living room. Except, he realized, they weren't towering, exactly. It appeared they were too heavy for the floor to support because there was splintered wood around the statues, with carpet heaved up around the knees of both of them.

"What did you say?" he whispered. "Who are...*friends?*" At that moment, each gargoyle statue blinked at him.

"So, we're in danger, you say?" Peter said to Kimar.

"Yes," Kimar replied.

"But," Amy interjected, her face still pale, "we need to get Peter to a hospital. His hand needs looking after…probably stitches…" Her voice quavered as she looked at Ercen, then at Kimar, and finally at Peter's left hand.

Peter was having trouble stabilizing his nervous system and how to respond to their…guests. Danielle had spent half an hour recounting what had happened to her since she'd left the house many hours earlier. He'd observed Amy's face during Dani's report, and he could see she was struggling with reconciling her scientific mind with these two creatures that defied any rational explanation. It was difficult to take everything seriously, except for the fact that the evidence stood before them.

There they were, two enormous creatures standing in the front room of his house. *What exactly are these things? Animals? Mammals? Prehistoric?* Peter wondered. He'd seen statues, of course, but that didn't prepare him for real gargoyles standing in—through—his house. The floor was destroyed. When Kimar had attempted to climb out of the instant hole he'd made when they had—*What did they call it again? "Parted" into our house?*—Amy had just been walking into the front room to see what the racket was about. Her nerves had already been on edge, what with Danielle missing and Peter gone over an hour searching for her. At the sight of a living gargoyle postholing through the living room like a lost hiker through deep snow, she'd simply fainted, rather than screamed. Danielle had just revived her with an ice compress and gentle words when Peter came blasting through the front door.

Peter flinched when Ercen added, "The danger grows the longer we linger here."

He gathered that the facial changes on the face of the female gargoyle were intended to be a smile. *Whew, this is going to take some getting used to,* he thought. He returned a wan smile back to her.

Peter looked down at his left hand, wrapped in the huge wad of paper towels that Danielle had retrieved from the kitchen. He was still annoyed with himself for not paying more attention. If he had, he wouldn't have shoved his left hand into a dozen shards of broken glass while getting up off the entry floor. His hand throbbed with pain, even after washing it out in the kitchen sink and taking three aspirin. He was pretty certain he'd gotten all of the glass pieces out.

"Peter, will you come here?" asked Ercen.

Peter hesitated, looking at the massive gargoyle with conflicted feelings. Disbelief battled with his curiosity.

"It's OK, Daddy. Really, it'll be OK," Danielle added.

Slowly, Peter walked over to the hole in their front room filled with the gargoyle his daughter called Ercen. His mind was awash with competing arguments. One argument was making a case for how silly it was to be entertaining—even for a moment—the notion that mythical creatures from children's fairy tales were real...and could carry on an intelligent dialogue. *This is absolutely nuts!* he thought. Another voice in his head was arguing that science is all about discovery, and he and Amy might just have made the discovery of the decade, perhaps even the century. *This could make us famous! Maybe even rich!* he mused. A third voice challenged his caution at approaching a creature upon which no study had been done. *Would they allow us to research them,* he wondered? The fourth argument, however, was the strongest: *Can we really trust these, these...things...to not harm us?*

Peter now stood in front of Ercen, the enormous being occupying the punctured floor by the coffee table, which was now propped up somewhat due to the heaving floor beside it. His breathing was slightly ragged, and he was unsure of why the creature had called him over. "Yes?" he said, not knowing what to expect. He heard Amy shifting in the couch, directly behind him.

Ercen, he could see, was making that face at him again. Assuming it was safest to conclude she was smiling, he gave a small grin back to her.

"May I take your hand?" she asked.

"Uh...I guess so," he replied, not sounding convincing, even to his own ears. He stretched out his white and crimson wrapped hand towards Ercen. It was clear he'd been steadily bleeding into the paper towels.

She took his wounded hand in both of hers. Until that moment, Peter had not noticed what had been there all along: Ercen's hands had talons as long as butter knives, and they looked as sharp as his wood-carving tools in the garage. He heard Amy faintly gasp behind him.

The most peculiar sensation Peter had ever felt began pulsing through his hand. It reminded him of the intense tingling he'd experienced as a kid when he'd played in the snow for hours without gloves. But instead of the painful freezing that normally caused the tingling, this sensation seemed to be caused by heat. Or was it both? He had trouble isolating the feeling.

After a moment, he realized the confusion was because there was also the awareness of enormous pressure being applied to his skin. But it wasn't like his hand being crushed under accidentally loosened rock; he'd experienced that unpleasantness during their dig in Ethiopia! No, this pressure was vaguely like the pressure on his eardrums when he and Amy went snorkeling in the Mediterranean during their honeymoon. The pressure became uncomfortable enough that he wished there was some way to equalize the heaviness on his hand like he had been able to do with his ears.

Abruptly, Ercen pulled her hands away from Peter's. "You may remove your dressing. Your hand is healed," she said.

Skeptical, Peter glanced at Kimar and Danielle, who had sat down beside him, turned to Amy and thrust his wrapped hand towards her.

Saying nothing, her eyes wide, Amy carefully unwound the ghastly wrapping that encased her husband's hand.

"Oh, Peter!" she cried, gently pulling the last of the soiled towels away. "Your hand! It's…it's completely healed. That's not possible!"

"Sure enough," Peter grunted, slowly turning his hand back and forth in front of his face. He had needed stitches before, but now the only evidence that he'd seriously cut the palm of his hand were the many, many thin scars that lined it. However, even the scars showed no signs of being recent. They perfectly matched the skin tone of his hand. *These scars should still be an angry red,* he thought, unbelieving. *What am I thinking? They should still be open wounds!*

"How…how did you do this?" he asked Ercen.

"It doesn't matter," replied Kimar.

"But—yes, it does! This is incredible!" Peter retorted.

Kimar lowered his head, looking intently at Peter. Danielle was reminded of a swashbuckling black and white movie she'd seen about a bullfighter, and how the bull he had fought dropped his head the same way before attacking.

"You misunderstand me," Kimar continued, his deep voice grumbling. "Ercen forced the wounds on your hand to not matter. Therefore, the damage you caused to your hand no longer exists in this realm of matter."

"Oh. Uh, right. Of course," Peter replied, sounding as nonchalant as if he'd made a simple mistake while speaking about the weather. He stared again at his newly-healed hand, moving his fingers back and forth in the air in the same way one does when drumming them on a table.

"Where are my manners?" he blurted out, eyes fixed on Ercen. Smiling, he said, "Thank you. Thank you very much!"

Ercen smiled back at Peter.

"Daddy," interrupted Danielle. "We really need to go. Soon. Please."

There was small gasp and a murmured, "Why is that again?" from the couch. All eyes—two human sets and two gargoyle—turned towards Amy. She was shaking, as if freezing. She tilted her head and smiled sheepishly at Danielle.

"Because, Mommy, we're in danger here," Danielle replied. "Kimar and Ercen explained it to me. We're being followed," she finished, with urgency in her voice.

"Um, OK," said Peter, with no conviction in his tone. "Please, Dani…explain it again. This has something to do with the key we found years ago, then?"

"Yes," Kimar replied flatly. "Will you get it? It is time for us to part."

Danielle noted that Kimar's reference didn't mean to "part ways" from each other, but meant something entirely different. She wondered how her parents would do with parting. With a start, she realized it was unclear *who* would be parting with the gargoyles.

Amy remained on the couch, still shaking.

"I'll get it," Danielle said, scurrying out of the room and running down the hall to her parents' study.

Just as she veered into their office, she heard a huge crash from the living room she'd just left. The house shook violently and she lost her footing, tripping over a mountain of books piled on one side of the room. Quickly, she got up and with one jumping motion, grabbed the plastic case holding the mysterious key. Misjudging her landing, Danielle slipped on a small stack of magazines and fell heavily to the floor a second time. There was another crash down the hall, followed by screaming and yelling. She recognized her mother's voice as the source of the scream. It was her father who was yelling. There was a third crash and the floor beneath Danielle buckled and heaved, just as she'd been told to expect in an earthquake. A moment later, all the lights went out.

"Mommy! Daddy! What's wrong?" she cried, just as a full shelf of books rained down around her.

Still clutching the case, Danielle struggled to her feet and started for the hallway.

She looked up just in time to see two bloodred eyes glaring down on her from near the ceiling.

CHAPTER SEVENTEEN

PURSUIT

Peter was gasping for air, partly because he was being squeezed by Kimar, partly because of the terror of what had just happened and mostly from abject fear for his daughter.

"We must go back! Let me go! I have to go back!" he yelled into the side of Kimar's head, over the roar of wind howling past his own face.

"That would be ill-advised, don't you think?" replied Kimar, who was now flying more than two hundred feet above the now-demolished roof of Amy and Peter's home.

Ercen, flying next to Kimar, was holding Amy tightly to her chest.

Although Amy looked terribly frightened to Peter, he could hear her shrieking, "I want my baby! Let us go!"

Only moments earlier, Danielle had run down the hall to fetch the key box. There was an enormous crash. Amy had screamed. Peter had twisted around, horrified to see a third gargoyle, with glowing red eyes, violently thrashing in the rubble of where their entry way had been. The gargoyle was stuck in the collapsed floor, just like Kimar and Ercen were. It was clear the gargoyle was enraged at being stuck in the floorboards and carpet. He was roaring and flailing wildly. He looked up just in time to see Kimar thrusting out his left hand, palm aimed forward, right at the slate-colored gargoyle.

Instantly, several bricks from the fireplace behind Kimar dislodged from the wall and flew past Kimar's shoulder, over Peter's head and into the chest of the gargoyle.

While Peter was trying to decide how Kimar had thrown bricks without touching them, Kimar lunged forward and grabbed him by the arm. Ercen seized Amy's foot, as she recoiled away from the coffee table.

As the red-eyed gargoyle fell backwards from the barrage of bricks, Kimar yelled, "Fly! Fly! Fly!"

With a huge thrust of his wings, Kimar blasted through the roof of the humans' home, clutching Peter, while Ercen broke through the roof, holding Amy.

Peter had watched, disoriented and disbelieving, as countless bits of splintered wood and roofing shingles fluttered below them into their backyard.

Ercen dropped her right wing and swerved over to Kimar. "Give him to me! Save the girl!" she wailed over the wind, reaching out her right arm. Her wings began flapping faster.

Without a word, Kimar eased Peter from his tucked position and swung him over to Ercen, who tucked him under her other wing.

Immediately, Kimar retracted his wings against his back, tipped his head forward and dropped like a meteor. Peter could see the edges of Kimar's wings thrust out slightly, and he watched the huge gargoyle veer back towards their home. Moments later, Kimar blasted a new hole through their roof.

Nauseating fear pulsed through Danielle as she stared at the horror hulking just twelve feet away from her. She was standing near the middle of the darkened office, clutching the box. Moments earlier, the power had gone out. Danielle screamed as the gargoyle lurched forward. Floorboards splintered into the air, along with torn carpet. Scrambling backwards, she slipped over some of the same magazines she'd tripped over just moments earlier and fell heavily to the floor.

"Give me the key, human!" snarled the gargoyle. "If you know what is good for you." He lunged at her again, slowed by the floor joists.

Danielle struggled to get back up. As the gargoyle grabbed at her feet, cracking the joist nearest him, she crab-walked backwards with one hand, tightly holding the box in the other, sliding over strewn books, magazines and papers. She was running out of room to retreat into. She was running out of time.

The gargoyle was difficult to see, due to his slate-colored skin and only filtered moonlight coming through the study's small square window. Except for his eyes. They were all too easy to find in the darkness.

She saw the gargoyle's head drop towards the floor and heard the sound of splintering wood. The floor heaved up in front of her as pieces of shattered lumber and bits of carpet fell around her. The gargoyle was making progress, ripping his way through the floor between them!

Danielle screamed. "No! Nooooo! You can't have it."

The gargoyle's head lifted slightly. Danielle's skin crawled as the creature stared at her again. His eyes narrowed into slits. The dark, ominous voice replied, "Oh, but I will, human. At last, my Master will have it again!"

His head dropped suddenly and, with a huge sweep of his massive arms, the floor in front of the gargoyle exploded.

With a desperate surge, Danielle shimmied hard into the rear wall.

The ceiling above her suddenly erupted downward, showering Danielle with sheetrock, insulation, bits of roof and a cloud of choking dust. A spasm of coughing shook her. As dust and debris settled to what was left of the floor, Danielle's heart leaped when she saw the powerful body of Kimar slowly come into focus.

"Danielle! Take my hand," shouted Kimar, amber eyes flashing.

She reached her right hand into the murky gloom until she touched the back of Kimar's taloned hand. Immediately, she felt his hand turn, lift her to her feet and swing her in front of him.

The other gargoyle bellowed angrily at Kimar and stabbed both fists, talons fully extended, straight at Danielle's belly.

Holding her tightly in his left arm, Kimar quickly twisted to the left, shielding Danielle. At the same time, he swept his right arm in a backwards motion, blocking his enemy's blow. Then, Kimar immediately swung his right arm down towards the floor, shredding up mounds of carpet and arcing it upwards towards the gargoyle's chest.

The other reared back just in time to dodge Kimar's razor sharp talons, while defensively hurling shattered floorboards at Kimar.

Kimar seized the opportunity to retreat from the battle with Danielle safely in his arms, still clutching tightly to the box. Vaulting off the ruined floor in a powerful leap, Kimar shot through the roof opening and flew rapidly away from what was left of Danielle's home. The Key of Kahrnahrgx glowed faintly within its plastic shelter. Quickly, he caught up to Ercen, whose flight was labored by the weight of two human adults.

"Nahgflint will not be far behind me!" he shouted at Ercen over the wind whistling past them and the steady thumping of their enormous wings. "We must drop to the earth and part away as soon as we can, before he—"

A high-pitched wail preceded the ball of flame as it hurtled in between the gargoyles, and was followed by the screams of Amy and Danielle as they looked behind them. The gargoyle Nahgflint was indeed in hot pursuit of his prey. In the night sky, he was visible only because of his flaming eyes and the glint of moonlight on his furiously flapping wings. Their enemy was gaining on them. Fast.

Immediately, Kimar and Ercen tucked in their wings behind them, rolled over on their backs, tipped their heads towards the ground and plummeted downward.

Amy and Danielle continued to scream as another ball of flame narrowly missed Ercen.

Peter could see that Nahgflint had also dropped into the same aerodynamic tuck but was no longer gaining on them. But he was still hurling fireballs.

"Kimar, watch out!" Peter yelled.

Instantly, Kimar rolled away to the right, barely avoiding a blazing orb, shielding Danielle from the fire with his wing.

Even though Peter's senses were overwhelmed with the pressure of being held tight by Ercen, the wailing of wind and pounding wings in his ears, the staccato screams of his wife and daughter, he felt Ercen's body tense and twist. Horrified, he guessed they were less than a thousand feet from impacting the ground. But Ercen wasn't even looking in that direction. What was happening?

"Now!" Kimar cried.

Ercen and Kimar simultaneously wheeled about and cast fireballs back at Nahgflint. Their aim was deadly accurate. The pursuing gargoyle's red eyes widened just before he covered his head. The first fireball smashed across Nahgflint's protective wing, sparks exploding outward like a campfire spitting flame. The second glanced off his back, leaving a plume of trailing smoke as he tumbled and rolled wildly in the gloomy sky behind the group.

With only seconds to spare, Kimar and Ercen thrust out their massive wings, arcing their flight away from their savage foe and dropping into a nearby small wooded knoll.

Landing heavily, the humans tumbled onto the dewy grass.

The animals slumbering on the knoll were frightened by their visitors. None had ever heard anything like Nahgflint's furious howl. They never wanted to hear it again, and scampered away as fast as their legs could carry them.

"Wow, that was close!" Peter said. "I thought we were goners. Either that gargoyle was going to get us or we were going to smash into the ground. Pretty nearly did both! Good thing you killed him!"

Ercen, who was lifting Amy to her feet, replied, "Nahgflint isn't dead! We have only slowed him down…hopefully enough. Now, grab hands. Quickly!"

Peter recognized the high-pitched wail before the fireball burst next to him. In the eruption of flame, he could see all hands joined, except his. He grabbed hands with Danielle and Kimar just as another blazing orb broke across Kimar's back.

And then they were gone. Only smoke and splattering sparks remained.

CHAPTER EIGHTEEN

RISKY BEHAVIOR

Tiny enjoyed these outings. He especially enjoyed exploring new places.

This cave was both new and strange. And it was strange in other ways than just being new. It smelled funny. Tiny had never smelled this sharp scent before. He didn't like it. The further he led their way into the cavern, the stronger the smell grew. He paced nervously from side to side as he ambled down the rough corridor leading to the main cavern.

What is that scent? he wondered. *Is it two-legged? No, that doesn't smell right. Hm. Is it four-legged...like the bear? No, not quite. But similar. Is it bird-smell? No, that's not right, either.* He stopped at the entrance to the large hall that his people were walking to, not far behind him. Their lanterns were swinging back and forth and tossing odd shadows in the corridor, but not much light into the hall. Freida, Paign and Anders seemed to be arguing again, he noticed.

This is not good. I know this is not a scent that is familiar, thought Tiny. *I know I don't like it, because it just…smells… wrong. I must protect my people. They should not enter here!*

Tiny stopped, turned and positioned his paws into a wide stance—a battle posture for those that know dogs—and blocked the entrance to the hall. The enormous and sweet-natured mastiff had not wagged his tail for the past few minutes, but the three friends had been too busy to notice, still debating the benefits and risks of revealing to their countrymen what they had learned from their parson.

"Come on, Anders! Surely you can see that sharing this news with everyone in town would bring a lot of pain to some of our neighbors there. Right?" Freida said.

"Yeah, I suppose so," Anders replied, still sounding unconvinced.

"Hey," interrupted Paign, who was trailing at the back of the small procession, "what's gotten into Tiny?"

Freida, who was in the lead and had been mostly looking over her shoulder at Anders during their debate, turned her attention to her dog, just a few feet in front of her now.

"What are you doing, Tiny?" she asked of her faithful companion, observing his stance. At first, she thought he appeared ready to play, as though a ball was about to be thrown for him to fetch. But the look on Tiny's face didn't look at all like when they played. He looked more like when strangers came to their gate. Tiny didn't welcome strangers well.

Tiny barked.

"What's this about, then?" Anders asked, as he stopped next to Freida, setting his pack on the ground. "He doesn't look happy."

Tiny growled.

"This is strange, don't you think?" Paign said, as he stooped to put his backpack on the ground next to Anders. "What's gotten into him?"

The light from their three lanterns flickered across the nearer walls of the main hall, but barely reached to the back of the chamber.

"I don't know," replied Freida, concerned. "He'll growl and bark at strangers. But he knows us, obviously, so that doesn't make sense."

Tiny whimpered.

"What's wrong, boy?" Freida asked, bending down to stroke his muzzle.

Wagging his tail a little, Tiny remained undeterred. *My friends must not pass. There is something wrong in this room.* He barked.

"Well, I haven't come this far just to stop in this hallway," Paign said, annoyed. He quickly pushed his way past Anders and Freida in the narrow passage, but stopped short when he got to Tiny, his lantern swinging just above the dog's head. Tiny had dropped his shoulders towards the floor of the cavern, in what appeared to be preparation for a fight. Paign thought the dog had a queer look in his large brown eyes. Was it anger? Or was it fear?

"What is it, boy?" Paign asked, as if expecting to hear an answer from the mastiff. Hoping to distract him away from this strange defensiveness—if that's what it was—Paign picked up a ball-sized rock and lobbed it into the left side of the dimly lit main hall.

Tiny watched the rock skip across the floor, deflect off a larger rock and roll to a stop near an opening that marked one of the far tunnels, where their lanterns' beams could not reach. Paign watched Tiny's tail swing once, like a very brief metronome, and then stop.

Tiny returned his attention to Paign. He stared at the human, tipped his head to one side and growled. *No, you can't pass...and no, I'm not chasing that rock.* But Paign didn't seem to understand him.

"So," Anders said, "what did you expect would happen? You're trying to play fetch with him? Here, of all places? This isn't exactly an ideal location for exercising him, you know."

Paign ignored his cousin and picked up another rock about the size and shape of a good snowball. Ignoring Anders, he pitched the roundish rock into the middle of the main hall, again hoping Tiny might chase after it and relent from obstructing their progress.

As before, Tiny twisted his head to watch the rock skitter across the rough cavern floor, bouncing unevenly as it caromed into other rocks. As the rock neared the middle of the main hall, it struck a jagged shard of stone, which deflected it upwards into the air. Just as it arched into the center of the cavern, there was a thunderous explosion. Part of the ceiling gave way and shattered to the ground, followed by a sickly green, throbbing glow that descended from the coarse roof of the hall all the way to the floor, like dripping honey.

"What the—" Anders gasped. Rearing back at the explosion, he flung out his arms to push Paign and Freida behind him.

Freida screamed.

Paign stumbled over his pack, cursing.

Tiny barked angrily at the column of putrid green.

Stunned, Paign saw the stone he'd thrown still tumbling from its momentum, but it now hovered in the middle of the cavern, surrounded by the pulsing green glow. The rock was still rolling along in midair, but it wasn't moving forward.

"Oh, my goodness, Paign!" cried Freida. "Can you imagine what would have happened to us if Tiny hadn't…"

Tiny enthusiastically wagged his tail, vindicated by this turn of events. *Better the rock than my people!*

Paign stooped to pick up another rock. Carefully, he tossed it at the other stone, still tumbling but suspended in midair. When it reached the columns of pulsing green, it bounced off. There was a sharp snapping like exploding sap from a burning log. A black wisp of smoke wafted upwards from where the rock bounced away from the sickly glow.

"Wow!" Paign, not often at a loss for words, dropped to one knee beside Tiny and vigorously stroked his head. "Good boy. Good boy!"

Anders slowly walked over to the undulating green columns that encircled the hovering, still-spinning rock. Holding his lantern high, he stepped carefully around the perimeter of the greenish shield.

From the far side of the column, he yelled back to Freida and Paign, "Have you considered what this means? This… this is not that far beyond where we stopped last time to eat our lunch. But obviously, this—thing—wasn't here then. It is some sort of cage—like a trap, I gather." Stepping around from the back rim of the glow, he looked intently at Paign and Freida, his eyes hard and cold. "Unless I am missing something, this cage was meant for us!"

"But…why?" Freida asked, her voice quavering.

"'Why' isn't important, Freida!" Paign replied hotly. "I want to know who left this trap for us. Or…or, *what*. Have you ever heard of anything like…like this?" Paign stabbed his finger in the direction of the tower of pulsing, glimmering green. He paced slowly behind Anders.

"And another thing!" Anders continued, still circling the luminous column. "Do you remember seeing all this broken rock here before? It's like something broke some stalactites right in the middle of this cavern. I mean, they might have simply fallen, you know, but why here? We sure didn't knock them loose. We couldn't have. We never got this far." Anders paced back and forth, staring at the ceiling, then at the shattered rock all over the center of the floor.

Tiny ambled over to Anders, whipping his tail back and forth like children wave flags at parades.

"Yes, Tiny, I'm sorry. You did great, boy! You've protected us from…from, well, we don't know from what. Or who. But you did it, boy!" Anders said, fondly patting Tiny's head.

"But how did he know?" asked Freida, walking over to them. She looked warily at the glowing column.

"Now, that's the question, isn't it?" Anders replied.

Paign, who had gone over to retrieve his daypack, dropped it down and sat in front of Tiny. He took the massive face in his hands. Pulling his head to Tiny's, he asked the dog, "Could you tell something wasn't right in here, Tiny?"

Tiny barked.

"Hm. Did it smell funny to you?" Paign asked, guessing at what abilities Tiny might be using to identify unseen dangers.

Tiny barked again.

"Could you tell if who—or whatever—did this is nearby?" Paign continued.

Tiny tipped his head to one side and sat down on his haunches.

"That's too complicated, Paign," Freida said. "Tiny, can you track the smell of, of…whatever did this?"

Tiny barked.

"Why on earth would we want to have Tiny track whatever did this?" Paign asked, a little too loudly. "We should get out of here!"

"Are you kidding? Because whatever set this trap will check on it, right? To see if anything has been caught? Maybe it can't track us. We don't even know what kind of creature can do this! But I'm telling you, Paign, I sure don't want to be here when it comes back to check on its trap," Anders answered.

"So, are you saying you don't want to track this—whatever it is?" Paign asked, confused. "You're not making any sense. Are you siding with me or Freida?"

"Blast it, Paign!" Anders snapped. "I'm saying that I'd rather that we be the hunters than the hunted. I'm pretty certain that whatever set this trap did so because it isn't skilled at tracking. Tiny smelled something was wrong here and warned us, right? That's why we're still alive. Tiny would be going crazy right now if he sensed whatever set the trap was nearby." Anders wasn't going to tell his cousin how scared he was, especially with Freida watching him.

"But maybe we can track it with Tiny," said Freida, hopefully.

Tiny jumped up and spun around, barking excitedly. *Of course! Of course!* He trotted over to the rear wall of the chamber, circling and sniffing. To Freida's great surprise, he came back holding an enormous jet-black feather in his teeth.

"What's this, boy? Does this have something to do with all this?" Freida swept the room with her gaze.

Tiny barked and jumped.

"Just the same, wouldn't it make more sense to just leave this place altogether?" Paign asked. "Why follow anything? Let's just get out of here!"

"Paign, if we leave now, we run the risk that whoever—whatever—did this…set this trap for us, mind you," Freida said, then paused, shuddering, like a strong burst of wind slamming against a tree. Taking a deep breath, she continued, "They'll set another one for when we come back. We've barely missed being ensnared in this one, thanks to Tiny. Coming back later, there might be a worse trap. Maybe a deadly one. If we don't seize this chance, we may not get another. I hate this place, but I agree with Anders. Whatever did this isn't here right now. I'm trusting that Tiny can sense…"

Freida's eyes welled up as Tiny slowly walked up to her and leaned against her leg.

"We can't go back on what we know," Freida pleaded, her voice cracking. "The widow…she deserves to have someone discover the truth about what happened to her."

Anders looked pale, but nodded. "That's right. If it isn't us, now, it'll never happen. We'll be careful. Tiny can lead us. Right, boy?"

Tiny jumped up and put his paws on Anders's chest, and barked. *Isn't that what I've been doing?*

"Hmphf," Paign retorted, shaking his head. "Truth be told, I think you're both being reckless. Foolhardy, even. I just hope you're right about whoever did this." He stared intently at his friends for a moment. Then he shrugged. "Well, if we're going to hunt strange creatures, we'd better eat something first. We've still not had lunch, and I'm not going anywhere until we do."

Without waiting or saying another word, Paign sat on the cavern floor, pulled his backpack up on his crossed legs, opened it and began rummaging about. A moment later, he pulled out a dish towel tied with string at the four corners. Untying it, he set into his lunch with great concentration.

Anders laughed. "OK, cousin! Fine idea. Fine idea, indeed." He sat down beside Paign and began making short work of his lunch.

Freida looked back and forth between her friends, her emotions swinging hard between fear and fondness. She finally smiled and kneeled on the hard floor, sweeping the rubble away from beneath her knees. Soon, she was eating her lunch, eagerly.

Tiny laid down beside her, patiently waiting his turn.

A few minutes later, Paign shoved the empty towel back into his pack. Freida chewed on her cheese sandwich, watching him as he pulled out his short sword and buckled it onto his leather belt.

"Think we'll need that, do you?" Anders asked, his mouth full of apple, pointing at the sword.

"Might. Better to have it ready and not need it than the other way round, eh?" Paign replied. He heaved his backpack onto his shoulders and adjusted the simple straps until it was snug.

"Hm. S'pose so," Anders nodded. Freida hadn't noticed before that Anders's bow was cinched to one side of his pack, with the quiver cinched to the other. Untying both, Anders adjusted the straps on his quiver and slung it over his left shoulder, so that it wasn't inhibited by the pack hanging on his right shoulder. The many arrow fletches sticking out above the quiver's top made them look like a bouquet of bizarre flowers to Freida. She knew that Anders's skill with the bow was almost as good as Paign's.

But seeing her friends arming themselves took away her appetite. She quietly put away her mostly uneaten lunch, but gave the rest of her cheese sandwich to Tiny. She put the black feather into the front pocket of her jacket. Fishing around in her pack, she pulled out her father's hunting knife and strapped it to her waist. The sudden trembling in her hands made this difficult. Finally, she slung her pack over her shoulders and smiled wanly at the boys. She knew, deep in her heart, that this mission was the right thing to do. It must be, or the boys wouldn't have agreed to it. Still, now that it was time to set out, her confidence wavered, and she found her mouth was parched.

Holding his lantern high, Paign looked at Tiny and said, "OK, then, boy! We're looking for whatever made this trap. Show us the way...wherever it is we're going. And let's be very careful, eh?" He laughed nervously, quietly troubled by how strange this adventure had become.

Tiny barked, happy to be going again, and gamboled down the center tunnel ahead of the trio of lanterns' light. Still, he had never been as aware of his surroundings as here in this cavernous realm. He was not about to permit anything to harm his mistress or his friends.

CHAPTER NINETEEN

BEACONS

"Stop squirming, you great beast!" Ercen scolded Kimar. "You are making this more difficult than it needs to be."

In the dim glow cast by the rocks that Ercen had "lit," Peter thought Kimar looked terrible. His right wing was partially severed. A very nasty burn, the size of a dinner plate, covered the creature's shoulder where he'd absorbed the fireball from the attacking gargoyle. Peter also realized with amazement that this "beast" had protected his daughter from certain death by shielding her. He shuddered at the vision of what could have been, had Kimar not taken the blow.

"Is there anything I can do?" he asked quietly, watching Ercen tenderly work across Kimar's damaged wing.

"Only if you can get him to stop squirming!"

"Ercen, we don't have time for this. And I'm fine," Kimar interjected. He shifted uneasily at her touch.

"Oh, you are not, not fine at all," she retorted, trying to hold him in place with one hand while healing him with the other. "Nahgflint's aim has improved, don't you think?" She must have put more pressure on Kimar's shoulder when she said this because he flinched, arched his back away from her and moaned. "Be still, will you?" Ercen said.

"Alright, then." He relented and became instantly motionless. Peter would have taken him for a statue, except for the events of the past day.

Peter watched Ercen for a while longer, putting her hands on Kimar the way she had on his own glass-sliced hand a few hours earlier.

Just a few feet away, Danielle lay sleeping on a bed of straw, embraced tightly by Amy, who had been observing Peter with half-shut eyes. "Everything OK?" she asked sleepily.

"Yes, Hon," he replied quietly. "It looks like Ercen can heal up Kimar's wounds...even as serious as they appear to me. But then, what do I know?" He looked over at Ercen for a moment. "You see, look at the way..." When he glanced back at his wife, he saw her breathing slowly, sound asleep, with a gentle smile on her face. He knew she was both exhausted and greatly relieved to have their daughter safe again.

Now that Kimar had accepted his treatment, and Ercen was in the thick of administering it to him, Peter decided there wasn't any reason for him to stay awake any longer, either. Feeling his legs threatening to cramp up from his extreme run home earlier in the evening and the countless crazy events that followed, he stretched himself out ramrod straight on the straw bed just behind Amy. Quickly, he drifted off to sleep, encircling Amy and Danielle with his outstretched arm.

Nestled against the rock above Danielle's head lay the plastic case protecting the Key of Kahrnahrgx. There was no glow coming from it.

Danielle awoke refreshed and alert. She was pleased with this outcome, but still puzzled. There was so much she'd been through—in what, just a few hours?—that it was remarkable she'd been able to sleep at all. Rolling onto her back, she stared into the dawn sky. The temperature was pleasant even though they were shrouded in a thin veil of drifting mist. As the light breeze created breaks in the mist, she could see steep rock faces vaulting into the air above them. Stunted, deformed fir trees clung to outcrops jutting beyond the sheer rock walls. As a shaft of sunlight broke upon the cliff face above her, she saw an eruption of pinks, purples, blues, yellows and magentas from various flowers embedded in the rock cracks. She sat up, beaming at the unexpected, dazzling beauty in such a harsh environment.

"How pretty!" she declared. Hearing a rustling to her right, she turned to see Ercen laying out food—human food—for her and her parents, who were still asleep.

"Good morning, child," Ercen said. "Kimar has obtained food for you and your parents."

Although she was curious how Kimar went about "obtaining" human food, Danielle suddenly realized how ravenously hungry she was and immediately set to remedy it.

While Danielle was finishing up her breakfast of small bread loaves, hard-boiled eggs, cheeses and apples, both of her parents stirred, sat up and rubbed the sleep out of their eyes.

"Hi, Dani," Amy said. "Been up long?"

"Hmphf," her daughter replied. Swallowing a huge mouthful, she said, "No, not long."

Peter stood, stretched and wiped straw bits off of his clothing. "So, where are we, exactly?" he asked, to no one in particular.

"We are in the Rookery of Ten Pinnacles. It is the home of our kind," Ercen replied. She spread her wings wide. "Behold!"

As Peter, Amy and Danielle looked at their surroundings, the mist dissipated and blew away. To their utter astonishment, they realized they'd slept on an outcropping many hundreds of feet above the valley floor. Far below was a patchwork of pine and oak forests scattered amongst meadows of green grass and wild flowers. The valley was almost completely ringed by steep ridges like the one they were perched on.

Danielle counted off the jagged peaks circling the valley and, sure enough, there were ten of them: Ten Pinnacles.

"So why is this place called the 'Rookery'?" Amy asked Ercen.

"Look closely at the rock face around us, and you will see," she replied.

Amy, Peter and Danielle would probably not have noticed them if Ercen hadn't said anything. Gargoyles tended to thoroughly blend into their mineral surroundings, and simply looked like more rock. But when the humans paused to focus on an area for long enough, they could first see subtle movement and then, finally, their eyes could distinguish the creatures that had been largely camouflaged. Within moments, the humans spotted countless gargoyles perched amongst the hundreds of outcroppings scattered above and below them.

Amy thought it somehow comforting to observe them going about simple daily tasks, like she did at home. She did note, though, that gargoyle sensibilities were different than human. Breakfast was drawn from the earth, as far as she could guess from watching Ercen and Kimar, although she observed some gargoyle families nearby eating fish that appeared cooked whole, but she didn't see how this was done.

And they didn't seem to mind sitting motionless on cold, damp hard rock.

"Anything I can do?" Peter asked Kimar. Peter could see that his wing was entirely mended, although the scars were more pronounced than those on his lacerated hand. It was still breathtaking to have seen, with his own eyes, such rapid healing.

"You know," Peter said to Kimar, "we didn't have a chance to tell you last night how grateful we are that you went back to save Danielle…from…from…"

Amy nodded briskly, in agreement. Tears welled up in her eyes.

Kimar lowered his head once. Slowly, he raised it and then looked at each human intently. "You are welcome. But it was not only to protect the human child that I went back to fight Nahgflint."

Ercen added, "It was necessary to retrieve the Key before he could part with it. Our future depends on it."

Danielle fidgeted some, and then asked, "You've told me that the Key of Kahrnahrgx was important for you to get back…and it sounds like you have been searching for it a long time, right? But why is it so important? Why does your future, well, depend on it?"

"Child, it is not just the future of our people that depends on the Key. It is also determines your future—the future of humans. Without the Key, Kahrnahrgx's power is limited. But with it…" Ercen's voice drifted away.

Although Peter found this news troubling, he'd been fascinated watching dozens of gargoyles leap from their high perches and fly over to the small lake at the northern edge of the valley. From a great height, they'd tuck in their wings behind them and plummet headlong into the water with a tremendous splash. A few moments later, they'd erupt from the water in a burst of foaming wake, having skimmed just under the surface before taking again to the air.

"What are they doing?" he asked, mesmerized.

"They are drinking," replied Kimar.

"Wow!" Danielle said. "It looks like they're having fun."

Kimar looked at her with a quizzical stare. "It is necessary to drink. But drinking in this way brings joy. Is that the meaning of 'fun'?"

"Yeah, I suppose it is!" she replied brightly. "Wish I could try it."

Kimar, who had also been watching the other gargoyles diving into the lake, turned to Danielle. Peter was sure it was a smile he saw cross the face of the protector of his daughter.

"As you wish," Kimar replied. He reached Danielle in three steps, scooped her up onto his back, and immediately plunged off the edge of the cliff.

Before Amy could scream—and Peter could see she was working on one—they both heard their daughter's shriek on the dissipating mist—"Ohhhh my! This is fantastic! Whoooooaaa, whooooooaa, whoaaa!"—followed by her uproarious laughter. Hundreds of feet below them, they could see Kimar rise out of his dive and float higher and higher towards the lake. Danielle twisted around on his back and waved back at them. Even from this distance, they could see her enormous smile, and her laughter drifted up to them on the slight breeze.

Kimar's powerful wings finally tucked behind him, forming small walls on either side of Danielle. Peter was reminded of the rollercoaster cars they loved to ride at the county fair. Danielle grabbed the ridge of Kimar's wings and tucked her head down onto his neck, as if she was listening to him. With a sudden twist, he rolled over so his belly was facing the sky, with Danielle upside down, under him. He then arched backwards and shot straight down into the middle of the lake. A gigantic spout and plume marked where they entered the water.

Amy, who had been standing next to Peter, grabbed his hand and squeezed it. "Do you think she's…"

Peter burst out laughing. Danielle's head was undulating along the surface of the lake, followed moments later by the rest of her, up to her waist, just like he'd seen dolphin trainers do on TV. Except his daughter wasn't riding on a dolphin, but on a massive gargoyle, who was swimming much faster than any dolphin could manage. His wings were propelling them through the water at over thirty knots, Peter guessed.

Soon, Amy was laughing, too. She was delighted, watching Danielle's arms flailing in the air, then scooping water up from the lake, all the while her wet blond hair flying wildly behind her. Her daughter's joyous screams echoed off the lake and rock canyon.

By the time Danielle slid, dripping wet, off of Kimar's back onto their high rock perch, grinning from ear to ear, her parents were wiping tears from their eyes, they'd laughed so hard.

"So, that looked like fun!" Peter chuckled.

"Oh, it was just fantastic, Daddy!"

Kimar shook himself from head to toe like a dog after swimming. Amy could see, unmistakably, a smile across his rough-hewn features.

The mist had burned off, now that it was midday. The sun had grown warm, and Danielle thought she might be getting a bit of a sunburn.

"How is it, then, that we—and the Key—are safe here? Can't your enemies part here like you were able to do?" Amy asked.

"We have beacons set around the world to monitor the partings of our foes, as well as our own," Ercen replied. "Especially here, within the Ten Pinnacles, we have special beacons—what you humans call 'sensors,' I believe, to alert us to a gargoyle's attempt to part into our territory."

"But," Peter interrupted, "how does that work? You must have some way of differentiating between your kind and your enemies. Is there something unusual about your enemies that trigger the warning beacons?"

"Darkness," Kimar replied, flatly.

"I'm sorry…what?" Amy asked. "Their 'darkness,' you say?"

"Yes," Ercen answered. "Our foes are very much like us in all ways, save one. They carry inside of themselves a darkness, a void, an emptiness. They were once our people, just as those you see flying around us this day. But long ago, one gargoyle, in the prime of his youth, believed that gargoyles—not humans—should rule the earth. As his strength grew, so did his arrogance. He challenged the wise of our tribes and clans. Some he swayed to his way of thinking. Others he intimidated with his power and insolence…"

Danielle thought Ercen looked to be in pain. After a moment, she continued.

"There were numerous councils…much discussion…many attempts to reach consensus. But it was no use. Our religion is very clear about this, that we are called to protect humans. In so doing, we fulfill our purpose as gargoyles. In rejecting this truth, our foes parted fulfillment from their hearts, leaving an emptiness they sought to fill with power and domination." Ercen lowered her head and sighed.

"As you might have surmised," Kimar continued, "the gargoyle leading this revolt was Kahrnahrgx. Many of our strongest leaders chose to follow him. They were attracted to his message of supremacy. They desired to rule the world. They desired dominion over humankind. They desire it still."

"But how would they, if you—gargoyles, I mean—were created to protect humans," Danielle replied, "how would they go about ruling us? Wouldn't that be, you know, like going against nature?"

"Child," said Ercen. "What is it that separates humans from the rest of the 'animal kingdom,' as you humans quaintly refer to all that is not you?"

Before Danielle could answer, Peter interjected, "Science, of course! What elevates us above other living things is our approach to understanding the world around us. We build and organize knowledge in logical, rational methodologies. We test theories repeatedly until patterns emerge that advance our comprehension."

Ercen said nothing. Kimar's head turned away, towards the ongoing choreography of diving gargoyles, a few still plunging into the lake.

"Hon, as important as science is to humanity, isn't the most important thing our creativity?" Amy said, glancing at Peter. "From the earliest recorded times, humans have engaged in a creative process, even painting crude stick figures on cave walls. So, wouldn't it be arts and literature, Ercen? That humans are always involved in creation, whether it is through music, writing, painting, or whatever?"

Danielle had been carefully studying her parents. She considered their arguments and, frankly, wasn't surprised by them. In fact, their comments here on their vaulted perch in the Rookery were much the same as she'd heard many times at home, around their dinner table. Sometimes, the discussion would evolve into more of an argument, especially when they hosted visiting faculty from other universities.

Ercen was watching Danielle, waiting.

"Um, well, I think it's important that humans, are—like you said, Daddy—scientific, and all. Obviously, some good things have come from that. But it's also true that some terrible things have come from science, too. For instance, we're certainly growing more powerful and able to kill more people…" She stopped, not sure if she'd said too much already.

Peter smiled a little, nodding for his daughter to continue.

"And it's great and everything that we're artistic and creative, like you said, Mommy. But sometimes it's through books and art that some people sway other people to believe—and to do—terribly wrong things about others.

"So, I guess, as far as I'm concerned," Danielle said, her voice quivering slightly, "what makes humans different than other creatures is that they can care about each other. You know…that they can love."

Kimar slowly turned his head to face Danielle. He nodded. "You are perceptive, young one. More perceptive than many of our own kind."

"To protect is to care, to love," added Ercen. "When some of our kindred chose to follow Kahrnahrgx and to part from protecting humans, they embraced the opposite of love. They rejected love. Within the void this left in their souls, they poured hate."

"Kahrnahrgx discovered great power in hate," Kimar continued, his deep, rumbling voice rising. "After a time, he and his followers built a temple where they could worship together. It is here that they delve deeper and deeper into hatred, making sacrifices to honor the destruction and domination of humankind. It is there that they devote themselves to violence against humans."

Ercen murmured, "It is there that they practice violence against humans…"

"What do you mean," Danielle asked, "'practice'?"

Very softly, just above the sound of the breeze filtering through the stunted pines around them, Ercen replied, "It is there that they have tormented humans."

All three of the Wheelens were quiet for several minutes as they considered what this horrible revelation meant to them. Amy's mind turned to alarm, urgent thoughts of retreat and a desire to put as much ground between her family and such an abominable place. Peter contemplated many images (far too many, he realized) of what "torment" might look—and feel—like, and to what end their enemies tortured humans. Danielle's thoughts were singular in scope and focused simply on rescuing anyone unfortunate enough to have fallen prey to these horrid, wicked foes.

"But why? Why would they harm us? What would their intention be of, of…tormenting people?" cried Danielle. "What is it they want?"

Kimar walked over to Danielle and slowly dropped to his knees. Amy marveled at how such a large, powerful creature could move so gracefully.

Danielle stared up into the rock-like features of her protector's face, expectantly.

Kimar gently took Danielle's hands and wrapped them with his enormous fingers, talons protruding outward precariously.

"Do you remember my question to all of you about what distinguishes humans from all other earthly creatures?" he asked, softly.

"Yes," she nodded. "Daddy said it was science and discovery. Mommy said it was creativity and artistic expression, and I, well, I said it was love."

Kimar nodded, sagely. "You are all correct. But you, Danielle, are most correct. For, as you said, not all scientific discovery has bettered humankind. Not all creative pursuits have enhanced your peoples. Both have also produced violence, destruction and desolation. It has been so over the entire lifespan of your race. So these do not distinguish your kind from the others that inhabit the earth."

"Only when humans show love, only when they demonstrate compassion for others of their kind, or even of other kinds of creatures, are they separated from the basest of animals," Ercen interjected.

"Kahrnahrgx understands little of how this power works," Kimar continued, "but he does absolutely understand *that* it works. Ever he desires to subvert this power to his own devices, to manipulate it, to multiply it, to wield it in domination over all things. He and his disciples mistakenly believe that its opposite is hate. In their ignorance and fetid arrogance, they sought to entrap the very essence of great human love after breaking their human prisoners' minds and tearing them from their sundered souls."

"How horrible!" Amy shuddered, her hands tightly clasped together.

"I'm not sure I want to know the answer to my question, but I observed you used a past tense, Kimar, when you said that Kahrnahrgx 'sought to,' well, capture human love and use

it like a weapon. Against us. Humans, I mean. Did he stop his
search, or did he…has he…trapped that power?" Peter asked.

"Yes," Kimar replied.

"Yes to which?" Amy asked, alarmed.

Kimar, still holding Danielle's hands in his own, lowered
his head, but said nothing.

Ercen replied, "Before we could stop him, Kahrnahrgx succeeded in parting, out of one poor human soul, the essence of
her love."

"How do you know it was only—" Peter began.

He was interrupted by Danielle asking, at the same time,
"But what happened to the—"

But Amy's voice rose above them when she asked, "How
was her love trapped? What device did he use to, to…encase
it?" She stared, pleadingly, into the eyes of Kimar, breathlessly
certain she already had guessed the answer.

Kimar looked long into her eyes and then, little by little,
turned his head until his gaze was aimed at the nook in the
rear wall of their granite eyrie.

Danielle felt a chill go down her spine as she gawked at the
plastic box in which her parents had encased the Key. A relic
of evil that, in turn, encased the sundered love of a tormented, shattered human soul. She felt soiled, stained. Revulsion
shook through her like a sudden surge of windblasts into a
tree. "Oh. Oh! Oh, oh, oh, nooooo," she cried.

From the corner of her eye, she saw her father jump up,
fists clenched so tightly she could see his knuckles turn white
with fury.

Amy, who was overcome with equal parts horror and shame,
simply turned away and violently threw up her breakfast.

CHAPTER TWENTY

TUNNELS

How long had they been at this? How deep had they delved into the bowels of this stupid mountain? After their party had skirted the pulsating column of luminous green, Paign had been trudging along behind Tiny for what felt like days. But now Paign was getting hungry, and when he was hungry Paign knew he could be unreasonable. Just about everyone had told him so. Right now, he didn't much care.

"Look." He stopped so abruptly that Freida walked right into him. "How long are we going to keep at this? Not sure about your lanterns, but I think mine has to be at about the halfway mark for kerosene!"

Tiny sat down farther along the tunnel, just within range of the cast lamplight, his tongue lollygagging off to one side.

"Hm," replied Anders, catching up to them. "Any reason we need *all* of our lanterns going at the same time? Why not just use one at a time? Our eyes will adjust well enough to one lamp, I should think. Could conserve fuel for, well, later, I suppose."

Freida, annoyed that Paign didn't seem to care about stopping so carelessly, was also getting hungry. Nevertheless, she appreciated Anders for his straightforward way of presenting things.

"Well, no," Freida said, glaring at Paign. "There's no reason we need all lanterns going at the same time." Then she realized that didn't answer Paign's question, but Anders's. "As far as how long…I don't rightly know. Why don't we stop for a snack break? I'm pretty hungry, and I expect you are, too. Do you have enough food left over to make something of it?" she asked the cousins.

Paign didn't bother to pause long enough for the courtesy of an answer to Freida's question, but proceeded to plop down in the upward curve of the tunnel's wall. He leaned his back into the wall and rummaged in his backpack.

"I didn't mean at this instant, Paign!" she retorted. "Just beyond where Tiny is sitting, it looks as if the tunnel opens up into another hall. Before we snuff out two of the lanterns, let's see what we're dealing with, huh? Maybe then we'll have a better idea whether we keep going or not."

Paign cast Freida a grumpy sneer, but picked up his lantern and dragged his bag down the tubular corridor.

Anders bent at his waist and tilted his upper body towards the tunnel's end, holding his hand out like a fancy butler. "After you!" he smiled at Freida.

She couldn't help but grin back at him. Snickering, she quickly fell in behind Paign.

Tiny bounded into the echoing emptiness of the spacious hall, eventually loping beyond the lanterns' beams. The three explorers could hear him scrambling around in the hall.

Occasionally, there'd be the crash of what must have been a thin stalagmite he toppled in his overly enthusiastic sniffing.

They hastened to the opening. Standing together at the very edge of the chamber, the tunnel stretching behind them, Freida held her lantern aloft but it couldn't pierce the far depths of the cavern. Anders and Paign hoisted their lamps over their heads. As one, they gasped.

In the middle of the hall was a dais of stone, roughly shaped in a huge disk. Anders thought it as wide as their entire church and several feet high. Standing at even intervals around the stone disk, columns of granite jutted towards the hall's high ceiling. Atop each column, twenty-nine in all, perched a gargoyle made of rock. Some stood with wings outstretched, while others squatted. All peered downward and outward from the circular platform. Most of the gargoyle statues were covered in gloom, with the lanterns' light largely absorbed by the darkness. However, as their lanterns' hissing flames danced back and forth against those closest to the intrepid explorers, the flickering light gave the statues a menacingly lifelike quality.

Unconcerned, Tiny continued to gambol about the cavern, trotting around the perimeter of the hall, then circling the dais and finally peeing on one of the columns. He sniffed his way back to Freida's side.

"So, nothing smells funny to you, boy?" she asked her faithful dog.

Tiny wagged his tail vigorously but said nothing.

"Hm," Paign grunted, uncertain what to make of Tiny.

Anders shrugged, and then picked his way across the scree-covered floor and occasional stalagmite, until he came to the stone platform. He pivoted back and forth on his feet so that he could cast lantern light across the dais. "Hey, this is interesting! Come and look at this!" he called out.

When Freida and Paign approached where Anders stood, their combined lamplight shone across the center of the platform, which had previously been blocked from view by one of the columns. There was a rough-hewn rock chair in the middle. Its tall back was facing them.

"What is this place, anyway?" Paign asked. "It looks like it might be a throne room or something, don't you think? Although the chair seems a wee small. Maybe a pygmy king!" He chuckled at his joke.

"No, I don't think so," Anders replied. "It's too...empty in here...to be a throne. Look around! There isn't any finery, you see. You know, like banners, or armament, or anything. Not even chairs or benches for others to sit on. Not much of a throne room, if you ask me. Not nearly impressive enough!"

"But who made this place? That's what I want to know. If any of our ancestors had a hand in building this, wouldn't we have heard about it?" asked Freida. "And what are all these doing here?" she added, picking up a half-dozen black feathers more than a foot long. Dozens more littered the floor. Some black, some slate, some grey. One white.

Tiny had started roaming around again. As he padded about the platform, dust kicked up from his paws. When he jogged around to the front of the stone chair, the kids heard him yelp like he'd been stung.

Tiny ran around the back of the chair , his head down. A low growl rumbled from his bared teeth. His gaze was fixed on the front of the stone seat.

Slowly, almost grudgingly, the children turned to face the rock chair, to see what Tiny was growling at.

Staring back at them were the vacant eye sockets of a mummified skeleton. A shock of disheveled brown hair adorned the skull. A dark cloak, coated in a deep layer of dust, wrapped the medium-framed body, from the neck to below the knees. Underneath it, however, they could see a colorful, but soiled, dress. In the very still, dry air of the cavern, there was no way to be sure of how long the skeleton had been here, but there was little doubt in their minds who these remains belonged to.

"Oh, no," sniffed Freida, tears welling in her eyes. "This has to be the Widow Vellhelmina."

Anders and Paign said nothing, but quietly nodded their heads. They didn't know what to say.

Tiny, sensing the disquiet of his mistress, sidled up to Freida's leg and leaned into it to reassure her of his presence.

Freida kneeled down in front of the widow's body, at once horrified and immensely curious. Noticeably shaking, she nevertheless visually inspected the body, carefully avoiding touching it.

Paign wondered if she was avoiding touching the remains out of respect or fear. He knew *he* didn't want to touch the body, and it wasn't due to respect.

As Freida's lamp bobbed up, down and around the mummified woman, Anders jumped.

"Hey, Freida! Swing your light back where you just had it," he cried. "Yeah, that's it. I need more light…right there… now, hold it!"

Freida was startled by Anders's outburst, and she'd felt her heart nearly launch itself up into her throat. Puzzled and quivering from head to toe, she held her lantern exactly where he'd said. Holding her eyes tightly shut, she worked at controlling her shallow breathing to bring it under control.

"Look!" she heard Anders blurt out right next to her. She followed his gaze, down his arm and beyond his pointing finger. Just beyond his finger, she could see, unmistakably, a thick, coarse rope binding the corpse's hands to the base of the stone seat.

Both Anders and Freida jerked when Paign, who'd been quietly standing behind them, said, "This isn't a throne room. It's an execution chamber."

No one had spoken much throughout the afternoon. The humans had been overwhelmed with the horrific discovery regarding the origins of the Key.

As dusk settled into the valley and shadows fell lower down the far ridge of the Pinnacles, Kimar parted to gather up more food for his human guests. Ercen proceeded to light and warm the shelf of rock that had been their nest for the past day.

After they'd eaten, Peter finally asked the question that had been gnawing at him throughout the midday.

"If I've understood your meaning," he said, looking first at Ercen, then to Kimar, "this fellow, this Kahrnahrgx, tortured and eventually murdered an old woman by parting her soul from her, and then encasing her love into that key over there." Peter pointed towards the box, without looking at it. "Is that pretty much it?"

"Yes," Ercen replied, "that's essentially it."

Kimar nodded, but said nothing.

"And this happened before you could stop him, I think you said."

Again, Ercen said, "Yes."

"So, you must have caught up to him...Kahrnahrgx, I mean? Right?"

"Of course," replied Kimar.

"Where was it you found him?"

"We caught him at his temple. But not in time to rescue the old woman," Ercen said.

"Well, that's the piece that puzzles me. If you have these beacons all around our world, sensing your enemies' movements and possible attacks...well, doesn't he do the same? Couldn't he tell you were coming?" Peter asked.

"We thought we'd managed a way to enter his realm undetected," replied Kimar. "In one respect, we were correct. We'd successfully parted many gargoyles sympathetic to our cause into the dominion of Kahrnahrgx to launch an attack on his Temple stronghold..."

Kimar began pacing back and forth along the cliff edge.

"However," he continued, "when we launched our surprise attack at the main gate, one of the Temple guards dodged his foe long enough to sound the alarm, before being struck down. Therefore, we lost many in the assault. Only a few of us got into the lower floors of the Temple, where Kahrnahrgx kept his prisoners, while the battle raged above. I, alone, reached his final dungeon."

Kimar stopped at the edge of the shelf, the talons on his feet protruding beyond the outermost rim and into the air. His shoulders sagged.

Amy noticed Ercen lower her head until her face was hidden.

"When I broke through the dungeon's door...the human was yet alive, although grievously broken. The faintest spark of life remained in her," Kimar spoke quietly into the air beyond the cliff.

Kimar gradually turned back to face his guests.

Danielle was shocked to see tears streaming down his face.

"What's wrong, Kimar?" she cried out.

"In that moment, I hesitated to strike down Kahrnahrgx. In that moment, he parted her soul from her body and killed her. Then he vanished. She died on my account."

"But, why? Why, Kimar? Why wouldn't you have destroyed him when you had the chance?" Danielle cried.

Kimar stood motionless, stone-like.

"Because," Ercen whispered softly, with tears now in her eyes, "Kahrnahrgx is Kimar's brother."

Anders pondered what Paign had said about the cavern being an execution chamber. He was convinced his cousin had it absolutely right. On his knees in front of the remains, he scanned the floor of the stone platform again. But this time, he applied all of his scientific analytical skills. There were several spots on the circular floor that were, for lack of a better description, bald. There were no flakes of shattered ceiling, no feathers. Only dust. Dust covered the area immediately around the cold chair on which the dead woman sat, as well as everything else in the chamber, but much less so in the bald spots.

Tipped up against one of the pillars was a wooden stool. Littering the base of another were bones. He thought they looked like chicken bones, like someone's refuse after lunch. Midway from the stone seat and the edge of the dais was a pewter cup, similar to the Communion cup at their church.

Picking up his lantern, Anders began walking carefully around the dais, holding the lamp close to the floor as he investigated.

"This doesn't make sense!" he said.

Squatting down, he lifted up a mostly used candle. Vague remnants of boot prints were all around it.

"Someone was here with this, uh, woman…with her before she died. Or maybe they were, you know, responsible for her death," he muttered.

"Huh? What do you mean?" asked Paign.

Before Anders could answer, Freida answered with more irritation than she felt, "Well, she didn't tie herself up and wait to die, did she?"

"Hmphf!" Paign snorted.

"Anders, who do you think tied up the widow, then?" Freida continued, ignoring Paign.

"Well, that's the rub, Freida. I don't believe this is the widow, after all," Anders said, scratching his chin.

"What? Why do you say that?" Paign asked his cousin.

"Hm," Anders replied, walking over to the mummy. "First, her hair is brown. We know the widow was quite elderly, right? Certainly not young enough to have hair any other color than white or grey."

Paign nodded.

"Second, her clothing doesn't fit what we know about the widow. She'd wandered about the valley, scorned by her neighbors until it undid her wits, eh? But as you can see, this woman has a colorful dress under this nice cloak."

Freida, swallowing hard, carefully touched the dead woman's dress, rubbing it between her fingers. It felt like silk.

"Third, this woman's shoes are in reasonably good shape. Not what you'd expect to find on a vagabond."

Paign only then realized the mummy had shoes on, but said nothing.

But it was true. This woman's shoes were scuffed up, as well as cracked from the dry air, Freida could plainly see, but that was to be expected since she'd gotten up Ruar's Ridge and all the way into this deep section of the cavern.

"Finally, we'd expect to find the widow still wearing her wedding ring to the Parson Vellhelmina. And this woman has a ring on, to be sure. But it isn't on her left hand ring finger like you'd suppose. It's on the wrong hand, as well as the wrong finger. And it looks very expensive, too!" Anders pointed, triumphantly, at the desiccated hand.

"But, if it isn't the widow, then who could it be?" Freida asked, feeling faintly nauseated and lightheaded. She sat down beside Tiny and hugged him.

"If I am not mistaken," Anders said excitedly, "this woman is none other than Maria Olson, the wife of the merchant suspected of murdering the Parson Vellhelmina and destroying the sanity of the widow."

"OK, let's say you're right," said Paign, quietly recognizing the impeccable logic of his cousin even as he resented it. "If this is Pers Olson's wife, then who bound her to this stone chair and killed her?"

Freida gasped and clutched Tiny's thick hair, at his neck. "I think it could only be one person, Paign. It had to have been her own husband. Pers must have killed his own wife!"

"OK, that's enough for me. Let's get out of here," Paign retorted. "I'm not that hungry anymore."

"Freida," Anders said, "that's probably a good idea. We're all getting a bit low on kerosene by now. We can always come back again."

Freida looked at the remains of the poor woman and sighed. "I suppose we should bring some men up here to collect this…uh, retrieve the…bring her back to be properly buried. Don't you think?"

Tiny jumped up and barked. The boys nodded.

Hurriedly, they re-shouldered their daypacks and retreated back the way they'd come, up the tunnel.

Tiny ran ahead, merrily barking from time to time.

Had Paign looked behind them, just as he reentered the main tunnel, he would have seen the shortest of the squatting gargoyles perched atop a rear column stand stiffly. He would have been alarmed to see a pair of red eyes grow bright in the deepening gloom. He would have jolted when the gargoyle, barely visible in the darkness, leaped off the pillar and dove in pursuit of them. But when Paign turned at the sound of crackling rock shards, fallen at the base of the column, he saw nothing at all. For the gargoyle had parted into thin air just a moment before.

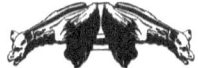

Anders walked quickly behind Tiny and was the first to arrive at the edge of the first hall. Of course, it was still filled with the sickly green hue of the throbbing beams sheltering the spinning rock Paign had thrown for Tiny to chase many hours earlier. He swung his lantern around to see how the others were doing.

Freida was not far behind. She looked very tired, he thought.

Paign was kicking at stones and scree, but was far enough behind Freida that he wasn't putting her at risk of a poorly aimed shot.

When they were gathered together again, Anders smiled. "OK, not far now. Around the…uh, this green wall, and then up the last tunnel. Let's get home to your place, Freida. I'm famished!" He had to nearly shout to be heard over the pulsing coming from the beams surrounding the floating rock.

The others simply nodded.

Anders struck out around the greenish cage, giving it a wide berth. He was still carefully examining the floor as he walked because of what he'd discovered in the great hall behind them. So it was only when he was a dozen paces from entering the final tunnel that he looked up. He stopped dead in his tracks.

Tiny howled, just as Freida and Paign tumbled into Anders. Freida screamed.

"You'll not be leaving here," the cowering gargoyle growled.

Anders reared back, horrified at what stood in front of him. He'd have sworn this creature looked just like one of the statues in the hall they'd just left. Except this one was very real, and it barred their way out.

"You know too much now, don't you?" the squat gargoyle said with a glare. Then he laughed. A hideous, chilling, mirthless laugh, reminding Anders of rocks shattering at the base of Ruar's Ridge, after a spring thaw.

Before he could do anything, Anders heard the twang of Paign's bowstring just over his left shoulder.

The gargoyle roared. Paign's arrow was protruding from the beast's upper right arm.

"Ha! You dare to fight Bahlkrum, mere children of men?" the gargoyle shouted. Reaching over his chest with his left hand, he pulled the arrow out of his wounded arm. He then pressed his left hand over the wound. When he removed it, to the astonishment of the children, only an angry scar remained where the arrow had struck him.

"Oh, my…" Freida whispered.

Bahlkrum laughed again, wickedly. "As I said, you'll not be leaving here. Leastways, not alive!"

Tiny barked furiously at the creature.

Stretching to his full height, the gargoyle spread his wings apart until they filled the tunnel's opening.

Paign reached for the hilt of his sword, just as Anders yanked his from its sheath.

Bahlkrum's hands thrust out from his chest simultaneously, palms upwards. Immediately, the swords fell clattering from each boy's hand.

"Ha, ha, ha! You'll have to do far better than that!" cried Bahlkrum.

Drawing his hands back to his chest, the gargoyle clenched them into fists. "My turn!"

Instinctively, Freida, who was standing in the middle of the group, just behind Anders and a little forward of Paign, dropped to her knees and shoved hard against the boys' waists, pushing them away from her. Each boy toppled to the floor just as a fireball burst from the gargoyle's fists and flew over the space their chests had just occupied.

Behind them, an eruption of colors and noises burst from the undulating force surrounding the spinning rock. Greens, yellows, flaming reds. Particles of fire dropped to the floor all around them, and the center of the cavern's ceiling collapsed in smoldering ruin. A plume of dust roiled behind them.

Whipping back around, Anders and Paign immediately nocked fresh arrows and prepared to fire.

Tiny's fury would no longer be contained. The huge mastiff leaped at the creature, growling, teeth bared to kill.

An instant later, he was flying backwards, over his mistress, and fell in a crumpled heap behind her.

"Oh, no! Tiny! What have you done to Tiny, you brute!" cried Freida. Enraged and frightened beyond reason, she seized the hunting knife from her pack and lunged at the monster.

Paign immediately grabbed her by the shoulders.

"Let me go!" Freida cried. "Let me go!" She struggled against Paign's grip, thrashing furiously, her eyes wild with rage.

Gloating, Bahlkrum snorted, "Ha! What the dog received awaits you, humans! I'll be very pleased to treat you next, girl, with the same tender ministra—"

Suddenly, the gargoyle twisted violently, severely arching his back into the yawning tunnel's opening.

"Aaaygh!" Bahlkrum bellowed.

His screaming quickly grew louder and shriller as he madly clawed the air behind his head, jabbing his talons into the gloom.

Abruptly, in the flickering light of the three lanterns, Paign, Anders and Freida all saw the point of a sword thrust out from the chest of the gargoyle.

Bahlkrum stopped moving, his eyes wide, their fire fading. "What...is...thi—"the gargoyle muttered. Then his head fell forward, his wings went abruptly limp and he slid into a heap upon the floor, dead.

So focused were the three on the unexpected and horrifying demise of their foe, they all flinched when a strong voice from the tunnel's gloom intoned, "Not if I have anything to say about it!"

Slowly emerging from the darkness of the tunnel, Johann Skulstad, Freida's father, stepped into the open, wiping the gargoyle's gore from his sword. A fierce, triumphant light danced in his eyes.

"Young lady, you and your friends are late for supper! Let's see to Tiny and then get back to the farm."

CHAPTER TWENTY-ONE

DEEP BREATH

After returning home, Johann quickly recounted for his wife the events of the day, in spite of constant interruptions from the boys, as well as Freida. Paign, especially, made it impossible to downplay the terrors of the battle with Bahlkrum. Nevertheless, his wife seemed to receive the news in her typically stoic fashion, making no comment. Although he sensed she needed time with Freida, father and daughter hastened to the barn to care for Tiny. The boys remained in the farmhouse kitchen.

"Is he going to be OK, Daddy?" Freida asked. She sat in the barn straw, nestling Tiny's head in her lap. Tears were in her eyes.

"Yes, Honey," he replied, stroking the mastiff's furry neck. "He took a nasty blow, to be sure. He'll be stiff for a few days. Had he been a smaller dog…well, I don't think he would have survived."

Tiny lifted his head slightly and wagged his tail.

Bending his head lower to meet the canine's eyes, he added, "Don't be getting any ideas, boy. You just lay up in here for a while. We'll come check on you before we turn in."

Tiny's thick tail flopped once, disturbing a considerable amount of straw in the process. He didn't appear ready to argue the advice.

Mr. Skulstad took his daughter's hand and held it as they walked back to the welcome warmth of the farm kitchen.

Paign and Anders were deep into their very late supper. Heidi Skulstad was still pale from the brief news her husband and daughter brought back from their adventures in the cavern below Ruar's Ridge. She kept ladling up more food to the boys, with an absent look in her eyes. When Freida came abruptly in through the back door, Heidi recoiled enough to spill some of the stew onto the well-used knotty pine floor.

"Oh, dear. Now look what I've done," she cried, staring at the mess but not moving to clean it up.

Freida hastened across the room, grabbed a dish towel and mopped up the wasted stew. "It's OK, Mom. I've got it."

Before she knew what happened, her mother had seized her in a tight embrace, her shoulders heaving up and down with silent, racking sobs. A moment later, her father enveloped them both in a brief hug. Anders found something intensely interesting to study on the floor by the stove. Paign's spoon simply hung in midair as he observed the Skulstads, his mouth partially open, awaiting the next delivery of his tasty supper.

After a minute, Heidi released her daughter. Smiling at Freida, she stroked smooth her daughter's hair. "That's better, now!"

"Alright, then. Let's all take a seat and sort this out completely," said Farmer Skulstad.

While the winter sunlight slowly paled into dusk, the intrepid friends described, for Freida's parents, what they'd done throughout the day and especially what they had discovered. The boys continued to devour their food while Freida and her father finally ate their own meals. Mrs. Skulstad looked pale and didn't eat much.

Eventually, they moved into the main room of the house and sat in front of the sturdy stone fireplace.

For the next two hours, it was mostly Anders who recounted details of their adventure, with occasional interruptions from Paign and helpful additions from Freida. Mr. Skulstad listened intently, sometimes asking for clarification. When Anders got to the place in their story where they discovered the desiccated corpse, he had each of the children carefully describe their experience in great detail.

"Jah, so, if I have this right, then," Farmer Skulstad said quietly, "the remains look to be that of a woman, dressed in finery, and with expensive jewelry still on her finger. Yes?"

"Yes, Daddy," Freida replied. Anders and Paign nodded in agreement.

"And her shoes were scuffed up, you say," he asked Anders, "but otherwise in good condition?"

"Uh huh," Anders said, then added, "although they looked more cracked than scuffed."

"I see." The farmer stroked his chin with the strong, gnarled, scarred fingers that all the farmers of the Highland Valley seemed to have.

"Seems to me you must have found the merchant's wife, then. Her shoes must have dried out after becoming drenched from hiking through the snow to get to the cavern. In the dry air of the cave, they must have shriveled and cracked…

in much the same manner that she did. It is clear she wasn't taken there to be robbed, or the ring would have been removed from her hand.

"Based on what you saw there, her death was no accident. She was, after all, bound to the stone chair as a prisoner. What is most disturbing to me, though, are the items you found nearby. The candles would help with lighting the dim chamber, but lanterns are much better. Candles point towards a very different meaning or purpose—and then there's the pewter cup.

"It appears"—the farmer paused, his forehead deeply furrowed—"her death was part of a ritual…perhaps the very focus of a, well, a depraved worship service. I believe the woman was sacrificed."

Farmer Skulstad got up and began pacing the length of the room.

"But then, who…who was involved in this…'worship service'?" Anders asked, shuddering. "Who would do such a thing?"

"What I want to know," Paign blurted out, "is who killed her. And why!"

"Wait! Wait! Stop!" Freida choked, panic lining her young face. "Who—or what—were they worshipping?"

Farmer Skulstad paused at the farthest, darkest corner of the room. Slowly, he turned to face the others. Firelight flickered across his rugged face, glinting in his pale grey eyes.

"To your question, Anders, I believe—like Freida—that those involved in the poor woman's murder must have included her husband, the merchant. We know from our Parson's research that the merchant had learned of his wife's terrible disclosures to the Parson Vellhelmina. Certainly, the merchant wouldn't have been pleased about his wife's exposing his deceitful business dealings. Or worse. It would have, at the very least, threatened his vast power and wealth. Perhaps even his life, if others had found out what he was involved in. However, I'm quite certain there were other merchants, of lesser power and wealth, also in the chamber at the time of her death. Perhaps even some of the town's tradesmen. There may even have been a farmer or two that participated in this fiendish act.

"As for your question, Paign, you have already guessed the answer. It appears undeniable that the woman's husband, the merchant Pers Olson, was the one who, in fact, actually killed her. His motive, of course, would have been to silence her to protect his interests, power and wealth. From what I know of his history, if he'd felt betrayed—even by his own wife—his rage could have fueled murderous revenge.

"It is your question, my dear," he said, looking intently into the eyes of his daughter, "that is the one we have no answer for. What—or who—were they willing to sacrifice the woman for? I wish we knew the answer to that."

Paign shifted nervously in his chair. "Sir. You've just said that Pers Olson killed his own wife out of a fit of rage, so as to protect his business interests and his 'good' reputation, I suppose. But you have also said that she was sacrificed to…to something. Or someone. Which is it? I don't see how it can be both."

The farmer stood, unmoved, bathed in the flickering firelight.

"I believe it *is* both, Paign. I believe she was killed by her husband, for the reasons—if one can think of them as such— that I've already described. But it appears that Pers Olson killed his wife not just for his own ends."

"Why do you say so, sir?"

"The candles you described are just like the candles we still use at our church. So, also, is the pewter cup."

Mrs. Skulstad gasped. "Oh, Johann! Oh, please...please. You aren't saying that—that they had some depraved kind of Communion service, ending with the sacrifice of the woman?"

"I"—he hesitated—"I really don't know. There are clues pointing at both conclusions. But I believe both are true."

"There were the feathers," Freida said quietly.

"Yes. Exactly," her father said. "Very much like those on the gargoyle creature that I killed moments before he was going to destroy you all."

"Do you think, Father, that there may be another creature like him? Perhaps...perhaps involved in the sacrifice?"

Her father drew a deep breath.

"It is that question we must find an answer to, as soon as possible!" His voice was so strong it made them all twitch.

Her voice quavering, Heidi Skulstad whispered, "Why? Why do we need to know that? And why do you feel it is urgent?"

"Because," Farmer Skulstad replied, steadily, "that thing I killed was surely a scout, or a guard, if you prefer. When he doesn't return to report to his commander, others will be sent to search him out. When he is found, quite dead, it is very likely that a raiding party will be dispatched to search out those responsible for his death."

Freida said, hoarsely, "You mean, they'll come looking for us?"

Paign leapt to his feet. "We need to get out of here! I don't know about you, but I don't want to bump into another one of those gargoyle creatures again anytime soon."

"How long do you think we have, Mr. Skulstad?" asked Anders.

"Honestly, I don't know. But I think we should leave here before first light. Freida and I will check on Tiny again. I'll keep watch tonight while the rest of you get some sleep."

An hour later, Tiny had been cared for and was fast asleep. All the lights in the farmhouse had been trimmed low. The bedrooms were dark. Nothing stirred anywhere on the farm. But none of the human occupants found any sleep during the long, still night.

CHAPTER TWENTY-TWO

CONVERGENCES

Peter had lost track of time, but guessed that it had been several hours since hearing the devastating revelations from Kimar and Ercen. He did know he'd been sitting next to Amy so long, with his arm tossed over her shoulder, that his hand had gone completely numb. He also knew he wasn't inclined to remove it.

Danielle had perched herself next to Kimar not long after learning about his relationship to Kahrnahrgx. The gargoyle's huge shoulders were hunched over so that he looked very much like the stone versions hanging off the sides of old church buildings. His hands were propped stiffly against the edge of the rock face. Silently, Danielle and Kimar both surveyed the comings and goings of other gargoyles, flying over the lake and occasionally plunging into it.

Danielle couldn't help smiling as she observed numerous gargoyles' cycles of flying and swimming. She remembered, wistfully, how she'd exulted in this cycle herself only a few hours earlier that day. But that wonderful experience seemed far behind in her past now, simply because of the terrible disclosures they'd learned.

Kimar had not moved the entire time she'd been sitting next to him. Impulsively, she placed her hand on his, carefully avoiding the protruding talons jutting into the air. Uncertain why she did so, she gave his huge hand a little squeeze.

She could feel a slight tremor ripple through his hand.

"Yes?" he asked, softly.

"Nothing," she replied, determinedly leaving her hand where it was.

Again, many minutes passed. It was as if Danielle and Kimar were all alone, castaways in a foreign place, sitting side by side.

Finally, Danielle cleared her throat.

"Kimar, where did Ercen go to? She's been gone a long time."

There was no response. Danielle turned so that she faced towards Kimar. He was so still, he truly did appear to be made of stone. A moment passed before he turned to Danielle. His amber eyes faintly glowed in the deepening dusk. There were smile lines creeping out from the corners of his limpid eyes.

"Child, she's gone for two reasons. First, she is conferring with leaders of our kind, seeking information from other field commanders. We need to learn what our enemy is up to. Second, she is obtaining human food for you and your parents. She'll be back momentarily."

A sharp snap sounded behind Danielle. She twisted around in time to see Ercen reappear on their eyrie. Her arms were full with all manner of food. A broken tree branch lay smashed and splintered beneath her feet.

Danielle jumped up and ran over to help Ercen. A moment later, she laughed.

"Hah! I don't suppose this load of groceries is really all that heavy to you, is it, Ercen?"

"No, Danielle. It is not, for me, what you call 'heavy.' Nevertheless, I thank you for helping me with it."

Within minutes, the granite perch high over the valley floor was busy with supper preparations. Kimar heated the sitting area, which had grown cool as night deepened.

"Thank you, Kimar!" Peter had come to think of their gathering area as the "fire ring," even though a fire hadn't been necessary.

The humans organized the food—a huge cheese round wrapped in wax, two long loaves, lightly browned, a cooked ham still bound in string—chattering as they went. Johann passed around a water jug. Ercen deftly swept remnants of the branch she'd crushed over the edge of the precipice with the tips of her wings.

The stars were twinkling brightly by the time the Wheelens had finished their ample supper.

"So, how is it that you 'obtain' our meals, anyway?" Peter asked, wiping his mouth with his sleeve.

"There are those of your kind who are sympathetic to our people, as well as our cause," Kimar replied.

"What? You mean we are not the first humans you've come in contact with?" inquired Amy.

"Mom! Of course not! Isn't it plain that they've had previous interactions with humans?" Danielle sniped. "Right?" she added, looking to Kimar.

Peter was grateful that Amy didn't respond to her daughter's imperious question. The expression on his wife's face revealed that it was just as well she didn't respond. At least not until she had calmed down.

Ercen broke the tension. "In a way, you are both correct. We have had, in fact, very limited experience with humans, beyond you three. However, the few we have come to know before you are of good character and are a credit to your species. It is from them that we obtain the appropriate provisions you need."

"Hm. Sounds like there may be quite a story behind that," Peter said.

"Please? What is your meaning?" Kimar asked.

"Oh, I just meant that it sounds like there must be an interesting story about these other humans you know. For instance, where did you get to know them? Or, perhaps, under what circumstances did you meet them? Was it by chance, or did it have something to do with your war?"

Kimar looked thoughtful, but said nothing.

Ercen stirred. With a flick of her wing, she sent the final splintered piece of branch over the side of their lofty shelter.

"It isn't so much where we met them, as when. And the conditions were much like they are now with you," she said.

"What do you mean, Ercen, when you say 'when' you met them?" asked Danielle.

"...'Like they are now'?" added Amy.

"The other humans we know are...farmers," Ercen replied.

"Ah, that explains the kinds of supplies you come back with. These people, then, are dairy farmers? Thus the eggs, cheeses, breads and whatnot?" Peter quipped. "Are they also in the Midwest?"

Kimar's expression was one of puzzlement, from what Danielle could see of his face.

"What is the 'Mid-West,'" he asked.

"Sorry, Kimar. It's the part of the country we live in. Just about smack in the middle of the United States. Lots of farming there. Lots of dairy farms. Lots of eggs and cheese. I guess I assumed that's where you'd be going to get the food for us, since it's close by. Or…at least it might be close by, if we're anywhere near our home town."

"No. We're not going to the 'Midwest' to obtain food supplies for you," interjected Ercen.

"We go somewhen else," added Kimar.

"Oh, I see, you go—what? I'm sorry. What did you say?" Danielle asked.

"We go somewhen else," Kimar repeated.

"Hm, excuse us, Kimar," added Amy. "Do you mean to be saying you go 'somewhere' else than the Midwest for our food?"

"No."

Amy cleared her throat. "So…you're saying you don't go somewhere else than the Midwest?"

"No."

"Uh…"

"We mean," Ercen stated, "we go somewhen else."

"You…you mean, then, that you, uh, 'part' into a different time than we're in now?" Peter asked, incredulous.

"Of course," Kimar replied.

"Fantastic!" cried Danielle. "That's fantastic! That is utterly cool!"

"Incredible!" Peter exclaimed. "So, Kimar, you didn't mean that 'when' you met these other humans it was under similar circumstances as ours, but that you met them in a different 'when' altogether!"

"Yes."

"But it was still under similar circumstances as yours," Ercen added.

"You mean that these other people, they were in danger, too? Kind of like we are?" Danielle fidgeted with her hair.

"Yes."

"Could you elaborate on that, please?" Amy asked.

"It would be more accurate to say that they *are* in danger, or continue to be in danger, for much the same reason you are. They are also in an age that Kahrnahrgx seeks to dominate," Ercen replied.

"He wishes to dominate all ages, Ercen. He would rule all creatures, in all times." Kimar had moved back to the eyrie's ledge. He stared unblinking into the deep darkness of a now overcast sky.

"Yes, of course, Kimar. I am aware of this, as you know," Ercen said. "Nevertheless, he cannot be in more than one place and time, even now, as powerful as he has become."

"Wait!" interjected Peter, jumping to his feet. "Are you really saying that Kahrnahrgx is so delusional that he intends to tyrannize not only creatures *now*, but also into the past? That's insane!"

"It is no delusion, Peter. Kahrnahrgx wields significant power already. With the recapture of his great key, his power will become enormous, perhaps even enough to conquer time," Ercen said.

"How horrifying!" cried Danielle. "Can his power reach into the future, also?"

"No," Kimar said flatly. "No created being has power over that which hasn't yet come into existence. Though my brother's thirst for domination is boundless, he has not grown so arrogant as to believe he can command time into the future."

"But how is it that he could 'command time' into the past, Kimar?" Danielle asked.

"He could not, if it were left to his strength and influence, and that of his followers. Although he wields much power and control, he does not even now dominate more than pockets within the human realm," Kimar grumbled.

"Well, then how—"

"With the great Key, his power could reach into the past."

Amy could see Danielle's face screw up and knew she was about to ask Kimar a third time, "How?" Gratefully, the hulking gargoyle continued. Perhaps he, too, noticed the look on his youthful inquisitor's face.

"We have told you the nature of the Key. You are aware of how it came to be, and what it contains. Yes?"

Danielle nodded.

"The power of human love is vast. It often wells up and fills the hearts of humans. It inspires deeds of great beauty. From the immense depths of human love come enormous acts of selflessness and sacrifice. Wondrous works are born from love, in your kind's music and art. Your most treasured writings and scriptures speak of love. Above all else, humans value and honor love. The abiding connections it provides from one soul to another are most prized. Love transcends space and time, even bonding hearts that were sundered from each other due to death. And it is that immense power of love, the power to span time—and even death—that Kahrnahrgx seeks to pervert and subjugate to his will. With that power, he believes he can wield dominion over not just this age, but all ages past."

Danielle noticed Kimar's fists had balled up so that his talons were thrust out.

"We, too, believe—and fear—that with the return of his Key…he can rule the present and the past," Ercen whispered.

His voice unnaturally tight, Peter asked, "Why do you not simply destroy the Key? What are you waiting for?"

"It is indestructible, Peter," Ercen replied, tolerantly. "As we have explained, it contains power unmatched, more than any earthly force that we have discovered. It cannot, therefore, be destroyed by any means of nature."

Still exhausted from the events of the prior day, Danielle rolled over to face the scratching sounds that had awakened her. In the predawn gloom, she was just able to make out Kimar dragging his talons through the dirt.

"What are you doing, Kimar?" she whispered.

"Thinking."

"About what?"

"About our conversation last evening."

"You mean about the Key?"

"Yes. I mean about destroying it."

"I thought you said it couldn't be destroyed."

"But," Kimar said as he squatted down, wings stretched out low behind him, scratching intricate designs into the dirt with his talons, "it may be possible to unmake the Key by not allowing its making in the first place."

Danielle heard sounds of stirring behind her.

"I'm sorry? What?" asked Amy, yawning. "Certainly, you don't mean going back in time, do you?" she asked, incredulous. A moment later, she giggled sheepishly. "Actually, I really am sorry, Kimar. With everything I've learned from you already—things that the scientist inside me still can't believe—I guess that going back in time shouldn't be impossible. For you, at least."

Kimar nodded towards Amy. "It is unclear if we could affect a different outcome than our first attempt. But it may be possible."

"Are you su—Kimar, do you really think so?" Ercen asked, her gravelly voice thick with emotion, while pensively rubbing her hands together. Her talons gently clicked as her hands moved back and forth.

"Is it not worth the attempt?"

For several minutes, the only sound in the eyrie was the rustling of leaves from the soothing breeze.

Peter shuffled over and sat down by Danielle. "Hm. I might have missed something earlier. But, let's say it works, at least to 'part' your way back to the moments just before your brother—before Kahrnahrgx—kills the woman. In fact, let's say it even works to the extent that he doesn't kill her after all. What happens to *this* key?" Peter asked, bobbing his thumb back and forth over his shoulder into the darkness where they all knew the perilous key lay in its box.

"I don't know." Kimar paced restlessly. "It is probable that it would be undone…that it would not matter."

"So…well…if this is true, what do you need us for?" asked Amy, imperiously. "Why didn't you just take the Key—that horrible, horrendous key—and be gone with it? Why did you take us along with you?"

Peter could hear how tired his wife was by the way she posed the question.

Kimar stopped and turned, facing Amy.

"Because you would still have been in danger. Nahgflint would not have been content to retrieve the key, only. He would have killed all of you for what your kind calls 'the sport of it,'" Kimar replied, calmly.

He shifted on his feet. Crushed rock spit out from under his toes.

"And because, if this is to work, we need Danielle to join us."

Farmer Skulstad's breathing was slow and measured. His chin rested on his chest, which was angled slightly into the side of the rocker he'd been sitting in all night. The fire had gone cold. Only a few embers still glowed a dim orange. The sky above Ruar's Ridge was just beginning to retreat from the deep dark.

Only the mouse scuttling out of the kitchen pantry noticed him twitch and moan. He appeared to be having a disturbing dream. But considering how disturbed the mouse's waking moments would become if the man awoke, the creature didn't linger but scurried into the tiny gap between the bottom row of fireplace stones and the chinking of the logs.

The farmer's dreams were, indeed, disturbed by the constant barking of a dog and a mounting sense of menace.

Like the gradual increase of light in the sky, Farmer Skulstad's growing awareness of being asleep finally woke him up. With a start, he realized he hadn't been dreaming at all, but had been hearing Tiny barking ferociously from the barn.

Leaping to his feet, he took one step and realized, too late, that his left foot had gone completely numb from sitting too long to one side in the wooden rocker. Flailing his arms wildly in a vain attempt to keep his balance, he fell heavily to the stone floor, just as the chair exploded into shards behind him.

At the same moment, a horrendous, guttural shout came from the corner of the living room, at the entry to the kitchen. "Garh!"

In the dim light, the farmer could barely make out the gargoyle's position. While grateful he'd not been hit by whatever the monster had thrown at him, he still rued the fact he was on the floor, without access to a weapon. His sword and bow were behind him, leaning up against the left side of the hearth.

Can the creature see me? he wondered. Not daring to breathe, he began to silently shimmy backwards towards the fireplace.

"Now where'd you be going?" croaked his assailant. "Unless you fall down again, all sudden like, I'll not be missing you a second time, farmer."

"What is it you want?" Farmer Skulstad asked calmly, slowly standing and brushing the rocker's debris from his clothing.

"A bit of brass you have, for a simple farmer, I'll give you that." The dark grey gargoyle was still very difficult to see in the predawn light, but it was clearly a smaller creature than the one he'd fought earlier.

"I want to know who it is that killed my comrade, Bahlkrum? He had quite the large orifice added to his chest, eh? Would that have been you that done it, master farmer?" sneered the gargoyle.

"That it was. I didn't take kindly to his threats against my daughter and her friends, so I ran him through. Perhaps I'll provide you some additional ventilation, too."

"Nahr! That'd be over my dead carcass, that would. It be my turn now, farmer!"

There was just enough light coming in through the east-facing window that Farmer Skulstad could see the gargoyle rear back, pulling his fists tight to his chest. There was a wickedly fierce look on the creature's face.

A plucking sound came from the hallway next to the kitchen.

And the creature tipped backwards, without stopping, until he finally pitched over and slammed into the kitchen's thick, hardwood floor.

"Well, not if we have anything to say about it!" came the voices of Paign and Anders, followed by the boys themselves as they stepped triumphantly into the living room, their bows swinging in their hands.

Johann Skulstad stepped into the kitchen. There lay the gargoyle, dead, with two arrows sticking in his throat.

"You know, he doesn't look much bigger than you, Paign," he said.

"But he does look meaner, if not uglier," quipped Anders, as he and Paign came alongside Farmer Skulstad.

Paign smacked his cousin in the arm. "What's next, Mr. Skulstad?"

"We should make a quick breakfast, gather up our gear and head back up to the cavern as soon as we can. But first we need to get…this…out of the kitchen before the women get up."

"We already are." Heidi Skulstad stood in the hallway opening, holding Freida's hand. The new dawn was gaining quickly, and in the growing light pouring into the kitchen doorway, the farmer could see that his wife's and daughter's faces were the color of ash. But they stood firm.

"Ah. So you are. Not quite the morning welcome I'd hoped for you. But then, thanks to Anders and Paign, it's still better than it could have been, all things considered," he said, smiling, throwing his arms wide.

While the Skulstads hugged tightly, Paign and Anders used the opportunity to drag the skewered gargoyle out the kitchen door, over the porch, down the steps and behind the barn.

Tiny began barking fiercely again—which is what had awakened the boys, too—but they didn't release him yet. First, they needed to bury the creature. About twenty minutes later, they had accomplished their mission, throwing old straw over the freshly turned soil. Unless a person knew exactly where the thing had been buried, the grave blended completely into the area behind the barn. The damp soil had packed down tight, defeating even the best bloodhound's sense of smell.

By the time they got back to the kitchen, with a newly freed and happy Tiny, Mrs. Skulstad and Freida had a hasty but hearty farm breakfast ready for them.

It didn't take long for the teenage boys to consume their meals. Before they were finished, Farmer Skulstad had their gear neatly stacked against the mudroom door next to the kitchen. Not long after, all of them—including Heidi Skulstad—were hiking back up to the threatening cavern at the base of Ruar's Ridge.

"Hey, Mrs. Skulstad! Is that a new walking stick?" Paign hollered up the slope to where the farmer and his wife were carefully picking their way through a steep slope of broken granite. "I didn't think she was old enough to need one of those," he muttered under his breath to Anders, so that Freida—who was halfway up the slope between the boys and her parents—couldn't hear him.

The senior Skulstads waited for the children to catch up to them on the far side of the talus field.

Mrs. Skulstad was leaning lightly on the highly polished wooden rod, smiling broadly, while being periodically encircled within swirling wisps of cloud breaking around them, so near the base of the ridgeline.

"So, young man," she said, with a curious twinkle in her eye that Paign had not seen before, "you are wondering if I've grown so old that I need a walking stick? Jah?"

"Um, well...no, not really. That's not it. I was just curious about the stick since I've never seen it before. That's all."

Heidi Skulstad began pacing back and forth in front of the group, tossing the rod back and forth, left hand to right.

"You see, Paign, it isn't so much a walking stick—although it can serve that purpose—as much as it's a fighting staff." As she spoke the word "staff," she seized the stick in both hands and began twirling it around so fast that Paign thought it looked like a windmill spinning in a hard storm. His eyes grew wide, mesmerized by the whirling of the staff and the whistling it made.

Abruptly, the staff stopped, perfectly vertical in her hands. She commenced to tilt the weapon—for he could plainly see that in her hands it would be exceedingly dangerous—violently from tip to tip, smacking the rocks to her left and right. All the while, she spoke with great calm.

"The staff has been in my family for generations. Legend has it that it came from the straightest branch of the oldest and strongest hickory tree on the farms belonging to my forebears."

She began swirling it over her head, angling it up to the right and down to the left, then reversing it the other way. Anders thought it looked similar to the funny leaves of the sugar maples that would spin round and round as they fell from the tree. He found it difficult to look away. Its motion made a throbbing, thumping sound.

Again, she stopped the staff abruptly, but this time the knurled knob of the staff was just inches from Paign's nose. It was much bigger than he'd realized, about the size of the hard leather ball he and Anders often played catch with. His stomach flopped when he considered what a blow from that knob, placed to the side of one's head, would do.

Swoosh.

Paign recoiled back from the other end of the staff, now hovering before his nose. There was a gleaming iron point on the hickory shaft. The iron was scarred and gouged from rough duty with the hard rock of the Honellaken Valley, where the Skulstad farm was located. Nevertheless, the point looked to be over three inches long and exceedingly sharp.

Heidi Skulstad set the iron-pointed staff down on the rock beneath her feet, and an enormous smile spread across her rosy face. There was a matching smile on Freida's.

Farmer Skulstad slapped Paign on the shoulder and gruffly asked, "So, young man! Are you satisfied that my wife isn't too old to be along with us?"

Before Paign could take offense at the tone of the farmer's question, everyone burst out laughing.

"Uh, yes. In fact, yes indeed, sir. Without question!" Turning to face her, he bowed low to Heidi. "Begging your pardon, ma'am. I am as ignorant as an ass and hardheaded as a mule. My apologies. I had no idea."

Turning to Anders, he asked, "Did you know about this skill?"

Anders had a somewhat dazzled look on his face. "Uh, no. I did not. Most certainly not. Quite surprised. Impressed!" He, too, bowed low towards Heidi. "However," he said, standing again, "I am *most* pleased she is on our side."

Freida's face beamed.

"Shall we be getting on then, lads?"

"By all means, sir." They re-hoisted their packs.

Tiny, who had lain quietly curled up on a large stone during his mistress's demonstration—he had seen all this before, after all—pranced happily around the humans, barking up a storm, ready for the next stage of their adventure.

Danielle yawned, stretched and sat up on her simple bed of straw grass bits, leaves, needles and detritus lying high above the valley floor, in their eyrie. The sun was just beginning to break over the Ten Pinnacles.

Her parents were still asleep. She was not surprised. They'd argued with Kimar and Ercen deep into the night, after Kimar's statement about Danielle's importance to their mission. Frankly, she had no idea why she was so important or what she could do that might be useful to Kimar or the other gargoyles. She did know, with certainty, that her parents didn't like the idea of her going anywhere near the Temple of Kahrnahrgx.

Ercen and Kimar sat hunched and motionless at the edge of their campground. She realized that placing themselves there would give them a commanding view of the valley below. But she also recognized they made a solid fence the humans could not roll through in their sleep.

Ercen turned to her. "How did you sleep, child? You seemed restless to me."

"Oh? I slept pretty well, thank you. Although some of my dreams were quite strange. Spooky, I guess."

"What is 'spooky'?" Kimar turned towards her.

"Sorry, Kimar. I keep forgetting you don't know all of our slang, although I don't know that 'spooky' is slang. Anyway, it just means that some of my dreams were bad. Disturbing. You know…scary."

"I understand."

"Really? Do you have bad dreams, too?"

"Perhaps…perhaps ours are like yours."

"Hm. Are yours kind of weird, where sometimes you can't quite figure out what's going on or who is doing what? And sometimes mine are in color!"

Ercen smiled.

Kimar tilted his head a little. "Ours are always in color. We always know what's going on and who is doing what. But we don't always know who else shared the dream."

"What? You share dreams? Like, when Ercen is dreaming—you have the same one? At the same time?"

Ercen's smile grew. "It's more a matter of being in the dream at the same time. We experience the same content but from our own points of view. Much like we are now, in the waking world."

Danielle could have sworn Kimar grumbled.

"But it is unlike the waking world in a critical way. The waking world is real. The dream world is possible."

"Kimar, what do you mean, 'possible'?" Amy asked.

Danielle jumped at her mother's question. She hadn't heard her get up. Her father was very busy rubbing the sleep from his eyes. All this talk about dreaming didn't seem to be helping him wake up.

"The dream world—*our* dream world—is the realm of possibilities. That is why we dream—to explore what *could be*, rather than what is." Kimar began scrawling in the dirt with his talons again. Danielle wondered if he did this when he was nervous. Or was he annoyed?

"So, you do problem solving in your sleep? Is that it?" Sometimes Danielle's father could be abrupt, even rude, when he was tired.

Kimar turned away and peered over the precipice again.

Ercen said, "In a way. But I believe it is more than what you call 'problem solving' because we are actually doing solutions in our sleep. Sometimes we will have others join us in creating a desired result together."

"I'm sorry," Amy said. "Are you saying that you invite other gargoyles into your dreams to collectively generate positive conclusions to problems you are dealing with?"

"Yes," Kimar and Ercen answered simultaneously.

"That...is...so...cool!" Danielle's eyes glittered.

"Uh, so, have you tried that approach to this Key problem? Seems like that could be useful." Peter was standing and stretching, arched backwards, with his arms spread high above his head. Danielle thought her father still sounded grumpy.

Even though he continued to face the valley and the rising sun, Peter heard Kimar just fine.

"Of course," growled the gargoyle.

Peter snapped back to a normal stance. It seemed to Danielle that he may have finally awakened, or noted the tone of Kimar's voice.

"Ah. Right, then. Was it...did you...were you able to come up with a 'desired result' together?"

Ercen replied, "It is what you would say is 'in progress.' The more complex the challenge, the more labored and difficult is the solution. Is that not so with humans?"

"Oh, yes, it is so. So…very so!" Amy said, grinning.

"Kimar, would you mind sharing with us how far you've gotten—in your dreams—at fixing, if that's the right word, this problem we have?" Danielle asked.

"Yes, Danielle," Kimar said, as he turned away from the sun and back to Peter, Amy and Danielle. "As you must know by now, this problem is vast in its importance to not only our race, but also yours. Much time and effort has been dedicated to its resolution. Not only by Ercen and myself, but also by many leaders of our kind. You should also recognize that some challenges are so difficult that many of the possible solutions we come up with will create new problems, perhaps even worse than the one being solved. This challenge—of Kahrnahrgx, his Temple, the Key—is more difficult than any other our species has ever been faced with. So far, we have not found a desirable solution. Only possibilities. Each one has at least one gargoyle dedicated to dreaming through it to its end. If there is time enough, we may discover that one is better than all others."

"We do not know this for certain, Kimar."

"No, Ercen. We do not. But we may hope. For that is the strongest weapon we have to wield in this battle."

"What's next, then?" Amy asked.

Kimar walked back to the middle of their island high above the valley floor.

"It is time for us to go from here. We must meet with others. There is a cavern, on a different continent than yours, which in the past has been used by those loyal to our beliefs.

But it has also been used recently, we believe, by followers of Kahrnahrgx. We made arrangements last night—in our dream—to meet our friends there. We need to learn what our enemy is planning. It has been many ages of men since we have been to the Cavern of Ruar's Peak."

Only moments later, Peter joined hands with Danielle, who was already holding Amy's. The Key box was tucked awkwardly under his wife's arm. He realized that his natural curiosity had won over his prior skepticism. Winking at Amy, he saw this was true for her, too. She was already holding Ercen's outstretched hand.

With a deep, somewhat uneven breath, and his heart pounding in his chest like a jackhammer, Peter smiled at the women in his life and grabbed Kimar's outstretched hand.

A little burst of dust blew up from where the group had been standing. They had parted.

CHAPTER TWENTY-THREE

PLUNGE

Heidi Skulstad stood quietly beside her husband, idly fingering her walking staff. Johann was bent over with his face close to the floor of the tunnel where, the day before, he'd skewered the gargoyle that almost killed the children. The body of the gargoyle was nowhere to be found.

Anders, Paign and Freida stood in a wide circle around the farmer, their lanterns held high as he inspected the area immediately around where the gargoyle had been slain.

Tiny sat quietly on his haunches, next to Freida.

"Strange," he said. "Look here!" He motioned to Paign for more light. "Do you see? There are two distinct sets of footprints near where the body was. That is, if you can call them footprints."

Anders squatted down next to the spot the farmer had pointed at.

"Yes, sir. There are two sets. But these are not human tracks. Or Tiny's. Although they are more like his than ours. They're similar to the gargoyle's, which you can see clearly just behind us. There's only one print that hasn't been trampled by us, but it is"—he twirled his hand in a wide circle—"the same pattern as these. Large, wide—and with curious scratches beyond the toe impressions."

"So, a gargoyle creature—or more than one—has been here and retrieved the body," Heidi said, matter-of-factly, as she leaned on her staff. "They know, then."

"Know what, Mrs. Skulstad?" Paign asked, noticing her tenseness.

"That someone killed their friend, or comrade, or whatever you want to call it…him. Presumably, more than Bahlkrum's comrade knows it was a human that dispatched Bahlkrum, since he died from a large, sword-shaped hole in his chest that ought not to have been there." She smiled at her husband.

"Ah, right. That…" Paign replied.

"But do we then assume that his comrade took care of Bahlkrum's remains, before coming for revenge? Or did some other gargoyle help him? In other words, when Bahlkrum's pal died in the farmhouse this morning, did the knowledge of what happened here—in this cave—also die? I'm hoping no other foe knows any of this. But if they do, makes you wonder what they might do about it, eh?" Anders pulled his bow back, pretending there was an arrow nocked on the string.

"Odds are, we'll find out soon enough," said the farmer. "Time for us to move on."

Tiny knew the way and trotted ahead of them all, smiling, with his tongue lolling to one side.

Danielle felt like she was experiencing a déjà vu of her first meeting with Kimar and Ercen. But she knew this was a different parting, even though she was in the deepest dark again, breathing dead, stale air that could only be from a cavern.

The rustling coming from the area to her right would be her mom. Her father's hand still held hers, comfortingly, on her left. She gave it a quick squeeze.

"Don't worry, Mommy and Daddy. In just a moment"— she heard the sound of rocks being shuffled—"we'll have light."

Quickly, the cavernous space they were in filled with the same golden light she'd first experienced with Ercen and Kimar.

"Wow!" her mother murmured. "This is fantastic." She slowly turned around, absorbing the entire glittering cavern in her gaze. "It's beautiful!"

The stone hall was shaped like the sanctuary he married Amy in, Peter thought. It was roughly rectangular, with a high vaulted ceiling. But instead of the standard suspended ceiling fans in midwestern churches, this sanctuary had rows upon rows of dazzling stalactites. Their limestone deposits were primarily golden in color, with sparkling silver mineral highlights.

Quietly, almost reverently, Peter asked, "Where are we, again? What is this place?"

"These are the caverns of Ruar," Ercen replied.

"This is one of many cavernous halls, connected by a labyrinth of tunnels," Kimar added. "It has been many an age since our last visit here."

"Is there something special about this place, then, that you decided to return now?" Peter asked.

"Our kind has used it as a gathering place during times of great unrest. We believe"—Ercen looked searchingly at Kimar—"that the 'others' have not found it yet. Therefore, we believe it to be safe."

Kimar's eyes glowed. "However, it has been long since we were here. We will assume nothing about our safety. I ask that each of you be alert and aware of your surroundings. The danger we face in a place like this is that gargoyles can easily blend into rock formations. They can even become disguised so that they appear to be a thick stalagmite. Be vigilant. Watch out for each other. Listen careful—"

From the depths of the furthest tunnel opening from their group, they could hear the far-off sound of a barking dog. Immediately, the golden light died, and they were plunged back into darkness.

Kimar spoke urgently, in a hushed voice. "I do not know what this means. Gargoyles do not know the ways of dogs. It is possible that this one—"

"Wait!" Peter whispered, then pointed ahead of him. "There's light growing in that tunnel." He shook his head, feeling stupid. Because of the darkness, of course, no one could see where he was pointing.

Sure enough, Danielle's eyes hadn't been playing tricks on her like she'd thought at first. Her father was right. A yellowish light flickered oddly in the furthest tunnel from where they had parted to. Someone—or something—was down there in that tunnel, with a lantern. And they were coming towards the cavern the group was huddled in.

"Be quiet. Perhaps they won't see you," Ercen said softly.

"What do you mean, 'you'?" Amy asked, just barely audible. "Why not 'us'?"

Neither Kimar nor Ercen answered.

The humans grew still. From the increasing backlight in the tunnel, they could see that an enormous dog had entered into their cavern. It had begun eagerly sniffing the air, while trotting back and forth.

At the tunnel entrance, the light was growing quickly. Peter decided that the source of the light must have come around the final turn behind the opening. A moment later, the light bloomed, filling the cavern. A large man stood in the breach, holding an old-fashioned kerosene lantern. At least that's what it looked like to Peter.

The man turned to face back into the tunnel and appeared to be speaking. He was too far away to hear.

Suddenly, more light framed the man. Then a woman entered and stood next to him. She, too, was holding a lantern.

Amy and Danielle were crouched low, mostly hidden behind a large stalagmite. Danielle's heart was beating so fast she was sure her mother could hear it pounding in her chest. She reached her right hand out in the inky darkness, still untouched by the lanterns, until she found her mother's hand. With her other hand, she steadied herself against the stalagmite. It was surprisingly warm to the touch. Only then did Danielle realize it was quite warm in the cavern.

Peering back towards the tunnel opening, she was astonished to see that there were now five people standing in it. The latest three were smaller than the first two. She thought they looked like children, perhaps her age, based on their size. One was a girl. She was watching the dog's search, while the others appeared to be having a discussion. Although they could hear nothing from this distance, the two boys, the man and the woman seemed to be having a heated argument.

The girl glanced up at the others. Danielle could see she was saying something to the group. The adults stepped away from the children. After a minute or two, they rejoined the others, and all five started into the cavern, following the path the dog was taking.

"They have weapons," her father murmured into her ear. Danielle started. She felt foolish that she'd forgotten her father was even with her, so focused was she on the group of strangers…and their dog. The dog kept getting closer to where they were hidden among the limestone columns of the ancient cave.

It was true. Lantern light glinted off of swords held tightly by the man and one of the boys. The boy held it with authority. She was sure they both knew how to use them. The woman walked with a long wooden staff, which seemed out of place. The other boy held a bow, arrow nocked at the ready. The girl was in front of the four by several paces, trying to keep up with the dog.

With a deepening sense of dread, the Wheelens watched the dog get ever closer to their position.

Peter, in spite of his gnawing uncertainty about their safety and growing conviction that they were just moments from being discovered, was impressed with the lumbering canine giant. The dog's search pattern at first appeared to be completely random, as one would normally expect. But this dog used a zigzag approach to the right, then the left, that moved forward with each pass. The beast was carefully, relentlessly examining every meter of the cavern's floor. It was only a matter of time before they were found out.

Peter gently pushed his face between his wife's and daughter's.

"It seems certain we'll be discovered," he whispered. "I can't be sure, but perhaps this is just a family out for a, uh, spelunking expedition. But given their weapons, it's best if we act with caution…and calm."

Just as he whispered "calm," the dog stopped, head low to the uneven floor, about fifty yards away.

But it couldn't have heard me. Not from this distance! Peter stared, astonished.

The dog's head suddenly snapped up. Sniffing furiously, its nose bobbed up and down, then side to side. Then its head turned and looked directly to the area where the Wheelens were hiding. With a great leap, the hound bounded over to their hiding place. They'd been found!

Before the dog's people arrived, Peter slowly stood up, instantly bathed in the fierce glow of five oncoming lanterns. He kept his arms limp at his side. In no way did he want the dog to feel threatened, especially now that the gargantuan beast stood only three paces from him, a low growl leaking through its bared teeth.

"Stay where you are! Don't move," the tallest stranger said, still twenty yards away, but closing quickly. "Or it will likely be the last thing you ever do."

Danielle jumped up. "Hey, there's no reason to threaten my dad like that! We haven't done anything wrong. We're just exploring…like you." She had to squint because of the combined brightness of all the lamps.

Tiny stopped growling. His head tipped to one side.

"Hmphf," Paign grunted. "Without lanterns? Sure way to get yourselves killed—exploring caves without the benefit of light, eh?"

Amy stood up and stretched her legs lazily, yawning. "Now that you mention it, it is kinda dark in here 'without the benefit of light.' Eh?" She had not been amused by the smart tone of the young man with her daughter.

By now, the other party had surrounded them with their beaming, hissing lanterns, as well as drawn weapons. Tiny had not resumed growling, but sat unconcerned on the rough surface of the stone hall.

"So, what have we here now?" The man speaking looked to be a farmer, near as Peter could tell. "Or shall I say...*who* have we here now?"

"What person in their right mind goes traipsing around in caves without any light?" Paign asked, loud enough that his voice echoed. "And what kind of clothing have you got on? Where are you folks from, anyway?"

Turning to Anders, he muttered, "Must be from the other side of Ruar's Ridge. What's the name of that valley again?"

Freida had been quietly studying the other girl. She saw the girl doing the same of her.

Ignoring Paign's outburst, Freida said, "Hello. I'm Freida Skulstad. These are my parents. These boys are our friends. This is Anders Knutson. The loud one is Paign Macy. Oh, and this is Tiny, our dog."

Tiny's tail flopped on the floor three times. Anders bowed, doing his best to appear older than he was by smiling just a little. Paign scowled.

"Uh, hi!" replied Danielle, uncertain of how her parents were feeling about this encounter. Her father had a most curious look on his face. She couldn't tell if he was afraid or amused. Her mother was looking intently at Freida's mother. Impulsively, she decided she liked Freida. "My name is Danielle Wheelen. These are my parents. But you probably already guessed that."

Peter immediately reached out to shake the farmer's hand. "I'm Peter. It's a pleasure to meet you, sir." He grinned at the sound of this formal greeting in such an informal place.

The farmer gave a quick nod and bowed slightly, and shook Peter's hand. "I am pleased to make your acquaintance. My name is Johann."

Danielle squatted down on her knees and reached out her hand for Tiny to smell. "Is your dog friendly, Freida? Hello, Tiny! Can you shake, boy?"

Before Freida could reply, Tiny's tail began swinging so hard it swatted Paign's leg.

"Oh my goodness! He's enormous! He must be over two hundred pounds, at least." By now, Tiny had shaken with each of his paws. Danielle was giggling and patting him on his massive head.

Freida dropped to her knees beside Danielle. "Well, I don't know anything about 'pounds.' He's about ninety-five kilos. But then he's not full grown yet."

While observing this exchange between the girls, Peter noticed that the boy named Paign looked annoyed or, perhaps, bored. When Peter looked over at the boy named Anders, he was surprised to see puzzlement on his face.

"Something wrong, son?" Peter asked.

"Hm? What, sir?" Anders replied, embarrassed. "Well, it's just that you're all dressed in a peculiar fashion."

"I was going to say the same of you," Amy smiled.

"Well, it's clear that we all have questions about each other," Johann said, smiling. "Might I suggest we all sit down and sort it out?"

"That depends," Amy said, then pointed her finger three times, "on what you plan to do with those."

"Ah. Of course. Forgive us. We were prepared for...well, uh...no matter. Yes, we'll put them away since you pose no danger to us." Johann sheathed his sword. "Paign, please put away your sword. Anders, your bow. Thank you."

Heidi bowed gently at the knees and reached her hand out to Amy's. "Hello. I am Heidi Skulstad."

This began a cascade of introductions that lasted several minutes of grown-up awkwardness, a stream of giggles from the girls and joyous leaps from Tiny.

"So! Now that we have all been properly introduced to each other, might I inquire as to what—here in this particular cavern—you are 'exploring,' as the young lady stated some time ago?" Johann asked.

"We, uh, are searching for something," Peter replied.

"But, you are here without lights! That just doesn't make any sense." Paign was pacing a short path between the two squat stalagmites the strangers were found behind. "And furthermore, I just don't—hey, what's that you have?" He pointed at the ground behind Danielle.

She was horrified to discover that she'd not adequately hidden the plastic box holding the Key of Kahrnahrgx. "It's nothing! Nothing at all. It's just a...souvenir...that I brought along."

"A souvenir? That you brought along on a caving expedition?" Paign cried, very doubtful of Danielle's honesty. "Here, let me see it!"

Before Danielle, Peter or Amy could answer, Paign made a lunge for the box.

What followed took less than a minute but felt much, much longer. Peter had anticipated Paign's brash move and had stepped into his path, only to be confronted by the burly farmer. Danielle and Amy began yelling loudly at Paign to stop, which set off Tiny, who was alarmed by all the shouting and ruckus. Heidi and Freida immediately dove for Tiny and wrestled him to the rocky floor, which is when he howled like he'd been set on fire. But he stopped as soon as he'd started. Puzzled and disoriented, it took the girls a moment to realize that it suddenly became very still.

"So what's gotten into everyo—" Freida choked off when she looked up at the entangled mass of family, friends and strangers. "Oh, no! Get back, get back, GET BACK!"

Just beyond Paign—who appeared frozen in his tracks—stood two enormous gargoyles, both much bigger than the one Freida's father had impaled the day before. One of them had apparently seized what Paign had lunged for and was now holding onto the unusual box. Freida had never seen a box made of glass before.

Heidi screamed. She'd not, as yet, seen a living gargoyle, of course. Now that she faced not one, but two of them, her nervous system was overwhelmed with fear. Johann stepped in front of her protectively, while he drew his sword and prepared to strike the nearest beast.

He saw out of the corner of his eye that Paign and Anders had also unsheathed their swords.

Johann's world instantly shrank to a single thought. "Get back, you foul creature!" he yelled. The gargoyle nearest him was smaller than the other that held the box. "Or I shall run you through like I did your friend!" It was as if all the others—and all of the strange happenings of the previous few minutes—had vanished. Now, the tall farmer stood alone, unaware even of Paign and Anders, prepared to protect his family. He expected it would be to the death. All of their deaths.

So he was astonished when the creature replied calmly, "There is no need for that." Its voice was strangely coarse, but feminine. "Unless you find other enemies to kill..."

Johann couldn't decide which was the more shocking, the calm—even warm—voice, or that she smiled at him. At least he took it to be a smile.

"I...you...what?"

"Perhaps I can help." Peter stepped in between Johann's sword and where it was pointed, at Ercen's mid-section.

"These are our friends," he continued. "Ercen you have already...met." He gestured towards her with a little flourish of his wrist.

"Friends?" Heidi whispered, stepping next to Johann.

"And this is Kimar. He saved us from a gargoyle that sounds pretty much like the one you—dispatched. Nasty disposition. Unpleasant demeanor. Seemed bent on bringing great harm and hurt to humans. Ring a bell?" Peter couldn't tell if his attempt to dispel the tension, at least some of it, was working. He was still trying to put his finger on what made these strangers so...strange.

No one made a sound. Peter's attempt didn't appear to be helping.

Anders broke the silence. "Sir, please forgive us. We would like to believe you. In fact, if I may be so bold, *I believe you*. Had you intended us harm, I am quite certain we'd all be dead by now, by your"—he paused, then motioned to Kimar and Ercen—"hands." He stared for a moment at the numerous knife-like talons at the gargoyles' disposal. "It's just that we were recently attacked by one of these...by a gargoyle creature, and narrowly escaped from this cave. Then, earlier this day, we were attacked again, at the Skulstads' farmhouse, not many hours ago. So, to find that what we took to be oddly-shaped stalagmites were actually the creatures we were hunting…well, I trust you understand our reaction…and strong hesitation."

Paign shifted on his feet, looking none too happy. "Well, I am *not* convinced." He sat down abruptly, sulking.

"Well, I guess that is understandable," Amy said. "Actually, we were more than a bit surprised when Ercen and Kimar vanished right after we got here."

"See!" Paign snarled. "Can't be trusted. Anders, I'm telling you."

"I'm sorry you had something bad happen to you," Danielle bristled. "But you speak from ignorance about these gargoyles. They are kind, gracious, desperately brave…they are certainly good. They—they are our friends!"

Amy could see her daughter was getting herself really worked up, so she quickly intervened. "As I said, it is understandable. And as Johann suggested, let's try this again, shall we?" She sat down and motioned for the others to do the same. Except for Paign, who was already sitting, and still sulking, by the look on his face.

"Let us do this, as you say, to 'try again,'" Johann agreed, sitting down after putting his sword back into its scabbard.

The others also sat down, fidgeting until they eventually found a comfortable position. Even Ercen and Kimar lowered themselves to their knees. They looked just as Danielle had first seen them, in the Cave of Osberg the Great.

Johann reviewed the disturbing events of the preceding several days. Especially Freida, but Paign and Anders, too, were surprised to hear their story from a different point of view. Until then, they hadn't considered how stressful and frightening their explorations could have been to Freida's parents. As the unfolding story reached the points where others played a key role, Johann would defer to them. Thus, in the end, the Wheelens and the gargoyles heard firsthand what Anders, Paign and Freida had experienced in the cave during both of their explorations. By the time they were finished, Tiny's ears lay flat against his head.

"Hopefully, it is now clearer why we reacted the way we did when you leaped up," Anders said, looking at each member of the Wheelen family. "And, more so, when you two appeared out of stalagmites," he added, nodding to Kimar and Ercen.

"Yes, indeed!" Peter said. "Actually, it showed restraint, on your parts, to not swing your swords first and ask questions later," he continued, looking intently at Johann, then the boys. "OK, Dani, how about you start us off."

Danielle shared her experiences, beginning at the house with the portico, how she was introduced to Ercen and Kimar, the disastrous attack by Nahgflint, and the ensuing destruction of their home. Amy picked up their story line with the airborne retreat away from their house, after Kimar had saved Danielle. Peter wrapped up their summary with the eyrie at the Ten Pinnacles.

"Jah, that's something!" Johann bellowed.

Paign's pale blue eyes flamed with the same enthusiasm as the farmer's. Anders was thoughtful. Freida continued stroking Tiny's neck. Danielle sat on the other side of the great mastiff, content to be leaning into him. Tiny was pleased with the attention.

Heidi, however, was not as excited as her husband seemed to be about the recent gargoyle experiences of the Wheelens.

"You say that Danielle was—how did you say?—'foretold.' What does that mean, exactly?"

Ercen stirred. "Our kind does not have written scriptures as humans do. We keep the central stories of our faith within an oral tradition, over many generations. Long ago, there was a prophecy about a time of great unrest within our kingdom and that a child—a human girl—would be…important."

"This is all very interesting, but shouldn't we be on our way, Mr. Skulstad?" Paign stood up and stretched. "We're not far from where that strange green, pulsing light ensnared the rock I threw."

"Wait!" Heidi interrupted. "Paign, please be still."

Paign immediately sat back down.

Heidi continued, staring at Ercen, "How did you know the 'human girl' was Danielle?"

"Because of the Key. The prophet's revelation made clear that she would lead us to the Key," Ercen replied, softly.

For a moment, the only sound in the cavern was Tiny's snuffling, as he cleaned his toes.

"Hm. Paign, you were saying the green tube of light is nearby, right? I would like to see what's left of that," Peter offered. "OK with you, then, Johann? Heidi?"

Paign was irritated that the strange man ignored him in the equation of who to ask from his group, especially when it had been his idea to go in the first place. But when it was clear that the entire group was preparing to move out, he shouldered his pack, hoisted his lantern and started off. Tiny bounded after him, with a bark. Freida and Danielle brought up the rear.

"It is strange, don't you think, that you are so special to these gargoyles?" Freida asked gently.

Danielle kicked at a small rock chip that was in her path. "I suppose," she said, faintly. "I certainly don't feel special. If anything, I just feel small and terrified, especially now that I've heard the story about the poor, poor widow Vellhelmina, or whatever her name is. It's just…so very horrible…and heartbreaking…and I…." Her voice trailed off and grew quiet.

Freida was at a loss what to say. Glancing at her friend, she observed that Danielle was staring at the back of the larger gargoyle. The peculiar glass box was tucked under Kimar's right arm.

Sensing that a different topic was needed before her new friend would talk more, Freida decided to ask Danielle about something that hadn't made any sense to her earlier.

"Danielle? What is a 'paper route'? I don't know what that means. Is it a pathway you make out of paper?" Freida asked, wide-eyed.

Danielle stopped in her tracks. "What did you say?"

Freida repeated her question.

Danielle knew better than to laugh at Freida, because it was certain to hurt her feelings. She could tell that Freida was quite serious. Still, the question puzzled her, but even more so the tone in which Freida asked it. She sounded intimidated, perhaps frightened. *Why would my having a paper route frighten her?* she thought. *Unless they don't have newspapers where she comes from. Perhaps she is very poor.*

"Freida, how do you share news with each other?"

"I'm sorry…news?"

"You know, stuff that's—newsy. Something noteworthy, different, things that people will talk about. Could be politics. Or some cataclysmic disaster. You know, stuff like that."

"I'm not sure about some of the things you mentioned. But we would just share these 'news' when we see each other. The best time for this is after church on Sunday when the whole town gets together."

"The whole...town?" Danielle asked, incredulous. "How many people live in your town, anyway?"

"Well, at last count, what with the latest Skogstann baby a few weeks back—they have seven children now!—and if we're counting all the farm families in the Honellaken Valley, that puts us at ninety-six. I'm pretty sure, anyway."

Danielle had stopped walking so abruptly that Freida had to quickly step to the left and swing her lantern out of the way. Danielle plopped down next to a stalagmite.

"What's wrong?" she asked.

"What kind of time bubble are you in? Even the smallest towns have more than ninety-six people! My junior high class has more than that many in it. This is the twentieth century, after all!" Danielle's arms were waving back and forth.

"This is...what?" Freida choked out. She desperately wanted to understand what Danielle was saying. So far, it was sheer madness. But before she could continue, many things happened at the same time.

She heard Paign yelling about black feathers he'd found. She heard "more" and "last time." There were screams. Women's screams. She figured that they came from her mother and Danielle's, but she had no idea why. Men were yelling, too. A lantern seemed to have exploded near where Paign's voice had been coming from. Freida could see Danielle was peering in between two thin stalagmites, also trying to determine what was going on. Then there was a ghastly, gravelly roar. It must have been Kimar. But, why? He sounded very angry. Freida's ears were hammering. She realized, with a shock, that it was from the racing of her own heart.

Panic was rising in her like a fast-moving storm. She reached out to clutch onto Danielle's hand, when suddenly Ercen appeared in her way. Before she could grab her friend's hand, both Danielle and Ercen vanished.

Blinking back hot tears of rage and unbridled terror, she recoiled violently when Kimar materialized directly in front of her. Disconcertingly, the gargoyle's amber eyes grew wide with fear.

His hands thrust out, grabbing wildly at her. Distraught, she pulled back. "Nooooo!" he bellowed.

But it was too late. She felt her shoulders seized by fists of iron. Reflexively, she turned her face backwards. Two fierce, bloodred eyes narrowed.

And she was gone.

CHAPTER TWENTY-FOUR

SUNDERED

Even with the great span of experience with humans that Ercen and Kimar had collected over generations, they had never experienced the unbridled, shattered hysteria that Freida's abduction unleashed. Never had they witnessed the volcanic emotions—first exploding, then seething, then erupting, then spewing—of a mother whose child is stolen from her. Heidi's fury only relented when she had utterly exhausted her terror-spawned anger. Finally, she collapsed in a heap, whimpering softly to herself. Amy had tried valiantly to keep Heidi from harming herself—and everyone else in their remaining party. Johann, stricken to his core, was altogether inconsolable for a long time. Peter, though speechless from his own tidal flow between guilty gratitude that it wasn't his daughter and nauseating horror that Freida was taken, simply stayed near Johann, hoping to lend comfort.

Immediately after Freida's abduction, Kimar had hastened after Anders, who had eagerly followed Paign's tunnel hunt for

the gargoyle. Only Kimar and Ercen fully knew the dangers
these tunnels held. "Do not leave this place! I will return with
the boys," Kimar said.

Within moments of Freida's disappearance, Ercen had
shrouded Danielle, encompassing the girl in a canopy made
by her wings. She sobbed uncontrollably, even as she held fast
to Tiny, who was, quite possibly, the most distraught of them
all. Danielle clutched at the huge mastiff's chest, as the dog
quaked from head to toe, his right leg spasmodically twitching. Little had she known that a dog could groan.

Amy stood next to Heidi, struggling to control her own
fear, as her hands lay gently on the shoulders of Freida's distraught mother.

No one paid any attention to the passage of time, so it
wasn't clear how long it took Kimar to return with the boys.
Paign was in a foul temper. Anders had finally given up on
trying to calm his cousin.

"Look, what's next? How do we retrieve Freida?" Paign
snapped, frenzied, looking mostly in the direction of Ercen.
"There must be a way, and we must find it!"

Then Paign bellowed in fury, and hurtled a fist-sized shard
of stalagmite nearly across the cavern's width. Peter estimated
his throw at sixty yards. *Wow, that kid has an arm*, he thought.

While the shard was still clattering off in the distance, Ercen
slowly withdrew from Danielle and rose to her full height.
"Yes, Paign, it is a certainty that we must rescue Freida."

Ercen gazed at Heidi, whose face was a mottled mess
of tears, fury and fear. "She is in grave peril, but she is not
yet in imminent danger. It will take time for the minions
of Kahrnahrgx to alert him about her. Neither Kimar nor I
recognized the gargoyle that captured her. But he is of the

obsidian class and therefore very dangerous and likely a high-ranking scout. But he—the scout—will need time to discover the whereabouts of Kahrnahrgx, or perhaps he'll first report to a senior officer. Still, we need to leave this place, soon."

Peter had been listening and watching Johann and Heidi carefully. The blood seemed to drain out of both of them.

Peter cleared his throat. "This is"—he paused to take a deep breath—"promising news." He fervently hoped he sounded like he believed it. "What, then, would you suggest we do to locate Freida? Because it sounds like, well, it may be difficult, or somewhat challenging, to find him. The gargoyle, I mean."

"We can't know exactly where the gargoyle parted to with Freida," Kimar intoned. "He is a strong one." He nodded to Danielle. He'd explained to her that especially powerful gargoyles could part without leaving a trace. "But he is not so strong that he didn't leave us some clues…"

Unexpectedly and unmistakably, a smile emerged upon the great gargoyle's face, like a long wished-for but unexpected thaw after an unforgiving, bitter winter.

"What?" Danielle cried. "Kimar, are you saying you can trace where the gargoyle parted with Freida? Honest and true?"

Slowly, he nodded. "Yes. He is very strong indeed. But I have tracked him. I know where he went with her."

Johann jumped up, flailing his arms. "But how can you be certa—"

His question was interrupted when his wife leaped in front of him and threw her arms wide around the startled gargoyle's neck, tears streaming down her face like drops running down a window pane in a rainstorm. Her feet dangled cheerfully off the ground.

"Please, please," she cried, "help me save my baby, Kimar!"

"Jah!" Johann yelled, his eyes welling up. "Let me at them!"

Paign and Anders pulled out their swords, thumping their chests with the hilt, the blades aimed straight at the ceiling, right in front of their noses.

Kimar gently and carefully grasped Heidi and lowered her to the cavern floor.

"It is my honor to serve you. And it is my promise to ransom Freida, no matter the cost. We shall find them. We will be certain to encounter resistance, and we will, no doubt, be fiercely opposed."

Danielle had not before seen the smoldering fire that was now in Kimar's eyes. She shuddered.

"We must first finalize our plans," he continued. He motioned for everyone to sit.

Peter guessed that it took half an hour for Kimar to lay out his rescue plan for Freida. It was impressive that the plan included not just general information about who they would be facing, but also elaborate tactical battle plans. He covered where each of them would be positioned, as well as how they would be armed. Only when each of the humans could repeat back to Kimar what their positions and purposes would be during this perilous mission did he relent to a meal break.

It must have been several hours since their chance meeting in the cave, as well as Freida's capture and all that came after. It was astonishing how hungry they all were.

As the boys plunged into the enormous load of food they'd brought with them, Peter half-expected to see most of it wolfed down by Paign. *Only boys can get away with that!* Peter thought ruefully. *At least I hope he gets away with it and doesn't lose it later.* "Thanks for sharing, boys," he said, gratefully.

As they made ready to leave, the Wheelens explained again to the others how parting worked, based on their admittedly limited experience. Anders kept asking technical questions they weren't equipped to answer.

"I don't care *how* it works," Paign stated, "just *that* it works. I'm tired of waiting around." He swung his sword idly around in front of him. Stab. Parry. Slice.

Anders jumped in front of him, deftly blocking a thrusting maneuver with a swinging, downward strike. Paign responded by swinging his sword in the same direction Anders had blocked him, using the added momentum to arc it around at his cousin's head. Anders brought his sword over his head to deflect Paign's slice. Back and forth they went for several minutes, until they were both bathed in sweat.

"That's enough, boys," Johann said. "Very pretty work, to be sure. But we need you to be sharp when we arrive at the enemy's stronghold. Your swords, too, for that matter."

"Don't worry, Mr. Skulstad," Paign replied, enthusiastically. "We'll be ready, just wait and see!"

"That's right, sir," Anders added. "We just needed to get warmed up, is all." Both boys immediately set to sharpening their blades back to a fighting edge.

Peter felt completely pathetic. He'd witnessed the awesome skills with a blade that each of the boys commanded. He was quite sure the farmer's would be even better, since he may have been involved in their training. While Heidi, the farmer's wife, still seemed distraught over the kidnapping of her daughter, Peter had a feeling that the woman's staff wasn't just for walking. If she needed to, he was quite sure she'd be able to protect herself—and others—with it. It brought him some comfort to consider that Freida may possess some of the same defensive talents.

But now he was faced with the demoralizing reality that his family spent more time talking about or watching athletic efforts than being involved in the actual experience. It had been years since he'd played football. He'd been able to throw an effective tackle in his day, but he wasn't so confident about his ability now. Amy still enjoyed running, as he did. But it was hard to see a useful application of jogging against the likes of gargoyles bent on his destruction.

Amy felt the same way. "Hon, we should get some pointers on how to be…more useful…when we are…required to be." She nodded in the direction of the boys. "You used to teach archery back during summer camp, didn't you, Peter?"

"Ha! You've got to be kidding, right? That was ages ago, Ames. I doubt my fingers will rememb—"

Amy cut him off. "All the more reason we should get busy getting reacquainted with the weapon, eh?"

"Uh. Yeah. I guess that would be the thing to do…we, huh?"

Anders had overheard the conversation and brought the bows over to them. "Jah! With Paign and me using our swords, we can't very well use the bows, too. It is much better to have them in use than on our backs, what with where we're going to." Smiling, he handed them over to Amy and Peter, along with fully loaded quivers.

"Well, what am I supposed to do?" asked a very agitated Danielle.

Ercen stepped alongside her. "You," she smiled, "need to protect this Key. That will be more than enough challenge."

Amy looked uneasily at Peter. She disliked this reminder of what was at stake. This mission ultimately was about more than saving Freida. If they succeeded, all of humankind would be saved. If they failed…that she didn't want to consider.

Kimar cleared his throat. At least that is what Peter took the gravelly outburst to mean.

"It is time for us to go. We won't part directly to where I've tracked the obsidian gargoyle. You are not yet ready. First, you must practice with the bow until you are as prepared as you can be on such short notice and need. Since you cannot practice in here without destroying the very arrows you practice with, we will go to a forest."

"Trim your lanterns, but leave them here," Ercen stated. "Where we are going we will not need them. When we return—and we do need to return, for we still need to discover what happened in the chamber containing the remains—they'll be waiting for us."

Danielle remembered that was just what their group was about to do when Freida was taken. She hated the memory of the look on her friend's face the moment she was seized by the glistening black gargoyle. More than anything, Danielle wanted her new friend back. Safe and sound.

Moments later, with the lanterns' flames quickly flickering out, she hoisted the dreadful box under her left arm. With her free hand, she grabbed Kimar's outstretched hand. Everyone else was already holding hands. The final lantern's fire sputtered out, leaving only a glowing wick. Completing the circle of hands, Ercen reached out to Danielle's left hand, so that her grip on the box wasn't disturbed.

They immediately vanished, leaving only darkness and quiet in the cave.

CHAPTER TWENTY-FIVE

THREATS

A grey, cold mist swirled around the shadowed figure. Light shifted up and down the spectrum of grey, like late sunlight dappling tree trunks on a summer day.

Freida wondered about the figure. Who was it? Where was this place? What time was it? Suddenly, her need for answers to these questions became urgent, overwhelming. But try as she might, she couldn't seem to reach the girl—yes, the mist shredded enough for a moment that she could make out that it was a girl. But why was she there in the first place? And why—why!—could she not get to her? What was holding her back from reaching the figure? It was like she was marching in hot sand.

Freida struggled again to reach the hooded figure. Mightily, she pushed and thrashed. Wait! She'd gotten closer this time. Just…a…few…more…steps. With each move closer, Freida's curiosity grew more intense, until it had bloomed into physical pain. Her feet felt like they were on fire, but, oh, she was so close! Now that she had only to reach out and turn the girl before her, each movement agony, the searing pain made her scream. The grey mist suddenly darkened. Freida's hand plunged desperately through the gloom, but the girl was no longer there. She screamed again.

The second scream finally woke Freida up. However, there was no dappled mist. It was utterly dark, wherever she was. On the other hand, the pain she'd experienced in her dream was real enough. Then it all came rushing in again. The strange new friends she'd made, the chaotic confusion of the moments before...before she was taken. If only she had not been frightened by Kimar...frightened of Kimar! Had she not reared back from him, she wouldn't even be here. Trapped.

Perhaps this is what Hell is like. It was an unbidden and crushingly unwelcome thought. Freida couldn't help it. Folding over so that her chin touched her knees, her small body was racked with sobs. Freida wept, rocking back and forth in the inky twilight.

Slowly, almost against her will, she became aware of another sound, rising over the gaspings of her sobs. At first, it reminded her of the rockslides at the base of Ruar's Ridge. Sometimes, when she and her friends traversed the scree fields, enough stone would dislodge that it triggered a small avalanche. But the noise increased so that it sounded more like the much more dangerous spring rock falls at the ridge, when the sun would thaw the cliff face enough that an occasional boulder would loosen and come thundering down. Finally, Freida recognized the sound for what it was: harsh, pitiless laughter.

As the laughter intensified, wicked red light burst all around Freida. The cruel face of her captor leered at her, the mirthless laughter quickly fading from his malicious features.

"Is the little human unhappy with her new surroundings?" he snarled. His breath was foul and smelled like the skunk cabbage that grew along the edges of the streams outside her village.

Freida's head throbbed from the thunderous pounding of her heart. Her pulsating fear was almost nauseating. She said nothing, not trusting her voice.

"Cat got your tongue?" The obsidian beast grabbed at the rope it had cruelly tied her feet with, giving it a jerk to make sure it was holding tight.

The unexpected eruption of pain made her cry out.

A cackling noise that reminded Freida of the town blacksmith's hammering exploded from the gargoyle.

Anger surged through Freida. "You just wait, you hateful thing. My father will—"

"Your father will WHAT?" the gargoyle bellowed. "He is not here. He has no idea where you are. He has no way of finding you. He is no match for Gahrspat. It won't be long before the minions of Kahrnahrgx come to 'collect' you. The least of your worries, human child, are these ropes. Perhaps, when you have spent some time receiving the ministrations of the great Kahrnahrgx, you will wish to be returned to my *tender* care!" Apparently this amused the gargoyle, since it ignited a second round of cackling from Gahrspat.

"You beast!" Freida spat back at her captor. *You don't know my father. He will find me. He will rescue me. And he will match you!* Her shoulders aching, her arms tied tightly behind her back, Freida silently heaped scorn upon the brute before her. Deep in her heart, though, a worm of doubt squirmed.

Johann was remarkably patient, Amy thought. She could see that Peter's skill with a bow was certainly coming back quickly; even she wasn't doing poorly with it. But when she put herself in the shoes of the farmer and his wife, she was humbled by how focused they could be with teaching them when, she was certain, more than anything they wanted to charge into the lair that Kimar had identified as Freida's prison. She thought it would have required a greater level of sophistication—of 'mental fortitude,' her old philosophy teacher used to say—than these simple peasants could muster. *And yet, here they are, patiently teaching two university professors how to shoot an arrow so that it would at least threaten what it was aimed at.* Then it occurred to her how harsh and condescending she was being. Amy felt deeply ashamed.

The tension in Heidi was more evident to Amy than it was in Johann. Nothing in her behavior or speech gave any indication that something was amiss, but her face unveiled the constant anxiety of a mother whose child is missing. Worry lines creased her lovely face, making her appear twenty years older.

"Ha! That's more like it!" Peter yelled, exultantly. "Yes!"

"Way to go, Daddy!" Danielle rushed over and gave Peter a hug.

Amy looked at the rotting stump they'd been shooting at for the past hour. Only when she studied it closely did she realize that he'd placed a second arrow so close to the first that it blended together from the angle she was looking.

"Wow! Well done, Peter!" she exclaimed.

Kimar effortlessly pulled the arrows out of the moist stump. He'd chosen it because it made a sufficiently good backstop without damaging the arrows. Amy wondered how many arrows Kimar thought they'd need to rescue Freida. But she didn't wonder enough to ask him. *Some things are better to just find out on your own,* she thought.

Kimar pointed to a stand of trees across the small clearing next to them. "There's an apple tree over there. Shoot the biggest apple, on the long branch to the right side of the second tree."

"Uh, OK." Peter was feeling somewhat less confident than he did moments earlier. *Sheesh,* he thought to himself, *I'm glad it's a fat apple.*

Acutely aware that he was being watched by Paign and Anders, Peter gritted his teeth, determined to calmly maintain focus. Holding the bow high, he drew the arrow fletches to his ear. Slowly, he lowered the bow so that the arrow was nearly parallel to the ground. Aiming carefully, he took a deep breath, gently exhaled and fired.

Thwap.

The arrow's flight was true. It neatly plucked the apple from the tree. Paign came running back with the neatly impaled apple and Peter smiled, relieved.

"Very good," Kimar intoned. He handed an arrow to Amy. "Now, the large apple on the left side of the same tree, four branches up from the ground." Looking intently at Amy, he added, "If you please."

Like her husband, Amy used the same steps for preparing to shoot. Unlike Peter, she didn't have archery experience in her past. But she'd always had good hand-eye coordination.

Thwap.

A moment later, Paign whooped when the apple fell from the tree. It took him several minutes to return. No one knew what to make of the delay. When he came back, he held the apple in one hand and the arrow in the other. The apple was perfectly whole.

"Ma'am, you made a great shot. But you didn't actually hit the apple, as you can see." Paign turned the apple so everyone could witness that it was, indeed, not punctured.

"Then, I'm confused," Anders said, grabbing the apple to inspect it himself. "The apple fell right after she shot it. So what happened, Paign, if she missed it? Why did it fall?"

Paign's face sprouted a wide smile. "Hah! She didn't miss it, Anders. Look, everyone! Look at the stem!"

"Well, I'll be. Mom, you hit the apple's *stem* with your arrow!" Danielle beamed at her mother.

Once again, Anders held up the apple for everyone to see. But this time he tilted it so the focus was on its severed, ragged stem.

"Well done, Ames!" Peter hollered.

"Yes, indeed. Both of you. Now you are ready. You are able to protect yourselves, as well as your companions." Kimar nodded to Amy and Peter.

"It is time for a break. You will need food and rest before we go after Freida." Ercen motioned for everyone to go back to the center of their campground, sheltered deeper in the woods.

As Amy turned to follow the others, Kimar leaned over and whispered in her ear, "Just drop your arrow a little before you shoot next time. Your hand lifts a tiny bit on your release."

He was smiling at her. Unmistakably. Surprisingly. Amy smiled back, encouraged. As she walked back to camp, an enormous gargoyle at her side, she marveled at how they'd gotten here…why they were here. What would have happened had she never found that fossil outside of Ghorlikharka, Nepal?

Freida awoke with a splitting headache. She could tell she was awake only by the change of her position from prone to upright. Even in the pitch-black of this cave, she could tell that much. Plus, the agony of moving her tightly-bound hands confirmed she was awake. She wondered if the skin around her wrists would ever grow back. The headache, she knew, came from sleeping with a rock for a pillow. *Must never do that again*, she thought. *Better to sleep on my back, even if I snore. Maybe it will keep that nasty gargoyle awake!*

"I'm thirsty," she said into the lightless cavern.

There was no answer.

"I'm thirsty," she said again, louder.

"What is that to me, human?" Two fiery red slits opened up to her right.

Freida figured he must still be in the same position as he was in when she fell asleep. *He's been scrunched down on his haunches for ever so long now*, she marveled to herself. *His eyes seem to be as close to the floor as last night.*

"I'm thirsty," she said a third time. "I'll keep saying it until you do something about it."

The wicked red light returned, followed by Gahrspat's smirking face thrust into hers. "You are a fool! Do you wish to tempt me? For I can certainly 'do something about it,' if you'd like," he snarled.

"I would simply like to drink some water because I am thirsty."

There was an immediate increase in the red glow, enough so that Freida could make out most of the cavern that now served as her dungeon.

"Behind you, human!" Gahrspat stabbed a finger over her shoulder. "Water."

Turning awkwardly, Freida saw that there was indeed a small pool of crystal clear water about fifteen feet behind her.

She concluded that it was the result of collected droplets falling from the stalactites above. Suddenly her mouth felt parched.

"And how do you suppose I should drink it? My hands are tied, and I have no cup, even if they weren't."

Gahrspat had already closed his eyes.

Freida realized with a start that she had no idea where the blood-red light was coming from. Not knowing how long it would last and worried she wouldn't get a second chance at the water, she wriggled over to the pool, sliding on her bottom by digging her heels into the floor, then wiggling forward , while pushing awkwardly with her hands trailing behind. It was very difficult, but she was finally able to get her legs under her and rise up on her knees. Waddling the final few yards on her knees, she crouched slowly down at the edge. Careful to maintain her balance—she did not want to fall headlong into the water—she sipped directly from the pool. The water was surprisingly warm and brackish, almost to the point of being bitter. But she drank her fill anyway.

Well, she thought, *if that doesn't kill me, then I'll be wanting something to eat soon enough.*

CHAPTER TWENTY-SIX

BEST OFFENSE

"So, you know *exactly* where that gargoyle took Freida?" Anders asked Kimar, dubious. "…Sir."

"That's fantastic!" Paign added. "Let's go, shall we?"

"In a moment, Paign," Kimar replied. "And yes, Anders. I know exactly where the gargoyle who took Freida is. That does not, however, mean that I know exactly where *Freida* is. We judge her to be in the same area that he is. While it is imperative that we move quickly, and gather her back to us before Kahrnahrgx's cohorts find them, we must be careful and finalize our plan of attack."

For the next ten minutes, Kimar, with help from Ercen, reviewed their plan for rescuing Freida. It would require simultaneously parting everyone into the cave together. The assumption was that the cave would be completely dark. Ercen would be responsible for casting light. Kimar would immediately engage the gargoyle in combat. Freida's parents were tasked with grabbing her and getting her to safety, while

Danielle, her parents and the boys would provide cover to Heidi and Johann, in case there were more gargoyles present by the time they parted in.

Kimar said for the third time, "Surprise will provide us our best chance of retrieving Freida. Obsidian gargoyles are very fast, and because he's trusted as a scout we know the one we are facing is a leader. Therefore, we can expect him to be one of their fastest. He is very dangerous, especially when surprised."

"Be very careful, and watch out for each other," Ercen added, quietly.

Kimar scanned the faces of the humans he would be leading into a fight beyond their comprehension. He deeply hoped they would be up to the task of facing such a daunting enemy. The faces looking back at him were resolute, even if pale.

"Weapons at the ready," Kimar cried. "Remember, do not face the gargoyle unless you have no other option. Use the stalagmites as shields."

As they formed their parting circle, everyone faced outward this time. The boys clutched their swords tightly and offered their fists for the other to grab. Farmer Skulstad did the same. Heidi Skulstad cradled her staff in the crook of her arm, awkwardly holding her husband's fist, as he grasped his sword. Again, Danielle tucked the Key box under her left arm, while holding onto Paign's hand. With her right hand, she clutched at Tiny's scruff. He made a deep, gutteral growl, anticipating what was to come. Anders gripped hold of Tiny's collar.

Kimar grabbed Ercen's free hand. "Now."

"Are you going to get me food or not?" Freida growled at Gahrspat. She thought it a fitting name for the unpleasant gargoyle. He made her want to spit at him.

Gahrspat snarled back at her. The red glow in the cave increased abruptly. He rose to his full height and started towards her.

"Perhaps you didn't understand my meaning, human. So it would seem that you need further instruction."

Freida feared she had pushed him too far this time, and she began crawling backwards. But with her hands still tied tightly behind her, numb at the fingers but burning at the wrists from the horrid cutting rope, it was hopeless. She moved too slowly.

Gahrspat loomed over her, his eyes ablaze with a wicked red fire. His right hand was aimed at her head. Slowly, a sneer crept over his face. His hand thrust suddenly at her, as if he was pushing her away.

Even though he had not touched her, Freida felt like her head was being crushed under a freight wagon. She writhed around on the floor, mashing her already damaged hands under her back, against the loose stone shards littering the cave floor. Pain exploded in her head. All Freida could do was crawl for the nearest stalagmite on the other side of the brackish pool. It was instinctive. Thinking was impossible.

Gahrspat began cackling again. A cold shiver ran down Freida's back.

"So, human. Is this not to your liking? Do you wish for me to sto—"

The searing pain in Freida's skull abruptly ended. She opened her eyes, which had been clamped tightly shut from the pain. The cave was glittering with a bright white light, not the red glow that had filled it earlier. A thunderous roar echoed off the dense walls of the chamber, but it was not the hateful voice of Gahrspat.

Freida was momentarily frightened when hands slipped under her arms and pulled her behind the very stalagmite she'd been making for. She was face-to-face with her mother! But she couldn't hear a word her mother was saying because of the deafening crash of stalagmites all around them. For a horrifying moment, Freida thought Gahrspat had pulled on the rope binding her hands. Pain shot up her arms. Then her father suddenly appeared before her, smiling broadly. While still holding the severed rope in one hand and his knife in the other, he hugged her fiercely.

"We've got to help!" he yelled, his lips tickling her ear. "Stay here!" He kissed her on the cheek.

Turning to peer around her protective stalagmite, Freida stared, amazed. Stalactites were crashing all over the cave. Gahrspat was thrusting out his fists, back and forth, like a drummer in the town parade. But he aimed at the ceiling, not at a drum.

She then saw that Kimar was directly under where the stone spears were falling. Kimar was furiously returning fire, while crouching under a canopy of his own wings. Stalagmites exploded next to Gahrspat. Astonished, Freida noticed that Paign and Anders had sheathed their swords and were now trying to flank to the right of the obsidian gargoyle. *Reckless boys!* Her assessment proved true enough because moments later the ceiling above the boys was crumbling around them, too. On the far side of the cavern, she could see her father and Ercen attempting a flanking maneuver. The farmer was firing arrows with enormous speed, as Ercen pumped her fists at the ceiling over Gahrspat's head.

"Wow! Have you ever seen anything like this?" Danielle yelled into Freida's ear.

"Where'd you come from?" gasped Freida. "You gave me a nasty start!"

"Oh, sorry! I've been hunkered down one stalagmite back." Danielle was clutching the case holding the Key. Her parents were kneeling just behind her, nocking arrows in their bows. They stood together and fired.

The Key! Freida thought. *What is it about this key that should bring so much threat and horror to me and my parents?* But there was no time to consider such things at a time like this.

With a cataclysmic crash, a huge section ruptured and cascaded down upon the obsidian enemy. Just in time, his wings linked into a canopy over his head. His attention diverted from the humans, a renewed volley of arrows set to flight. When the rock fall debris cleared, it was obvious that several arrows had found their mark. Gahrspat swore loudly and plucked a pair of arrows from his chest. From the angle they'd hit him, Freida determined they'd come from Peter and Amy, and not her father.

A fiendish red radiance erupted around him. He'd spotted the boys and would wreak his vengeance upon them. Clapping his wickedly taloned hands together, the resulting boom dislodged much of the ceiling above Anders and Paign. Freida and Danielle could see them leap out of the way just as an enormous section of the roof came crashing down.

But in that moment, Kimar threw out both fists together and all of the stalagmites between he and his enemy shattered, like a wave breaking onto shore, bursting up into the air. With a great thud, Gahrspat was launched off his feet, sailing through the air, slamming through numerous stalagmites until he finally crashed into the cavern's farthest wall.

"All right, all of you. Is anyone hurt?" Ercen yelled into the cave. Without waiting for an answer, she continued. "We don't have much time. It is certain that this gargoyle has alerted his comrades of our presence here. An attack is imminent. Be vigilant!"

Running quickly between the stalagmites, Paign and Anders hastened back to where the girls were huddled together with the adult Wheelens, not far from where they had arrived. A few moments later, the Skulstads hurriedly joined them.

"Where are Ercen and Kimar?" the farmer asked, sharply. "Why aren't they here?" He was looking at Danielle, as she held the box.

"Uh, I don't know, sir." It made Danielle uncomfortable the way he looked at her. He was bleeding from his shoulder.

"Daddy! What happened?" cried Freida.

"Jah, well that wicked creature dropped a lot of ragged stone all around me. I was caught by a large fragment that blew up from the floor." He ignored his shoulder, while his wife examined the wound. He was covered in dust.

Suddenly, Ercen appeared. "Let me see, please," she said to the startled man. Heidi faltered backwards. Ercen stepped up to him, placing a hand on his shoulder.

"What is she doing?" Heidi asked, her voice quavering.

"Don't worry, ma'am," replied Danielle. "I've seen them do this before. It's pretty neat."

"What?" Freida wondered out loud. "'Neat'? What does this mean?"

Before Danielle could answer, Ercen removed her rough hand. The farmer's shoulder was healed, plainly seen through the still-shredded shirt he wore. The lacerations still looked angry but were sealed as if they had been stitched.

"These won't bother you again," Peter said, revealing his recently healed wounds to the farm family. "I have no idea how it works, but sure am glad that it *does*."

"What do you know?" Johann exclaimed. "Have you ever seen such a thing?" he asked, looking at Peter, even though Peter had just indicated that, in fact, he had just seen such a thing. Flexing his shoulder and spinning his arm around, he added "Jah...well, now that's something, isn't it?"

Heidi smiled sheepishly. "Thank you, Ercen. I'm...this is...there's been so many...what I'm trying to say is"—she shrugged—"we're grateful."

After the dust had settled near the area Paign and Anders had been firing from, the boys went back to investigate the destruction. They were amazed they'd not been killed, so much of the ceiling had hurtled down upon the outcropping where they'd volleyed arrows towards the obsidian demon. Loose stone, shards and thousands of bits of stalagmites and stalactites littered the area. Their way back to the rest of their group was slow and treacherous.

From the top of the heap, they could see Kimar nosing around the area where Gahrspat had crashed. Given the unnatural position of his glistening black body, Anders was confident the gargoyle was dead.

Anders felt dampness on his shoulder. A steady dripping of water fell from a massive crater in the ceiling above them.

"So, what do you make of that, eh?" He noticed his cousin staring up at it.

Paign cleared his throat. "Not knowing where we are, I don't know whether that beast ruptured enough of the cavern's roof that he's let in melting snow…or an overhead lake or stream. As you know, any of these are possible along the length of Ruar's Ridge. All I know is that it's not encouraging. We should plan on leaving. Sooner than later."

Anders was staring at the cave's entire ceiling. Many sections were as this one directly over them. The ruptures seemed to all have water streaming down from them. But Anders noticed the water was not pooling as one would expect.

"Paign…are you seeing what I am seeing?"

"What the…"

Kimar's voice exploded like thunder from across the glittering cavern. "Everyone! Get to Ercen! Get to Ercen. NOW! We're under attack! The Vannveps have come! Run! RUN! HURRY!"

Paign and Anders were hard-pressed to slide-run down the enormous heap of shattered ceiling they'd just been standing upon. It would have been difficult enough to do carefully, but much more so with great haste. Not knowing what Kimar was warning them about didn't make their descent any easier. Their eyes were locked on the lowest depression at the base of the mound.

"Anders!" Paign yelled, as he slid nearly out of control to the base of the slag. "Are you seeing what *I'm* seeing?"

Anders tilted his head up long enough to look where Paign was pointing.

Many streams of water fell from the cavern's ceiling, but rather than pooling at the cavern's lowest point, the water instead ran slowly up the hill the boys were scrambling to get away from.

"Oh, my! This can't be happening…it's not possible!" he shouted in reply, just as he crashed to the lowest edge of the mountainous heap.

Now, above and to the right of where they stood, Anders and Paign watched the water rush up the hill from numerous rivulets cascading from the roof. To their horror, they watched the water pool *upwards*, like there was an invisible bowl being filled at the crest of the slope.

"What the…" Paign repeated, louder.

The collected bowl of water erupted up and out, but not in random drops. Instead, the water flew up in thin rivulets, gathering into shimmering, transparent orbs. Then those shapes split into more, smaller forms, all suspended in midair. It reminded Paign of a bizarre snowball fight frozen in time. The orbs quickly transformed into something more recognizable, with translucent wings wildly beating the air, holding their segmented bodies in place.

"Paign! We need to get out of here. Those things look like—"

"We must leave! Now!" The gravelly, intense rumble startled Anders and Paign. Neither boy had heard Kimar part directly behind them, so focused were they on the bizarre vision unfolding in front of them.

The gargoyle's enormous hands clapped down on each of their shoulders. A moment later, they'd joined the others.

"By all things that are holy," Paign cried, "what on earth were those things, Kimar? They look like overgrown bees or something! What'd you call them again? Van-steps?"

"Vannveps," Ercen corrected him. "Water wasps. Their sting is very—"

"There's no time to discuss this!" Kimar yelled. "Ercen! We must gather everyone together. It is perilous to stay here any longer!"

Kimar began hastily—and roughly—shepherding the humans together into a tight circle. Ercen, following his lead, began doing the same.

Quickly, Danielle found herself in the middle of a shuffling group of people. Her parents stood nervously in front of her. Freida and her parents were jostling behind her. Kimar held Anders and Paign in his grip.

Peter quickly grabbed the bow from Amy and handed it, with his, back to the boys. "Looks like you might need these again!" No sooner had the boys retrieved them, Ercen cried out.

"Too late!" Ercen's wings snapped out to their full width.

As if out of thin air, the Vannveps were flying in from all directions.

"Defend yourselves!" Kimar roared, leaping behind Freida and snapping his wings wide over the girl's head as a protective canopy.

"Child!" he yelled at Freida. "Grab Danielle and pull her under my wings!" Kimar punched out his fists simultaneously and two of the water wasps disintegrated into mist.

Danielle, desperately trying to stay low, was already hastily crawling back towards them with one hand while the other tightly clutched the box. Freida grabbed her under the arms and hauled her the rest of the way under Kimar's wings to get her out of harm's way. Danielle was startled to land, roughly, beside Tiny, who immediately began licking her face.

When Freida looked up, she could see her father wickedly slicing the air where a pair of Vannveps had just been. Her mother's staff was spinning over her head so fast it made a whooping sound. When a water wasp flew into it, however, the sound was more like a pig flopping into fresh mud.

Paign and Anders stood back-to-back, swords flying, thrusting, jabbing. There was an enormous smile on Paign's face.

"Not very bright, are they?" he cried. "Even after we've killed several of their friends, they just keep coming in the same way." He stole a glance at Anders. "They ought to change tactics, don't you think?"

Anders leaped to one side, stabbing a wasp just as it flew up from the floor, aiming straight at his cousin. "It appears they heard you, Paign!"

To their left, Danielle's parents crouched low to the floor, arrows aimed upwards.

"Dang it!" Amy yelled. "These things are hard to hit. They're stinking fast, the little creeps." She fired at a hovering wasp but missed.

"Who says they're little?" Peter yelled. "They look to be about half the size of this crazy dog."

Tiny had been barking madly at all the wasps, trying to bite them as they flew past. He began howling.

A moment later, a fireball flew in from the far corner of the cavern, near where Gahrspat had fallen. It exploded against the stalagmite next to where Ercen stood. Then, in quick succession, three more fireballs burst all around the group.

Freida screamed. "Tiny! Tiny is on fire!"

Anders spun around to see what was happening. To his horror, Tiny was running around in a tight circle right behind him, yipping in pain and fear. The upper half of his tail was smoking. The stench and smoke of burnt hair filled the air. Hearing a now-familiar buzzing sound closing in, Anders whirled around and slashed a Vannvep that was aiming to sting him on his shoulder. The water wasp blew apart over his head, splashing next to Tiny, and largely putting out the fire on his tail.

"We must part. We're outnumbered and in danger of being overrun. Gahrspat's reinforcements have come. Draw closer!" Kimar shuffled towards the center of the group, as he bellowed out orders. He carefully kept Danielle and Freida under the canopy of his wings. All the while, he kept pumping his fists, twisting one way, then the other, returning volleys of fireballs back at their obsidian enemies.

"Well, at least Gahrspat's comrades are taking out some of the wasps in their eagerness to get us!" Paign quipped, as he sliced another flying predator out of the air. It splashed close enough to Tiny to completely put out his smoldering tail. "Anders, what do you think of Kimar's flying fists?" Paign bellowed over the din. "It's as if he's throwing invisible hammers! It's incredible!"

Being in such close proximity to each other made it difficult for the humans to defend themselves without threatening the welfare of their friends. Heidi nearly smashed her staff into Peter's head as he rose up to shoot a glistening black gargoyle closing in on them. The attacker fell heavily to the floor, tumbling right past where the Skulstads were fighting more wasps.

"Ercen! Quickly now!" Kimar bellowed urgently. He stretched his wings farther than Anders thought possible. Just as Ercen's wings shrouded the other humans between her and Kimar, fireballs began exploding all around them. Sparks skittered under the protective shelter, singeing Paign's boots.

"Kimar…now! NOW!" Her wings spread over the heads of the adults and touched those of Kimar. "Please, my husb—"

An explosion of withering heat and crushing brilliance enveloped the humans just as they parted out of the cave below Ruar's Ridge.

And Freida was rescued.

CHAPTER TWENTY-SEVEN

REDEPLOYED

Paign had instinctively raised his arms up to cover his face when the blast of blinding light and heat assaulted them all. Perhaps it was for this reason that he was the first to recover from the excessively harsh parting. He had to shake his head to clear the ringing in it from the blast that had engulfed them the moment before they left the chaos of the cave.

"Well, that was close, eh? Eh? Yo, there! Anders?" he ran over to his cousin. Anders's face was filthy, covered with grime, tiny grains of blasted stone, spots of blood and what looked like ash. *I suppose the ash came from Tiny's burnt hair*, he thought to himself.

"Hey," he said, gently shaking Anders. "Are you hurt?"

Slowly, Anders sat up. "Hm. Feel a bit cooked, as you might say. It got plenty hot right at the end there…you know, before we came here. And—where is that, anyway?" Paign had been watching his cousin closely and was relieved to see he was unhurt. Anders surveyed their new surroundings. His eyes suddenly grew wide.

"Why are we so far apart from each other, Paign?" he cried. "Did you move me over here for some reason?"

"Uh, no, of course not. What are you talking about?" he replied, suddenly annoyed with Anders. But as he looked around the meadow they were in, he finally noticed that, unlike their last parting, this time their group was strewn all around the meadow. Or at least some of them were. With deepening dread, he realized that some of his friends weren't moving yet.

Without the need to say anything to each other first, they both ran over to the girls, who were about a hundred and fifty meters away. They were hunched around Ercen. As the boys drew near, they could clearly hear the girls crying.

"What do we do now?" Freida asked Danielle. "You know more about these creatures than I do. Isn't there anything we can do?"

Danielle's face was wet with tears. "How would I know that? It's not as if I've had loads of experience with gargoyles, you know. It was only two—maybe three days ago, I guess— that they showed up in our lives!" Her hands were clenched so tight her knuckles were white. "Is she…is she…dead?"

The boys couldn't help but gasp when they looked at Ercen.

"Oh, my!" Paign cried. "Her wing—it's gone!"

Anders had already kneeled quickly beside the creature. She was horrendously damaged. She was lying on her left side. Virtually all of her left wing—which should have been lying on the ground under her—was blown off. Ragged fragments remained on her back where the wing merged into her ribs and back muscles. Her right wing, what was left of it, curled over her side and lay tucked in front of her. There was a huge hole in the middle of it. Most of her back was scorched and covered in sooty ash, from her own incinerated skin and feathers. Under the hole in her wing, blisters had formed. It was the most gruesome thing Anders had ever seen.

Paign ran into the nearby trees and vomited.

Gently, breathlessly, Anders placed his index finger on Ercen's neck.

Anders had no idea of how a gargoyle's pulse, healthy or sick, should feel. But he had to try. While it was faint, he felt a pulse.

Immediately, he stood up and said, "She's alive. I don't know if her pulse is normal or not."

Freida, Danielle and Paign, who had come back looking sheepish, stared at him without saying a word.

"Look, she seems to be unconscious. Maybe it is their way of protecting themselves from further stress. I don't know. But this is a poor place to have her…well, lying around. We need to move her," he said, looking quickly around at their surroundings, "over to those trees, into the shaded area over yonder. And—wait a minute!—where is everyone else, anyway?"

"I've been meaning to ask that, too. Where on earth are Kimar and the grown-ups?" Paign demanded, louder than necessary. "Where are your parents?" he said, staring at each girl in turn. "And why did we land so far apart from each other, I wonder?"

"We don't know the answers to any of your questions. We didn't even know you were anywhere nearby until you walked up to us. We thought we were alone…alone with Ercen." Danielle's voice quavered. "We've been here for over an hour, I think."

"You haven't seen—what do you mean—did you say 'an hour'?" Anders stared at her, disbelieving.

"Yes," Freida chimed in. "That seems about right. We didn't notice when you, uh, arrived."

"But that doesn't make sense!" Paign snorted. "We would have 'arrived' at the same time as you did!"

"Well…we don't know that to be true, Paign. It makes sense to assume we'd all come together, I suppose." Anders stroked his chin. "At least, that's what happened the last time. But, clearly, something really bad happened just as we were parting out of that cave." He nodded towards Ercen's prone body. "Something explosive…powerful. If it was strong enough to tear her wing off, perhaps it was enough to disrupt a 'normal' parting. Although that sounds a little crazy to say out loud, since until recently there was nothing 'normal' about parting…or gargoyles, for that matter."

"But if that's true," said Danielle, "where is everyone else?"

"And where's Tiny?" asked Freida.

Peter couldn't remember a headache this bad, even as a college student on a weekend bender. How his ears rang. What had he just been doing? It was so difficult to formulate thoughts.

Slowly, he sat up and carefully opened his eyes. Surprised that the light of day didn't make his headache worse, he opened his eyes fully. What he saw shocked him.

He was in a field of tall grass, blowing in a gentle, warm breeze. But Amy lay nearby, apparently unconscious. Her pants were smoldering. *That's strange,* he thought to himself. But he couldn't quite seize on the niggling, troublesome worry inside. It was so hard to focus. *Of course, it's strange, you fool. No one should have smoldering pants. Besides, that is my wife—*

"What the—" he yelled. "Amy! Amy! Honey…what's happened to you?" He began crawling over towards her but collapsed almost immediately. A searing pain shot through his left thigh. The headache was immediately replaced by the appalling awareness that he had a stone shard wedged into his leg. Blood had oozed out and stained his pants. He knew better than to pull it out. Until he was better prepared to staunch the wound, which felt nauseatingly deep, it was best to keep the shard lodged where it was. Gasping from the pain, he continued towards Amy, dragging himself slowly along.

By the time he reached his wife, she was already stirring.

"Hey," she said dreamily. "What are you up to?"

"I was hoping you could tell me," he quipped, gritting his teeth into something he hoped passed for a smile. "Your pants seem to be on fire, Hon." Grimacing at the effort, he leaned awkwardly and tried patting out her smoldering clothing with his bare hand.

"What?"

"And I've got a hole in my leg I was hoping you could help me with."

"Peter!" Amy screamed. She quickly pulled her button-down shirt over her head, leaving her undershirt stuck to her sweaty skin, and tore it into strips. She expertly and efficiently created a tourniquet above the jagged rock sticking out of Peter's thigh. He was grateful for her first aid classes.

"Where's everyone else?" she asked.

"Who else?" Peter replied.

"The others, Hon. In the cave…where you must have received this little souvenir." She pointed to his leg. Troubled by his vacant stare, she continued, "You know, Johann, Heidi, the gargoyles, Tiny, the kids...our daughter?"

Like the moon's slow rising above the horizon, awareness dawned across Peter's face.

"Oh, man. Amy. I...I don't have any idea where they are." His eyes were wide with worry. "I suppose the others could be hidden in this tall grass. We should start looking for them."

"Not before we get that out of your leg," she said, pointing at his impaled thigh. "Bite on this." She handed him a chunk of broken tree limb, which was lying on the ground next to where Peter had found her.

Peter half-expected to chew through the piece of oak, he bit it so hard when she yanked the rock out of his thigh. She quickly wrapped the open wound with more of her shredded shirt.

"We need to get this cleaned out. There are certain to be little stone fragments and dirt left in there. You could get an infection. That wouldn't be good," she murmured, stroking his face.

"Fair enough, Hon. But first we need to find our daughter and her—our—new friends." Peter struggled to his feet, using the broken limb like a staff, grimacing as he put weight on his leg. "Dani!" he yelled, swaying like the waist-high grass.

For several minutes, Amy and Peter hollered in all directions. Amy circled out further and further away from Peter, looking through the tall grass for their companions.

Peter swayed unevenly on his damaged leg, like the grass behind her, but continued to call for Danielle. He was roughly thirty yards away when Amy heard a moan.

"Peter! Shut up, Honey! Someone else is out here."

Peter watched the back of Amy's head getting smaller as it weaved away through the tall grass, moving in the direction of the trees at the edge of the glade. It dropped so suddenly out of sight he thought she may have tripped.

Gingerly, using his borrowed bow as a cane, he shuffled through the grass towards where he'd last seen her standing. When he got there, he could hear voices. Female voices.

"Honey? Amy? Where are you?"

Amy's head popped up about twenty yards to his left. "Over here," she waved. "I've found Heidi and Johann. Come quickly. As quick as you can, anyway," she shrugged. Then her head dropped from view.

He was sweating profusely when he finally found them.

Heidi's head was nestled in Amy's lap, and Amy was stroking the hair of the farmer's wife. There was dried, crusted blood on the side of Heidi's face, just below her left ear. Johann lay next to her, breathing slowly.

"So, what do you make of this?" he asked Amy quietly, sitting down heavily, his wounded leg set stiffly in front of him.

"Looks like they were both knocked out cold. My hunch is that they both suffered a concussion." She stared at Heidi. "I think she's trying to come out of it…she cries from time to time. Just before you arrived, she called out for Freida."

"Any sign of the others…of the kids?"

She shook her head achingly slowly. "No. No sign of Tiny, Ercen or Kimar, either." Her face was flushed.

Peter had never hoped to sound as confident as he needed to now. For Amy. For *himself*. "Hm. Well, that must mean the kids are with Kimar and Ercen, right? It's only logical. They'll be along shortly, I'm sure."

Amy smiled wanly.

"Hon, can you hear a little stream burbling? Sounds nearby to me. How about if I stay here and watch over these two? You can check it out."

Nodding, Amy got up and trudged off towards the trees, vanishing almost instantly into the grass.

Kimar's body still smoldered and fumed. At least, it would if he could break free. Vaporous smoke was frozen in a swirl near his right wing. Remnants of a fireball still glowed in his wing. But there was no pain. No movement. There was, in fact, nothing at all.

In the ancient archives of the gargoyle's collected oral histories, only one legend described what Kimar was experiencing in truth. He had, against all odds, been parted out of space and time. The only light within his view, ironically, came from his wounded wing, where the fireball burned with no heat, no fire. Several more fireballs were frozen in flight, suspended in time and space just moments before impacting Kimar. Otherwise, Kimar was surrounded by abject darkness. The darkness of the Void.

He struggled mightily to move, to generate any energy or force at all. Nothing. He had no sense of time elapsing. This was normally true for him, as one of the Great Ones. He was accustomed to parting in and out of time periods, as he needed.

But this was different. Time was critical now. Not to him. But to Ercen, his beloved mate. As they had winked out of the ruinous cavern below Ruar's Ridge, he'd witnessed the massive fusillade of fireballs hurled by the minions of Gahrspat. He and Ercen had instinctively thrown out their wings as a protective shield around their human colleagues. Scores of the obsidian beasts must have been assembled just before their parting. The fury of their assault was staggering! It was everything he could do to maintain the integrity of the group's members at the inception of their parting. But he could sense that Ercen had been brutally damaged, even before she accidentally released, taking the children with her. His shock was so great that he'd lost his own focus, released the adults before he'd been ready and landed himself out of time and space. He needed to get to Ercen!

Furious with himself, with the situation, he roared. But there was no sound and no one else to hear it.

"Look who I found!" Amy yelled as she burst through the tall grass next to her husband.

A very wet, boisterous Tiny came leaping along right behind her. Before he could defend himself, Peter had been completely slobbered down by the enormous canine.

"Hey, boy! It *is* good to see you, too!" Laughing with joy, Peter was surprised at his own tears. "Boy, yes, it is *good* to see you, fella!" He gave Tiny an awkward bear hug, not wanting to move his wounded leg. Tiny seemed to sense this and immediately quieted down and happily accepted the hug from his new friend.

A minute later, Peter's face emerged from the dog's rough, tears streaming down his face. He smiled at Amy.

"Yeah. I feel the same way," she said, tears welling in her eyes.

"Jah, he's always been a smart one. But he eats like a small horse!"

Peter and Amy whipped their faces around to see Johann sitting up, rubbing his hands through his hair. Dust, soot and flecks of stone flew off his head.

"What a relief!" Amy cried. "You're a sight for sore eyes, Johann!"

"Eh? What's that you say?" he laughed. "You have sore eyes? Jah! I thought mine were going to dry right up inside my head, just before we left that hateful place. Felt like I'd stuck my head into the woodstove, it did!"

"Oh, never mind!" Amy replied. Then she leaned over and kissed the farmer on top of his tousled head.

Peter smiled, amused at the look of utter confusion that sat on Johann's face. "Welcome back, my friend!"

"So, then. I see you didn't fare so well, eh, Peter?" Johann pointed at Peter's wrapped leg. Blood had seeped into the shirt-strip bandages.

"You, on the other hand, look to be enjoying the life. Yes, Amy?"

Amy giggled. "What a curious—and delightful—expression! Yes. Such as it is, I'm well enough."

"How is my wife?" He leaned over and kissed her gently on her forehead. "Heidi? 'Tis time to wake up." He reached under her arms and softly lifted her up to his chest, rocking her back and forth.

A moment later, her eyes fluttered. "What a horrible dream I had! It was the worst imaginable, my dear." She opened her eyes fully and looked into her husband's open face. Reaching up first to wipe away the grime on his nose, she kissed him. "But it wasn't a dream, was it, my Johann?"

"No, my dear," he whispered. "Unfortunately, not a dream. Not a dream."

A cloud scudding overhead darkened her face. "Where are the children?" she whispered back.

CHAPTER TWENTY-EIGHT

RAGE

The ferocity that Evalcohr meted out upon the first strike team to reach Gahrspat's cavern beneath Ruar's Ridge was horrifying, even to the squads with him, made up of his most loyal followers. His fury over the team's failure to capture—or at least obliterate—those who killed Gahrspat was seemingly unquenchable. Even though he'd arrived just in time to witness their fiery onslaught, he was not satisfied with their enormous effort. It didn't change the fact that they had singularly failed. It was the result that mattered. And it was that at which they'd miserably failed.

Despite the murmuring from his troops, he'd dispatched with ruthless precision all twelve of the strike team, one at a time, beginning with the lowest-ranking grunt and working his way up to the commanding officer.

Until he reached the top gargoyle, he'd been satisfied to simply impale them with a rapid thrust of his talons into their chests. With the commander, however, Evalcohr wanted to make a special point and leave a lasting memory for those under his command.

So, when Tiunarz came forward, Evalcohr had the carcass of Gahrspat brought forth. Six soldiers laid it on the floor. The body lay face down, but it was still plain that he'd been pierced by several arrows. It appeared he'd had time to heal some before being struck down by the crushing aerial blows thrown by Kimar.

Four of Evalcohr's senior lieutenants stepped out from the ranks and stood three meters away from the body, positioned at equal lengths from the feet and shoulders, facing each other in two rows. His eyes burning with a red flame, Evalcohr nodded slightly. Their four heads dropped low, their fists thrust out and the body of the slain leader rose off the gritty cavern floor. Gahrspat's body hovered in between Evalcohr and Tiunarz, stiff as a plank, his dead arms hanging inert, talons dangling and his lifeless eyes staring at the floor.

Evalcohr's voice broke against the walls of the cavern like a volcano erupting.

"You see before you the result of your failure, Tiunarz." His words boomed throughout the cave. "You were not, of course, responsible for the death of our friend and comrade Gahrspat. No, that guilt belongs to the traitor, Kimar, and to his pathetic mate, Ercen, as well as their human followers. And the time draws near when they all will pay!" he shouted. In several places around the cavern, ceiling sections cracked and crashed to the floor.

"Your guilt, Tiunarz," he howled, "is not snaring the one, above all others, who should stand here for their treacherous sin! Kimar was within your grasp. Yet you allowed him to escape! This is offensive to the obsidians!"

Dozens of gargoyles roared their approval.

"Either you succeed…or you die. It is the way of things."

"Success or death! Success or death! Success or death!" the mob chanted.

"You failed, Tiunarz. Therefore, you die!"

"Success or death! Success or death! Success or death!" The chant grew in volume with each shout until it became deafening.

Evalcohr's arms slowly rose from his sides, fingers pointed down towards the floor, palms aimed out at Tiunarz. And slowly the body of Gahrspat moved until it stopped in front of Tiunarz.

"Success or death! Success or death! Success or death!" More sections of the roof collapsed.

The lifeless hands of Gahrspat rose up from the floor until they hovered just in front of each shoulder of the condemned leader. The dead fingers balled up, clenched into fists so that the wicked talons protruded past the neck of Tiunarz.

But Tiunarz was not overwhelmed with fear. He suffered no mindless quivering of the flesh or faintness of heart. He cared not for whatever slim mercy Evalcohr might deign to give unto him. Indeed, he despised Evalcohr and his syco- phantic ways with Kahrnahrgx. He knew of the many in- trigues and plots that the supposed "right hand" of the Great One had employed to get to his vaulted position.

He tipped his head back and burst into uproarious laugh- ter. The chanting abruptly ceased.

"Ha! You amuse me! Of course you can kill me, Evalcohr! Certainly I expect no less from you than a violent demise. The evidence is before me, as all can see!" He tipped his massive head first to the right, bumping the talons hovering beside his ear, then to the left. He laughed harder.

"Yes, you can kill me...and you will, soon enough. But you cannot defeat me, Evalcohr. You cannot defeat me! You cannot DEFEA—"

Even as Tiunarz bellowed his ultimate defiance, the right hand of Gahrspat's carcass suddenly swung down and to the left, while the left hand swung down and to the right, cutting completely through Tiunarz. The only noise in the cavern was a queer gurgling sound coming from Tiunarz. His head tipped upwards, as if he was going to laugh again. But it continued tipping backwards until it rotated off his shoulders, rolled down his back and landed on the floor with a thud. Then, sections of his multiply-severed torso slid away to the floor until only his waist and legs remained. Without the massive weight of his head, chest and wings, the lower half of Tiunarz took a moment before finally folding at the knees and collapsing backwards in a heap on top of the wing remnants.

The chant resumed with renewed vigor. "Success or death! Success or death! Success or death!"

Evalcohr had made his special point. The lasting memory had been implanted.

Kimar's anger kept building, energy piling up like the un-released tension of tectonic plates accrued over millennia. His wrath surged higher and higher until his body was throbbing with it. Ercen had to be reached! Time was his enemy because it was her enemy. He was ensnared in timelessness; she was not. As more time trickled through her and whatever damage she had sustained—and he grew more convinced that it was severe—the more difficult it would be for him to heal her. Wave after wave of fury pulsed through him. His body began to cast off bursts of light, like lightning in a dark sky. Even in the throes of his passion and pain, his mind—his heart—was ever on Ercen. Shards of light crackled in the Void, sparking out from the center of Kimar. All the energy and strength he could muster was directed towards searching for Ercen. The mighty gargoyle bent all his will to focus on nothing else but locating the trail of where she'd parted, where she'd landed. Then, he found her!

"Now!" he wailed. "Aaaygh!" Dazzling radiance erupted out from Kimar, as if an advancing thunderhead unleashed its entire arsenal of lightning at the same instant. A ferocious explosion shattered the Void, tearing it asunder. Kimar was gone, parted away. This mattered not to the Void. The momentary vacuum left where Kimar had been encased was instantly reabsorbed into nothingness, being "momentary" only to Kimar.

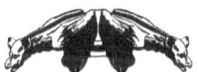

"What in the world is that?" Paign yelled over a sudden windy blast. "What's going on, anyway?"

"Wow! Never seen anything like that," Anders replied. "Whoa! It's coming right at us!"

It was as if a small tornado had formed in the clear sky, then rolled into a ball of swirling violence, and finally came rocketing towards the ground.

Freida grabbed Danielle's hand. "Should we move Ercen again? It seems to be coming our way!"

"No. I've got a funny feeling about this," Danielle replied. "Let's wait..."

Less than a minute later, the cloud-like orb splashed into the stream next to where they'd made a sheltered camp for Ercen.

Steam erupted from the cold mountain runoff. To the astonishment of the kids, Kimar emerged from the steam, waded across the creek and stepped out onto the short grassy area where they had placed Ercen.

A moan emanated from Kimar, so deep that Danielle almost thought it had come from the earth itself.

"Thank you for protecting her," he said quietly, looking long at Danielle and Freida.

"You're welcome, of course, Kimar." Danielle spoke softly, hoping to not disturb Ercen.

"Sir?" Anders said. "Is she in a stupor of some kind? You know, so as not to stress the body…given what she's been through and all."

"Yes, Anders." Kimar seemed anxious. "She's been terribly wounded. Her body is in a kind of sleep…a forced rest."

"Is there anything…anything that can be done for her, uh, damage?"

"Perhaps, yes." Kimar shifted nervously on his huge feet. "It may be too late already, but I must try. I must retrieve her wings."

"What?" shouted the two boys and girls simultaneously.

"That's completely mad, Kimar, even for you!" Paign's face was a deep red.

"If her wings are not reattached—and soon—she'll never be able to fly again."

"Well, then she won't be able to fly, but at least she'll be alive!"

"Without flight, she would rather not live."

"That's just stupid!" Paign yelled. "What a crazy notion! You must be joking, even though I see no humor at all in this. Come on, Anders. Help me out!"

"Kimar, it seems mad to go back to that cave. She was almost killed on our last trip there. You don't look so good, either," Anders said, noticing rancid smoke wisp away from the hole in Kimar's wing.

"That can be mended later. It is not urgent. There is no time for arguing this with you. I must go. Do not delay me any longer!"

"Hmphf! If you *must* go, then we're going with you!" yelled Paign. "Right, Anders?"

Anders blinked. "Uh, that's right, Kimar."

"You're both crazy," Freida cried at the boys, then at Kimar. "All three of you—completely mad!"

"Are you sure you know what you're doing?" Danielle asked Anders.

"Not a clue, really. But you must admit that Kimar's chances of finding the—locating what's needed—is increased dramatically with some help."

"Well, that counts me in. I'm going with you, too!" Freida yelled.

"No, child. You must…I ask that you stay with Ercen, as you have already, for which I am grateful beyond words. If we are to succeed, we must leave now. I fear we may be too late already. If luck favors us, we won't be long. If it doesn't, we will never return."

"Ah, great," quipped Paign, strapping on his sword tightly. With a flourish, he ran his fingers through his hair, slung his bow over his shoulder, bowed to Freida for a moment and then winked at Danielle. He very much hoped to look braver than he felt.

Anders gave the girls a wan smile, then cinched his sword belt. Both boys wished they had their bows to use.

"We'll return soon." Kimar, still dripping from the pond, reached out his hands to each boy.

And with that, Kimar, Paign and Anders were gone.

"So, now what do we do?" Freida asked.

"We wait," Danielle replied. "And pray."

Anders assumed that their parting was complete because he could feel warm, acrid air on his face and grit under his feet. It was black as pitch and he recognized the smell of burnt hair. And worse.

"We won't have long," Kimar whispered in Anders's ear. Apparently, the sound frightened Paign because he yanked his hand away from Anders's. Kimar continued, "Begin looking. We have parted back to as close to where we stood as I am able to identify."

A dim golden light grew out from Kimar's feet.

"It is certain that guards have been posted nearby, if not in this cave itself, and that my presence here will set off a warning."

"Oh, great," Paign hissed.

"Hey, it was your idea to come! Let's get this done and get out of here," Anders hissed back.

"Pst. Anders. Do you see a couple of red spots over to your far right?" Paign's voice was so low, he was barely audible.

Anders squinted in the direction his cousin had indicated. Back and forth he scanned. And then he saw them: two red orbs. Then, another pair appeared close to the first.

"You're right, Paign. We've got unfriendly company," Anders murmured, dropping to one knee and fluidly sliding his bow off his shoulder, then nocking an arrow on the string.

Anders knew from the faint rustling he heard that was Paign doing the same. He also noted that the dim golden glow was gone.

"You take the one on the right," Paign whispered. "Three. Two. One."

The combined thwap of their bow strings was startlingly loud compared to the deep stillness that had greeted them. Even more so were the grunts that came from both gargoyles when the boys' arrows found their marks. A pair of thumps followed, as the guards fell to the cavern floor.

"Not bad shooting," whispered Paign. "That was pretty—"

A hideous wail broke the stillness. "Intruders!" squawked one of the dying guards. "Intruders! Intrud—aaaygh!"

"Well, that tears it!" Paign spoke under his breath, urgently. "Time to get out of here! Where the dickens is Kimar?"

Red light erupted throughout the cavern. Obsidian gargoyles began appearing all over the perimeter. Anders's hasty scan counted at least eight.

"There! Over there!" a coarse, brash voice bellowed. "Fire on them, you fools!"

"Duck, Anders!" yelled Paign, tackling him to the floor. Three fireballs exploded just beyond where he'd been standing a moment earlier.

"Thanks, mate!" Anders choked out, nearly breathless from being knocked to the floor. Then, he shoved Paign away, quickly nocked an arrow and fired, still uncomfortably seated on a pile of rubble. A gargoyle, mid-flight, crashed through a stalactite and careened into the floor behind them.

Thwap. Paign fired at another gargoyle just as it began to hurl a fireball. It veered away to avoid the arrow; the ball of flame flew wildly into a nearby stalagmite.

"The traitor! The traitor is here! GET HIM!"

Kimar had emerged behind a thick cluster of stalactites and stalagmites, not far from where they had been ambushed when rescuing Freida.

"Paign, the obsidians have seen Kimar. Start firing as fast as you can!" Anders yelled, as he jumped up and fired on another flying gargoyle.

Before Anders could reload, Paign had shot two enemies who were perched on the rear wall, from where most of the fireballs had been coming.

"Nice shooting, Paign!" Anders had to duck to avoid being hit. Flame engulfed the scree field behind him.

Kimar ran low to the ground with his good wing forming a partial canopy over his back. Plumes of flame exploded all around him. "Quickly now! Grab hands, boys!"

Paign and Anders fired their ready arrows and then dove into a small opening that was encircled by broken columns from the earlier combat. If Kimar could make it that far, Anders was sure they'd be able to get out.

But their enemies had discerned their intentions and mounted a furious assault of flaming orbs, as well as the highly destructive "flying fists," as Paign called them. Kimar was cut off. The area between him and the cousins was awash in fire and exploding stone.

"Anders!" Paign screamed over the din. "We must create a diversion! It's his only chance. It's *our* only chance!"

Before Anders could reply, Paign jumped up and began running, weaving in and around the mineral stumps, firing as fast as he could nock his remaining arrows. His aim was lethal, every shaft finding a mark. His success enraged their enemy. They responded by lobbing a barrage of flame-balls and energy bursts at him. For a moment, Anders couldn't see him through all the exploding rock and dust.

With the gargoyles' attention focused on Paign, Anders seized the chance to jump up and fire off three arrows as he hastily covered the distance to where he'd last seen Paign hunkered down. Even so, he was under fire long before he reached Paign. He lurched as he ran, weaving around obstacles, and finally jumped into the same gap between stalagmites where he'd seen Paign go.

"You all right, then?" Anders asked.

"Well enough," Paign replied. "A few scratches is all. And some dandy bruises by tomorrow, I expect." Blood oozed from a deep cut on his chin. "Where's Kimar gotten to?" he yelled over the cacophonous eruptions of stone blasted by fireballs and more flying fists.

"Hey, look!" Anders yelled. A mountain of rubble about ten meters away from them blew upwards as Kimar emerged from it. He'd been momentarily buried under it, although the boys had not seen it happen. But at this close proximity, Anders could plainly see that Ercen's wings were tucked tightly under Kimar's right arm, sheltered under his wounded wing.

"He's coming, Paign! Run!" Anders could see the fierce resolve in the great gargoyle's amber eyes. Quickly glancing at his cousin, he realized Paign was instead looking over his right shoulder towards the biggest concentration of their foes. Anders grabbed Paign by the collar and yanked him away from their embattled shelter.

It would only take a second to reach Kimar, he thought. Three strides and they'd grab hands and part away from this hellish place, finally and forever. Out of the corner of his eye, Anders noticed an inbound streak of fire, followed by an eruption of heat that washed over him. Paign nearly jerked his hand away from Anders's. But they'd reached Kimar.

Anders had come to appreciate the brief moment of stillness that parting brought. It was as if they passed through a dark, quiet, peaceful place before arriving at the next location.

It didn't last long. Screaming filled the cool dusk. Paign's screaming.

CHAPTER TWENTY-NINE

CONFRONTATIONS

Johann had been the better fisherman, but Peter had been the better guide, albeit haltingly because of his leg wound. They'd spent a few hours together, fishing with sharpened sapling switches. Peter had, of course, known it could be done and had even watched natives doing so during a remote archeological dig. He was grateful that Johann had actual experience. From his own extensive scientific research, he knew it was vastly different to know how to do a thing versus actually having done it.

Although Johann was very slow to admit it, he recognized that while he was incredibly knowledgeable about his homeland in the Honellaken Valley, it was because he'd traipsed all over it since he was a child. However, Peter had developed an ability to keep a mental map of where he'd traveled to, due to the many expeditions he'd led in very remote parts of the world.

They walked back into their makeshift camp, Peter in the lead, half a dozen good-sized trout skewered on a switch.

"The intrepid hunter-gatherers return!" Amy quipped.

"What's that, now?" Heidi asked.

"Oh, don't mind me. I'm just being silly," Amy replied. But she noticed that Heidi still looked puzzled.

It didn't take long before they had a fire going, with the rich smell of roasting fish wafting through their campground, carpeted in pine needles. As the sun set the evergreen trees alight with dappled yellows and oranges, the adults settled in for a quiet evening in front of an open fire. Parting here was an accident, of course, and they'd gone to rescue Freida armed only with weapons, not camping provisions. The fish they'd returned with were sufficient for everyone to feel full, although it made for a messy and simple meal. The fifth fish was shared between the men. The last fish made Tiny very happy.

When they had all finished, it was quiet except for the crackle of their small fire.

"How do we get back to our kids?" Peter asked bluntly, restarting a conversation they'd stalled on earlier in the afternoon.

"Jah, like we said earlier, it seems we have just the one choice, eh? We must wait for Kimar or Ercen to retrieve us." Johann scratched his head as he spoke, firelight flickering across his open face. His pale blue eyes appeared almost golden from the setting sun beaming through the tree trunks, in addition to the dancing firelight.

"But what if they don't come?" Heidi wondered out loud. "Parting here appears to have been accidental; I believe we all agree on this. And what if they were injured? What if they...died?"

"Well, I don't even want to think about that possibility. We must remain positive!" Amy retorted. "We should plan on being 'retrieved' by Kimar or Ercen—I don't care which one it is—and being reunited with our children."

"Hm. Yes. And let's not forget that we came in useful to both of them in rescuing Freida," Peter added. "Based on what little we know, they'll be needing us again. Probably very soon."

"You are probably correct, my friend. But it does not mean that we *must* help them again," Johann countered. "We are away from our children because of this very thing. Our daughter and the boys have been threatened many times in just these recent days. Our farmhouse is damaged because of these foul creatures. We buried one of them behind our barn after it attempted to slaughter my family! Why don't they fix their own problems?" It was difficult to determine if Johann's face was flushed red from only the fiery sunset's glow.

Peter nodded slowly. "Yes, Johann. We understand. Our house was destroyed entirely. Most of the roof is gone. The floor has either been crushed in by the gargoyles' weight or ripped up by Nahgflint. For all we know, it's burned to the ground by now."

Taking a deep breath, he continued. "So, we do understand the desire to tell them all to leave us out of this fight." Peter grabbed a fistful of pine needles, grimacing as he squeezed them hard. He opened his hand, palm down. While most of the needles fell back to the floor, many were sticking out of his hand like it was a porcupine. "The problem is this," gesturing at his wounded palm. "Now it's our fight, too. We may not have asked for it. We'd rather be left out of it. But we're stuck with it now, like these needles in my hand."

Long after the sun had set, Peter and Amy finished telling the Skulstads about what they had learned from Ercen and Kimar about the nature of their immense conflict. It was, ultimately, a fight for the survival of humankind.

"You've seen the hatred of humans that some gargoyles share. It nearly cost Freida her life," Amy said quietly.

Heidi nodded nervously, her tears glittering in the firelight.

"Jah, that's so." Johann shifted his weight around against the log he was using as a chair back. But Peter could see that it was something else making him uncomfortable. "Our friends, we again thank you for placing yourselves at dire risk to rescue our child. We are simple people and don't have all the proper words to express ourselves as you do." He had difficulty getting his words out. "But we are grateful...so very grateful."

Again, Heidi nodded, but this time she was smiling. "'Tis so."

Amy went over to Heidi and hugged her fiercely, brushing her light blond hair away from her tear-stained face. "We know you would do the same for us...for our Danielle."

Johann and Peter, both uncomfortable with the women's emotions, became suddenly intensely interested in the stars twinkling overhead through the evergreen canopy above.

After a moment, Johann asked, "What kind of work is it you do, again?" while looking at both Amy and Peter.

"We're archeologists, Johann," Peter replied. "Why do you ask? Is there a specific question you have about archeology, my friend?"

"Well, yes. I mean, no...ah, spytte!" Johann yelled, as he jumped up. "Yes, I have a question—but it is not about your work. It is about your *words*. We know—Heidi and I—that you are from another country than ours. But there are some words we don't understand even when you have explained them to us. They describe things we do not understand. For instance, Danielle's *paper route*—you have described as a series of homes that she delivers a *newspaper* to, for which she is paid. We have homes and we have books in our country, of course. But we do not have anything like your newspapers. And these rooms in your homes called *'garage'* are unknown to us, also. I think you might be referring to what we have barns for…"

Amy's eyes had grown wide. "What do you mean, Johann? Do you mean to say that you don't have newspapers in your country—I mean, out in the country where you live? Come on, really? This is the twentieth century, after all!"

Heidi and Johann looked stricken.

"What?" Peter asked, confused by their reactions.

"The twentieth century?" Johann whispered.

"Well, of course, what do you think we would mean?" Peter jumped up. "Oh, my. Do you mean to say you're not just from a different country…somewhere other than…oh, man…you're from a…different *time*?"

"Jah," Heidi murmured, barely audible. "This…this is the nineteenth century…for us."

"But, that's impossible!" Amy cried.

Peter let out a long whistle. "Whoa!" A huge smile nearly split his head in half. "Have we got a lot to learn from each other! This is going to be a long night."

Danielle could not sleep. Her head hurt as she tried to sort out all that happened. There were too many things to worry about…so many people she loved who were in mortal danger. But as she glanced over at her friend, a smile stole across her face. Freida was breathing deeply, sound asleep, exhausted from her perilous kidnapping and rescue and despite her still being very hungry.

Careful to not snap any sticks, Danielle slowly got up to go check on Ercen.

The gargoyle had remained unmoved since they'd landed in this place. Danielle, trembling a little, laid her hand delicately on Ercen's neck. It was as if she was, in fact, stone, except that she was warm to the touch. Not knowing what else to do, she wept for her friend. Although her spiritual experience was more limited than she wanted to admit to herself, she prayed for Ercen. In the stillness of the night, stars circled overhead, and Danielle fell asleep, nestled up against Ercen.

She hadn't slumbered long before being awakened by screaming. Startled, she jumped up, fearing it was Ercen. But the wounded gargoyle was still unconscious. So, she ran over to Freida, who was bathed in the brilliant moonlight. Yet she, too, slept. Where was the screaming coming from? Trembling, only in part from the cool night air, Danielle ran towards the frightful sounds.

Bursting into a nearby clearing close to the stream, Danielle was shocked to see a luminous amber glow encircling a small patch of ground. Inside the circle, Anders stood next to Kimar, who was leaning over the prone body of Paign; he was the source of the screaming, but she couldn't see him because the others' backs blocked her view. Kimar was yelling something into Anders's ear, which she couldn't hear. Kimar then quickly ran off towards the stream. Danielle could see Paign clearly now. And everything else around him. Horrified, she screamed.

Kimar, startled, wheeled around with fury in his eyes. Frightened by him, she screamed again. This seemed to grab Paign's attention long enough that he stopped his own screaming.

Anders crashed through the thick brush on the other side of the clearing nearest to Paign, and yelled, "What's going on? Let's stop this incessant screaming, shall we?" At the same time, he threw his soaking wet jacket onto Paign. There was a brief hissing sound.

"Oh, that's loads better!" Paign howled, sarcastically. "Now, how about the shoulder? That would fall under Kimar's range of skills, would it not?"

Danielle still couldn't believe what she was looking at. Paign's right shoulder was horribly disfigured, twisted up around his ear, with his arm sticking out sideways from his body at a peculiar angle. Much of his jacket was burned away. She could see angry reddened skin through the numerous holes in the burned fabric, and what appeared to be several blisters forming. She felt terrible for her friend. But what made her scream the first time were the dismembered wings lying on the ground, next to Paign.

"Hey, Danielle, could you give me a hand with these?" Anders asked her, pointing at the wings. "They're kind of heavy together. We need to get them over to wherever you have Ercen." He'd noticed the vacant look in her eyes as she stared at the torn wings. "As quick as we can. Kimar's going to be busy here—and we should probably go."

Reluctant to touch them, but anxious to help her friend, she ran over to Anders and grabbed hold of the smaller remnant. Timidly, she tried lifting it but it fell to the ground; she'd barely nudged it because it was astonishingly heavy. Determinedly, she seized hold of it and hoisted it up, holding her hands tight just below her chin, and shuffled as fast as she could to where Ercen lay still, the wing bouncing against her knees as she walked. Anders grunted along close behind her, with the heaviest of the wing remnants. As they left the clearing behind, she could hear Kimar's low voice rumbling something to Paign. She hoped that Kimar could put his shoulder right again.

Freida was already beside Ercen. "How horrible!" she cried, her eyes fixated on the objects they carried. "The poor thing. But I suppose that without these, uh, pieces, she couldn't be made whole again."

"That's about the size of"—another burst of Paign's yelling came from behind them, causing Anders to pause mid-sentence—"it, yes. I'm just glad we made it back. It was nip and tuck for a moment there." His voice drifted off.

"Please, tell us about what happened, Anders," Danielle asked.

Anders tried to give a brief summary of their treacherous journey back to the cave that nearly cost them their lives, but before he could finish, Kimar walked quickly into the clearing, Paign just behind him, looking grim, but very much improved.

Anders shrugged at the girls. It would have to wait.

Kimar dropped to his knees beside Ercen and laid his huge hands on her. His eyes were shut tightly, but a moment later, he said, "Something has changed. Has one of you touched her?"

Danielle, trembling, replied, "Uh, yes, Kimar. I actually fell asleep next to her earlier tonight, when I was praying for her. I just wanted her to have a friend nearby in case she woke up...I hope it was OK."

Kimar opened his eyes and looked at Danielle, quietly but intensely. "Yes, of course, Danielle. Not only was it 'OK'—as you say—it was better than 'OK.' Your touch has deepened her resting, so that her internal healing was increased both in power and speed. This is certainly one of the reasons you are so important to us, child, although this...gift...was not foretold. I thank you." And then, remarkably, Kimar stood and bowed to Danielle.

"I've got some serious damage that could use some of your special healing touch," Paign quipped. "I'd be grateful, too."

Freida slugged him. Hard.

Danielle flushed, while Anders rolled his eyes.

It wasn't until sunrise that Kimar had finished bringing Ercen back to wholeness. All of the kids had fallen asleep, either from well-earned exhaustion, or simply because of the very late hour. By the time they awoke, Ercen had already parted to wherever it was she went to get human food, and returned with an ample and, to famished teenagers, fantastic breakfast. She'd come back with hard-boiled eggs, pastries, apples, peaches and three long loaves of bread.

"So, how are you feeling, Ercen?" Freida asked, her mouth full of pastry. Danielle thought Freida didn't look as pale as she had the night before, but maybe that was just because she was in daylight now. Still, she looked better than when they had rescued her from Gahrspat.

"I am well, thanks to you...and Kimar." Ercen smiled, unmistakably. "My deepest thanks to all of you, especially Anders and Paign, who risked so much to retrieve my wings." She walked over to Paign, who was focused completely on consuming an entire loaf of bread by himself. Bending over, she shocked him, first with her presence—which was imposing at such a close distance—and then by kissing him on his head. His hand paused midway to his mouth, a huge piece of bread dangling awkwardly.

"Hrm, ur elcom," he murmured.

Freida and Danielle burst out laughing. The sight of a nearly speechless Paign was hilarious. Anders simply shook his head.

A moment later, Anders asked Ercen, "So, when do we go to find the Skulstads and Wheelens? They've been gone a long time and are probably crazy with worry. And we're hoping Tiny is with them."

"Ah, yes. It won't be long now. We won't be going to them. They'll be coming to us. Kimar discovered their parting location shortly after completing my healing. Before he was willing to rest, he went to get them. They should be back any time."

Not far behind Ercen, a pile of pine needles begin to lift off the ground and spin quickly. Freida's parents parted into the shelter of the evergreens, her father holding onto Tiny as best he could manage the large dog. Danielle's parents were next to them, holding onto Kimar's hand.

"That's better!" Peter exclaimed. "Been too long without my girl! Just happy we're all back together and everyone is whole again!"

Kimar smiled, squatted down and immediately turned into stone. His rest was long overdue.

CHAPTER THIRTY

PLAN OF ATTACK

"Silence!" The booming command of Quarastohr echoed in the enormous rocky ravine.

Danielle glanced around the high canyon walls and marveled at how many gargoyles were perched above them. After Kimar had rested, there'd been a hasty meal and then they had all parted to the Valley of the Ten Pinnacles. Of course, Danielle and her parents had fond memories of the place, during their stay high above where they sat now, in the Rookery. But it was foreign to their new friends. It was difficult to reconcile in her mind that her dear friends, who were technically "new" in terms of having met them only days ago were, in fact, "old" in functional terms. They were here next to her, but were from an age hundreds of years before she was even born. Freida was probably older than Danielle's own long-dead great, great, great grandmother. And yet here she was sitting next to her, about the same age as she was. It was confusing. And unsettling.

But now Quarastohr, a huge beast with a bluish soapstone tint, had called the War Council to order. Ercen had explained that he was the gargoyle in charge of penetrating the defenses at the Temple of Kahrnahrgx. Ercen didn't seem to think much of him, though.

"Silence!" he bellowed again.

Danielle guessed there to be several hundred gargoyles positioned around the canyon. She and the others sat on the valley floor, in front of the dais on which sat the War Council. In addition to Quarastohr, there were eleven other gargoyles on the dais, including Kimar, each seated upon an ornately carved, immense stone chair. They were already in the deepening shade cast by the mountains behind them, as the sun began to dip behind the ridge. But they were easy to spot because of their glowing eyes. The sight reminded Danielle of sunlight glinting off of broken, colored glass. She felt a shiver go down her back, thrilled and awed by what she saw.

"As you have all heard from Kimar, it is clear that Kahrnahrgx and his followers intend to reacquire the Key, which these humans found unwittingly," Quarastohr said, then gestured towards the entire group of humans, not distinguishing between Danielle and her parents and all the others. Although Ercen was sitting with them, she didn't seem to be included in Quarastohr's wave.

"What is that supposed to mean?" Paign hissed under his breath. "That didn't sound very nice."

Before anyone could respond, the large gargoyle continued.

"Whether we wish it or not, it is now come to us…this Key. Its evil has twice entered into this valley, our haven, the rookery of our young ones. It cannot stay. But whither shall it go?" His voice reverberated throughout the canyon.

A cascade of voices fell down from the cliffs above, in support of Quarastohr's question.

Ercen shifted next to Danielle. "Well, there's not much question about that, is there?" she murmured. "It can't stay here. You can't take it back to your time…"

Before she could finish, a squat gargoyle, with a deep reddish hue, rose to his feet, just a few chairs to the right of where Kimar sat. "My esteemed colleagues of the War Council," he said, then bowed, his voice so low it seemed to Peter that he felt it, more than heard it. "Quarastohr." He bowed even lower. "My countrymen," he said, lifting his hands into the air and slowly circling around the dais.

"That's Uud-Rement. He's a fierce commander," Ercen whispered in Danielle's ear. "And he's absolutely fearless. Some would say even reckless. This should be interesting."

From the look of him, Paign thought that all of Uud-Rement's body had at some point been torn off and pressed back on. He couldn't believe how many scars covered the beast.

"It is true that the Key of Kahrnahrgx has come to us, unbidden. Perhaps even unwanted. Yet, I need not retell you the stories we all learned from our birth nests. That Osberg the Great led an assault upon Kahrnahrgx and his minions long ago. That he did, indeed, assail Kahrnahrgx himself, and capture his Key even as he suffered mortal hurt in the battle. Nevertheless, despite being moments from dying, he parted away with the Key, thus frustrating the plans of Kahrnahrgx, lo these many years upon years."

While speaking, Uud-Rement continued to pace back and forth across the dais, focusing his attention on the crowd perched above, rather than those directly before him. Peter

wondered if this meant that Uud-Rement felt he didn't need
to convince the dignitaries before him.

"Now we have learned the mystery of where the Key parted
to. Osberg's remains—parted into vast ages past—and the
perilous Key were safe until recently found by these humans,
along with his fossil."

Murmurs of agreement came from above.

"We are at a meeting of pathways, where tunnels merge,
where stalactite joins stalagmite. We may choose to accept
that it was through great providence these humans have come
to us now…with the Key!"

Shouts echoed off the canyon walls around them.

"It is time for great courage," Uud-Rement shouted. "But
it is also a time for great confidence. For we have in our possession the very device our enemy seeks above all else—the
weapon he has imbued with otherworldly powers."

Many of the gargoyles perched up the canyon's walls gave a
huge shout. Johann recoiled at the bloodlust flaming in their
glowing eyes.

"If there was ever a time to attack the strongholds of
Kahrnahrgx, that time is now!" Uud-Rement returned to his
seat, a smug look on his face.

The followers of Uud-Rement shouted down from the heights,
"Now!" Their roar turned into a chant, "Now! Now! Now!"

Freida shivered at the terrifying sound. The mood
turned dark and fiery, as if to match the blazing rays of the setting sun that were bursting against the eastern spires of the Ten
Pinnacles. Her mother grabbed her hand and squeezed it tight.

Slowly, Quarastohr stood again. The chanting continued,
so he raised his hand to silence the enthusiastic followers.

"My esteemed colleague, Uud-Rement, speaks inspiring words," Quarastohr intoned sarcastically. The echoes of "Now!" dissipated into nothingness. "It is one thing to have possession of the Key. It is quite another to not become possessed by its wickedness. Let us not forgot how it came into being."

Anders was surprised by the murmurs above them, from presumably the same gargoyles that just moments earlier had agreed with Uud-Rement.

"It must be remembered that it was through the destruction of a human soul that Kahrnahrgx made this Key of power."

The murmurs grew in volume.

"It would be a fool's errand to take it into the citadel of our enemy."

Uud-Rement scowled darkly at Quarastohr. Danielle shuddered at the grim look on his disfigured face.

"Where, then, Quarastohr," he growled, leaning forward on the high-back stone seat, "would you have us take the Key? If, in your vast wisdom, we fear to make use of its untold power for our collective good, would you have us hide it? Or, as suits your nature, would you simply have all of us hide instead?"

An eruption of cries cascaded down from the Rookery walls. Freida thought some seemed to be yelling their support for Quarastohr, incensed by the direct challenge from Uud-Rement. But others sounded supportive of Uud-Rement against Quarastohr. All of the gargoyles sounded angry. Many were standing on their outcroppings, shaking their fists at their neighbors. Some had thrust their wings out to their full span, as if to intimidate others.

Then, a gargoyle sitting at the very end of the dais stood. He was taller than any other and his body was a warm orange color. He stretched his oddly narrow wings out languidly, as if he was just rising from a nap and had not a concern in the world, oblivious to the raucous shouting all around and above him. His behavior was so incongruous with what was happening that the Rookery soon grew quiet.

Ercen whispered so that only those in their party could hear. "Oh, that's Prohximus. His clan is mostly from limestone lineage. While not the strongest of our kind, he is certainly one of the smartest. And he's the fastest in flight."

"My brethren," he said very quietly, almost in a whisper. Peter noticed that many gargoyles leaned forward to hear him. It was a technique he and Amy used many times as teachers to get a class of rowdy students to calm down and pay attention. "Works here, too," he whispered, then winked at Amy, who was still clutching Danielle's hand, just as Heidi held onto Freida's.

With the faintest grin on his face, Prohximus stepped into the center of the dais and bowed low, first to Quarastohr, then to Uud-Rement and finally to Kimar. Then he gazed upwards into the Rookery above.

Still speaking quietly, he continued. "We have heard compelling arguments from Quarastohr, the chief of the War Council, to safeguard our kind by hiding the Key of Kahrnahrgx."

Shouts broke out above.

"And we have heard compelling—even rousing—testimony from Uud-Rement, perhaps our most battle-seasoned general, to take the fight directly to the stronghold of our mortal enemy, using the immense power of the Key to defeat him."

More voices joined in the fracas cascading down.

"It would seem," he said, speaking louder and with a quickening pace, "that we must choose between these two competing options. And compete they do, yes? The one would have us storm the gates of the Temple of Kahrnahrgx, using the Key to unmake our enemy and his fortress. The other would have us seeking out the best hiding place, in great stealth, for the Key that would unmake us all."

A smattering of cries fell down from the cavern's walls. The assembly didn't seem clear on what Prohximus was driving at and sounded unsure of how to respond.

The towering, orange-hued gargoyle paced slowly back and forth on the dais.

Amy marveled that the only sounds she could hear now were of his talons clicking rhythmically on the polished marble surface of the dais and the slight breeze filtering through the boughs of the huge cedar trees encircling them. *Wow, this Prohximus character could be a politician back home,* she thought.

"My friends, perhaps the answer is not choosing between one or the other, but choosing"—he dropped his voice to a sigh—"both together."

For a moment, only the rustle of wind through the majestic evergreens could be heard.

Then, like an incoming ocean wave, the voices above first muttered gently amongst themselves, then more loudly to each other, until finally they were all yelling questions down to those on the dais.

Danielle couldn't make out whether there was overall support or not because of the raucous crashing of voices. But, like a wave, the voices reached an abrupt crescendo and then quickly dissipated.

Prohximus smiled and gave a little wave to his countrymen above. "Some of you may wonder how it is we can join these two approaches together when they seem to be quite opposed to each other…not unlike their authors."

Danielle and Freida glanced at each other quickly, both puzzled by the way the statuesque gargoyle seemed to be baiting the other speakers. They noticed that Uud-Rement scowled. Quarastohr appeared somewhat bemused. Kimar, who had so far been silent during the proceedings, shook his head almost imperceptibly.

"What's he going on about, do you think?" Danielle asked under her breath.

"I really have no idea…it's like he wants to make the others angry," Freida said quietly.

"We cannot storm the gates of the Temple of Kahrnahrgx using the Great Key without thus becoming like our very enemy," Prohximus continued, his voice rising in pitch and volume. "To do so would mean we have become like him and his minions, employing the power of enormous pain and suffering to our own ends! To do so would make them no longer our enemies…but our brothers!"

An eruption of curses, growls and cries fell from above. To Paign, it sounded just like an avalanche of scree—rock tumbling down a steep slope—on Ruar's Ridge.

"So, we cannot use the Great Key as a weapon. But we cannot seek to hide it away, either!" Prohximus strode back and forth across the dais, thrusting his fists upwards emphatically. His talons glinted fiery orange-red in the dying beams of the setting sun. "It is now clear that the Key will be found, wherever we would conceal it. No one could have guessed the manner in which it has been found. Certainly, Osberg intended to part so far into the past that he—and the Key— would be lost to the vast depths of time over time, ages upon ages, until it had fallen from memory. Yet, it was discovered by these humans while looking for something different, but of great importance to them."

Well, he parted far enough back into time that he was there long enough to become fossilized, Peter thought, sardonically. *That certainly seems to fit 'ages upon ages.'*

A clamoring of voices and clattering noise was rising above Danielle's head. Freida, no longer whispering, leaned over and said into her ear, "Are they cracking rocks together?"

"If we cannot lead an assault with the Key," Prohximus bellowed up into the Rookery, "and we cannot spirit the Key away into hiding." He paused, and it grew alarmingly quiet. "We must take the Great Key into the dungeons of Kahrnahrgx, where it was created through the darkest magic…and there we must destroy the Key! In so doing, we will unmake the power of our foe!"

The tumultuous roar that followed Prohximus's speech was beyond anything the human visitors had ever heard. It was deafening. Small bits of rock and shale tumbled down beyond the rear edge of the dais, broken away from the vertical walls of the Rookery. All but Paign clapped their hands over their ears.

Paign's eyes, frightened wide, stared into the dusk above them. "They're glowing!" he bellowed, although no one could hear him over the din. He pivoted on his knees so that Anders and the others could see his face. Again, he bawled, "They're glowing!" and stabbed his finger into the night sky.

Anders, unable to hear Paign even with his cousin shouting directly into his face, was able to read his lips. He looked up and was astonished. All around the Rookery, from just above the treetops to just below the edge of the highest ridgeline, countless gargoyles glowed against the ancient granite rock face. Their radiating shapes covered the entire span of colors: greens, yellows, blues, reds, purples, greys, browns, golds and oranges. Anders's jaw dropped. "It's beautiful!"

He turned to his left to make sure the others were also seeing this wonder, but he need not have. Freida, Danielle and their mothers were standing in a semicircle, holding hands, tears streaming down their cheeks.

Freida turned to Anders, her eyes reflecting the myriad colors above, and smiled. "It's like an enormous rainbow, but in small pieces!"

Almost forgetting the men with him, Anders turned to his right. Peter and Johann had huge smiles on their ruddy faces, their arms draped on each other's shoulders. Beyond them, Paign was dancing wildly in the brilliant colors carpeting the floor of the Valley of the Ten Pinnacles, Tiny leaping after him.

Anders felt a tap on his shoulder. Ercen bent down to his ear and said, "Now watch, child! Behold the wisdom of Prohximus."

The volume and tone of the shouting gargoyles shifted lower. Anders remembered enough of his piano lessons to recognize that the voices were beginning to blend into one syncopated rhythm. It reminded him of a blacksmith's bellows, pulsing faster and faster as he increases the volume of air over the coals. As the pace quickened, the hundreds of gargoyles' individual colors thinned and dissipated like paints when too much water is added. The colors vanished into brilliant white just as their pulsating cries reached their crescendo. The sudden brightness nearly matched the noonday sun. Anders instinctively squinted.

Just as quickly as it had begun, the brilliant white dimmed so that only tiny points remained where each gargoyle stood, the clamorous shouting abruptly shifting into a deep, gentle unified hum.

Anders heard the girls gasp. His eyes quickly adjusted to the darkness and, looking upwards, he, too, gasped.

The night sky was full of twinkling stars beyond the ridge-line of the Ten Pinnacles. But the starlight—for that is exactly what it looked like—came all the way down the granite face of the Rookery, each gargoyle's tiny point of brilliance emanating from its chest like a star.

Danielle cried, "It's as if we've been joined to the universe!"

"I think my heart is breaking," Amy sobbed.

An orb of light, larger than the other stars spread around them, bobbed slowly up and down in the near-total darkness. As it drew close, Danielle realized it was Ercen walking towards her, holding hands with Freida and Heidi.

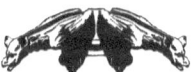

"I'm not understanding what it is you say," Johann said, frustrated. "Could you please go over it again?" He tore off a huge chunk of bread and began chewing.

After the War Council concluded, the humans gathered on the same eyrie that Danielle and her parents had used on their last visit. It was utterly dark except for the rocks Kimar had set glowing. Danielle had warned the others about the precipice and sat near the edge as a guard. She was sure if anyone went over the side, it would be Paign.

Ercen nodded. "Yes, of course. Our ways are not your ways, as I'm sure you have noticed by now. To you, it probably appeared that Uud-Rement and Quarastohr are foes."

"Yeah, I'd say so!" Paign agreed, enthusiastically. "Thought they were going to come to blows there, for a moment."

"They don't seem to like each other very much," Danielle chimed in. "Especially when Quarastohr sniped at his 'inspiring words' after Uud-Rement had basically called him a coward for wanting to hide the Key!"

"Kids," a very tired Peter interjected, "how about we let Ercen finish?"

Ercen smiled. "As I said, our ways are different than yours. While it is true that these two leaders may not be in agreement on all issues, there is great respect between them. They simply represented each of the most commonly held viewpoints among our people, and argued those points as vigorously as possible."

"So…you're saying they were acting as spokesman for the two primary positions of your people on how to resolve this challenge?" Peter asked, dismayed.

"Yes."

"Did they—*do they*—actually hold to those positions themselves?" Peter continued.

"Not necessarily," Ercen replied.

Kimar added, "It is irrelevant." The sound that followed from reminded Peter of a lion's growl.

"It's irrelevant what their personal perspective is?" Amy questioned.

"Yes," Ercen replied simultaneously with Kimar.

"You'd think it would matter to them," Peter said flatly.

"It does not," Kimar stated, matter-of-factly.

"You see, their role of stating and arguing a position is critical in assisting our kind to come to a consensus," Ercen continued.

"You mean, you go through this process for everything you discuss? Are you kidding?" Amy quipped.

"No, Amy, this is a matter of great consequence to us," Kimar retorted. "We use this 'process' when the matter being discussed is of critical importance."

"There has never been anything as important in the history of gargoyles as this issue," Ercen added quietly. "I am sure you can see this."

"Yes, that makes perfect sense," Freida, who had been listening carefully, nodded. "I have witnessed something like this during important discussions by our town's leaders."

"What?" Johann asked.

"You know, Father, like when the town council meets after church services to discuss issues with the mayor about the workings of our town."

"Well," he replied, shrugging his shoulders. "I had no idea you were listening!"

"But Uud-Rement sure scowled a lot during the 'discussion,'" Anders said, shifting around on the dirt and needles, trying to get comfortable.

Ercen replied, "Uud-Rement simply scowls a lot."

"So, what about Prohximus? What was he doing?" Danielle asked, bringing the conversation back. "He's the one who brought the consensus, right? At least, that's how it seemed to me."

"You are correct, child," Ercen smiled. "Prohximus quickly recognized what some of us knew from the beginning. The positions that Quarastohr and Uud-Rement argued would result in an unacceptable outcome. As you heard, the one would leave us—at some point in the future—in the same predicament we are in now…possessing the Key with no wish to use it. The other opinion would be to use it and thus become possessed by it. Prohximus simply argued for our position."

"I'm sorry...what?" Peter asked. "If he conveyed your position—but wait. You were right here, all along. Why didn't Ercen argue your position? She's presented it clearly to us. But, for that matter, why didn't you, Kimar?"

"Because females are not permitted to speak at War Council gatherings...and because she is my mate, and no one here has forgotten that I am the brother to the creator of the Key," he said softly. "They do not trust me."

"And only when the two opposing stances had been strongly argued by prominent and well-respected leaders could Prohximus make the winning case as he did," Ercen added.

"Well," Paign yawned, "all I know is that the light show at the end of all the arguing was just plain unforgettable, and that if I don't get to sleep in the next minute, I'm likely to sleepwalk right off this cliff!"

Tiny was already snoring.

CHAPTER THIRTY-ONE

GATHERINGS

Danielle awoke to a soft scrunching sound, like light footfalls in the dirt. Deep darkness still filled the night sky, but it was less gloomy beyond the eastern ridge, so she guessed it would soon be dawn. She was lying on her side, with just a soft bed of leaves for a cushion. Drowsy, she looked to where she heard the noise, expecting to see her mother's feet before her. Though it was very dim, enough light came from the rocks Ercen set glowing earlier that, with a start, she realized the feet just inches from her nose were those of a marble-colored gargoyle, but a much smaller one than she'd ever seen so far. Before she could sit up, the gargoyle dropped his face down to her level, very close, parallel to the ground. Pale lavender eyes gazed at her. Of course, Danielle was looking at him sideways, so she pushed up on her elbow to get a better look at him. She'd never seen such a big smile on a gargoyle. In fact, she'd concluded there was some muscle group missing in their faces that kept them from making a good smile. Before she knew what was happening, Danielle grinned back.

"Hullo there!" she said.

"Good morning, small human! Did you sleep well?" the gargoyle's voice was gentle, with a curious raspiness. Now that she could get a good look at the creature, Danielle was struck by how small he was.

"Uh, I guess, although I'd still like to be asleep. And what do you mean calling me 'small human'? You're smaller than me. In fact, you're the smallest gargoyle I've seen. Are you a child, then?"

"No, young one! I'm not a child—I am Lohxnahr," the gargoyle stated clearly, as if he was making a momentous pronouncement and had just made everything abundantly clear by doing so.

"Oh, I see…now I don't need to ask your name," Danielle replied, giggling.

"No, of course you don't since I've just told you my name. I am Lohxnahr!"

"Yes, thank you! I remember…" Danielle couldn't help but giggle some more.

"Is there something I can do for you, Lohxnahr?" she continued, grinning from ear to ear. She'd not had such a pleasant wake-up alarm as this, ever.

"Oh my, yes!" Lohxnahr's cheeks were all scrunched up from his enormous smile.

Since no further explanation seemed to be coming, she asked, "And what might that be?"

"What might what be?"

"What might I help you with?"

"I have no idea what you might help me with," Lohxnahr replied, his cherubic face beaming in the strengthening sunrise. "But I'm sure it would be most welcome, whatever it is."

"I'm sorry," replied an increasingly confused Danielle. "I thought you said you needed my help."

"No, I didn't!" he replied enthusiastically.

"So, you don't need me to do something?" Danielle asked.

"Of course you do!" he replied.

Danielle sat up completely and rubbed her eyes, wondering if she was in the middle of not a bad dream, but a most confusing one. Opening her eyes again, the still-beaming Lohxnahr gazed back at her. *Not dreaming, after all*, she thought. Her head was beginning to hurt.

Glancing around, she confirmed that her fellow travelers were still scattered all around her, fast asleep. Tiny snored lightly, twitching.

"OK, let's slow down." She hoped starting over would help. "You don't need my help," she continued, speaking each word slowly, like she talked to her elderly grandparents, except without the yelling. "But you do need me *to do something* for you. Is that right, Lohxnahr?"

"Exactly right!" he replied, jumping a few inches off the ground.

"What, then?" Danielle quipped, feeling stuck somewhere between very amused and quite frustrated.

"Hold my hands," Lohxnahr answered, holding out his slate-grey hands.

Without hesitating, Danielle placed her hands in his.

Tiny woke up from the gentle poof caused by their parting, looked around for a moment, then laid his head back down onto his front paws and immediately went back to twitching.

Danielle let go of Lohxnahr's hands so she could cover her eyes. The sun had just been rising above the eastern ridgeline where they'd been. Now, it was in full flame.

"Where have we come, Lohxnahr?"

"We are come to the mystic's cavern on Zarentil's Peak. It is the tallest of the Ten Pinnacles." Turning to the side, she saw behind him the small entrance to a cave behind Lohxnahr. He bowed and motioned for her to enter with a little flourish of his wrist.

"Why, thank you, sir!" she smiled. Then she dropped to her knees to crawl through the low, narrow opening, keeping her head down to avoid smacking it on the rough ceiling of the low tunnel. Danielle could hear Lohxnahr humming as he followed her. Occasionally, he'd knock stones past her as he crawled clumsily along.

Although darkness filled the tunnel, Danielle sensed that she'd reached the end of it because things sounded more hollow than before, like she had entered into a room. Slowly, she stood, brushing dirt and pebbles off of her pants, afraid to bang her head on the unseen ceiling. A moment later, Lohxnahr stood beside her.

"Please follow me," he said. But before moving his feet, his small hands thrust out in front of him and the cavern quickly lit up.

Danielle gasped. The other caves she'd seen in her gargoyle journeys had been beautiful in their own way, full of stalactites and stalagmites and colors of limestone and granites. But, this room! This room reminded her of the sea anemones she learned about in last year's biology class. Instead of various lengths and widths of stalactites and stalagmites, here they were virtually uniform. The room was large and roughly in the shape of a ball, with the shafts of stone poking towards the center, like an anemone turned outside in. Yet there was no uniformity to the colors. Here there were quartzite purples, pale blue soapstones, travertine oranges, onyx silver-whites, even brilliant jade greens and granite pinks.

"This…this is incredible, Lohxnahr," she whispered. "I feel like I'm in a chapel unlike any on earth. At least that I have seen, anyway."

The small gargoyle nodded reverently and smiled. *But then maybe he's always smiling*, she thought. With another flourish of his wrist, she knew he meant for her to follow his lead through the chamber of colorful stone.

Danielle fell in behind Lohxnahr, stepping lightly as he did around the myriad anemone-like spires spread across the cavern's floor. They had not gone far when the chubby gargoyle waved both hands in a curious set of circles. A moment later, a tunnel grew from the wall before them, widening out from a spot into a portal wide enough for them to walk through.

"Oh, my," she inhaled. The tunnel remained dark until it stopped growing and then immediately bloomed into sparkling golds and reds. The tunnel's interior of rock appeared to be made of tangible light. She touched the wall out of sheer wonder, but hadn't realized she had stopped walking until she looked up and saw Lohxnahr a dozen yards ahead of her. But she could tell from the gentle swaying movements of his head that the beauties of Zarentil's tunnel dazzled him, too.

Moments later, Danielle caught up with Lohxnahr, where he'd stopped at the other end of the passageway. They emerged together into a vast chamber. Its vaulted ceiling, roughly in the shape of a cone, must have reached all the way to the summit of Zarentil's Peak. Danielle suspected that the roof of the chamber opened to the sky. A soft light filtered down to the floor where they stood. At the back of the chamber, an ornate stone chair sat upon a dais. Candles beyond counting, stacked on the dais and hanging from the walls, flamed brightly. But the occupant sitting upon the chair commanded Danielle's attention.

Lohxnahr stepped forward, bowing so low his horns and the tips of his tall ears gently tapped the stone floor. "Behold, Zarentil. We are come." As he stood up, he turned and swept his hand back to indicate Danielle. "This is the human child."

"Come near, child," Zarentil said softly, in a voice both liltingly light and resonantly deep.

Danielle couldn't decide how she felt about the gargoyle. In some ways, he alarmed her. Smaller—much smaller, she realized—than Lohxnahr, he looked more like an infant gargoyle. Except his eyes! His eyes were the color of a brand new copper penny, but looked so old, like he'd witnessed the dawn of time. His leathery body glimmered a pearlescent white, cloaked in a robe of pale lavender. And yet, she found something comforting, even inviting, about the way he looked at her.

But before she had determined what to make of him, Zarentil spoke.

"In order to be, see.
Attend your ear, hear.
Withhold not, free.
Defeat fear, run near.
Ambiguity, embrace.
Throw open, heart.
Radiance upon your face.
The evil, part."

Anders awoke to Tiny's muzzle tickling his face. When he opened his eyes, Tiny licked his nose and whimpered.

"What's wrong, boy?" Anders asked.

Tiny turned his head away from Anders's now very wet nose and looked over to where Danielle and her parents were sleeping. Except Danielle wasn't there.

Anders sat up and peered around their elevated campground. He'd found it a bit unnerving to sleep hundreds of feet above the valley floor. Several times throughout the night, he'd awakened unpleasantly to dreams of rolling off the edge.

Tiny turned back to Anders, delicately closed his teeth around the boy's dangling hand, tugging him so that he got up on his feet, and continued to pull him into the center of camp until they stopped in front of the fireless pit. Letting go of his hand, the enormous dog sat on his haunches and whimpered again.

"Hm," Anders remarked. "Worried about Danielle, are you, boy?"

Tiny barked, which woke up Paign.

"Something the matter?" he asked Anders, his hair wild from sleep.

"Well, I think Tiny is worried about Danielle," his cousin replied. "She doesn't appear to be in camp."

"Maybe she rolled over the side!" Paign quipped.

"That's not funny," Peter retorted, rubbing the sleep from his eyes.

By now, everyone was stirring.

"So," Johann groaned, as he stretched his long, muscular body, hands aimed towards the sky. "What is next for this day?"

"Well, unless I am missing the point here, Tiny is upset because he doesn't know where Danielle's gotten to," Anders said. "Actually, so am I. Anyone know where she is?"

"No, we don't!" Amy replied, clearly agitated, anxiety washing over and contorting her delicate face. "In fact, where are the gargoyles? Where are Ercen and Kimar?" she cried, anger and fear choking in her throat.

She and the others ran off in all directions in search of an answer, yelling Danielle's name. Tiny chased after one, then another, barking furiously.

Peter guessed the eyrie was sixty yards long and fifteen yards deep, at best. Numerous gnarled trees of various sizes sprang out of unlikely cracks in the rock, most of them in the area immediately around where they made camp. A few larger trees clumped together towards the edges of their lofty encampment. It didn't take long to check behind them all, as well as the numerous boulders and outcrops.

"She's not here!" Peter yelled from the eastern edge.

"Nor here, either, Peter!" Johann yelled back, standing atop the largest boulder at the western end.

Just as the search party returned back into the center of the camp, Kimar and Ercen parted into the shadowed rear of the eyrie, where a thin section of rock thrust out from the vertical face, waist-high, like a natural shelf. They set their food supplies onto it.

Peter and Amy ran up to them, immediately peppering the gargoyles with angry questions. Kimar stood dispassionately, waiting. Ercen continued laying out the breakfast items, like any good hostess, Heidi marveled, as if nothing else mattered.

When the frenzied parents had depleted their energies enough for a momentary pause in their interrogation, Kimar replied. "She's safe with Lohxnahr."

"What? Who on earth is Lohxnahr?" Amy cried.

Kimar replied, "Lohxnahr is the High Priest of our order. He's taken Danielle to Zarentil the Mystic. They are with him even now, at the summit yonder." He pointed to the highest peak, on the other side of the valley. "He's summoned her. She is the Chosen One."

"I…who…what?" Amy sputtered. "You just can't take our daughter like that. It's not right, Kimar!"

Ercen stopped organizing the humans' breakfast, turned to Amy and said, "Danielle was not taken, Amy. She permitted it. We have no power over her. She is the Chosen One."

"What exactly…does…that mean?" Peter struggled to spit out the words, nearly breathless from competing fury and fear.

"We do not fully know, Peter…Amy," Ercen continued, focusing on each parent, in turn. "We know that Danielle has been foretold, as we have told you. We know she is of great importance, at least, to defeating the power of the Key. We suspect that her importance is tied to her exposure to the Key when she was an infant."

"I wish we'd never found that Key," Amy snarled.

"It matters not," Kimar replied, "Danielle is the Chosen One."

"Well, you shouldn't have taken her. You had no right!" Amy continued, seething.

"Amy," Ercen replied quietly. "We did not take her, nor can we make her do something against her will. She is a strong person. Did you not raise her to be so? She freely chose to go with Lohxnahr."

"Ames," Peter said, looking at his wife. "Ercen has a point. Danielle is no pushover. She's smart, like you. She's industrious, even pigheaded, like me. Right? I guess we may have been over—"

Suddenly, Peter's face went taught, his eyes wide with alarm. An unearthly howling erupted high above their eyrie and from numerous high points around the Ten Pinnacles.

In a single bound, Kimar leapt over the heads of the humans, landing in front of them, positioned so that he had a commanding view of the valley and ridgeline. Immediately, he turned back and yelled, "Arm yourselves! We're under attack!"

Paign, Anders, Johann and Peter all went for their weapons; they had not been wearing their swords or bows, for there had been no need to. Heidi quickly had her long staff at the ready. Ercen jumped over to the fire ring in the middle of their campsite, to better protect her human charges.

Freida's scream rose above the din of the howls and people yelling. "Look! They're coming!"

Anders had just retrieved and belted his sword, slinging his bow over his shoulder. Paign was swearing at his gear, as if it was purposefully slowing him down. Both gasped when they looked to where Freida was pointing.

More than forty gargoyles emerged in full flight, just over the far ridge of the Pinnacles. Twice as many fireballs were already impacting defensive positions upon the vertical walls thrusting up from the valley.

"Prepare yourselves!" Kimar bellowed, his hands thrusting like pistons, balls of flame blasting outward .

Paign was startled when a huge cloud of dust blew up a few feet away from him, and he stared, confused and frozen, at the swirling dirt when an obsidian gargoyle emerged out from it. Only because of his quick reflexes, he ducked as a fireball smoked over his head. Rock chips flew back over him as the flaming orb exploded on the granite behind him.

The gargoyle bellowed angrily and charged at Paign. He had no time to nock an arrow, so he fell back, nearly tripping over a fallen tree branch, grabbing for his hilt. Pulling his sword from its scabbard, he prepared for a slashing stroke at the legs of the attacking beast.

Leaping high, the gargoyle bore down on Paign from above, his wings spread out to slow his descent. But Paign calculated he didn't have adequate time to react, and he instinctively raised his forearm to block, expecting it wouldn't be enough. He clenched his eyes tight.

The gargoyle's foot brushed across Paign's head, knocking him over. Paign couldn't believe he was still alive and swung around, his sword poised for a defensive move. There was no need.

The gargoyle was piled up in an unnatural heap of wings, arms and legs, two arrows sticking prominently out from the obsidian beast, one from its neck and the other from its temple. Before Paign could determine if the arrows came from Anders's or Johann's bows, women's screams and Tiny's enraged barks echoed from the other end of camp.

Horrified, Paign saw at least ten obsidians attacking Heidi, Peter, Amy, Ercen and Freida. Three others kept Kimar and Tiny occupied.

Johann bellowed, "Get thee away, you beasts!" and charged recklessly into the fray, his sword flailing back and forth like he was threshing grain. Anders fired arrows as fast as he could nock them, which was fast enough to enrage two of the attackers.

Nevertheless, the attacking gargoyles maintained their relentless, furious onslaught.

Paign grasped his sword tightly and charged at the nearest foe, screaming at the top of his lungs.

Just as he swung his sword viciously down at the rear of his enemy, a huge dust cloud kicked up in front of him, knocking him backwards and onto his back. He sat up immediately, shaking the grit from his hair and wiping his eyes clean. Appalled at what he saw before him, he walked slowly up to the others, barely aware that Anders was beside him.

Heidi's staff was broken nearly in half, her attacker dead at her feet. Blood dribbled down both of her arms. Peter lay on the ground, his legs askew, his body leaning heavily against the rear wall. His face was a mess of grime, sweat and smudged blood. Paign couldn't tell if it was Peter's or another's. What was clear were multiple stains emerging from his chest. Amy sat on a rock, next to Peter, who was panting hard but appeared to be whole. While his grin was less robust than normal, he was grinning as she gently stroked her husband's head, whispering something Paign couldn't hear. Johann was sprawled face down, breathing heavy. Two more foes lay crumpled nearby. One of them still had Johann's sword sticking out of its throat.

Shocked, Paign slowly turned back to the edge of the eyrie. Ercen was bent over Tiny. The mastiff's limp body lay on top of his dead enemy, the dog's huge jaws still clamped tight on the gargoyle's neck. Kimar, fresh slashes across his back, seemed to be assisting Ercen, his hand pressing into the dog's fur.

Anders stepped up next to his dazed cousin and quietly said, "Let's see if we can help."

Startled, Paign stared at Anders. "Right," he replied, his voice quavering.

As they drew up beside Ercen, they heard her whisper, "Now, Kimar." Only now could they see what had been blocked by Kimar's wounded back. Tiny's foe had thrust its talons fully into Tiny, even as the mastiff choked the life out of his foe, crushing its throat in his powerful teeth. At Ercen's signal, Kimar seized the dead arm of the Obsidian and pulled the clenched fist and talons away from Tiny's motionless body. Instantly, Ercen clamped her slate palm over the bleeding wound.

"Oh, my," Paign groaned. "He can't have survived a wound like that."

Anders put his hand on his cousin's shoulder and murmured, "It's going to be all right, I think, Paign. My fear was that his horrible wound *wouldn't* bleed like that. But it did. It means he's still alive. Tiny's alive. He's going to—"

Without warning, a high-pitched, blood-curdling cry burst against the granite walls of the Ten Pinnacles. A woman's cry. A mother's cry. Heidi's cry. "Where is my Freida?"

CHAPTER THIRTY-TWO

ARMED AND DANGEROUS

"OK, let me see if I'm getting this," Peter said, frustration in his voice. "We were attacked…here, even though you have strong defenses around the Ten Pinnacles, because Kahrnahrgx and his followers are desperate." He glared at Kimar, struggling hard with the impulse to blame someone for what happened to Freida.

"Yes," Kimar answered.

"Well, it seems not so desperate as incredibly bold!" he said, beginning to engage his mind over his shaken emotions. "And your sentries, or guards, or whatever you call them, only became aware of the attack moments before it took place, because the enemy found a way to hide plans of his attack somehow."

"Yes," Kimar said again.

"And the reason for the attack was to capture…Danielle," Peter continued, his voice catching at his daughter's name. "But they took Freida, at great cost to their troops, because they're convinced that Freida, not Danielle, is the Chosen One."

"Given that Danielle was not here at the time of the attack, but with Lohxnahr and Zarentil, there was no question that they would take the one human female child they found," the great gargoyle explained.

"So, why can't we just keep Danielle up in Zarentil's cavern until this all blows over?" Amy asked tensely.

"Because this will not blow over," Kimar replied calmly. "The advance team of Kahrnahrgx sensed the presence of Danielle in the valley below the Ten Pinnacles. But because they were presented with a human female girl, especially when they have already had Freida captive for a time, they took the only human girl they found. But that doesn't mean that they would not eventually sense and find Danielle, even if she were sheltered within Zarentil's Peak."

"Mom!" Danielle interrupted, so agitated she stood with clenched fists. "Dad, this is pointless. We need to go after them! There is only one way to end this. We need to go and save Freida. I can't tell you why, and this probably sounds stupid and obvious, but I don't think we have a lot of time. I feel there's something different about her capture than mine... something even more dangerous. Please!"

Just a few minutes earlier, after Heidi screamed out for Freida, their party was surprised and alarmed when Danielle parted back onto their eyrie, accompanied by the short, squat, smiling Lohxnahr. An alarming array of weapons swung out at the two at first, the group was so twitchy after their pitched battle with the shock troops of Kahrnahrgx.

Somehow, Danielle and the little gargoyle already knew what had happened.

Lohxnahr did not seem the least bit concerned about these events. But Johann and Heidi looked grim, indeed.

Ercen created a new staff for Heidi out of the same tree limb that tripped—and saved—Paign during the recent ambush and kidnapping. Anders and Paign gawked as the female gargoyle quickly stripped away twigs and bark by shaving the limb clean with four talons at once. Ercen held the finished staff tightly for a moment. A faint glow emerged from in between her gnarled, thick fingers. Still squatting, she handed the completed branch to Heidi. "This staff will not easily break," she said.

"Say, could you do something like that for us?" Peter asked Ercen. "Amy and I would, you know, prefer to arrive with something of an offensive nature to our foes."

Kimar overheard his question and strode over to Ercen. "Yes."

Without a word, Ercen twice repeated the process she'd used for Heidi's staff, but used narrower branches.

While she worked on the bows, Kimar reached over his shoulder and to the utter astonishment of the humans plucked about a dozen of the longest feathers from his wings. He then quickly shaved short lengths of feather from the shaft, reattaching it to the end, until the shaft had an arrow's full fletch. Already about the length of an arrow, he wrapped his fingers tightly around the middle of the feather's shaft and slowly slid them outward , straightening the shaft. The same faint glow came from the shaft until he set them down to work on the next. The entire process took only a few seconds for each arrow.

Ercen rose up and handed the new bows to Peter and Amy. Looking at Heidi, she said, "We now need bow string to complete the weapons."

"Ah, of course!" Heidi smiled, instinctively understanding. She tipped her long hair towards Ercen.

Ercen carefully reached into Heidi's long hair with a single talon. With the thumb and index finger of her other hand, Ercen gently rolled the length of hair back and forth, rolling out what wasn't needed until she'd thinned it to the proper thickness. Deftly, she snapped her talons together and snipped away the length of hair. In a moment, she had two lengths. Spinning the lengths between the fingers of both hands, the hair glowed faintly and appeared to gell together.

That's amazing! Peter thought. *It looks more like braided fishing line!*

Kimar, finished with the arrows, placed his right hand on the dirt next to him, and within a few seconds it glowed like molten lava.

"What the—" exclaimed Paign and Anders, closest to the fire, stepping back.

Kimar quickly jabbed in all the unfinished arrows directly into the molten dirt. Although it was only a few inches wide, it threw off tremendous heat.

Despite the gravity of the situation, Amy giggled, thinking it was the queerest bouquet she'd ever seen. *A dozen of your finest deadly flowers, please!*

Kimar rapidly pulled arrows out, one at a time, and grabbed the glowing gob of lava that tipped each, squeezing it into his left palm. With his right hand, he pushed the blunt edge of a talon into the other end of the arrow to create a notch for the string. A second later he lay down on the ground in front of him a shimmering, four foot, perfectly straight and supple, razor-sharp, stone-tipped arrow.

By the time Ercen finished stringing the new bows, which had just minutes earlier been Heidi's hair, Kimar finished the dozen arrows.

Grinning as far as his face allowed it, Johann hastily rummaged in his pack before pulling out a thick shirt.

"How about these for quivers?" he said to Peter and Amy, chuckling. "You'll be needing something to keep those for the ready!"

Johann held out the sleeves of his shirt to Kimar, who deftly sliced them off, with enough fabric still attached to fashion a shoulder sling for the inventive quivers.

Just before handing the new bows to Peter and Amy, Ercen sliced an arrow rest into the middle of each bow.

In less than five minutes, Peter and Amy were armed with weapons that were the envy of Anders and Paign.

"Come," Kimar said in a commanding voice. "Take food, build your strength, for we leave soon for battle!"

"What are you thinking about, Danielle?" Anders asked quietly, as he checked his quiver and arrows for the third time. He sat with his back against the same tree she leaned against.

The tension in the valley was thick like a deep morning fog. Besides a gentle rustling of wind through the evergreens, the only sound was Paign's whetstone being repeatedly drawn against the length of his sword's edge. A huge contingent of gargoyles gathered for battle preparations in the large open meadow near where they sat. Danielle stared at the frenetic activity, distracted, tense and vexed.

With all these gargoyles, shouldn't there be more noise? And what on earth is making that incessant, unpleasant scraping sound? Danielle thought it sounded like fingernails being dragged down a school chalkboard. "We shouldn't be here!" she hissed. "We need to go."

Paign, sitting on the remains of a stump and hidden in shrouds of fog, worried about Danielle's remoteness. She'd withdrawn into herself when it became clear that they wouldn't be leaving right away with a rescue party for Freida. Convinced his heart was beating hard enough to be heard by the others, from his own gnawing anxiety over Freida, he sharpened his already razor-sharp blade fiercely. It was about all that kept him from exploding.

Tiny lay in a heap, depressed, next to Paign, and whimpered from time to time. He kept licking the wounds healed by Ercen.

"Danielle?" Anders asked again. This time, he delicately touched her arm.

Danielle recoiled, startled out of her swirling apprehension. "What...yes?"

Anders gently drew his hand down her arm until it rested on Danielle's hand. He gave it a little squeeze but didn't let go. "I was just wondering what you are thinking about?"

"Oh, uh, well, I don't—you know—about Freida," she stammered. Then, suddenly, "We're wasting time! We need to go. Now!" Tears welled up in Danielle's eyes. "I...I don't know about me being some sort of 'Chosen One.' But I...she...it should have been *me* who was kidnapped." Her mottled face contorted in anger and fear. Then she threw her arms around Anders's neck and sobbed on his shoulder.

Tiny rose up with a groan, trotted over to Danielle and Anders and laid his immense head in her lap.

Paign, although shadowed in the fog, wasn't so far away that he couldn't hear the quiet voices of his friends. He felt awkward, as if he shouldn't be able to hear them, and was very relieved at that moment Peter and Johann walked into their gloomy camp.

"'Tis time to go," Johann declared, a fierce glint in his pale blue eyes. "The gargoyle army is prepared to part at once." Paign noticed that the farmer's wide hand gripped the hilt of his sword so tightly his knuckles were white. But nothing in his voice betrayed the anxious suffering raging inside Freida's father.

Peter's jaw was set hard. "Let's get going."

Tiny went and stood next to Farmer Skulstad, his feet planted firm, his stance wide, a look of death in his eyes.

Out of the shadows behind their impromptu camp, Lohxnahr walked lightly towards them. As always, he smiled and appeared completely unconcerned, when he said, "The time has come to part into the lair of Kahrnahrgx and battle our brethren to the death. Who will prevail? Will we be victorious, or will they? Won't it be interesting to find out? Yes…I do believe this will be quite enlightening!"

That sounded almost cheerful, Paign thought, even more agitated than before. *Do we really want this little fellow with us?*

Paign was still shaking his head and muttering about how strange the little gargoyle's speech sounded in light of the severity of their situation. "He's not right in his head!" he hissed at Anders.

Annoyed at the lack of response, Paign continued, "So, do you have any idea what the war plan includes, especially as it involves us?" He paused. "Well, do you?"

But Anders wasn't paying attention to his cousin's grumbling. Now that their rescue group had been summoned back to council area and stood among hundreds of gargoyles, his attention was drawn elsewhere. All of the gargoyles had just turned to face the lower portion of the eastern ridge. There were more important matters to listen to.

A great blaring, like a trumpet, burst the air. Paign looked for the source of the blasts and realized it came from Lohxnahr! Paign could see the little creature standing near the base of the ridge.

Everyone's attention fixed on a long, shallow ledge above the tree line. The War Council stood, assembled, across the length of the ledge, with Quarastohr and Uud-Rement next to each other.

Quarastohr's wings already outspread, he cast his arms wide and declared, "Comrades! My brothers! My sisters! Behold! The time is upon us!" Bowing, Quarastohr turned to the other gargoyle standing with him.

"We can expect that they expect us!" Uud-Rement bellowed down into the great gargoyle host arrayed upon the valley floor. The commanders perched against the vast, vertical eastern wall of the Ten Pinnacles, about two hundred feet above the base. This provided them a clear view of the entire army. Peter realized this also meant that every gargoyle could see them, unimpeded. *Smart*, he thought. *It's as if they speak to each individual this way.*

"Therefore, we will not have surprise on our side," Uud-Rement continued. "So we must go with the full conviction that our cause is just and then prosecute our battle with unrelenting forcefulness until we win complete supremacy!"

The assembled gargoyle force shouted as one, "Supremacy!"

"My brothers and sisters, do you share this conviction?" Uud-Rement shouted from his high perch, his deep voice resonating off the granite cliffs.

"Conviction!" echoed back.

"Shall we prosecute with unrelenting forcefulness?" the commander bellowed, leaning far out from the cliff face, his wings spread wide.

"Forcefulness!" erupted hundreds of gargoyles, like an exploding volcano. "Forcefulness! Forcefulness! Forcefulness!"

"Our mission is twofold. First, Freida must be saved!"

"Freida!"

"Second, we destroy the Key!"

"Destroy!"

"Battalion commanders, form your companies!" Uud-Rement roared. "We part when the sun reaches its zenith!"

Anders and Paign were dazzled by how quickly the gargoyles assembled into their units. For Peter and Johann, it reminded them of their younger years, when they had served in the military.

Kimar and Ercen strode up to them. Kimar announced, "We will be divided into two special squads. The rescue squad will be led by Ercen and include Johann, Heidi, Paign and Tiny, along with five other gargoyles. The squad assigned to the destruction of the Key, I will lead, along with Danielle, Amy, Peter and Anders. This squad will also include five more of our best fighters."

At first, Paign was upset that someone assigned him and Anders to different squads. They fought well together and could depend on each other in battle. But when he observed the relief on Anders's face—that he would be on the same squad as Danielle—he realized that he probably had a similar look on his face. His desire to rescue Freida, he guessed, was just as strong as Anders's was to protect Danielle. Nothing would divert him from being part of Freida's rescue team. Not even Kimar, had he chosen to keep the cousins together.

Ercen added, "We part at the sun's zenith, which is about twenty of your minutes from now. Make your final preparations, at once." Then she walked off with Kimar in the direction of Uud-Rement, who now stood on the valley floor alongside Quarastohr and the other members of the War Council.

The entire area of the Ten Pinnacles was electric. Tiny began barking and jumping up on humans and gargoyles alike, overcome with excitement and nervousness.

Peter leaned over to Johann. "Well, my friend, I don't know about you, but I wish I'd eaten something now. Guess it's too late." Peter clapped the farmer on his stout shoulder. "Good luck to you. I'm sure she'll be fine!" he added, hoping he sounded more confident than he felt. Even more, he hoped to bring calm and certainty to his friend. He knew, firsthand, the agony of not knowing if his daughter was safe.

"Thank you, Peter," the farmer replied, a little too firmly. "And to you...I wish for you good hunting and better fortune!" He smiled broadly at Peter and Amy, while squeezing Heidi's shoulder tight against his own.

Amy smiled anxiously and hugged Heidi tightly. Before she could say a word, Lohxnahr shuffled up with nine gargoyles. "I am come with the rest of your squads." Looking at Johann and Heidi, he said, "These are Rutahn, Gustlab, Stenring, Lohmong and Urchzahv. Battle seasoned. All good lads and lasses."

Johann bowed to welcome the new recruits to his squad.

Lohxnahr faced Amy and Peter. "And these additions will prove most helpful to your squad. This is Ita-Mudak, Mahtrance, Conomorg and Recknab," the gargoyle happily continued. Each gargoyle bowed when named.

"But, Lohxnahr," Danielle said, looking puzzled, "Kimar said each squad would have an additional five fighters. You've only brought four. Right?"

"Yes, but no. This would be true if I had not also brought myself." With a little flourish of his wrist, just like he did in the cave on the way to Zarentil's, the diminutive creature bowed. "I am the fifth gargoyle warrior added to your squad."

"Oh, fantastic!" she cried. Had Danielle looked at her parents, she'd have seen, for a fleeting moment, something less enthusiastic on their faces.

"Boy, could they have picked any hotter time of the day than the zenith?" Paign complained. "There'll be less of me going into this fight because there's a lot of me dripping off while we wait."

"Wait no more, child," Ercen chided. "Seize my hand! All of you, gather in!"

Paign, one hand clamped on a weapon, like the others, thrust his free hand upon the tangle of fingers, paw and talons made by the gargoyle, Johann, Heidi and Tiny. Glancing over at Anders, he saw a similar mashing of claws and hands. Suddenly, he realized that none of the other gargoyles needed to join hands for parting. Only the non-gargoyle members of the special-mission squads needed help for that. Their two squads were, in fact, the only groups in a circle, rather than in a line formation.

A huge storm of dust and grit blew up from the valley floor. Only Zarentil the Mystic remained in the valley of the Ten Pinnacles. The battle had commenced.

CHAPTER THIRTY-THREE

WAR

Again, it was discomfort that made her wake up. Freida's shoulders ached where her abductor seized her before parting; he'd clamped down so fiercely that his talons twice pierced her upper back and on both sides of her collar bone. Whenever she moved, the dull, throbbing ache jumped to stabbing, breathtaking pain.

Still, she continued making careful observations of her surroundings. There was no question in her mind that a rescue party was on its way. The only unknown factors, as far as Freida was concerned, were who was coming for her…and when.

This time, her captors showed complete disregard and contempt for her. *My last abductor wasn't exactly kind*, she thought, ruefully. But although Gahrspat had treated her cruelly, he'd also seemed terribly anxious about what would happen when Kahrnahrgx himself came for her. Otherwise, Freida decided, the obsidian devil would not have gone to such lengths at trying to scare her. He didn't want to face his own fear and so he scared her instead.

Here, though, they treated her as if she was nothing at all. It seemed purely accidental that there was a little water pooled in a natural basin in the stone cage she was being kept in. She'd noticed it shortly after she'd been thrown into her prison cell, and although it tasted bitter, she still drank it. But the leftover meat, already molding on the bone and of a suspicious origin, she immediately discarded into a corner after smelling it.

Freida guessed that her cell—and it was truly a cell this time—was roughly fifteen feet square and about nine feet high. *Just big enough for about three or four gargoyles to fit in here at the same time*, she realized, darkly. *I wonder how many it takes to form an execution party?* She could not find a door. She decided that her captors must have parted in with her and then left without her.

A small hole at the far corner, although set high into the wall, provided her a commanding view of the area outside her cave. But she had to stand on her tiptoes, propping one foot against the opposing wall while pushing up on a small stalagmite below the window with the other.

Her window looked onto a large meadow surrounded by very tall evergreens. But the trees were different than those around the Honellaken Valley she called home. Freida choked up as she thought about her home and all the beautiful trees surrounding the Skulstad farm. She missed her parents so! They must be nearly mad with worry, especially her mother. But Freida knew that her father, though very stoic on the outside, was probably more worried even than her mother. And yet she knew that Tiny would be the worst off of all. She knew a dog's love to be simple compared to a parent, but also un-yieldingly loyal, total, immensely forgiving and fiercely selfless.

For a few long minutes, Freida wept, her forehead leaned against the top of her meager window, tears dripping and roll-ing down the outside wall below the opening. Her legs began to cramp up from the awkward position she was holding. She lifted her head and shifted her weight, scanning the surround-ings outside her prison.

There was a very large stone platform at the far side of the meadow, near the forest. It reminded Freida of the dais in the cavern she discovered below Ruar's Peak, where they'd found the desiccated woman tied to the stone chair, except it was much, much bigger. The platform was surrounded by many tall columns, as if there had once been a magnificent roof over the raised area. Most of the capitals at the top of each column were damaged or completely missing, darkened from fire and smoke.

"What was this place?" Freida wondered out loud. "And what happened to it?"

A scraping sound jolted her out of her thoughts. She spun around, jumped down from her window perch and glared at her jailor—very imposing, in the center of her cell—despite the fear gnawing at her.

The gargoyle leered back at Freida. "Dreaming up a jail-break, human?" he sneered. "There is no chance of that, you pathetic creature, for I am Strohrnahq."

"What do you want, you vile beast?" she spit back at him.

His backhand was wickedly fast. She didn't have time to dodge his swing and was flung sideways into the middle of her cell. When Freida stood up, she rubbed away the blood drib-bling from the multiple cuts on her bruised cheek. Glaring at him, she realized there was an opening behind where he stood.

It must have been not only where he came through *but where he'd been hidden all along*. Strohrnahq himself had been a part of the wall!

"What do I want? What do I WANT?" he screamed back at her in a blind rage. "I want you—all of you wretched wingless bipeds—to die! To vanish! To leave this world at once! Since the dawn of time, you have been a scourge upon the earth. We would be rid of you, once and for all, finally. Kahrnahrgx has something special planned for you, human—the 'Chosen One,' indeed! But for what you have been 'chosen,' he has not said. That is his special little secret. He doesn't seem inclined to share it with me!" The gargoyle exploded in guttural, mirthless laughter.

By now, Strohrnahq's face was just inches from Freida's, his wings spread out to their full span and shook, his hands so tightly fisted that his talons flailed around her face and his spittle landed on her arms. His rage was horrifying.

Though filled with loathing and fear of Strohrnahq, Freida began to wonder why this creature, even allowing for his being a loyal minion of Kahrnahrgx, was so driven by hatefulness. She looked at him, studying him, and realized she'd seen a face like his before. There was something dreadfully familiar about him—tall, obsidian, fierce, narrow but muscular build, deadly red eyes. *Oh, no!* She recoiled, overwhelmed with terror, but unable to make a sound. *Strohrnahq is Gahrspat's brother!*

Freida backed away from the enraged beast, frantically thinking of something she might do to protect herself from his fury. She didn't look behind her for fear of taking her eyes off of him, and tripped over a rocky bump on the floor of her cell. Freida fell heavily onto the hard surface, badly bruising her tailbone. When she cried out in pain, Strohrnahq laughed viciously.

"Ah, one less fresh place to cause you pain and suffering! Pity. And yet my master will make full use of the unharmed places upon you. For he will reveal to you how much agony a human can endure before the end! Especially for you, 'Chosen One,' he will linger at his work, taking into full measure all of his many resources. With you, a new standard will be se—"

Freida instantly recognized the unearthly wail that blew into her cell like a siren. It was so similar to the warning cry at the Ten Pinnacles just as they were attacked, it must have the same implication here. But that would mean…

Strohrnahq's eyes went wide with alarm, and he ran to the cell's opening, where he'd been disguised as part of the wall. No longer afraid, Freida ran to her window, jumped up, planted her feet and peered out onto the meadow. She gasped.

From the farthest point away, right at the edge of the forest, all the way up the huge platform, gargoyles swarmed. Many were already in flight, hurling fireballs on those below. Dozens of pairs were locked in mortal combat, talons glinting madly in the bright sunlight. Several columns had collapsed from misfired and deflected implosions. Freida found it impossible to tell which gargoyles were from Kimar and Ercen's side of this fight. The action was too fast to recognize any gargoyles she knew. Between the thrusting fists and the destructive forces that followed them, the multitude of hissing fireballs, and the sheer numbers of fighters, she quickly realized her focus needed to be closer to her prison.

"Why aren't there any gargoyles coming nearer?" she cried.

"Oh, you'll see!" Strohrnahq's voice rasped in her ear. She hadn't heard him come up behind her because of all the noise outside. Startled, Freida's left foot slipped off the narrow bit of rock she was perched on. Losing her grip, she fell back into her cell, just as the rock face on the other side of her window exploded into the air. Before Freida's eyes could register what they were seeing, her ears recognized the sound of dozens of Vannveps, flying into the melee below her window.

"Oh, no!" she wailed.

The obsidian creature cackled into her neck, his hot breath making her skin crawl. His finger closed down hard on the wounds he had made when kidnapping her. She winced and closed her eyes tightly.

"What is it, human? You do not like this turn of events? Perhaps we should retrieve a few wasps for your enjoyment inside this cell…or perhaps it would be more accurate to say that it would be for my amusemen—aaaygh!" His hands immediately fell away from her.

Freida whipped around, turning her back on the massive battle taking place in the meadow, only to find the battle had entered her cell. A frenzy of wings, arms, fireballs and chaos filled the view beyond Strohrnahq's back. Both of his wings were pierced by several arrows, but it was clear that her captor wasn't seriously wounded. Alarmed, Freida saw that Strohrnahq was phenomenally skilled at defensive fighting.

An explosion of flame and dust just over Freida's head knocked her off her feet. She landed in a heap behind Strohrnahq. Through his legs, she could see the legs of another gargoyle—Ercen, she was certain—and several humans. She recognized Paign's trousers and boots.

Even through the cataclysmic, shattering noises of swords, fireballs and explosions, Freida made out the roar of her father's outraged shouts and Tiny's furious, frightened barking. Strohrnahq was single-handedly keeping Ercen, Paign and both of her parents at bay. Only Tiny seemed to cause Strohrnahq any concern. Even with the gargoyle blocking nearly all of her view, she could see most of his fireballs seemed to be directed towards her companion. Tiny just narrowly missed a direct hit, and his rear haunches already smoldered.

Freida became enraged at her beloved dog's yelps and, without thinking it through, spun around on the floor. Spreading her arms out for stability, her back firmly grounded, Freida pulled her knees up almost to her chin and then kicked out with all her might, directly into the back of Strohrnahq's knees.

His legs buckled momentarily, and he let out a furious roar.

But the kick had been enough, causing him to misfire and lose his balance. In the bare moment he needed to right himself, Ercen's fist punched out and arrows flew from Johann's and Paign's bows.

Strohrnahq staggered back from the force of Ercen's blasts. Freida scrambled out of his path, narrowly avoiding being impaled by the enormous talons on his heels. Rolling over, she looked up to see two arrows still shuddering in his chest. Even though grievously wounded, defiance glared from his contorted face. His right arm swung rapidly up towards the ceiling. He formed a fist, violently sweeping it back down towards her face, intending to kill her with his immense talons. Instinctively, she ducked and rolled into his legs. The beast howled in fury, angry that his death blow went unconsciously wide to avoid severing his own leg.

"You filthy spawn of a human, I will destroy you!" he roared.

Abruptly, he yanked his right fist up to his chin, eager to deliver his killing blow straight down upon her. Freida screamed, knowing she didn't have time to roll away. Horrified, she glanced up into her foe's eyes, just as something flashed over his head, followed by a sickening, moist crack. Strohrnahq's eyes stared at Freida for a moment, lost focus and then rolled up and back into his head.

"You will not, you beast!" Heidi yelled, pulling her heavy wooden staff away from Strohrnahq's cratered skull. As the gargoyle slowly slumped and fell towards the floor, Johann's sword lopped off his head.

"Nei!" the farmer bellowed. "We human spawn have destroyed you!"

"Quickly, we must move!" Ercen sprinted to the cell's doorway, yelling as she ran. After first giving Freida a huge lick, Tiny bounded off to follow Ercen. Johann and Heidi helped their daughter to her feet, relief quickly winning over the fear and fatigue written on their faces.

Grinning from ear to ear, Paign simply nodded at Freida. "Hi. Good to see you!"

Joining Ercen in the wide stone tunnel outside her cell, Freida was astonished to find five more gargoyles. Paign jumped in front of Freida and with a flamboyant swing of his arm, announced, "You may wish to thank Rutahn, Lohmong, Gustlab, Urchzahv and Stenring for guarding the entrance to your cell during our rescue. Without them, things may not have gone so well for us, eh?"

Dropping into a formal curtsy, Freida smiled. But her eyes grew wide when she realized that what she'd first taken to be a large pile of rock behind these soldiers was actually a huge mound of foes. "Oh, my! Uh, thank you very much," she whispered.

Dust filtered down from rupture lines in the ceiling behind the five gargoyles. Wisps of smoke curled up from Stenring's wings and Lohmong's chest. But all five fighters bowed low to Freida's curtsy.

Danielle was immediately overwhelmed by chaos. She'd heard a strange howl getting louder and louder during their parting, a sound like they'd heard when they'd come under attack earlier in the day. Then she'd landed roughly in harsh scrub grass, next to a huge stone platform, in a gigantic plume of dirt and grit. Anders crawled up beside her. Within moments, the air was full of shouts, fireballs, implosions, flying bits of stone, ash, smoke and screams. Suddenly, her parents heaved themselves over the side of the platform and landed next to her. Kimar and the other gargoyles in their squad formed a protective circle around them. Lohxnahr stood above Danielle's head, atop the platform. Flanking him, Ita-Mudak and Kimar were firing their fists towards unseen foes somewhere on the platform. Danielle didn't want to chance a look. Conomorg, Mahtrance and Recknab stood behind them, firing balls of flame in all directions, including up.

"Vannveps, Kimar!" Mahtrance yelled. "Vannveps are coming!"

Kimar's head dropped down to the edge of the platform and bellowed over the din, "Follow us! Come, now!"

Peter leaped over the top of the dais and pulled up Amy and Danielle. Anders sprang over after, first laying his bow on the platform, then retrieving it. He didn't have many arrows left.

"Now! This way!" Kimar sprinted towards the very center of the raised area.

Surrounded by their gargoyle squad, the humans ran as fast as they could while keeping their positions in the middle of their sheltering, winged friends. It was difficult to avoid getting entangled in the rubble, the slain bodies of friend and foe, and especially the wildly shuffling feet and talons of their own group. A fireball erupted just in front of Kimar and Lohxnahr, who absorbed the fire and heat.

The rest of their group was enveloped in dissipating smoke and fume as they leapt through it. Amy nearly doubled over, gasping and clawing for clean air. Peter, who had been running behind her, quickly thrust his hands under each of her arms and dragged her along, off to one side, as fast as he could. But Anders, who had been just behind Peter, was momentarily blinded by the choking smoke; he tripped on Amy's outstretched feet, lurching headlong into Peter, causing the three to fall into a heap. The other gargoyles were protecting the rear. Recknab was fully engaged in battling a hive of Vannveps in hot pursuit, along with Conomorg and Mahtrance. Because they were all running backwards, they didn't see the collision of humans. Recknab's heel talon landed across Anders's leg, gashing it deeply.

"Aaaygh!" Anders screamed, this time crumpling to the ground.

Recknab lost his balance, falling hard just behind Amy's dragging feet.

Their squad came to a complete standstill, nearly in the center of the fiercest fighting. Debris and grit rained down on them.

Danielle's heart pounded so hard, as she clutched the grimy plastic box protecting the hideous key tight against her chest, that she could hear it even over the din. She knew they were in grave danger, now fully exposed to their enemy. It was only a matter of time before—

Her mind was overcome by a strange, deep humming, almost more felt than heard. Something immensely gentle grazed her face. Glancing upwards, she realized it was one of Lohxnahr's gossamer wings that swept by her. Danielle felt the same odd way she did after jumping off the sheer bluff near her home, into the deep end of Parkside Pond. The moments between plunging into the water and breaking the surface were both exciting and terrifying, full of strange sensations and noise, like time itself held its breath.

Mesmerized, Danielle watched Lohxnahr fluttering so slowly over their group that remaining airborne didn't seem possible. But then everything else had also slowed to a crawl. The cluster of Vannveps appeared almost frozen in air. The humming grew louder and louder. Lohxnahr's arms stretched up over his unhurried thrumming wings, as his hands clasped together to form one fist, fingers wrapped tightly around each other.

Still, it was plain enough that time had not stopped. From all around the battlegrounds, Danielle saw fireballs gradually forming on the outstretched fists of hundreds of gargoyles. Countless flaming orbs were already in flight towards the group.

The humming reached a level that was astonishing to Danielle. It was like the pressure on her ears when she swam to the bottom of their pond back home. She thought her head would burst from it. Weakness washed over her body, and the box nearly slipped from her hands. It was growing difficult to focus her eyes, but she was able to make out Lohxnahr clasping his hands together into a large fist, just behind his head. Just when she felt she could not take it anymore, Lohxnahr slowly brought the fist down to the nape of his neck and then suddenly snapped it over his head. An enormous burst of light exploded out from his fist. A concussive detonation ended the oppressive hum. Abruptly, time returned to the tempo Danielle was used to, like she had finally broken through the surface of the pond. The diminutive gargoyle's wings beat the air furiously. A shockwave rapidly expanded away from him in all directions, vaporizing all of the inbound fire. As it slammed into their foes, they were knocked to the ground below or far into the forest.

"Now, Kimar!" Lohxnahr yelled. "Now to the Temple's door!"

"Follow me!" Kimar bellowed to his companions, running again towards the center of the platform.

Enemies were already launching off the ground and rising above the tall trees where they'd been felled by Lohxnahr. A volley of fireballs filled the sky above the rescue party.

Recknab hurriedly scooped up Anders, who was writhing in pain from his punctured leg, and ran past Kimar and to the front of their group. As Recknab's wings expanded into a protective canopy over her friend, Danielle glimpsed the gargoyle's left hand pressed hard into Anders's horrible wound. She couldn't hear what he yelled at Anders.

Conomorg seized Danielle by the waist—nearly dislodging the Key from her grasp—and sprinted to catch up to Kimar. His wings snapped up into a canopy. Startled, she looked to either side but couldn't see past his wings. Alarmed, she yelled up into his face, "Where are my parents?"

"Safe, child!" he bellowed, staccato, blurting the words out in between gasps of air. "Do not fear!" Tucking in his wings momentarily, she saw her mother sheltered by Mahtrance's wings, while Lohxnahr flew just above her father's head. Although fireballs were crashing down all over the platform by now, there was some sort of protective glowing dome over Lohxnahr, safeguarding him while he ran.

Danielle swung her head back, looking forward, beyond the shadow of her protector. Smoldering ruin and fury lay between Conomorg and Recknab. She hoped that Anders and Recknab would get through the onslaught of incoming fire,

because she and Conomorg didn't appear to have a chance.
A swarm of Vannveps swept down low and broke over the
far edge of the dais, flying just a meter above the floor. She
guessed they had only seconds before they'd crash into them.
Without warning, Recknab dropped out of sight. Anders still
held tight, his feet visible for just a moment, bouncing under
his protector's wing. Then Kimar vanished, as if the stone floor
swallowed him. Danielle gasped as her father disappeared, with
Lohxnahr right after him. Just as she concluded there must be
a hole in the center of the dais, Mahtrance fell out of view
with just her mother's feet seen bouncing beyond his right
wing before they disappeared. Finally, she and Conomorg
dove headlong into a wide, dark stairwell. The blast of withering heat and light that followed them in told Danielle how
close they'd come to being incinerated by the volley of fireballs from their foes. Screams from dozens of Vannveps broke
over her like a horrifying wave of heartbreak and despair; they
had been destroyed by Kahrnahrgx's army, their own allies.
Danielle understood, with sickening clarity, that the swarm of
Vannveps had just been sacrificed, intended only to distract
and delay their prey's retreat. But the Vannveps hadn't discerned their fate until it was too late.

Danielle caught her breath at the sight of stairs vanishing
into utter darkness below, and the speed their party descended
into them was frightening. She tightly gripped the box containing the key Kahrnahrgx was willing to destroy even his
own forces to recover. Conomorg veered hard to the right of
the stairwell. Fireballs flew past them, up towards the opening. The upper sections collapsed not far behind Danielle and
Conomorg, and all were plunged into darkness.

Recknab leaned against the stone wall at the end of the long, dark corridor. He'd lit the floor and ceiling but the dust and fume from the collapsed stairs made it difficult to see and breathe.

Anders, still held by Recknab, hacked hard but managed to choke out, "All right, then. Thanks. You can put me down now. Please!"

The gargoyle smiled wanly and set him gently on the gritty floor. "I'm sorry about stepping on you…my attention had been elsewhere."

"We've been over that," Anders replied. "Don't worry about it." He bent down and ran his finger over his long, nasty new scar.

"OK, so where are we, and why are we here?" Peter said hoarsely.

Kimar slowly scanned his squad. "We have come to the entrance to the Temple of Kahrnahrgx," he intoned.

"Ah." By the tone of Peter's voice, Danielle could tell he wished he'd not have asked.

"Why did we have to risk annihilation in running—and flying—here?" Amy asked. "Couldn't we have just parted in, done our business, and then parted out?"

Lohxnahr smiled. "Simply impossible."

"Why is that?" Amy pressed.

"Too many defenses are in place now," the little gargoyle replied, beaming.

"Kimar, we don't have time for this!" Mahtrance muttered, his head awkwardly tipped forward because of the corridor's low ceiling. "The rubble above is already being cleared away. Our time grows short!"

"Agreed, Mahtrance," Kimar replied, speaking quickly. "Amy, we cannot part into the Temple. Kahrnahrgx has mounted too many defenses for us to get through. This makes our mission much more difficult. But our enemies also cannot part into the Temple. So they, too, must come down the stairwell. But come they will." He paused, motioning behind him. "On the other side of this door is the special Temple room. It is certain that it will be defended by sentries long stationed here. My comrades and I have already devised an attack sequence. We need Danielle to unlock this door with her key and then get to the center of the dais, which is in the far right corner, and then—"

"Wait! Where's Kahrnahrgx? Where is he, Kimar?" Amy yelled. "Is he in…there?" She stabbed her finger towards the stone door.

Recknab stepped in front of the door. "We do not know, Amy. We have not been able to sense his location. We know he's near."

"Oh, that's just great!" she hissed. "Just fantastic, really! So, you propose we simply march into this Temple—this certain trap!—and assist our daughter in…somehow…destroying…"

"Kimar!" Recknab interrupted. "We absolutely do not have time for thi—"

A horrendous explosion blew Recknab off his massive feet. Anders instinctively ducked his head and rolled into the hallway as much of the roof over the doorway collapsed inches behind him and onto Recknab.

With unearthly speed, Conomorg jumped in front of Danielle and her parents and unleashed a rapid barrage of fireballs into the now-open Temple dungeon.

Because there was no room to fly, Kimar leapt to the right of the opening and dove precisely in between Conomorg's defensive barrage, rolling past the rubble-filled doorway into the cavernous room behind. Mahtrance hurled himself through the left side. Both immediately began a barrage of fireballs to match Conomorg's.

Amy knelt beside Recknab, oblivious to the chaos erupting all around them. She stroked the gargoyle's massive face. A ragged spire of rock jutted from his chest. He was dead. "I...I'm sorry, Recknab. If only I hadn't argued with you..."

Conomorg moved just inside the rubble of the doorway and, in between volleys of fireballs, motioned to Peter to follow. So far, between Kimar, Mahtrance and Conomorg, the minions of Kahrnahrgx were pinned down.

"Ames! We've got to go!" Peter yelled, jerking her arm away from the gargoyle's body. "We've got company!" He pulled at her arm and, with a massive heave, threw her directly into the cavern, filled with their enemies, beyond the destroyed doorway. Danielle ran in behind them, with Anders in pursuit.

The Temple room was hot, the air acrid from smoke and fume. Danielle found it difficult to see because of it. Mahtrance, Kimar and Conomorg fired volley after volley into the depths of the vast space. She couldn't see Lohxnahr in the gloom. In fact, she couldn't remember seeing him even enter the large hall.

A huge explosion behind her destroyed more of the area where the door had been.

"What's making the walls collapse, Kimar?" Anders roared. "I don't see any fireballs from the enemy's side!"

Before he could answer, Kimar and Conomorg suddenly dove to the floor, away from the wall. A shockwave swept violently past Anders and Danielle and what was left of the Temple's entrance collapsed into ruin behind them.

"We've been cut off, Anders!" Danielle screamed. "There's no way out now!"

A horrific roar howled from across the deep cave.

"What on earth was that?" Peter yelled.

Amy cowered next to him.

Kimar bellowed, "Vanntorden! Cousins to the Vannveps."

"Except much bigger…slower," added Conomorg, firing off two more fireballs. "And they cannot fly."

Mahtrance yelled over the din, "They have very poor aim, but their blasts carry the force of a hundred years of glacial movement…all at once!"

"Oh, terrific!" Peter hollered back. "Just terrific!"

Violent yellows, oranges and reds exploded off the cavern's walls like a massive holiday fireworks display. *Except we're indoors*, Danielle thought. *We've got to get out of here.*

In the undulating light and dark, Kimar grabbed Peter and Anders and dashed across to the left of the cavern, finding cover behind some large stalagmites. When Conomorg and Mahtrance let fly another volley of fireballs, Kimar ran ahead of the humans, as Anders and Peter fired off a round of arrows into the cluster of Vanntorden. Amy stole over to Danielle, crouching as close to the floor as she could.

Danielle recoiled, frightened speechless, when a raspy voice spoke urgently into her ear, "We must go now, child. Bring your mother." Lohxnahr smiled pleasantly, hovering in the air next to her. He was covered in soot, grit sloughing off his shoulders like dripping sand.

"But…can't you see? There are still sentries down at the other end, Lohxnahr. It's too dangerous to move," Amy shouted at him.

"Amy, those aren't the sentries," he replied, barely audible over the cascade of yells, roars, explosions and crashing stone. He waved his right arm in an arc around them. "These are."

Only then did Danielle and her mother see the bodies, or what was left of them, of six obsidian gargoyles.

"Wha—when…" Amy croaked. "You?"

"Just as you came through the entryway." Lohxnahr beamed.

Impulsively, Danielle reached up, took the little gargoyle's face in her hands and kissed him fiercely on the forehead, even as he hovered.

"Will you lead us?" she asked.

"Of course," he grinned. "But first, we must deal with our remaining foes. Pardon me for a moment."

Lohxnahr surged higher into the room to midway between the floor and the ceiling, and then he began spinning. A curious whirring pulsed faster, in time with his rotations. Danielle thought of the girl from her school who competed in ice-skating events. She'd spin so fast it was hard to make out the girl inside the spin. All of a sudden, she'd stop, ice would fly up from her braking skate, and the girl would curtsy. But Lohxnahr's spin was even faster. Like the ice-skater, he suddenly came to a complete stop. But as he did so, a silver wave pulsed out from his wings, straight into the rear corner from where the Vanntorden continued to hurl concussive blasts. The roof of the cavern above them cracked, groaned and then collapsed on the shrieking water wasps.

Stillness enveloped the cavern like a thick blanket.

Amy jumped at the sound of crumbled rock settling where the doorway had been. Similar noises came from the far end of the cavern, where the roof had crashed down on their adversaries.

"All well, then?" Lohxnahr inquired, his gossamer wings humming rhythmically. "Shall we proceed?"

Danielle and Amy followed close behind. Behind them, Mahtrance, Ita-Mudak and Conomorg examined the ruination of the doorway, presumably looking for a way out, Danielle hoped. The rest of their party carefully picked their way through the debris of battle, looking for any surviving foes. Kimar frequently glanced back at Danielle.

Lohxnahr slowly flitted over to the corner dais and hovered above the altar at its center. A silverish light emanated from the small gargoyle and fell across the altar area.

It was a horrifying place. Danielle fought against the overwhelming impulse in her to turn and run back, heedlessly, to the ruined entrance to this chamber. Revulsion washed over her like the pulsing of her heartbeat. Gaping at the massive columns of carved stone—embellished throughout with hellish images intricately woven together—encircling the sacrificial table, Danielle's feelings surged between nauseating sorrow and mind-numbing wrath. *After the long years of persecution she suffered at the hands of her own kind, the poor, wretched widow came...here...to this hideous place and*—Danielle wouldn't allow herself to complete her thought.

When she came to the edge of the dais, Danielle looked up at Lohxnahr, who shimmered strangely through her tears, and instinctively reached to clutch her mother's arm. She couldn't get any words to come from her mouth, so she nodded upwards in his direction.

Great sadness washed over the face of Lohxnahr. Tears fell from his large, limpid lavender eyes and splashed into the dust layered deep upon the altar and floor around it. Small, damp pockmarks remained.

Danielle began to weep. Something inside her ached at the sight of Lohxnahr's tears falling into ages of accumulated dust...dust that almost buried the true nature and horrors of the altar. From the sniffles coming from her side, Danielle knew her mother was also experiencing something powerful from this place.

Lohxnahr's tears made virtually no sound as they fell into the dust. But as Danielle wiped her face, she heard a nearly inaudible tinkle come from the top of the altar. Something glinted in the silvery glow falling down from Lohxnahr, wet from the tear that had just fallen on it.

Danielle stepped lightly onto the dais and walked timidly towards the edge of the altar. Curiosity and revulsion competed for emotional dominance inside of her. Midway, she stopped. Her knees became rubbery and she felt faint. With great effort, she forced herself to swallow hard and breathe normally, at least as regularly as she could manage. Glancing back at her mother did nothing to quell the waves of fear washing over her. Time had slowed to the point that her mother's moist eyes blinked with the speed of a crawling worm. This bizarre altered sense of time only added to Danielle's anxiety.

Steeling herself, Danielle exhaled deeply and commanded her legs to continue walking. Dust erupted up and around her feet as she waded through the layers of time it represented.

Lohxnahr's wings flapped with agonizing sluggishness just a meter over her head. But the silver light coming from him fell onto the altar, glittering off of what she'd seen. Danielle reached out her hand and scooped up the little object, along with a fistful of grime that had hidden it for—*how many years?*

she wondered. She blew the remaining soil off of it and caught her breath.

"This is a…woman's ring, a wedding band," she whispered. The inscription inside the band was faint, but still readable: *To my beloved Anna.* Danielle bowed her head, sobbing at the realization that she held in the hollow of her right hand the Widow Vellhelmina's long-cherished wedding ring. "The poor woman must have been wearing it right up to the…the…final…moment," she choked out.

Deep within Danielle churned an emotional storm. In a rush, as in a waking dream, she saw the long years of harsh treatment the old woman had suffered. Fragments of vision, scenes of the widow's terrible imprisonment, flashed across Danielle's mind, right up to the moment of her murder by the foul Kahrnahrgx. Shreds of long-distant conversations played in her mind. Shouts and cries. Accusations and defenses. Gentle words of endearment alongside vile screams of hatred. Decades of great loneliness, followed by years of dreaded isolation, ending in horrible wretchedness. Danielle, in the present, glared at the ring, the altar, the cavern, seething. Fury erupted inside her.

Enraged by the vast wrongs perpetrated on the old woman, Danielle took the heavy Key of Kahrnahrgx out of its box. She'd been holding onto the box so tight with her left hand for so long that it had gone numb. Now that the Key was in her hand, like a monster wave crashing into a beachhead, the waves of revulsion and rage she'd felt finally erupted. With a scream filled with fury, misery and defiance, she focused all the energy her body could muster and smashed the Key down on the altar. A huge plume of dust and grit flew up from the Key. But where she'd held it, there was a sickening crunch.

Danielle had not let go of it, smashing her fingers between the stone table and the unyielding metal. Reflexively, she dropped the Key and, faltering backwards, fell down a step.

"Aaaygh," she cried out. Her fingers throbbed piteously. "Oh, that was just brilliant! What was I thinking?"

Sparks flashed out from the Key of Kahrnahrgx, at first just around the surface of the altar. Where it struck piles of dust and grit, it left blobs of molten glass. Alarmed, Danielle recoiled backwards. Spasms of light flashed above and through the altar below, farther and farther until they finally pulsed from the floor to the ceiling overhead. Almost immediately, Lohxnahr was surrounded by the pulsing bolts of electricity, but as before, he seemed to be suspended, his wings beating laconically, at a different speed of existence than Danielle's. Quickly, she stole a glance back at her mother. Yes, she was still stuck in the same sluggish universe as Lohxnahr. She was surprised, though, to see that Kimar now stood next to her.

Danielle, horrified, could see plainly that at any moment an arcing ribbon would slice through Lohxnahr. She felt like a fool for throwing down the precious Key in a rage, not only smashing her fingers in the process but risking their entire mission. A mission that other friends had already died for. "No way I'm going to let something happen to Lohxnahr!" she yelled.

Hoping against hope that it wouldn't hurt too much, Danielle clenched her fists, shoved her feet hard against the dais and threw herself up onto the altar and over the wildly sparking key.

The piercing, wincing pain never came. Not realizing she'd clamped her eyes shut in anticipation of agony, Danielle opened them, puzzled. Although she could still feel the cold stone under her dust-covered hands, she could not see it. She couldn't see anything, really. Everything in the cavern was now bathed in a brilliant, dazzling light. In fact, it was so bright that she wasn't sure it had a color unless there was something beyond white. Yet, she didn't need to squint.

A far-off ripple, the barest of shadows, seized her attention. Slowly, the ripple grew, becoming more and more substantial, until it finally took enough shape that Danielle could see someone walking towards her through the brilliance. A fragrance, subtle but very strong and unlike anything she'd ever smelled before, wafted out from the shadowy form.

"Greetings, child," came a clear, pure voice.

"Hello," Danielle replied, timid but also excited. "Who are you, please?"

"Do you not know, dear one?" The smell reminded Danielle of a famous flower garden she had visited with her mother when she was in kindergarten. Except this was far better.

"I…I believe that I do, ma'am."

"Oh, that is wonderful. You are indeed a special child, Danielle." The shadowy form shifted again, stepping forward until it was just a few paces from Danielle and the altar upon which she lay. "Thank you, child," said the most beautiful woman Danielle had ever seen.

"Are you the Widow Vellhelmina, then?" Danielle asked quietly, wondering why the woman thanked her.

The woman who stood before her, neither old nor young, paused for moment, seemingly confused by the question.

"What's that, you say?" she murmured. "Ah…yes, that's right. That's what most people called me. But to my husband, and my family before him, I was Anna."

"Am I dead, then, ma'am? Seeing as how you are dead, I mean, then I must be, too."

"Well, why would you say that, child? Do I look dead to you?"

"Uh…no, ma'am," Danielle replied, flustered. "It's just that we came to save you—well, not you exactly, because you had already been destroyed by Kahrnahrgx ages ago. But we came to destroy the Key of Kahrnahrgx because he—Kahrnahrgx, I mean—is going to use the power of your soul, that he harnessed into the Key, against his own kind…and ours, too."

"No."

"Ma'am?"

"No, you are not dead. I had not properly answered your exceedingly important question."

Danielle didn't know what to say. On the one hand, she was delighted beyond words to be speaking with the widow—or at least dreaming she was—and yet, on the other hand, she was utterly confused by their conversation.

Suddenly, she remembered the ring clutched in her hand. Her hand shaking a little, Danielle handed it to the woman.

The woman's eyes twinkled brightly. "Child, I again thank you. What you have done is born out of a brave heart that carries great love and is full of kindness. You have ransomed me, did you not know?"

"I've what?"

"You've ransomed me, child." Her smile was full of warmth and wonder, like an embrace.

"But…but," Danielle stammered, growing more and more upset. "I haven't really done anything. They've been calling me the 'Chosen One' but won't tell me—or maybe they can't—what it is I am chosen to do!" She began shaking, unsure of what to feel. "I've never been all that special. There are only a few kids at school who talk to me. I'm pretty good in most of my classes, but I'm not very 'sports-minded' like the popular kids." Her hands opened and then clenched tight. "My parents love me…I know that. But it's their job to do that, isn't it? I mean, ever since they found that cursed Key, my mother has been kind of crazy about it—and me—demanding that I stay away from it, without telling me why. And now we find out it's like the most important thing in this world, when these gargoyles—gargoyles, mind you!—snatch me away from my town, hide me in a cave and scare me half to death, then tell me I'm this special person to them, like it's up to me to save them! Me? Me, save *them*? It's like I've been in a sick dream for many days now and…and…I just want to wake up! Except I'm pretty sure this hasn't been a dream and that my house is completely destroyed by that nasty Nahgflint fellow…"

The woman gazed at Danielle with ageless, embracing eyes. But she could see no judgment in them, only complete acceptance and boundless joy. Still, confusion raged inside of her.

"I don't know what I am supposed to do!" she blurted out. "What is it I am supposed to do? How can I be the Chosen One when I have no idea how to be her?"

"There is nothing for you to do to be the Chosen One, dear child." The widow smiled, stepped forward and gently stroked Danielle's cheek. "You *are* the Chosen One."

"But what does that mean?"

"Dear one, it is not about doing but about being. You are the Chosen One not because of what you've done or need to do…but because of who you are."

"But…but…"

"Were you not given a prophecy, Danielle?"

"Well, yes, ma'am. Little Lohxnahr took me to see Zarentil, who is a mystic, I guess. But what he said didn't make any more sense than—begging your pardon—than what you are saying to me."

"And yet, you have fulfilled his prophecy. Of that I am certain, for, behold, I am ransomed and set free! Again, my dear child, I thank you."

The woman smiled, stepped back and slowly turned away.

"Wait!" Danielle cried. "I don't understand. Please, don't go! What have I done? How have I changed anything?"

The intense brilliance behind the woman dissipated like shredding fog as she gradually walked away from Danielle. Before vanishing, the shadowy figure turned and waved. A final burst of her lovely fragrance wafted over Danielle, along with, "Thank you, child."

Looking down, Danielle saw at once that she still lay on the altar, her hands buried in inches of powdery dust. She could feel the massive Key pressed into her belly exactly where she'd landed on it. For a moment, she wondered if her conversation with the widow had been nothing more than a dream. But the ring was no longer in her hand.

"Wow. What exactly just happened?" she said out loud, dropping her forehead down onto the back of her hands. She closed her eyes tightly and, very frustrated, blew a huge plume of dust away from her face. When she looked up again, Lohxnahr was beaming at her, his head tipped to one side just like when she first met him. He squatted on the altar next to her head, most of the dust blown off of his thick, strong toes. Chagrined, she realized she'd blown the plume up and over him and now it was now drifting down on his head.

"Zarentil's prophecy has come true. You did well, Chosen One!" he exclaimed, jubilant. Then he took Danielle's face in his hands, careful to keep his talons wide, leaned forward and kissed her on the forehead.

"I did what?"

CHAPTER THIRTY-FOUR

REUNIFICATION

"This doesn't look very good, eh?" Paign said flatly. He stood staring at an enormous pile of rubble scattered all down the long stairs. "It's still hard to believe there was ever a Temple back up the steps behind us. Also hard to believe that anyone made it through the devastation that took place on that Temple floor above! Were those...uh, what was left...you know, Vannveps? Looked like it. Mostly."

No one answered him. The gargoyles were either closely watching the opening into the long, stepped passage they'd already come about halfway down or were searching for enemies in the tunnel below. The other humans were relieved to have survived their desperate race across the Temple's floor just moments earlier.

Freida was still shaken from her encounter with the blood-thirsty Strohrnahq, only minutes before. She couldn't get any words out of her parched mouth and shrugged without any enthusiasm. She clutched a fistful of Tiny's scruff. The dependable dog was happy to oblige his master's need for support, physical and otherwise.

Johann strode wildly down the stairs into the gloom below, sometimes jumping over the considerable rock debris in his way. Occasionally, he'd swing a leg over a boulder and then slide down the back of the stone, almost vanishing from sight. Often, he dislodged a minor avalanche of loose fragments.

Heidi followed along behind him but at a more leisurely pace. Now that Freida had been rescued, Heidi found it much harder to concentrate. She struggled to articulate her thoughts and felt a little dizzy. Like a metronome, her staff swung back and forth, helping her maintain balance on the exceedingly uneven remaining surface of the steps. Her mind's eye kept replaying, over and over, the vision of Strohrnahq's head being impacted by her staff. She vaguely wondered how her friends were, but the emotions about their well-being were distant, even remote, as if they belonged to someone else.

Ercen swept past her to catch up to Johann. "It just won't do to have that human running so far ahead of me and the other gargoyles," she muttered. Although she felt pretty certain that Kimar's squad had succeeded in their mission, a nagging disquiet kept pulsing through her. Something felt... wrong. She needed to *see* Kimar, touch his face, confirm that those with him were also safe. She'd ordered the other gargoyles to go back up and stand guard at the top of the steps. Her fear—at least the only fear that was clear in her mind— was that Kahrnahrgx and his minions might set up an ambush in the ruins of the Temple floor when their group retreated back up the steps and exited the chambers beneath. There was, therefore, some comfort knowing that Urchzahv, Lohmong, Gustlab, Rutahn and Stenring made a highly experienced, dependable and strong rearguard. But the desire to get down to the chamber below, where she expected to locate Kimar and the others, was gnawing at Ercen, more and more.

By the time Freida and Paign caught up to the others, Ercen had cast an intense golden light into what was left of the corridor at the base of the long, wide steps. Between Johann and Ercen, a surprising amount of loose stone had been heaved into the far end of what was left of the corridor. There was no telling how long the tunnels may have stretched in either direction from the base of the steps, had they not been filled with rubble.

"This is worse than I expected," Ercen sighed. "I'll be back in a moment. Do *nothing*," she said to Johann. She parted before he replied, "Jah."

Heidi stepped gingerly between two large, loose blocks of stone. "These look like they're carved, don't you think? There's not much left but this one has...yes, I'm certain! It has runes or something carved right into the face. Maybe it was a lintel over a doorway?"

Johann stopped next to the rubble Heidi was pointing at. "Hm," he muttered, examining the rock from numerous angles. "I think so! But who carved it?" He poked at it with his sword.

A cloud of dirt and debris blew up behind him. Startled and still very twitchy, he wheeled around so fast that he nearly lopped the head off of Gustlab. Only because of the farmer's strength and agility did he stop his blade in midair.

Ercen had returned with Rutahn and had already set to heaving massive boulders down the side halls and took no notice of Johann and Gustlab. Their only focus, for the moment, was to clear debris away from the doorway into the sacrificial chamber.

"That was excellent, Mr. Skulstad!" Paign gushed.

"It depends on one's point of view, boy!" Gustlab barked. "Ercen needs our help in getting through what used to be the main entrance to the lower dungeons of Kahrnahrgx's fortress. We will be faster at completing this task when you get out of our way," he said with a glare.

Freida pulled on Paign's sleeve to motion him back up the stairs until they stood to the side. Her parents joined them a minute later. She was amazed to see that Tiny was asleep at a time like this, let alone with his tongue splayed carelessly into the dust and grime. She couldn't help but grin at her contented beast.

Paign guessed that they sat in the surging dust for about twenty minutes before Ercen reappeared a few steps below.

"It is time," she said, without any enthusiasm.

"What is wrong, Ercen?" Freida asked.

"Come. See."

The debris on the remaining steps was largely untouched, but at the base of the stone steps, and to either side, the floor of the tunnel was now nearly completely cleared. Freida thought it strange that there was one dark boulder still lying prominently near the—

"Oh, no!" Freida cried out. She'd drawn close enough to see that it was the body of Recknab she'd taken to be a boulder. She gasped, horrified by the terrible damage wreaked upon the massive gargoyle, and quickly turned away. Struggling with her emotions, Freida was only vaguely aware of the sounds that Rutahn and Gustlab made retrieving the body of their friend. A moment later, a strong arm wrapped around her shoulders and she turned into her father's embrace and buried her face in his chest, sobbing.

Paign stood nearby, angrily kicking loose debris across the steps. He wished there had been more time to get to know Recknab better. Even though he was a gargoyle, Paign felt they had a similar sense of humor and way of looking at things. His sense of loss was similar to what he experienced when he'd been told about his father's death. He kicked more debris and stomped down the corridor.

Debris skittered and a dust cloud blew up when Gustlab and Rutahn parted back into the tunnel. They'd taken Recknab to where Lohmong, Stenring and Urchzahv continued to stand guard. No one asked where they had gone or what they had done with the body of their friend. Ercen hadn't moved.

"Come." Ercen's voice sounded odd to Paign. It was forceful but strained at the same time. "We still have the collapsed doorway to get through. If the others are safe—and are on the other side—then they should be able to help in clearing the way. You," she said, looking at the humans, "please stay away from this area."

Johann led them all down the tunnel about a dozen paces, where they sheltered behind a mound of debris that served as a protective wall. Even before they settled in, the three gargoyles began their work.

What astonished Paign the most was how quiet they were. Ercen, Rutahn and Gustlab stood close to the destruction of what had been the doorway. In unison, their hands formed fists, palms out and facing the debris. At first, nothing seemed to happen. But then he could hear a low throbbing. The debris shifted some, with small rock falling down the heap. Paign shook his head and blinked. The pile began to glow faintly orange, like the first few moments of a sunrise. The throbbing sound grew louder and louder, just as the color deepened and intensified. A deep groan came from beneath the pile, followed by a horrendous grating of stone on stone. Then, the mass of boulders, stone and grit slid down the opposing tunnel, grinding a multitude of gashes into the floor.

"Now, that's a sight to see, jah?" exclaimed the farmer. "That pile of rock would have filled our barn and then some. A month of Sundays would not have been enough time to do what they've done in a bare minute!"

All that movement of loose stone disrupted enormous clouds of dust, enough so that it was difficult to peer beyond the opening into what they presumed was a great hall behind it.

Quickly, the dust settled and Paign could plainly see some light coming from the other side. Then a silhouette formed in the doorway.

"What took you all so long?" Anders asked.

A moment later, Lohxnahr fluttered out, followed by Danielle, her parents, Mahtrance, Conomorg, Ita-Mudak and finally, Kimar.

The sun had set about half an hour earlier, and dusk was settling in with a slight chill in the night air. Peter sat in front of an old-fashioned fire that he built with help from Ita-Mudak. It crackled merrily under a huge canopy of evergreens, in a small meadow not far from where Freida had been imprisoned. By now, he and Johann, as well as Anders and Paign, already had thirds for supper. Paign was seriously considering fourths. "Fighting a war sure works up an appetite," he said in between bites. The women and girls mostly pushed their food around.

Anders watched gargoyles flying all around the valley. It was easier to see those in the western sky. Those in the east were almost invisible in the deepening gloom. "So, Kimar. What are they all doing, then?" He poked his finger into the air and waved it around.

Kimar took a moment to notice the question. "Oh, there are numerous squads assigned different tasks. Some are looking for survivors—ours…or theirs. Some are hunting, searching out any remaining enemies. Many are simply beginning the massive cleanup that is needed."

"Is it done, then?" Amy asked. "Is the battle won?"

"Yes. It appears so," Ercen replied.

"'Appears'?" Peter quipped. "That doesn't provide quite the level of conviction or comfort I'm looking for. Wasn't the spell broken? You know…the Key and all?"

"Undoubtedly!" came Lohxnahr's raspy voice from a large branch hanging over the open fire. "I witnessed it! Danielle shattered the power of the Key."

Danielle sat hunched on a log near the fire, making designs in the dirt with a stick. Freida sat close by on her left, with Tiny on the right.

Paign blurted out, "How's that, again? I'm still confused how that worked."

"Simple!" Lohxnahr replied, as he swooped down to a patch of thin grass just beyond Danielle's stick. "As you've already learned, she met the Widow Vellhelmina and fulfilled Zarentil's prophecy."

"Uh, that's the place that confuses me," Paign said. "The prophecy didn't make any sense. So, what did she do to fulfill it?"

Firelight danced on the faces of the girls while Lohxnahr paced in front of them.

"Paign," he said, "it was not what she *did* but who she *is*. These are the words of his prophecy:

In order to be, see.

Attend your ear, hear.

Withhold not, free.

Defeat fear, run near.

Ambiguity, embrace.

Throw open, heart.

Radiance upon your face.

The evil, part.

"Without knowing what she must do, Danielle neverthe-less did. She faced grave danger many times. Horrors had been perpetrated at the Temple's altar, by means of the terrible Key, upon the poor widow. This Danielle knew well. Therefore, suffering and horror Danielle fully expected to meet there. With open heart and clear eye, she welcomed grievous hurt when she jumped upon the arcing Key. She did that to protect me, who she barely knows. She could have run from the altar, but she did not. Rather, she leapt upon it.

"In so doing, she broke the horrific spell cast upon it ages ago, destroying the power of it and releasing the imprisoned woman. Even then, she could not know who or what ap-proached her within the brilliance. Again, she embraced the moment despite her uncertainty. She threw open her heart when first she heard of the widow's sad, sad story.

"When she finally met her, what did she do? She returned the woman's stolen ring. Danielle knew that a wedding ring embodies the love of the giver. This ring carried the lifelong love of her husband. It was then that Danielle, out of an open heart, brought the means of redemption to the widow.

Returning it freely to the widow restored her to a wholeness that Kahrnahrgx had broken asunder.

"The forces at work here are much larger than any of us. What Danielle *did* came from who she *is*. Otherwise, her actions would have been different, as would the outcomes. This is why she is the Chosen One. Can you not see? Do you not hear?" Lohxnahr bowed low before an astonished Danielle.

Movement beyond Lohxnahr caught Danielle's eye. A deep sense of wonder and—what was it?—joy, she realized, washed through her. Ita-Mudak, Mahtrance, Conomorg, Rutahn, Lohmong, Gustlab, Urchzahv and Stenring formed a circle around the campers. They, too, bowed low. Ercen and Kimar, beaming, walked over and dropped to one knee. Tiny jumped up and began running in circles in front of the circled gargoyles, barking madly while kicking up plumes of dirt.

"We honor you, Danielle. You are, indeed, the Chosen One!"

CHAPTER THIRTY-FIVE

MANY PARTINGS

The Wheelens felt out of place, certainly, if not even "out of time," staying with the Skulstads for a few days. Peter enjoyed rising while it was still dark to help Johann with his chores. Some of the farm animals were in dire shape upon their return and needed urgent attention. But they had gotten them cared for in time. For her part, Amy felt like she was on a special research assignment, tasked with immersion, learning as much as possible about northern European agricultural-based living in the nineteenth century. The simplicity was breathtakingly inviting to her. There was nothing easy about helping Heidi run a farm without electricity, combustion-based equipment or running water. Without the added distractions of radio and television, the focus was so narrowly—and appropriately—on family, it was easy to embrace even while accepting the hardships of living that came with it. Johann and Heidi welcomed the help and deepening friendships.

Conomorg and Ita-Mudak joined Kimar and Ercen in parting the humans back to the Honellaken Valley, partly as a way of expressing gratitude for what the humans had done for them. But because no sign of Kahrnahrgx was ever discovered in the Temple ruins or surrounding area, it was vital to search out locations known to have been used by him or his minions. So, shortly after arriving with their humans, Freida, Paign and Anders took them all up to Ruar's Ridge, along with Danielle. The gargoyles had stayed in the mountain region for more than two days before returning. Though the humans didn't know it, Rutahn and Lohmong stayed in the valley, near the Skulstads' farm, disguised as boulders, to watch over the humans. Although it was unlikely that anything might happen so soon after their victory, because Kahrnahrgx had not been found, Kimar wanted guards set.

Of course, Anders and Paign had a lot of explaining to do with their mothers. Although it wasn't uncommon for the boys to stay overnight at the other's farm, without any forewarning, their mothers were not amused at not knowing their whereabouts for many days. It took many apologies from the boys, and hearing about their adventures several times, especially from their interesting new friends, to smooth things over.

In the days that followed, the girls and boys had been inseparable. Some of the time they'd simply wandered around the valley, talking over their experiences, trying to make sense of it all. Passersby marveled at the strange garb on the girl with Freida, but they went on their way with no comment. Tiny gloried in these walks, gamboling around like an uncoordinated puppy, often making the foursome burst out laughing.

Peter had largely repaired the kitchen floor by himself, for which Johann was especially grateful. In the twilight hours after supper, they'd gather around the Skulstads' fireplace and talk well into the evening. It helped them each fill in the blanks of the individual pieces of their great adventure. On the third night, the gargoyles returned, so they took the conversation into the small meadow next to the Skulstads' barn. Neither Peter nor Johann desired any more floor repairs.

"Still no sign of Kahrnahrgx, then?" Peter asked.

"No." Kimar replied, staring into the brilliantly clear night sky.

Heidi, Amy and Danielle lay side by side and stared into the mesmerizingly beautiful canopy of stars. Johann stared, instead, at Ita-Mudak, who had perched himself on the western edge of the barn roof. The farmer was reasonably certain that the barn's timbers could support the weight of the gargoyle. *Jah, he is the smallest of the lot, eh?* he thought.

"Well, then, what's next?" Peter continued.

"That is unclear, Peter," Ercen interjected. "We believe that with the destruction of Kahrnahrgx's Key, his power was critically diminished. Perhaps it was even destroyed, but Kimar doesn't think so. What we do know for certain is that our scouts have not been able to sense a location for him...or many of his most loyal followers, for that matter. However, many of his junior minions *have* been found and imprisoned. It is our hope that some may be redeemed back into our fold. But that path is difficult and long..."

Only the sound of a crackling fire disturbed the solitude of the gathering.

"My friends," Johann said warmly, turning to face Peter, Amy and Danielle, "what is next for *you?*"

"Well, it's high time for us to be on our way home," Peter replied, smiling broadly back at Johann. "Except that we're quite sure we don't have a home anymore. It was on fire the last time we saw it, you remember. So, it's a certainty we'll have some serious explaining to do…to law enforcement, to our insurance agent, the homeowner's association, the dean, Danielle's principal…" He sighed. "And who knows who else?"

Johann and Heidi, who had sat up to participate in the dialogue, smiled without understanding most of what Peter meant. They were still sympathetic to the challenges that lay before their friends.

"Now, then?" Kimar asked.

"Oh, uh, sure!" Amy cried.

Within moments, Ita-Mudak observed a flurry of human hugs down in the meadow, with so many arms flailing around it reminded him of a gargoyle youngster's first flight. A smile crossed his angular face as he watched the antics of Tiny, who seemed to want in on each of the many hugs and couldn't decide which one to join first. The dog ended up just running wildly around.

Ita-Mudak flew down from his perch, landing next to Conomorg. Johann wiped his brow when he heard a groan come from the barn once the weight of the gargoyle had lifted. The deep voice of Conomorg rumbled, "We beg your leave, Kimar. Ita-Mudak and I will go back to the Ten Pinnacles and begin preparations for your return." Kimar nodded. Conomorg and Ita-Mudak bowed and parted, leaving little swirls of dust in their wake.

After hugging each of the Wheelens, Paign stepped back for Anders's turn. He felt sorry for his cousin because it was clear to him by now that Anders had taken a real fancy to Danielle. Since it was nearly certain he'd never see her again, Anders was in a lot of turmoil. The awkwardness that came with being from two different places *and times* made it especially hard. Paign wished he could do something—any-thing—to encourage Anders, but felt just as helpless. So, he busied himself kicking dirt and, consequently, he didn't see that when Anders went to Danielle to bid her goodbye, she leaned over and kissed him gently on the cheek. Anders walked, like a sailor in rough seas, back to where Paign's cloud of dirt floated. His cheeks were flushed.

"Did she say anything to you?" Paign asked his cousin.

"Yes!"

After waiting for more and not getting it, Paign followed up with, "Well? What did she say?"

"I'm not telling you!" he said, then slugged Paign halfheart-edly. But from the enormous smile on his face, Paign couldn't muster enough of a grudge to slug him back. He burst out laughing, which set Anders laughing, too.

The last goodbye was between Danielle and Freida. The girls held each other tight, wishing they could stay together but knowing that vast distances and ages separated them.

"Take good care of Tiny, will you?" Danielle said.

Freida nodded her head as tears welled up in her eyes.

"I'll remember you always," Danielle added.

"And me, you," Freida choked out. "But somehow I think we'll see each other again. Don't you?"

This time, it was Danielle who nodded her head, with tears in her eyes. She gave Freida another fierce hug, wiped her eyes and joined her parents, who already held hands with Ercen and Kimar.

Danielle gave a final wave to her friends before taking Kimar's open hand, and they were gone.

EPILOGUE

The old cathedral had been standing for nearly two hundred years. Its gothic design was consistent to the era in which it was built. For some, it seemed strange that a church building's exterior included any decoration, but especially a substantial number of handwrought gargoyles of various sizes. Stonemasons had, for several generations now, been a lost profession. Consequently, a landmark with such a deep history, combined with a severe lack of interest in the skills that brought it into being, suffered from complete disregard from the citizens that hastened past it every day.

Except for Franklin. Many who knew him—and even Franklin himself—would say he'd never had much luck in his life. For years beyond his counting, Franklin had been a vagrant living on the streets around the cathedral, homeless and taken to what he called the "demon drink." And so it was that one cloudy day, blustery and threatening, Franklin lay across the street from the cathedral shouting out loudly, to anyone who would listen, his keen observation that a new gargoyle had perched atop the great cathedral's center spire. But no one listened much to his bellowing, except to snicker uncomfortably at his vigorous protests. "That one...up yonder there...it's got the glowing, ya know?" he'd say. "At night, ya see? Them eyes it's got—they gleam a fiendish red, I'm telling ya! Mark my words! It be looking around even now. I'm warning ya!"

But no one heeded Franklin's words. Indeed, once the storm had passed through, no one noticed they never saw Franklin again.

If you enjoyed *The Quest for the Temple Key*, please consider adding a review on Amazon. I would be grateful if you could spare five minutes to do that. It need only be a line or two and it makes a huge difference for an author.

Best wishes,
Brandon

PLEASE LEAVE A REVIEW

APPENDICES

GLOSSARY

Alcove	A recessed space; vaulted room
Archaeologist	A scientist who studies ancient peoples, species or civilizations
Detritus	Debris; disintegrated material; small particles broken or worn away from a mass
Escarpment	A long, cliff-like ridge
Nodule	A small, rounded lump or mass
Portico	A structure to fortify a gateway, usually attached to a building as a porch
Roil	Combining the words "roll" and "boil"; disturb; stir up
Rookery	A nesting area for winged creatures, typically very high up and sheltered among cliffs

Scree   A steep mass of detritus on the side of a
                 mountain

Stalactite   A mineral deposit, shaped roughly like an
                 icicle, hanging from the roof of a cave

Stalagmite   A mineral deposit, shaped roughly
                 like an icicle, that rises from the ground;
                 made from drippings from stalactites

Umbrage   Annoyance; displeasure

CHARACTERS

CREATURES

Tiny
The Skulstads' enormous dog, a mastiff. Very protective of his family, especially of Freida, his mistress. Fond of Anders Knutson and Paign Macy, Freida's best friends.

Vannveps
Literally means: *water wasps.* Very dangerous, especially when flying in large numbers.

Vanntorden
Literally means: *water thunder.* Very dangerous, but slower than their cousins, the Vannveps. It is unlikely they would sting their opponents, because they cannot fly. Their roars generate the destructive force of a hundred years of glacial movement, condensed down to moments.

GARGOYLES

Bahlkrum   Pronounced: "Ball-crum." Minion of
                Kahrnahrgx, middle rank. Obsidian class.

Conomorg   Pronounced: "Con-oh-morg." Superior
                fighter. Granite class.

Ercen   Pronounced: "Ur-sen." Mate to Kimar.
                Protector, especially of human children.
                Granite class.

Evalcohr   Pronounced: "Evil-core." Commander.
                Ruthless. Obsidian class.

Gahrspat   Pronounced: "Gar-spat." Minion of
                Kahrnahrgx, senior rank. Obsidian class.

Gustlab   Pronounced: "Goost-lab." Superior fighter.
                Basalt class.

Ita-Mudak   Pronounced: "It-ah-moo-dack." Superior
                fighter. Granite class.

Kahrnahrgx   Pronounced: "Car-narx." Brother to Kimar.
                Leader of the gargoyle rebellion. Created the
                powerful and dreaded Key of Kahrnahrgx by
                murdering the Widow Vellhelmina. Killed
                Osberg the Great. Granite class.

Kimar   Pronounced: "Key-mar." Mate to Ercen, brother
                to Kahrnahrgx. Leader of the gargoyle defenders
                and protector of humans. Granite class.

Lohmong   Pronounced: "Low-mong." Superior fighter.
                Granite class.

Lohxnahr Pronounced: "Locks-nar." Friend of Kimar and Ercen. Guide for Danielle. Slate class.

Mahtrance Pronounced: "Mah-trance." Superior fighter. Basalt class.

Nahgflint Pronounced: "Nog-flint." Comes to the Wheelens' home to capture Danielle. One of Kahrnahrgx's special hunting units. Slate class.

Osberg Pronounced: "Oss-burg." Great leader of the gargoyle clans. Killed by Kahrnahrgx while capturing the Key. Gabbro class.

Quarastohr Pronounced: "Koo-war-uh-store." Senior commander of forces opposed to Kahrnahrgx. Leader of the War Council. Soapstone class.

Prohximus Pronounced: "Procks-e-muss." Senior commander. War Council member. Very tall. Supremely intelligent. Limestone class.

Recknab Pronounced: "Wreck-nab." Superior fighter. Granite class.

Rutahn Pronounced: "Rue-tan." Superior fighter. Soapstone class.

Stenring Pronounced: "Stenn-ring." Superior fighter. Granite class.

Strohrnahq Pronounced: "Stro-ar-nock." Fierce, very mean. Gahrspat's brother. Obsidian class.

Tiunarz   Pronounced: "Tea-oo-nar-z." Senior squad
                leader. Obsidian class.

Urchzahv   Pronounced: "Urch-zahv." Superior fighter.
                Granite class.

Uud-Rement   Pronounced: "Ood-rement." Battle-seasoned
                general of opposition. Gabbro class.

Zarentil   Pronounced: "Zair-entill." Mystic High Priest
                and prophet. Ancient. Copper class.

HUMANS

Amy Wheelen	Mother of Danielle. Archaeologist. Professor.
Anders Knutson	Cousin to Paign Macy. Friend of Freida Skulstad.
Anna Vellhelmina	The widow of Parson Vellhelmina. Murdered by Kahrnahrgx.
Danielle Wheelen	The "Chosen One." Abducted by gargoyles.
Freida Skulstad	Inquisitive, hard-headed friend of Anders Knutson and Paign Macy. Becomes best friend to Danielle Wheelen.
Heidi Skulstad	Mother to Freida.
Johann Skulstad	Burly father to Freida. Primarily a sheep and goat farmer.
Paign Macy	Cousin to Anders Knutson. Friend to Freida Skulstad. Name pronounced like "pain."
Pers Olson	Wealthy Honellaken merchant. Believed by some to have killed the Widow Vellhelmina. Leader of a secretive society of merchants and important townspeople.
Reverend Pearsson	Pastor to the people of Honellaken. Confidant to Freida, Anders and Paign.

PLACES

Honellaken Valley	A mountainous Nordic valley, where Freida, Anders, Paign and their families live.
Ruar's Ridge	A ragged ridge, vaulting high above the Honellaken Valley. Named after the historic Norwegian adventurer Hans Ruar.
The Temple of Kahrnahrgx	An ancient place that had originally been the primary worship center for all gargoyles. Site of battle between the followers of Kahrnahrgx and those loyal to Osberg the Great. Now a ruin.

The Rookery of Ten Pinnacles	The majestic, rugged primary nesting grounds for the granite, basalt and slate gargoyle classes.
Ghorlikharka, Nepal	The area where Amy and Peter Wheelen discovered the remains of Osberg the Great, along with the Key of Kahrnahrgx.

www.ingramcontent.com/pod-product-compliance
Lightning Source LLC
Chambersburg PA
CBHW030635260626
47157CB00007B/2333